DE

HIGH STAKES

Dick Francis has written over forty-one international best-sellers and is widely acclaimed as one of the world's finest thriller writers. His awards include the Crime Writers' Association's Cartier Diamond Dagger for his outstanding contribution to the crime genre, and an honorary Doctorate of Humane Letters from Tufts University of Boston. In 1996 Dick Francis was made a Mystery Writers of America Grand Master for a lifetime's achievement and in 2000 he received a CBE in the Queen's Birthday Honours list.

Dick Francis

DECIDER

&

HIGH STAKES

PAN BOOKS

Decider first published 1993 by Michael Joseph.
First published in paperback 1994 by Pan Books in association with Michael Joseph.
High Stakes first published 1975 by Michael Joseph.
First published in paperback 1976 by Pan Books in association with Michael Joseph.

This omnibus first published 2006 by Pan Books
an imprint of Pan Macmillan Ltd
Pan Macmillan, 20 New Wharf Road, London N1 9RR
Basingstoke and Oxford
Associated companies throughout the world
www.panmacmillan.com

ISBN-13: 978-0-330-44668-6
ISBN-10: 0-330-44668-1

Copyright © Dick Francis 1993, 1975

The right of Dick Francis to be identified as the
author of this work has been asserted by him in accordance
with the Copyright, Designs and Patents Act 1988.

1 3 5 7 9 8 6 4 2

A CIP catalogue record for this book is available from
the British Library.

Printed and bound in Great Britain by
Mackays of Chatham plc, Chatham, Kent

DECIDER

My thanks to my godson

ANDREW HANSON
Dip Arch (Edin) RIBA

and love to my grandchildren

Jocelyn
Matthew
Bianca
Timothy
William

CHAPTER I

OK, so here I am, Lee Morris, opening doors and windows to gusts of life and early death.

They looked pretty harmless on my doorstep: two middle-aged civil Englishmen in country-gent tweeds and flat caps, their eyebrows in unison raised enquiringly, their shared expression one of embarrassed anxiety.

'Lee Morris?' one of them said, his diction clipped, secure, expensive. 'Could we speak to him?'

'Selling insurance?' I asked dryly.

Their embarrassment deepened.

'No, actually . . .'

Late March evening, sun low and strong, gold light falling sideways onto their benign faces, their eyes achingly narrowed against the glare. They stood a pace or two from me, careful not to crowd. Good manners all around.

I realised that I knew one of them by sight, and I spent a few extended seconds wondering why on earth he'd sought me out on a Sunday a long way from his normal habitat.

During this pause three small boys padded up the flagstoned passage from the depths of the house behind me, concentratedly threaded a way around me and out through the pair beyond and silently climbed like cats up into the fuzzy bursting

1

leaf-bud embrace of an ancient spreading oak nearby on the lawn. There the three figures rested, becoming immobile, lying on their stomachs along the old boughs, half seen, intent, secretive, deep in an espionage game.

The visitors watched in bemusement.

'You'd better come in,' I said. 'They're expecting pirates.'

The man I'd recognised smiled suddenly with delight, then stepped forward as if in decision and held out his hand.

'Roger Gardner,' he said, 'and this is Oliver Wells. We're from Stratton Park racecourse.'

'Yes,' I said, and made a gesture for them to follow me into the shadowy passage, which they did, slowly, tentatively, half blinded by the slanting sun outside.

I led them along the flagstones and into the cavernous room I'd spent six months converting from a rotting barn into a comfortable house. The revitalising of such ruins was my chief livelihood, but recently the inevitable had finally happened and my family were currently rebelling against moving to yet another building site and were telling me that this house, *this one*, was where they wanted to live.

The sunlight fell through tall west-facing windows onto the sheen of universal slate-grey flagstones which were softened here and there by rugs from Turkey. Round the north, south and east sides of the barn now ran a railed gallery bearing a row of bedrooms, with a staircase giving access at either end.

Under the gallery, a series of rooms stood open-fronted to the great room, though one could close each off with folding doors for privacy. They offered a book-lined room for watching television, an office, a playroom, a sewing room and a long capacious dining room. A breakfast room in the south-east corner led into a big half-visible kitchen with utilities and a workshop wholly out of sight beyond. The partition walls between the open-fronted rooms, partitions which looked merely like space dividers, were in fact the extremely strong load-bearers of the gallery above.

Furniture in the central atrium consisted chiefly of squashy armchairs scattered in informal groups, with many small tables handy. A fireplace in the western wall glowed red with logs.

The effect I'd aimed for, a dwelling built like a small roofed market square, had come out even better than I'd imagined, and in my own mind (though I hadn't told the family) I had intended all along to keep it, if it had been a success.

Roger Gardner and Oliver Wells, as was usual with visitors, came to a halt and looked around in frank surprise, though they seemed too inhibited to comment.

A naked baby appeared, crawling across the flagstones, pausing when he reached a rug, wobbling onto his bottom and looking around, considering things.

'Is that yours?' Roger asked faintly, watching him.

'Very probably,' I said.

A young woman in jeans and sweater, fair hair flying, came jogging out of the far part of the kitchen in businesslike trainers.

'Have you seen Jamie?' she demanded from a distance.

I pointed.

She swooped on the baby and gathered him up unceremoniously. 'I take my eyes off him for *two seconds* ...' She bore him away, delivering a fleeting glance to the visitors, but not stopping, vanishing again from our view.

'Sit down,' I invited. 'What can I do for you?'

They tentatively sat where I indicated and visibly wondered how to begin.

'Lord Stratton recently died,' Roger said eventually. 'A month ago.'

'Yes, I noticed,' I said.

'You sent flowers to the funeral.'

'It seemed merely decent,' I agreed, nodding.

The two men glanced at each other. Roger spoke.

'Someone told us he was your grandfather.'

I said patiently, 'No. They got it wrong. My mother was once married to his son. They divorced. My mother then married again, and had me. I'm not actually related to the Strattons.'

It was unwelcome news, it seemed. Roger tried again.

'But you do own shares in the racecourse, don't you?'

Ah, I thought. The feud. Since the old man had died, his

heirs, reportedly, had been arguing to a point not far from murder.

'I'm not getting involved,' I said.

'Look,' Roger said with growing desperation, 'the heirs are going to *ruin* the racecourse. You can see it a mile off. The rows! Suspicion. Violent hatreds. They set on each other before the old man was even cold.'

'It's civil war,' Oliver Wells said miserably. 'Anarchy. Roger is the manager and I'm the Clerk of the Course, and we are running things ourselves now, trying to keep the place going, but we can't do it much longer. We've no *authority*, do you see?'

I looked at the deep concern on their faces and thought about the difficulty of finding employment of that calibre at fifty-something in the unforgiving job climate.

Lord Stratton, my non-grandfather, had owned three-quarters of the shares in the racecourse and had for years run the place himself as a benevolent despot. Under his hand, at any rate, Stratton Park had earned a reputation as a popular well-run racecourse to which trainers sent their runners in dozens. No Classics, no Gold Cups took place there, but it was accessible and friendly and had a well laid out racing circuit. It needed new stands and various face-lifts but old die-hard Stratton had been against change. He appeared genially on television sometimes, an elder conservative statesman consulted by interviewers when the sport lurched into controversy. One knew him well by sight.

Occasionally, out of curiosity, I'd spent an afternoon on the racecourse, but racing itself had never compulsively beckoned me, nor had my non-grandfather's family.

Roger Gardner hadn't made the journey to give up easily.

'But your *sister* is part of the family,' he said.

'Half-sister.'

'Well, then.'

'Mr Gardner,' I explained, 'forty years ago my mother abandoned her infant daughter and walked out. The Stratton family closed ranks behind her. Her name was mud, spelt in capitals. That daughter, my half-sister, doesn't acknowledge

4

my existence. I'm sorry, but nothing I could say or do would carry any weight with any of them.'

'Your half-sister's father . . .'

'Particularly,' I said, 'not with him.'

During the ensuing pause while the bad news got chewed and digested, a tall fair-headed boy came out of one of the bedrooms on the gallery, skipped down the stairs, waved me a flapping hand and went into the kitchen, to reappear almost at once carrying the baby, now clothed. The boy took the baby upstairs, returned with him to his bedroom and shut the door. Silence fell.

Questions hovered on Roger's face but remained unasked, to my amusement. Roger – Lt. Colonel R.B. Gardner, according to the Stratton Park racecards – would have been a thorough flop as a journalist, but I found his inhibitions restful.

'You were our last hope,' Oliver Wells complained, accusingly.

If he hoped to instil guilt, he failed. 'What would you expect me to *do*?' I asked reasonably.

'We hoped . . .' Roger began. His voice faded away, then he rallied and manfully tried again. 'We *hoped*, do you see, that you might knock some sense into them.'

'How?'

'Well, for one thing, you're big.'

'*Big?*' I stared at him. 'Are you suggesting I *literally* knock some sense into them?'

It did seem that my appearance had given them instant ideas. It was true that I was tall and physically strong; very useful for building houses. I couldn't swear I'd never found those facts conclusive in swinging an argument. But there were times when to tread softly and shrink one's shoulder-span produced more harmonious results, and I leaned by nature more to the latter course. Lethargic, my wife called me. Too lazy to fight. Too placid. But the ruins got restored and left no trails of rancour in local official minds, and I'd learned how to get round most planning officers with conciliation and reason.

'I'm not your man,' I said.

Roger clutched at straws. 'But you do own those shares. Can't you stop the war with those?'

'Is that,' I asked, 'what you mainly had in mind when you sought me out?'

Roger nodded unhappily. 'We don't know where else to turn, do you see?'

'So you thought I might gallop into the arena waving my bits of paper and crying "enough", and they would all throw down their prejudices and make peace?'

'It might help,' Roger said, straightfaced.

He made me smile. 'For one thing,' I said, 'I own very few shares. They were given to my mother all those years ago as a divorce settlement, and I inherited them when she died. They pay a very small dividend now and then, that's all.'

Roger's expression went from bewilderment to shock. 'Do you mean,' he demanded, 'that you haven't heard what they are fighting *about*?'

'I told you, I have had no contact with them.' All I knew was what I'd learned from a brief paragraph in *The Times*'s business pages ('Stratton heirs dispute over family racecourse') and some blunter remarks in a tabloid ('Long knives out at Stratton Park').

'I'm afraid you will soon hear from them,' Roger said. 'One faction of them want to sell off the racecourse to developers. As you know, the course lies just to the north-east of Swindon, in an area that's growing all the time. That town has exploded into a centre of industry. All sorts of firms are moving there. It's heaving with new life. The racecourse land is increasing in value all the time. Your few shares might now be worth quite a lot, and they might be worth even more in the future. So some of the Strattons want to sell now, and some want to wait, and some don't want to sell at all, but to go on running the racecourse for racing, and the sell-now lot should have been onto you by now, I would have thought. Anyway, some day soon they'll remember your shares and they'll drag you into the fight whether you like it or not.'

He stopped, feeling he'd made his point; and I supposed he

had. My sincere desire *not* to be dragged into any fracas looked like being a casualty of 'the real world', as one of my sons described all calamities.

'And naturally,' I commented, 'you are with the faction that wants racing to continue.'

'Well, yes,' Roger admitted. 'Yes, we are. Frankly, we hoped to persuade you to vote your shares *against* selling.'

'I don't know that my shares even have a vote and there aren't enough of them to sway anything. And how did you know I had any?'

Roger briefly consulted his fingernails and decided on frankness.

'The racecourse is a private limited company, as I expect you know. It has directors and board meetings and the shareholders are informed each year when the annual general meeting is to take place.'

I nodded resignedly. The notice came every year and every year I ignored it.

'So last year the secretary who sends out the notice was ill, and Lord Stratton told me just to do it, there's a good chap . . .' – his voice mimicked the old man's splendidly – 'so I sent out the notice and it happened that I put the list of names and addresses in a file for the future . . .' he paused, hovering, 'in case I had to do it again, do you see?'

'And the future's upon us,' I said. I pondered. 'Who else owns shares? Did you by any chance bring the list with you?'

I saw from his face both that he had brought it and also that he was unsure of the ethics of passing it over. The threat to his job, though, conquered all, and after the briefest of hesitations he reached into an inner pocket in the tweed jacket and produced a clean once-folded sheet of paper. A fresh copy, by the looks of things.

I opened it and read the ultra-short list. Shorn of addresses it read:

William Darlington Stratton (3rd Baron)
Hon Mrs Marjorie Binsham

Mrs Perdita Faulds

Lee Morris Esq

'Is that all?' I enquired blankly.

Roger nodded.

Marjorie Binsham was, I knew, the old lord's sister. 'Who is Mrs Perdita Faulds?' I asked.

'I don't know,' Roger said.

'So you haven't been to see her? You came here, though?'

Roger didn't answer, but he didn't need to. That sort of ex-soldier felt more at home with other men than with women.

'And,' I said, 'who inherits the old man's shares?'

'I don't *know*,' Roger answered exasperatedly. 'The family aren't saying. They've shut up like clams about the will, and of course it's not open to public inspection before probate, which may be *years* away, at the rate they're going. If I had to guess, I'd say Lord Stratton left them all equal shares. He was fair, in his way. Equal shares would mean that no single one of them has control, and that's the nub of the problem, I'd think.'

'Do you know them personally?' I asked, and they both nodded gloomily. 'Like that, is it?' I asked. 'Well, I'm sorry, but they'll have to sort it out themselves.'

The young fair-haired woman strolled out of the kitchen with a glass in one hand and a feeding bottle of milk in the other. She nodded vaguely in our direction and went up the staircase and into the room where the boy had taken the baby. My visitors watched in silence.

A brown-haired boy rode a bicycle up the passage from the front door and made a controlled circuit of the room, slowing slightly as he passed behind me and saying, 'Yeah, yeah, you told me not to,' before returning along the passage towards the outside world. The bicycle was scarlet, the clothes purple and pink and fluorescent green. The very air seemed to quiver with vibrant colour, settling back to quiet slate when he'd gone.

Tactfully, no one said anything about obedience or keeping children in order.

I offered the visitors a drink but they had nothing to

celebrate and murmured about the length of the drive home. I went with them into the softening sunlight and proffered polite apologies for their non-success. They nodded unhappily. I walked across with them to their car.

The three pirate-ambushers had de-materialised from the oak. The scarlet bicycle flashed in the distance. My visitors looked back at the long dark bulk of the barn, and Roger finally came out with a question.

'What an interesting house,' he said civilly. 'How did you find it?'

'I built it. The interior, that is. Not the barn itself, of course. That's old. A listed building. I had to negotiate to be allowed windows.'

They looked at the neat dark oblongs of glass set unobtrusively into the timber cladding, the only outward indication of the dwelling within.

'You had a good architect,' Roger commented.

'Thank you.'

'That's another thing the Strattons are fighting over. Some of them want to tear down the stands and rebuild, and they've engaged an architect to draw up plans.'

His voice was thick with disgust.

I said curiously, 'Surely new stands would be a good thing? Crowd comfort, and all that?'

'Of course, new stands would be good!' Irritation finally swamped him. 'I implored the old man for years to rebuild. He always said, yes, one day, one day, but he never meant to, not in his lifetime, and now his son Conrad, the new Lord Stratton, he's invited this dreadful man to design new stands, and he's been striding about the place telling me we need this and we need that, and it's all rubbish. He's never designed stands of any sort before and he knows bugger all about racing.'

His genuine indignation interested me a lot more than a fight about shares.

'Building the wrong stands would bankrupt everybody,' I said thoughtfully.

Roger nodded. 'They'll have to borrow the money, and

9

racing people are fickle. The punters stay away if you don't get the bars right, and if the owners and trainers aren't pampered and comfortable, the buggers will run their horses somewhere else. This lunatic of an architect looked totally blank when I asked him what he thought the crowds did between races. Look at the horses, he said. I ask you! And if it's raining? Shelter and booze, I told him, that's what brings in the customers. He told me I was old fashioned. And Stratton Park will get a horrendously expensive white elephant that the public will shun. And, like you said, the place will go bust.'

'Only if the sell-now or sell-later factions don't get their way.'

'But we *need* new stands,' Roger insisted. 'We need *good* new stands.' He paused. 'Who designed your house? Perhaps we need someone like *him*.'

'He's never designed any stands. Only houses . . . and pubs.'

'*Pubs*,' Roger pounced on it. 'At least he'd understand the importance of good bars.'

I smiled. 'I'm sure he would. But you need big-building specialists. Engineers. Your own input. A team.'

'Tell that to Conrad.' He shrugged dejectedly and slid behind his steering wheel, winding down the window and peering out for one more question. 'Could I possibly ask you to let me know if or when the Stratton family contact you? I probably shouldn't trouble you, but I *care* about the racecourse, you see. I know the old man believed it would carry on as before, and he wanted it that way, and perhaps there's something I can do, but I don't know *what*, do you see.'

He reached into his jacket again and produced a business card. I took it and nodded, making no promise one way or another, but he took the acknowledgement as assent.

'Thank you very much,' he said.

Oliver Wells sat impassively beside him, showing his certainty that their mission had been, as he'd all along expected, unproductive. He still failed to raise guilt in me. Everything I knew of the Strattons urged me strongly to stay away from them in every way I could.

Roger Gardner gave me a sad farewell and drove off, and I went back into my house hoping I wouldn't see him again.

'Who were those people?' Amanda said. 'What did they want?'

The fair-haired woman, my wife, lay at the far side of our seven foot square bed, emphasising as usual the distance between us.

'They wanted a white knight act on Stratton Park racecourse.'

She worked it out. 'A rescue job? You? Those old shares of yours? I hope you said no.'

'I said no.'

'Is that why you're lying there wide awake in the moonlight, staring at the canopy?'

The pleated silk canopy roofed our great four-poster like a mediaeval sleeping tent, the only way to achieve privacy in those days before separate bedrooms. The theatrical glamour of the tester, the tassels and the bed's cosy promise beguiled friends: only Amanda and I understood the significance of its size. It had taken me two days of carpentry and stitching to construct, and it was understood by both of us to be a manifestation of a hard-won compromise. We would live in the same house, and also in the same bed, but apart.

'The boys break up from school this week,' Amanda said.

'Do they?'

'You said you'd take them somewhere for Easter.'

'Did I?'

'You know you did.'

I'd said it to de-fuse an argument. Never make rash promises, I told myself. An incurable failing.

'I'll think of something,' I said.

'And about this house . . .'

'If you like it, we'll stay here,' I said.

'Lee!' It briefly silenced her. I knew she had a thousand persuasions ready: the scattered hints and sighs had been unmistakable for weeks, ever since the gravel had been laid in the drive and the building inspector had called for the last time. The house was freehold, finished and ready for sale, and we needed the money. Half my working capital lay cemented into its walls.

'The boys need a more settled existence,' Amanda said, not wanting to waste her reasons.

'Yes.'

'It's not fair to keep dragging them from school to school.'

'No.'

'They worry about leaving here.'

'Tell them not to.'

'I can't believe it! Can we afford it? I thought you'd say you couldn't afford it. What about the mansion near Oxford, with the tree growing in the drawing room?'

'With luck I'll get planning permission this week.'

'But we're not going there, are we?' Despite my assurance, her anxiety rose sharply.

'I'll go there,' I said. 'You and the boys will stay here for as long as you want. For years. I'll commute.'

'You *promise*.'

'Yes.'

'No more *mud*? No more *mess*? No more tarpaulins for roofs and brick dust in the cornflakes?'

'No.'

'What made you decide?'

The mechanics of decision, I thought, were mysterious. I could have said it was indeed because it was time to settle down for the children's sake, that the eldest had reached the examination time zone and needed continuity in teaching. I could have said that this area, the smiling countryside on the Surrey–Sussex border, was as wholesome as anywhere nowadays. I could have made the decision sound eminently logical.

Instead, I knew in my private mind that the decider had been the old oak. It had appealed to me powerfully, to the inner boy who had been brought up in London traffic, surrounded by landscapes of stone.

I'd seen the oak first a year earlier, fuzzy then as now with the promise of leaf. Mature, perfect, its boughs invited climbers, and as I'd gone there alone I climbed it without embarrassment, sitting at home in its ancient embrace, looking at the rotting great eyesore of a barn that the hard-up landowner had been forbidden to demolish. A historic tithe barn! A local landmark! It would have to stay there until it actually fell down.

A lot of crap, I'd thought, descending from the tree and walking into the ruin through a creaking gap doing duty as a doorway. History-worship gone mad.

Parts of the roof far above were missing. Along the west side the timbers all leaned drunkenly at wild angles, their supports wholly weathered away. A rusted abandoned tractor and heaps of other assorted junk lay among saplings struggling up from the cracked concrete floor. A stiff breeze blew through the tangled desolation, unfriendly and cold.

I'd seen almost at once what could be built within there, almost as if the design had been hovering for a long time in my mind, awaiting life. It would be a house for children. Not necessarily for my own children, but for any. For the child I'd been. A house with many rooms, with surprises, with hiding places.

The boys had hated the place at first and Amanda, heavily pregnant, had burst into tears, but the local planners had been helpful and the landowner had sold me the barn with a surrounding acre of land as if he couldn't believe his luck. When each son found he would be having a separate bedroom as a domain all his own, the objections miraculously ceased.

I'd brought in a conservationist to check the oak. A superb old specimen, he'd said. Three hundred years in the growing. It would outlive us all, he said; and its timeless strength seemed to give me peace.

Amanda repeated, 'What made you decide?'

I said 'The oak.'

'What?'

'Common sense,' I said, which satisfied her.

*

On Wednesday I received two direction-changing letters. The first, from an Oxford District Council, turned down my third application for planning permission for restoring the mansion with the beech tree growing in its drawing room. I telephoned to discover why, as I'd understood the third plan had met with their unofficial approval. They now were of the opinion, a repressive voice told me, that the mansion should be restored as one dwelling, not divided into four smaller houses, as I'd suggested. Perhaps I would care to submit revised plans. Sorry, I said. Forget it. I phoned the mansion's owner to say I was no longer a potential buyer, sending him into predictable orbital rage: but no planning permission, no sale, had been our firm agreement.

Sighing, I disconnected and dropped three months' work into the wastepaper basket. Back, literally, to the drawing-board.

The second letter came from solicitors acting for the Stratton family, inviting me to a Stratton Park shareholders' extraordinary meeting the following week.

I phoned the solicitors. 'Do they expect me to go?' I asked.

'I don't know, Mr Morris. But as you are a shareholder, they were required to alert you to the meeting.'

'What do you think?'

'Entirely your decision, Mr Morris.'

The voice was cautious and non-committal, no help at all.

I asked if I held voting shares.

'Yes, you do. Each share has one vote.'

On Friday I did the end-of-term school run, collecting the boys for their Easter break: Christopher, Toby, Edward, Alan and Neil.

What, they wanted to know, had I planned for their holidays?

'Tomorrow,' I said calmly, 'we go to the races.'

'Motor?' Christopher asked hopefully.

'Horses.'

They made vomiting noises.

'And next week . . . a ruin hunt,' I said.

Deafening disapproval lasted all the way home.

'If I don't find another nice ramshackle ruin, we'll have to sell this house after all,' I said, pulling up outside. 'Take your pick.'

Sobered, they grumbled, 'Why can't you get a *proper* job?' which I took as it was meant, resigned acceptance of the programme ahead. I'd always told them where the money came from for food and clothes and bicycles and because they'd suffered no serious shortage they had inexhaustible faith in ruins, and were apt to point them out to me unprompted.

Since the thumbs-down letter on the mansion, I'd checked through the file of replies I'd had to an advertisement I'd run in the *Spectator* three months earlier:

'Wanted, an uninhabitable building. Anything from castle to cowshed considered.'

I enquired of several interesting propositions to see if any were still available. As, owing to a recent severe slump in property prices, it seemed they all were, I promised an inspection and made a list.

I hardly admitted to myself that the uninhabitable buildings niggling away on the fringes of my mind were the grandstands at Stratton Park.

Only I knew the debt I owed to the third baron.

CHAPTER 2

It rained on Stratton Park's steeplechase meeting, but my five elder sons – Christopher, fourteen, to Neil, seven – grumbled not so much about the weather as about having to wear tidy, unobtrusive clothing on a Saturday. Toby, twelve, the rider of the red bicycle, had tried to avoid the trip altogether, but Amanda had packed him firmly into the mini-van with the others, providing a picnic of Coca-Cola and ham omelettes in burger buns, which we dealt with in the car park on arrival.

'OK, ground rules,' I said, collecting the wrappings into a single bag. 'First, no running about and banging into people. Second, Christopher looks after Alan, Toby takes Edward, Neil goes with me. Third, when we've chosen a rallying point, everyone turns up there immediately after each race.'

They nodded. The family crowd control measures were long established and well understood. The regular head counts reassured them rather than irked.

'Fourth,' I went on, 'you don't walk behind horses as they're apt to kick, and fifth, notwithstanding the classless society, you'll get on very well on a racecourse if you call every man "sir".'

'Sir, sir,' Alan said, grinning, 'I want to pee, sir.'

I trooped them in through the gates and acquired Club

16

enclosure tickets all round. The white pasteboard badges fluttered on cords from the sliders of the zips on five blue-hooded anoraks. The five young faces looked serious and well intentioned, even Toby's, and I went through a rare moment of being both fond and proud of my children.

The rallying point was established under shelter not far from the winner's unsaddling enclosure and within sight of the gents. We then went all together through the entrance gate into the Club itself and round to the front of the stands and, once I was sure they all had the hang of the whereabouts, I let the paired elder ones go off on their own. Neil, brainy but timid when not in a crowd of brothers, slid his hand quietly into mine and left it there as if absentmindedly, transferring his hold to my trousers occasionally but running no risk of getting lost.

For Neil, as for imaginative Edward, getting lost was the ultimate nightmare. For Alan, it was a laughing matter; for Toby, an objective. Christopher, self-contained, never lost his bearings and habitually found his parents, rather than vice versa.

Neil, easy child, made no objection to walking around in the stands instead of going to see the horses currently plodding wetly round the parade ring before the first race. ('What are the stands, Dad?' 'All those buildings.') Neil's agile little brain soaked up vocabulary and impressions like a sponge, and I'd grown accustomed to hearing observations from him that I would hardly have expected from adults.

We popped our heads into a bar that in spite of the rain was uncrowded, and Neil, wrinkling his nose, said he didn't like the smell in there.

'It's beer,' I said.

'No, it smells like that pub we lived in before the barn, like it smelled when we first went there, before you changed it.'

I looked down at him thoughtfully. I'd reconstructed an ancient, unsuccessful and dying inn and turned its sporadic trade into a flood. There had been many factors – reorganised ground plan, colours, lighting, air management, car parks. I'd deliberately *added* smells, chiefly of bread baking, but I didn't know what I'd taken away, beyond stale beer and old smoke.

'What smell?' I asked.

Neil bent his knees and put his face near the floor. 'It's that horrid cleaning stuff in the water the pub man used to wash his lino tiles with, before you took them all up.'

'Really?'

Neil straightened. 'Can we go out of here?' he asked.

We left hand in hand. 'Do you know what ammonia is?' I said.

'You put it down drains,' he explained.

'Was it that smell?'

He thought it over. 'Like ammonia but with scent in it.'

'Disgusting,' I said.

'Absolutely.'

I smiled. Apart from the wondrous moment of Christopher's birth I'd never been a good man for babies, but once the growing and emerging minds had begun expressing thoughts and opinions all their own, I'd been continuously entranced.

We watched the first race, with my lifting Neil up so that he could see the bright action over the hurdles.

One of the jockeys, I noticed in the racecard, was named Rebecca Stratton, and after the race, when the horses returned to be unsaddled, (R. Stratton unplaced), we happened to pass by while she was looping girths round her saddle and speaking over her shoulder to downcast owners before setting off back to the changing rooms.

'He moved like a torpid stumblebum. Might try him in blinkers next time.'

She was tall with a flat body and a thin scrubbed face with high hard cheekbones, no compromise with femininity in sight. She walked not in a heel-down scurry like the male jockeys but in a sort of feline loping strut on her toes, as if she was not only aware of her own power but aroused by it. The only other woman I'd seen walk like that had been a lesbian.

'What's a torpid stumblebum?' Neil asked, after she'd gone.

'It means slow and clumsy.'

'Oh.'

We met the others at the rallying point and I issued popcorn money all round.

'Horse racing is boring,' Toby said.

'If you can pick a winner I'll pay you Tote odds,' I said.

'What about me?' Alan said.

'Everyone.'

Brightening, they went off to look at the next race's runners in the parade ring, with Christopher explaining to them how to read the form line in the racecard. Neil, staying close to me, said without hesitation that he would choose number seven.

'Why seven, then?' I asked, looking it up. 'It's never won a race in its life.'

'My peg in the cloakroom at school is number seven.'

'I see. Well, number seven is called Clever Clogs.'

Neil beamed.

The other four returned with their choices. Christopher had picked the form horse, the favourite. Alan had singled out Jugaloo because he liked its name. Edward chose a no-hoper because it looked sad and needed encouragement. Toby's vote went to Tough Nut because it had been 'kicking and bucking in the ring and winding people up'.

They all wanted to know my own choice, and I ran a fast eye over the list and said randomly, 'Grandfather', and then wondered at the mind's subliminal tricks and thought it perhaps not so random after all.

Slightly to my relief, Toby's Tough Nut not only won the race but had enough energy left for a couple of vicious kicks in the unsaddling enclosure. Toby's boredom turned to active interest and, as often happened, the rest responded to his mood. The rain stopped. The afternoon definitely improved.

I took them all down the course later to watch the fourth race, a three-mile steeplechase, from beside one of those difficult jumps, an open ditch. This one, the second to last fence on the circuit, was attended by a racecourse employee looking damp in an orange fluorescent jacket, and by a St John's Ambulance volunteer whose job it was to give first aid to any jockeys who fell at his feet. A small crowd of about thirty racegoers had made the trek down there beside ourselves, spreading out behind the inside rails of the track, both on the take-off and the landing sides of the fence.

The ditch itself – in steeplechasing's past history a real drainage ditch with water in it – was in modern times, as at Stratton Park, no real ditch at all but a space about four feet wide on the take-off side of the fence. There was a large pole across the course on the approach side to give an eye-line to the horses, to tell them when to jump, and the fence itself, of dark birch twigs, was four feet six inches high and at least a couple of feet thick: all in all a regular jump presenting few surprises to experienced 'chasers.

Although the boys had seen a good deal of racing on television I'd never taken them to an actual meeting before, still less down to where the rough action filled the senses. When the ten-strong field poured over the fence on the first of the race's two circuits, the earth quivered under the thudding hooves, the black birch crackled as the half-ton 'chasers crashed through the twigs, the air parted before the straining bunch risking life and limb off the ground at thirty miles an hour: the noise stunned the ears, the jockeys' voices cursed, the coloured shirts flashed by kaleidoscopically . . . and suddenly they were gone, their backs receding, silence returning, the brief violent movement over, the vigour and striving a memory.

'Wow!' Toby said, awestruck. 'You didn't say it was like *that*.'

'It's only like that when you're close to it,' I said.

'But it must be always like that for the jockeys,' Edward said thoughtfully. 'I mean, they take the noise with them all the way.' Edward, ten, had led the pirate ambush up the oak. Misleadingly quiet, it was always he who wondered what it would be like to be a mushroom, who talked to invisible friends, who worried most about famine-struck children. Edward invented make-believe games for his brothers and read books and lived an intense inner life, as reserved as Alan, nine, was outgoing and ebullient.

The racecourse employee walked along the fence on the landing side, putting back into place with a short-handled paddle all the dislodged chunks of birch, making the obstacle look tidy again before the second onslaught.

The five boys waited impatiently while the runners continued round the circuit and came back towards the open ditch for the second and last time before racing away to the last fence and the sprint to the winning post. Each boy had picked his choice of winner and had registered it with me, and when people around us began yelling for their fancy the boys yelled also, Neil jumping up and down in excitement and screaming 'Come on seven, come on seven, come on *peg*.'

I had put my own trust on Rebecca Stratton who was this time partnering a grey mare called Carnival Joy, and as they neared the fence she seemed to be lying second, to my mild surprise, my own expertise at picking winners being zero.

At the last minute the horse in front of her wavered out of a straight line, and I glimpsed the strain on the jockey's face as he hauled on a rein to get himself out of trouble, but he was meeting the fence all wrong. His mount took off a stride too soon and landed right in the space between take-off pole and fence, where, frightened, it dumped its jockey and veered across into the path not only of Carnival Joy, but of all the runners behind.

Things happen fast at thirty miles an hour. Carnival Joy, unable to see a clear path ahead, attempted to jump both the fence *and* the horse on the take-off side, a near-impossible task. The grey's hooves caught the loose horse so that its whole weight crashed chest first into the fence. Its jockey willy-nilly flew caterpaulting out forwards over the birch and in a flurry of arms and legs thudded onto the turf. Carnival Joy fell over the fence onto its head, somersaulted, came down on its side and lay there winded, lethally kicking in an attempt to get up.

The rest of the field, some trying to stop, some unaware of the mêlée, some trying to go round it, compounded the débâcle like cars crashing in a fog. One of the horses, going too fast, too late, with no chance of safety, took what must have seemed to him a possible way out and tried to jump right off the course through the nearside wing.

Wings, on the take-off side of each fence, were located there precisely to stop horses running out at the last moment and, to be effective, needed to be too high to jump. Trying to escape trouble by jumping the wings was therefore always a disaster, though not so bad as in the old days when all wings had been made of wood, which splintered and ripped into flesh. Wings at Stratton Park, conforming to the current norm, were made of plastic, which bent and gave way without injuring, but this particular horse, having crashed through unscathed, then collided with the bunch of onlookers, who had tried to scatter too late.

One minute, a smooth race. In five seconds, carnage. I was peripherally aware that three more horses had come to grief on the landing side of the fence with their jockeys either unconscious or sitting up cursing, but I had eyes only for the knocked down clutch of spectators and chiefly, and I confess frantically, I was counting young figures in blue anoraks, and feeling almost sick with relief to find them all upright and unscathed. The horror on their faces I could deal with later.

Alan, born seemingly without an understanding of danger, suddenly darted out onto the course, ducking under the rails, intent on helping the fallen jockeys.

I yelled at him urgently to come back, but there was too much noise all around us and, powerfully aware of all the loose horses charging about in scared bewilderment, I bent under the rails myself and hurried to retrieve him. Neil, little Neil, scrambled after me.

Terrified for him also, I hoisted him up and ran to fetch Alan who, seemingly oblivious to Carnival Joy's thrashing legs, was doing his best to help a dazed Rebecca Stratton to her feet. In something near despair I found that Christopher too was out on the course, coming to her aid.

Rebecca Stratton returned to full consciousness, brushed crossly at the small hands stretched to help her and in a sharp voice said to no one in particular, 'Get these brats out of my way. I've enough to contend with without that.'

She stood up furiously, stalked over to the jockey whose mount had caused the whole pile-up and who was now standing forlornly beside the fence, and uttered loud and uncomplimentary opinions about his lack of horsemanship.

Her hands clenched and unclenched as if, given half a chance, she would hit him.

My brats predictably detested her immediately. I hustled them with their wounded feelings off the course and out of further trouble, but as we passed near to the lady jockey Neil said, suddenly and distinctly, 'Torpid stumblebum.'

'*What?*' Rebecca's head snapped round, but I'd whirled my small son hastily away from her and she seemed more disconcerted than actively directing fire at anyone except the other unfortunate rider.

Toby and Edward, impervious to her, were more concerned with the mown down spectators, two of whom looked badly hurt. People were in tears, people were stunned, people were awakening to anger. Somewhere in the distance, people were cheering. One of the few horses that had side stepped the calamity had gone on to win the race.

As on most racecourses, the runners had been followed all the way round by an ambulance driven along on a narrow private roadway on the inner side of the track, so that help was at hand. The racecourse official had unfurled and urgently waved two flags, one red and white, one orange, signalling to the doctor and the vet sitting in a car out in the middle of the course that they were both needed at once.

I collected the boys together and we stood in a group watching the ambulance men and the doctor, in an identifying arm band, kneeling beside the fallen, fetching stretchers, conferring, dealing as best they could with broken bones and blood and worse. It was too late to worry about what the boys were seeing: they resisted my suggestion that we should go back to the stands, so we remained with most of the spectators already there, and were joined by the steady stream of new spectators ghoulishly attracted down the course by chaos and disaster.

The ambulance drove off slowly with the two racegoers who'd been felled by the crash through the wing. 'The horse jumped on one man's face,' Toby told me matter-of-factly. 'I think he's dead.'

'Shut up,' Edward protested.

'It's the real world,' Toby said.

One of the horses couldn't be saved. Screens were erected round him, which they hadn't been for the kicked-in-the-face man.

Two cars and a second ambulance swept up fast from the direction of the stands and out leapt another doctor, another vet, and racecourse authority in the shape of the Clerk of the Course, Oliver Wells, one of my visitors from Sunday. Hurrying from clump to clump, Oliver checked with the doctors, checked with the vets behind the screens, checked with first-aid men tending a flat-out jockey, listened to a horse-battered spectator sitting on the ground with his head between his knees and finally paid attention to Rebecca Stratton, whose brief spell of daze was still resulting in hyperactivity and a het-up stream of complaints.

'Pay *attention*, Oliver.' Her voice rose imperiously. 'This little shit caused the whole thing. I'm reporting him to the Stewards. Careless riding! A fine. Suspension, at least.'

Oliver Wells merely nodded and went to have a word with one of the doctors, who looked across at Rebecca and, leaving his unconscious patient, attempted to feel the all-too-conscious lady's pulse.

She pulled her wrist away brusquely. 'I'm perfectly all right,' she insisted. 'You stupid little man.'

The doctor narrowed his eyes at her and took his skills elsewhere, and across Oliver Wells's bony features flitted an expression that could only be described as glee.

He caught me looking at him before he'd rearranged his expression, and changed the direction of his thoughts with a jolt.

'Lee Morris,' he exclaimed, 'isn't it?' He looked at the children. 'What are they all doing here?'

'Day at the races,' I said dryly.

'I mean . . .' He glanced at his watch and at the clearing up going on around us. 'When you go back up the course, will you call in at my office before you go home. It's right beside the weighing room. Er . . . *please*?'

'OK,' I agreed easily. 'If you like.'

'Great.' He gave me a half-puzzled final glance and dived

back into his duties and, with things improving on the turf and slowly losing their first intense drama, the five boys at length unglued their feet and their eyes and walked back with me towards the stands.

'That man came to our house last Sunday,' Toby told me. 'He's got a long nose and sticking-out ears.'

'So he has.'

'The sun was making shadows of them.'

Children were observant in an uncomplicated way. I'd been too concerned with why the man was there to notice shadows on his face.

'He's the man who mostly organises the races here,' I said. 'He runs things on race days. He's called the Clerk of the Course.'

'A sort of Field Marshal?'

'Quite like that.'

'I'm hungry,' Alan said, quickly bored.

Neil said 'Torpid stumblebum' twice, as if the words themselves pleased his lips.

'What are you talking about?' Christopher demanded, and I explained.

'We were only trying to help her,' he protested. 'She's a cow.'

'Cows are nice,' Alan said.

By the time we reached the stands, the fifth race, over hurdles, was already being run, but none of my five much cared about the result, not having had a chance to pick their fancy.

No one had won on the fourth race. Everyone's hopes had ended at the ditch. Edward's choice was the horse that died.

I gave them all tea in the tea-room: ruinously expensive but a necessary antidote to shock. Toby drowned his brush with the real world in four cups of hot sweet milky pick-you-up and every cake he could cajole from the waitress.

They ate through the sixth race. They all went to the gents. The crowds were pouring homewards out of the gates when we made our way to the Clerk of the Course's office beside the weighing room.

The boys entered quietly behind me, unusually subdued and

giving a misleading impression of habitual good behaviour. Oliver Wells, sitting at a busy-looking desk, eyed the children vaguely and went on speaking into a walkie-talkie. Roger Gardner, racecourse manager, was also in attendance, sitting with one hip on the desk, one foot swinging. The colonel's worry-level had if anything intensified during the week, lines having deepened across his forehead. Civilised habits of behaviour would see him through, though, I thought, even if he rose to full height at our entrance, looking as if he had expected Lee Morris but not five smaller clones.

'Come in,' Oliver said, putting down his instrument. 'Now, what shall we do with these boys?' The question seemed to be merely rhetorical as he had recourse again to his walkie-talkie, pressing buttons. 'Jenkins? To my office, please.' He switched off again. 'Jenkins will see to them.'

An official knocked briefly on an inner door and came in without waiting for a summons: a middle-aged messenger in a belted navy raincoat, with a slightly stodgy expression and slow-moving reassuring bulk.

'Jenkins,' Oliver said, 'take these boys into the jockeys' changing rooms and let them collect autographs.'

'Won't they be a nuisance?' I asked, as parents do.

'Jockeys are quite good with children,' Oliver said, making shooing motions to my sons. 'Go with Jenkins, boys, I want to talk to your father.'

'Take them, Christopher,' I encouraged, and all five of them went cheerfully with the safe escort.

'Sit down,' Oliver invited, and I pulled up a chair and sat round the desk with the two of them. 'We're not going to get five minutes without interruptions,' Oliver said, 'so we'll come straight to the point.' The walkie-talkie crackled. Oliver picked it up, pressed a switch and listened.

A voice said brusquely, 'Oliver, get up here, pronto. The sponsors want a word.'

Oliver said reasonably, 'I'm writing my report of the fourth race.'

'Now, Oliver.' The domineering voice switched itself off, severing argument.

26

Oliver groaned. 'Mr Morris . . . can you wait?' He rose and departed, whether I could wait or not.

'That,' Roger explained neutrally, 'was a summons from Conrad Darlington Stratton, the fourth baron.'

I made no comment.

'Things have changed since we saw you on Sunday,' Roger said. 'For the worse, if possible. I wanted to go and see you again, but Oliver thought it useless. And now . . . well, here you are! Why are you here?'

'Curiosity. But with what the boys saw at that fence today, I shouldn't have come.'

'Terrible mix up.' He nodded. 'A horse killed. It does racing no good.'

'What about the spectators? My son Toby thought one of them, too, was dead.'

Roger said disgustedly, 'A hundred dead spectators wouldn't raise marches against cruel sports. The stands could collapse and kill a hundred, but racing would go on. Dead *people* are irrelevant, don't you know.'

'So . . . the man *was* dead?'

'Did you see him?'

'Only with a dressing covering his face.'

Roger said gloomily, 'It'll be in the papers. The horse came through the wing into him and slashed him across the eyes with a foreleg – those racing plates on their hooves cut like swords – it was gruesome, Oliver said. But the man died of a snapped neck. Died instantly under half a ton of horse. Best that can be said.'

'My son Toby saw the man's face,' I said.

Roger looked at me. 'Which is Toby?'

'The second one. He's twelve. The boy who rode his bike into the house.'

'I remember. Poor little bugger. Nightmares ahead, I shouldn't wonder.'

Toby was anyway the one I most worried about, and this wouldn't help. He'd been born rebellious, grown into a cantankerous toddler and had never since been easy to persuade. I had a sad feeling that in four years' time he would

27

develop, despite my best efforts, into a sullen world-hating youth, alienated and miserable. I could sense that it would happen and I ached for it not to, but I'd seen too many other suffering families where a much loved son or daughter had grown destructively angry in the mid-teens, despising attempts to help.

Rebecca Stratton, I surmised, might have been like that, ten years earlier. She came into Oliver's office now like a whirlwind, smashing the door open until it hit the wall, bringing in with her a swirl of cold outside air and a towering attack of fury.

'Where's that bloody Oliver?' she loudly demanded, looking round.

'With your father . . .'

She didn't listen. She still wore breeches and boots, but with a tan sweater in place of her racing colours. Her eyes glittered, her body looked rigid, she seemed half-way demented. 'Do you know what that stupid bloody doctor's done? He's stood me down from racing for *four* days. Four days! I ask you. He says I'm concussed. Concussed, my arse. Where's Oliver? He's got to tell that bloody man I'm going to ride on Monday. Where is he?'

Rebecca spun on her heel and strode out with the same energy expenditure as on the way in.

I said, closing the door after her, 'She's concussed to high heaven, I'd have said.'

'Yes, but she's always a bit like that. If I were the doctor I'd stand her down for life.'

'She's not your favourite Stratton, I gather.'

Caution returned to Roger with a rush. 'I never said . . .'

'Of course not.' I paused. 'So what has changed since last Sunday?'

He consulted the light cream walls, the framed print of Arkle, the big calendar with days crossed off, a large clock (accurate) and his own shoes, and finally said, 'Mrs Binsham came out of the woodwork.'

'Is that so momentous?'

'You know who she *is*?' He was curious, a little surprised.

'The old Lord's sister.'

'I thought you didn't know anything about the family.'

'I said I had no contact with them, and I don't. But my mother talked about them. Like I told you, she was once married to the old man's son.'

'Do you mean Conrad? Or Keith? Or . . . Ivan?'

'Keith,' I said. 'Conrad's twin.'

'Fraternal twins,' Roger said. 'The younger one.'

I agreed. 'Twenty-five minutes younger, and apparently never got over it.'

'It does make a difference, I suppose.'

It made the difference between inheriting a barony, and not. Inheriting the family mansion, and not. Inheriting a fortune, and not. Keith's jealousy of his twenty-five minute elder brother had been one – but only one, according to my mother – of the habitual rancours poisoning her ex-husband's psyche.

I had my mother's photographs of her Stratton wedding day, the bridegroom tall, light-haired, smiling, strikingly good looking, all the promise of a splendid life ahead in the pride and tenderness of his manner towards her. She had that day been exploding with bliss, she'd told me; with an indescribable floating feeling of happiness.

Within six months he'd broken her arm in a fight and punched out two of her front teeth.

'Mrs Binsham,' Roger Gardner said, 'has insisted on a shareholders' meeting next week. She's a dragon, they say. She's Conrad's aunt, of course, and apparently she's the only living creature who makes him quake.'

Forty years back she had implacably forced her brother, the third baron, to behave harshly in public to my mother. Even then Mrs Binsham had been the dynamo of the family, the manipulator, the one who laid down the programme of action and forced the rest to follow.

'She never gave up,' my mother said. 'She would simply wear down any opposition until you would do what she wanted just to get some peace. In her own eyes, you see, she was always *right*, so she was always certain that what she wanted was *best*.'

I asked Roger, 'Do you know Mrs Binsham yourself?'

'Yes, but not well. She's an impressive old lady, very upright. She comes to the races here quite often with Lord Stratton – er, not Conrad, but the old Lord – but I've never had any really private conversations with her. Oliver knows her better. Or at least,' he faintly grinned, 'Oliver has obeyed her instructions from time to time.'

'Perhaps she'll sort out the present squabbles and quieten things down,' I said.

Roger shook his head. 'What she says might go with Conrad and Keith and Ivan, but the younger generation may rebel, especially since they're all coming into some shares of their own.'

'You're sure?'

'Certain.'

'So now you have an informant in the nest?'

His face grew still; wary almost. 'I never said that.'

'No.'

Oliver returned. 'The sponsors are unhappy about the dead horse, bless their little hearts. Bad publicity. Not what they pay for. They'll have to reconsider before next year, they say.' He sounded dispirited. 'I'd framed that race well, you know,' he told me. 'Ten runners in a three-mile 'chase. That's good, you know. Often you'll only attract five or six, or even less. If the sponsor pulls out, it'll be a poorer affair altogether, next year.'

I made sympathetic noises.

'If there *is* a next year,' he said. 'There's a shareholders' meeting next week . . . did they tell you?'

'Yes.'

'They're holding it here on the racecourse, in the Strattons' private dining room,' he said. 'Conrad hasn't moved into the big house yet, and anyway this is less personal, he says. Will you be coming?' It was less a question, I thought, than an entreaty.

'I haven't decided,' I said.

'I do hope you will. I mean, they need an *outside* view, do you see? They're all too *involved*.'

30

'They wouldn't want me there.'

'All the more reason for going.'

I doubted that, but didn't bother to argue. I suggested collecting the boys, and found them 'helping' the valets pack the jockeys' saddles and other gear into large laundry hampers while eating fruit cake.

They'd been no trouble, I was told, and hoped I could believe it. I thanked everyone. Thanked Roger. 'Vote your shares,' he said anxiously. Thanked Jenkins. 'Well-behaved little sods,' he said helpfully. 'Bring them again.'

'We called everyone "sir",' Neil confided to me as we left.

'We called Jenkins "sir",' Alan said. 'He got us the cake.'

We reached the mini-van and climbed in, and they showed me all the jockeys' autographs in their racecards. They'd had a good time in the changing room, it seemed.

'Was that man dead?' Toby asked, reverting to what was most on his mind.

'I'm afraid so.'

'I thought he was. I've never seen anyone dead before.'

'You've seen dogs,' Alan said.

'That's not the same, plank-head.'

Christopher asked, 'What did the colonel mean about voting your shares?'

'Huh?'

'He said "Vote your shares." He looked pretty upset, didn't he?'

'Well,' I said, 'do you know what shares are?'

'Pieces of cake,' Neil guessed. 'One each.'

'Say you had a chessboard,' I said, 'there would be sixty-four squares, OK? Say you called each square a share. There would be sixty-four shares.'

The young faces told me I wasn't getting the idea across.

'OK,' I said, 'say you have a floor made of tiles.'

They nodded at once. As a builder's children they knew all about tiles.

'Say you lay ten tiles across and ten tiles down, and fill in the square.'

'A hundred tiles,' Christopher nodded.

'Yes. Now call each tile a share, a hundredth part of the whole square. A hundred shares. OK?'

They nodded.

'What about voting?' Christopher asked.

I hesitated. 'Say you owned some of the tiles, you could vote to have yours blue . . . or red . . . whatever you'd like.'

'How many could *you* vote on?'

'Eight,' I said.

'You could have eight blue tiles? What about the others?'

'All the others, ninety-two, belong to other people. They could all choose whatever colour they liked for the tiles they owned.'

'It would be a mess,' Edward pointed out. 'You wouldn't get everyone to agree on a pattern.'

'You're absolutely right,' I said, smiling.

'But you're not really meaning *tiles*, are you?' Christopher said.

'No.' I paused. For once, they were all listening. 'See, say this racecourse is like a hundred tiles. A hundred squares. A hundred shares. I have eight shares of the racecourse. Other people have ninety-two.'

Christopher shrugged. 'It's not much, then. Eight's not even one row.'

Neil said, 'If the racecourse was divided up into a hundred squares, Dad's eight squares might have the stands on!'

'Plank-head,' Toby said.

32

CHAPTER 3

Why did I go?

I don't know. I doubt if there is such a thing as a wholly free choice, because one's choices are rooted in one's personality. I choose what I choose because I am what I am, that sort of thing.

I chose to go for reprehensible reasons like the lure of unearned gain and from the vanity that I might against all odds tame the dragon and sort out the Stratton feuds peacefully, as Roger and Oliver wanted. Greed and pride . . . powerful spurs masquerading as prudent financial management and altruistic good works.

So I disregarded the despairing plea from my mother's remembered wisdom and took my children into desperate danger and by my presence altered for ever the internal stresses and balances of the Strattons.

Except, of course, that it didn't seem like that on the day of the shareholders' meeting.

It took place on the Wednesday afternoon, on the third day of the ruin hunt. On Monday morning the five boys and I had set off from home in the big converted single-decker bus that had in the past served as mobile home for us all during periods when the currently-being-rebuilt ruin had been truly and totally uninhabitable.

The bus had its points: it would sleep eight, it had a working shower room, a galley, sofas and television. I'd taken lessons from a yacht builder in creating storage spaces where none might seem to exist, and we could in fact store a sizeable household very neatly aboard. It did not, all the same, offer privacy or much personal space, and as the boys grew they had found it increasingly embarrassing as an address.

They packed into it quite happily on the Monday, though, as I had promised them a real holiday in the afternoons if I could visit a ruin each morning, and in fact with map and timetables I'd planned a series of the things they most liked to do. Monday afternoon we spent canoeing on the Thames, Tuesday they beat the hell out of a bowling alley, and on the Wednesday they'd promised to help Roger Gardner's wife clean out her garage, a chore they bizarrely enjoyed.

I left the bus outside the Gardner house and with Roger walked to the stands.

'I'm not invited to the meeting,' he said as if it were a relief, 'but I'll show you to the door.'

He took me up a staircase, round a couple of corners, and through a door marked Private into a carpeted world quite different from the functional concrete of the public areas. Silently pointing to panelled and polished double-doors ahead, he gave me an encouraging pat on the shoulder and left me, rather in the manner of a colonel avuncularly sending a rookie into his first battle.

Regretting my presence already, I opened one of the double-doors and went in.

I'd gone to the meeting in business clothes (grey trousers, white shirt, tie, navy blazer) to present a conventional boardroom appearance. I had a tidy normal haircut, the smoothest of shaves, clean fingernails. The big dusty labourer of the building sites couldn't be guessed at.

The older men at the meeting all wore suits. Those more my own age and younger hadn't bothered with such formality. I had, I thought in satisfaction, hit it just right.

Although I had arrived at the time stated in the solicitor's letter, it seemed that the Strattons had jumped the clock. The whole tribe were sitting round a truly imposing Edwardian dining table of old French-polished mahogany, their chairs newer, nineteen-thirtyish, like the grandstands themselves.

The only one I knew by sight was Rebecca, the jockey, dressed now in trousers, tailored jacket and heavy gold chains. The man sitting at the head of the table, grey-haired, bulky and authoritative, I took to be Conrad, the fourth and latest baron.

He turned his head to me as I went in. They all, of course, turned their heads. Five men, three women.

'I'm afraid you are in the wrong place,' Conrad said with scant politeness. 'This is a private meeting.'

'Stratton shareholders?' I asked inoffensively.

'As it happens. And you are . . .?'

'Lee Morris.'

The shock that rippled through them was almost funny, as if they hadn't realised that I would even be notified of the meeting, let alone had considered that I might attend; and they had every reason to be surprised, as I had never before responded to any of their official annual bits of paper.

I closed the door quietly behind me. 'I was sent a notification,' I said.

'Yes, but –' Conrad said without welcome. 'I mean, it wasn't necessary . . . You weren't expected to bother . . .' He stopped uncomfortably, unable to hide what looked like dismay.

'As I'm here,' I said amiably, 'I may as well stay. Shall I sit here?' I indicated an empty chair at the foot of the table, walking towards it purposefully. 'We've never met,' I went on, 'but you must be Conrad, Lord Stratton.'

He said 'Yes', tight lipped.

One of the older men said violently, 'This is a disgrace! You've no right here. Don't sit down. You're *leaving*.'

I stood by the empty chair and brought the solicitor's letter out of a pocket. 'As you'll see,' I answered him pleasantly, 'I *am* a shareholder. I was properly given advance notice of this meeting, and I'm sorry if you don't like it, but I do have a legal right to be here. I'll just sit quietly and listen.'

I sat down. All of the faces registered stark disapproval except for one, a younger man's, bearing a hint of a grin.

'Conrad! This is ridiculous.' The man who most violently opposed my presence was up on his feet, quivering with fury. 'Get rid of him at once.'

Conrad Stratton realistically took stock of my size and comparative youth and said defeatedly, 'Sit down, Keith. Who exactly is going to throw him out?'

Keith, my mother's first husband, might have been strong enough in his youth to batter a miserable young wife, but there was no way he could begin to do the same to her thirty-five-year-old son. He hated the fact of my existence. I hated what I'd learned of him. The antagonism between us was mutual, powerful and lasting.

The fair hair in the wedding photographs had turned a blondish grey. The good bone structure still gave him a more patrician air than that of his elder twin. His looking glass must still constantly be telling him that the order of his birth had been nature's horrible mistake, that *his* should have been the head that engaged first.

He couldn't sit down. He strode about the big room, snapping his head round in my direction now and then, and glaring at me.

Important chaps who might have been the first and second barons looked down impassively from gold-framed portraits on the walls. The lighting hung from the ceiling in convoluted brass chandeliers with etched glass shades round candle bulbs. Upon a long polished mahogany sideboard stood a short case clock flanked by heavy old throttled-neck vases that, like the whole room, had an air of having remained unchanged for most of the old Lord's life.

There was no daylight: no windows.

Next to Conrad sat a ramrod-backed old lady easy to identify as his aunt, Marjorie Binsham, the convener of this affair. Forty years earlier, on my mother's wedding day, she had stared grimly at the camera as if a smile would have cracked her facial muscles, and nothing in that way, either, seemed to have been affected by passing years. Now well into her eighties, she flourished a still sharp brain under disciplined wavy white hair and wore a red and black dog-toothed dress with a white, ecclesiastical-looking collar.

Rather to my surprise she was regarding me more with curiosity than rigid dislike.

'Mrs Binsham?' I said from the other end of the table. 'Mrs Marjorie Binsham?'

'Yes.' The monosyllable came out clipped and dry, merely acknowledging information.

'I,' said the man whose grin was now in control, 'am Darlington Stratton, known as Dart. My father sits at the head of the table. My sister Rebecca is on your right.'

'This is unnecessary!' Keith snapped at him from somewhere behind Conrad. 'He does not need introductions. He's leaving.'

Mrs Binsham said repressively and with exquisite diction, 'Keith, do stop prowling, and sit down. Mr Morris is correct, he has a right to be here. Face facts. As you cannot eject him, ignore him.'

Mrs Binsham's direct gaze was bent on me, not on Keith. My own lips twitched. Ignoring me seemed the last thing any of them could do.

Dart said, with a straight face covering infinite mischief, 'Have you met Hannah, your sister?'

The woman on the other side of Conrad from Mrs Binsham vibrated with disgust. 'He's not my brother. He's *not*.'

'Half-brother,' Marjorie Binsham said, with the same cool fact-facing precision. 'Unpalatable as you may find it, Hannah, you cannot change it. Just ignore him.'

For Hannah, as for Keith, the advice was impossible to follow. My half-sister, to my relief, didn't look like our joint mother. I'd been afraid she might: afraid to find familiar eyes hating me from an echo of a loved face. She looked more like Keith, tall, blonde, fine-boned and, at the moment, white with outrage.

'How dare you!' She shook. 'Have you no decency?'

'I have shares,' I pointed out.

'And you shouldn't have,' Keith said harshly. 'Why Father ever gave them to Madeline, I'll never know.'

37

I refrained from saying that he must know perfectly well why. Lord Stratton had given shares to Madeline, his daughter-in-law, because he knew why she was leaving. In my mother's papers, after she'd died, I came across old letters from her father-in-law telling her of his regret, of his regard for her, of his concern that she shouldn't suffer financially, as she had physically. Though loyal in public to his son, he had privately not only given her the shares 'for the future' but had endowed her also with a lump sum to keep her comfortable on the interest. In return, she had promised never ever to speak of Keith's behaviour, still less to drag the family name through a messy divorce. The old man wrote that he understood her rejection of Hannah, the result of his son's 'sexual attacks'. He would care for the child, he wrote. He wished my mother 'the best that can be achieved, my dear'.

It was Keith who later divorced my mother – for adultery with an elderly illustrator of childrens' books, Leyton Morris, my father. The resulting devoted marriage lasted fifteen years, and it wasn't until she was on her own one-way road with cancer that my mother talked of the Strattons and told me in long night-time outpourings about her sufferings and her fondness for Lord Stratton; and it wasn't until then that I learned that it was Lord Stratton's money that had educated me and sent me through architectural school, the foundations of my life.

I had written to thank him after she died, and I still had his reply.

> My dear Boy,
> I loved your Mother. I hope you gave her the joy she deserved. I thank you for your letter, but do not write again.
> Stratton.

I didn't write again. I sent flowers to his funeral. With him alive, I would never have intruded on his family.

With Conrad identified, and Keith, and Marjorie Binsham, and Conrad's offspring Dart and Rebecca, there remained two males at the meeting still to be named. One, in late middle-age, sat between Mrs Binsham and Keith's vacated chair, and I could make a guess at him.

'Excuse me,' I said, leaning forward to catch his attention. 'Are you . . . Ivan?'

The youngest of the old Lord's three sons, more bullish like Conrad than greyhound like Keith, gave me a hard stare and no reply.

Dart said easily, 'My uncle Ivan, as you say. And opposite him is his son Forsyth, my cousin.'

'Dart!' Keith objected fiercely. 'Be quiet.'

Dart gave him an impassive look and seemed unintimidated. Forsyth, Ivan's son, was the one, I thought, that had reacted least to my attendance. That is to say he took it less personally than the others, and he slowly revealed, as time went on, that he had no interest in me as Hannah's regrettable half-brother, but only as an unknown factor in the matter of shares.

Young and slight, he had a narrow chin and dark intense eyes, and was treated by the others without the slightest deference. No one throughout the meeting asked his opinion about anything and, when he gave it regardless, his father, Ivan, regularly interrupted. Forsyth himself seemed to find this treatment normal, and perhaps for him it was.

Conrad, coming testily to terms with the inevitable, said heavily, 'Let's get on with the meeting. I called it . . .'

'*I* called it,' corrected his aunt sharply. 'All this squabbling is ridiculous. Let's get to the point. There has been racing on this racecourse for almost ninety years, and it will go on as before, and that's an end to it. The arguing must stop.'

'This racecourse is dying on its feet,' Rebecca contradicted impatiently. 'You have absolutely no idea what the modern world is all about. I'm sorry if it upsets you, Aunt Marjorie, but you and Grandfather have been left behind by the tide. This place needs new stands and a whole new outlook, and what it doesn't need is a fuddy-duddy old colonel for a manager and a stick-in-the-mud Clerk of the Course who can't say boo to a doctor.'

'The doctor outranks him,' Dart observed.

'You shut up,' his sister ordered. 'You've never had the

bottle to ride in a race. I've raced on most courses in this country and I'm telling you, this place is terminally old fashioned and it's got my name on it too, which makes me open to ridicule, and the whole thing *stinks*. If you won't or can't see that, then I'm in favour of cashing in now for what we can get.'

'Rebecca!' Conrad's reproof seemed tired, as if he'd heard his daughter's views too often. 'We need new stands. We can all agree on that. And I've commissioned plans . . .'

'You'd no right to do that,' Marjorie informed him. 'Waste of money. These old stands are solidly built and are thoroughly serviceable. We do *not* need new stands. I'm totally opposed to the idea.'

Keith said with troublemaking relish, 'Conrad has had this pet architect roaming round the place for weeks. *His* choice of architect. None of us has been consulted, and I'm against new stands on principle.'

'Huh!' Rebecca exclaimed. 'And where do you think the women jockeys have to change? In a partitioned-off space the size of a *cupboard* in the Ladies loo. It's pathetic.'

'All for want of a horseshoe nail,' Dart murmured.

'What do you mean?' Rebecca demanded.

'I mean,' her brother explained lazily, 'that we'll lose the racecourse to feminism.'

She wasn't sure enough of his meaning to come up with a cutting answer so instead ignored him.

'We should sell at once,' Keith exclaimed, still striding about. 'The market is good. Swindon is still growing. The industrial area is already on the racecourse boundary. Sell, I say. I've already sounded out a local developer. He's agreed to survey and consider –'

'You've done *what*?' Conrad demanded. 'And *you've* consulted no one, either. And that's never the way to sell *anything*. You know nothing about business dealings.'

Keith said huffily, 'I know if you want to sell something you have to advertise.'

'No,' Conrad said flatly, as if that settled it. 'We're not selling.'

Keith's anger rose. 'It's all right for *you*. You inherit most of Father's residual estate. It's not fair. It was *never* fair, leaving nearly all to eldest sons. Father was hopelessly old fashioned. *You* may not need money, but none of us is getting any younger and I say take out our capital *now*.'

'Later,' Hannah said intensely. 'Sell when there's less land available. Wait.'

Conrad remarked heavily, 'Your daughter, Keith, fears that if you take the capital now you'll squander it and there'll be none left for her to inherit.'

Hannah's face revealed it to be a bull's eye diagnosis, and also showed disgust at having had her understandable motives so tellingly disclosed.

'What about you, Ivan?' his aunt enquired. 'Still of the same indecisive mind?'

Ivan scarcely responded to the jibe, even if he recognised it as one. He nodded with a show of measured sagacity. 'Wait and see,' he said. 'That's the best.'

'Wait until you've lost the opportunity,' Rebecca said scathingly. 'That's what you mean, isn't it?'

He said defensively, 'Why are you always so *sharp*, Rebecca? There's nothing wrong with patience.'

'Inaction,' she corrected. 'Making no decision's as bad as making the wrong decision.'

'Rubbish,' Ivan said.

Forsyth began, 'Have we thought about tax on capital gains ...' but Ivan was saying, 'It's clear we ought to shelve a decision until –'

'Until the bloody cows come home,' Rebecca said.

'Rebecca!' Her great-aunt's disapproval arrived automatically. 'Now stop it, all of you, because at the moment I and I alone can make decisions and I have the impression that none of you realises that.'

From their expressions it was clear that they neither knew nor cared to be told.

'Aunt,' Conrad said repressively, 'you have ten shares only. You cannot make unilateral decisions.'

'Oh, but I can,' she said triumphantly. 'You're so ignorant, all of you. You fancy yourselves as men – oh, and *women*, Rebecca – of affairs but none of you seems to realise that in any company it is the directors, not shareholders, who make the decisions, and *I* . . .' she looked round, collecting undivided attention, 'I am at present the sole remaining director. *I* make the decisions.'

She brought the meeting to its first taste of silence.

After a pause, Dart laughed. Everyone else scowled, chiefly at him, disapproval of a grandson being more prudent than defying the dragon.

The splendid old lady took folded sheets of paper from an expensive leather handbag and shook them open with an almost theatrical flourish.

'This is a letter,' she said, putting on reading glasses, 'from the Stratton Park racecourse solicitors. I won't bother you with the introductory paragraphs. The heart of the matter is this.' She paused, glanced round at her attentive and apprehensive audience and then read from the letter. 'As two directors are sufficient, it was quite proper for yourself and Lord Stratton to comprise the whole Board and for him, as by far the major shareholder, to make all the decisions. Now that he has died you may wish to form a new Board with more directors, and while these *may* be members of the Stratton family, there is no bar to your electing outside, non-shareholding directors if you should wish.

'We would accordingly suggest you call an extraordinary meeting of shareholders for the purpose of electing new directors to serve on the Board of Stratton Park Racecourse Ltd, and we will be happy to assist you in every possible way.'

Marjorie Binsham looked up. 'The solicitors were willing to conduct this meeting. I said I could do it and they weren't to bother. As the sole remaining director of the company I make a motion that we elect new directors, and as director I also second the motion, and although this may not be exactly regulation procedure, it will have the desired effect.'

Conrad said, feebly for him, 'Aunt . . .'

'As you, Conrad, are now titular head of the family, I propose that you become a director forthwith.' She looked down at the letter. 'It says here that any director may be elected if he obtains at least fifty per cent of the votes cast at a shareholders' meeting. Each share, in this company, bears one vote. According to this letter, if I and the inheriting family shareholders all attend this meeting, there will be eighty-five votes available. That is to say, my ten shares, and the seventy-five now inherited by the rest of you.' She paused and looked down the table to where I sat. 'We did not expect Mr Morris to attend, but as he is here, he has eight votes to cast.'

'No!' Keith said furiously. 'He has no *right*.'

Marjorie Binsham replied implacably, 'He has eight votes. He can cast them. You cannot prevent it.'

Her verdict had surprised me as much as it had astounded the others. I'd gone there out of curiosity as much as anything else, ready to upset them slightly, but not to this fundamental extent.

'It's *disgraceful*,' Hannah yelled, rising compulsively from her seat like her still-pacing father. 'I won't have it!'

'According to our solicitors,' her great-aunt went on, totally ignoring the tantrum, 'once we have elected a Board of Directors it is *they* who decide the future of this racecourse.'

'Make *me* a director,' Rebecca demanded.

'You need forty-seven votes,' murmured Dart, having done some arithmetic. 'Any director needs forty-seven, minimum.'

'I propose we elect Conrad at once,' Marjorie reiterated. 'He has my ten votes.' She looked round, challenging them to disagree.

'All right,' Ivan said, 'Conrad, you have my twenty-one.'

'I suppose I can vote for myself,' Conrad said. 'I vote my own twenty-one. That's, er, fifty-two.'

'Elected,' Marjorie said, nodding. 'You can now conduct the rest of the meeting.'

Conrad's manner regained confidence and he seemed literally to swell to fill his new role. He said kindly, 'Then I think we should vote to keep Marjorie on the Board. Only right.'

No one demurred. The Honourable Mrs Binsham looked as if she would chew any dissenter for breakfast.

'I, too, must be a director,' Keith asserted. 'I also have twenty-one shares. I vote them for me.'

Conrad cleared his throat. 'I propose Keith for director . . .'

Forsyth said too quickly, 'That's asking for trouble.'

Conrad, not hearing, or at least choosing not to, hurried on. 'Keith's twenty-one, then, and mine. Forty-two. Aunt?'

Marjorie shook her head. Keith took three fast paces towards her with his hands outstretched as if he would attack her. She didn't flinch or shrink away. She stared him down.

She said with starch, 'That's exactly why I won't vote for you, Keith. You never had any self-control, and you've grown no wiser with age. Look elsewhere. Ask Mr Morris.'

A wicked old lady, I saw. Keith went scarlet. Dart grinned.

Keith walked round behind Ivan. 'Brother,' he said peremptorily, 'I need your twenty-one votes.'

'But I say,' Ivan dithered, 'Aunt Marjorie's right. You'd fight Conrad all the time. No sensible decisions would ever get made.'

'Are you *refusing* me?' Keith could hardly believe it. 'You'll be sorry, you know. You'll be sorry.' The violence in his character had risen too near the surface even for his daughter, Hannah, who had subsided into her seat and now said uneasily, 'Dad, don't bother with him. You can have my three votes. Do calm down.'

'That's forty-five,' Conrad said. 'You need two more, Keith.'

'Rebecca has three,' Keith said.

Rebecca shook her head.

'Forsyth, then,' Keith said furiously, at least not begging.

Forsyth looked at his fingers.

'*Dart?*' Keith shook with anger.

Dart glanced at his sweating uncle and took pity on him.

'OK, then,' he said, making nothing of it. 'My three.'

Without much emotion, a relief after the storm, Conrad said flatly, 'Keith's elected.'

'And to be fair,' Dart said, 'I propose Ivan also.'

'We don't need four directors,' Keith said.

'As I voted for *you*,' Dart told him, 'you can do the decent thing and vote for Ivan. After all, he has twenty-one shares, just like you, and he's got just as much right to make decisions. So, Father,' he said to Conrad, 'I propose Ivan.'

Conrad considered his son's proposal and shrugged: not because he disapproved, I guessed, but because he didn't think much of his brother Ivan's brains.

'Very well. Ivan. Anyone against?'

Everyone shook their heads, including Marjorie.

'Mr Morris?' Conrad asked formally.

'He has my votes.'

'Unanimous, then,' Conrad said, surprised. 'Any more nominations?'

Rebecca said, 'Four is a bad number. There should be five. Someone from the younger generation.'

She was suggesting herself again. No one, not even Dart, responded. Rebecca's thin face was in its way as mean as Keith's.

Not one of the four grandchildren was going to give power to any other. The three older brothers showed no wish to pass batons. The Board, with undercurrents of gripe and spite, was established as the old Lord's three sons and their enduring aunt.

Without difficulty they agreed that Conrad should be Chairman ('*Chair*,' Rebecca said. 'Don't be ridiculous,' said Keith), but Marjorie had another squib in reserve.

'The solicitor's letter also says,' she announced, 'that if the shareholders are dissatisfied with any director, they can call a meeting and vote to remove him. They need a fifty-one per cent vote to achieve it.' She stared beadily at Keith. 'If it should become advisable to save us all from an irresponsible director, I will make certain that Mr Morris and his eight votes are encouraged to attend the meeting.'

Hannah was as affronted as Keith, but Keith, besides being infuriated, seemed almost bewildered, as if the possibility of his aunt's vitriolic disapproval had never occurred to him. Similarly it had never occurred to me that she wouldn't demand my execution rather than my presence. Marjorie, I then reckoned, would use any tool that came to hand to achieve a desired end: a wholly pragmatic lady.

Dart said with deceptive amiability, 'Isn't there some rule in the set up of this company that says all board meetings are open? I mean, all shareholders may attend.'

'Rubbish,' Keith said.

Forsyth said, 'Attend but not interrupt. Not speak unless asked.'

Ivan's voice drowned his son's. 'We'll have to read the articles, or whatever.'

'I did,' Forsyth said. No one paid any attention.

'It never mattered before,' Conrad observed. 'The only shareholders besides Father and Aunt Marjorie were Mr Morris, and of course before him, Madeline, and ... er ... Mrs Perdita Faulds.'

'Who exactly *is* Mrs Perdita Faulds?' Rebecca demanded.

No one replied. If they knew, they weren't telling.

'Do you,' Dart asked me directly, 'know who Mrs Perdita Faulds is?'

I shook my head. 'No.'

'We'll find her if necessary,' Marjorie declared, making it sound ominous. 'Let's hope we won't have to.' Her malevolent gaze swept over Keith, warning him. 'If we have to remove a director, we will find her.'

On the brief list of shareholders that Roger had shown me, Mrs Faulds' address had been care of a firm of solicitors. Messages to the lady would no doubt routinely be relayed, but actually finding her in person might take ingenuity. Take a professional bloodhound, perhaps. Marjorie wouldn't blink at that, I guessed, if it suited her.

It also occurred to me that if she were so certain the mysterious Mrs Faulds would vote as Marjorie wanted, then Marjorie, at least, knew who she was. Not really my business, I thought.

Conrad said, with a show of taking a grip on the meeting, 'Well, now that we have directors, perhaps we can make some firm decisions. We must, in fact. We have another race meeting here next Monday, as you know, and we cannot ask Marjorie indefinitely to be responsible for authorising everything. There was a lot Father used to do that none of us know about. We simply have to learn fast.'

'The first thing to do is sack the Colonel and stupid Oliver,' Rebecca said.

Conrad merely glanced at his daughter and spoke to the others. 'The Colonel and Oliver are the only people at present who can keep this place running. We need, in fact we rely entirely, on their expertise, and I intend to go on consulting them over every detail.'

Rebecca sulked angrily. Marjorie's disapproval grew vigorous runners in her direction, like a rampant strawberry plant.

'I put forward a motion,' Ivan said surprisingly, 'that we continue to run the races as before, with Roger and Oliver in their normal roles.'

'Seconded,' Marjorie said crisply.

Keith scowled. Conrad, ignoring him, made a note on a pad in front of him. 'The Board's first decision is to continue without change, for now.' He pursed his lips. 'I suppose we ought to have a secretary to write the minutes.'

'You could use Roger's secretary,' I suggested.

'No!' Rebecca jumped on it. 'Everything we said would go straight to bloody Roger. And no one asked you to speak. You're an outsider.'

Dart launched into verse, 'Oh wad some power the giftie gie us to see oursels as others see us! It wad frae monie a blunder free us, an' foolish notion.'

'*What?*' Rebecca demanded.

'Robert Burns,' Dart said. 'To a Louse.'

I smothered the least appearance of a laugh. No one else seemed to think it funny.

I said to Rebecca mildly, 'You could reposition the women jockeys' changing room.'

'Oh really?' She was sarcastic. 'Exactly where?'

'I'll show you. And,' I went on speaking to Conrad, 'you could double the take in the bars.'

'Ye *gods*,' Dart said comically, 'what have we here?'

I asked Conrad, 'Are there already detailed plans for new stands?'

'We're *not* having new stands!' Marjorie was adamant.

'We must,' Conrad said.

'We sell the land,' Keith insisted.

Ivan dithered.

'New stands,' Rebecca said. 'New management. New everything. Or sell.'

'Sell, but later,' Hannah repeated obstinately.

'I agree,' Forsyth nodded.

'Not in my lifetime,' Marjorie said.

CHAPTER 4

When the meeting broke up, it became apparent why it had
been held impersonally on the racecourse, as none of the
people attending lived with any of the others.

They walked out as individuals, each in a seeming barbed-
wire enclosure of self righteousness, none of them anxious to
acknowledge my continued presence.

Only Dart, halfway out of the door, looked back to where I
stood watching the exodus.

'Coming?' he said. 'The fun's done.'

With a smile I joined him by the door as he thoughtfully
looked me over.

'Care for a jar?' he said and, when I hesitated, added,
'There's a pub right outside the main gates that's open all day.
And, frankly, I'm curious.'

'Curiosity's a two-way street.'

He nodded. 'Agreed, then.' He led the way downstairs by a
different route than the one I'd come up, and we emerged into
an area, within the paddocks and near the unsaddling
enclosures, that had been crowded with people on the race
day but now contained only a number of parked cars. Into
each car a single Stratton was climbing, none of the brothers,
offspring or cousins grouping for friendly family chat.

Dart took it for granted and asked where my car was.

'Down there.' I pointed vaguely.

'Oh? Hop in, then. I'll drive you.'

Dart's car, an old dusty economical runabout, was standing next to Marjorie's chauffeur-driven blackly-gleaming Daimler, and she lowered her rear window as she glided slowly away, staring in disbelief at my acceptance by Dart. Dart waved to her cheerfully, reminding me vividly of my son Alan's similar disregard of the power of dragons, a lack of perception as much as a matter of courage.

Car doors slammed, engines purred, brake lights went on and off; the Strattons dispersed. Dart put his own car into gear and steered us straight to the main entrance, where a few forlorn looking individuals were slowly walking up and down bearing placards saying 'BAN STEEPLECHASING' and 'CRUELTY TO ANIMALS'.

'They've been here trying to stop people coming in, ever since that horse died here last Saturday,' Dart observed. 'The woolly-head brigade, I call them.'

It was an apt enough description, as they wore a preponderance of knitted hats. Their placards were handwritten and amateurish, but their dedication couldn't be doubted.

'They don't understand horses,' Dart said. 'Horses run and jump because they want to. Horses try their damnedest to get to the front of the herd. Racing wouldn't exist if it weren't for horses naturally busting their guts to get out in front and win.' The grin came and went. 'I don't have the instincts of a horse.'

But his sister had, I thought.

Dart by-passed the demonstrators and drove across the road into the car park of the Mayflower Inn opposite, which looked as if it had never seen Plymouth let alone sailed the Atlantic.

Inside, it was resolutely decorated with 1620 imitation memorabilia, but not too bad for all that. Murals of pilgrim fathers in top hats (an anachronism) and white beards (wrong, the pilgrims were young) were reminiscent of Abraham Lincoln two hundred years later, but who cared? The place was warm and welcoming and had at least tried.

Dart bought us two unadventurous half-pints and put them carefully on a small dark oak table, settling us into wooden armed, reasonably comfortable old oak chairs.

'So why,' he said, 'did you come?'

'Eight shares in a racecourse.'

He had steel grey eyes: unusual. Unlike his sister, he hadn't honed his bone structure to angular leanness. Not for him the agonies and bad-temper-inducing deprivations of an unremitting battle with weight. Thirty or thereabouts, Dart already showed the roundness which could develop into the all-over weightiness of his father. Unlike his father he was also showing early signs of baldness, and this did, I slowly discovered, upset him radically.

'I'd heard about you,' Dart said, 'but you were always cast as a villain. You don't look villainous in the least.'

'Who cast me as a villain?'

'Hannah, mostly, I suppose. She's never got over being rejected by her mother. I mean, mothers aren't supposed to dump infants, are they? Fathers do, regularly, male prerogative. Rebecca would kill me for saying that. Anyway, your mother dumped Hannah but not *you*. I'd look out for knives between the shoulder blades, if I were you.'

His voice sounded light and frivolous but I had the impression I'd received a serious warning.

'What do you do?' I asked neutrally. 'What do you all do?'

'Do? I farm. That is to say, I look after the family estates.' Perhaps he read polite surprise on my face because he grimaced self-deprecatingly and said, 'As it happens, we have a farm manager who runs the land and also an agent who sees to the tenants, but I make the decisions. That is to say, I listen to what the manager wants to do and to what the agent wants to do, and then I decide that that's what *I* want them to do, so they do it. Unless Father has different ideas. Unless Grandfather had different ideas, in the old days. And, of course, unless they've all been listening to my Great Aunt Marjorie whose ideas are ultimate.' He paused quite cheerfully. 'The whole thing's bloody boring, and not what I'd like to do at all.'

'Which is?' I asked, entertained.

'Fantasy land,' he said. 'Private property. Keep out.' He meant no offence. The same words in Keith's mouth would have been a curse. 'What do *you* do, yourself?' he asked.

'I'm a builder,' I said.

'Really? What of?'

'Houses, mostly.'

It didn't interest him greatly. He trotted briefly through the occupations of the other Strattons, or at least the ones I'd met.

'Rebecca's a jockey, I suppose you guessed? She's been besotted with horses all her life. She's two years younger than me. Our papa owns a racehorse or two and goes hunting. He used to do my own job until he decided I was too idle, so now he does even less. But to be fair, he does no harm, which in these days invests him with sainthood. My Uncle Keith . . . heaven knows. He's supposed to be in finance, whatever that means. My Uncle Ivan has a garden centre, all ghastly gnomes and things. He potters about there some days and trusts his manager.'

He paused to drink and gave me a glimmering inspection over the glass's rim.

'Go on,' I said.

'Hannah,' he nodded. 'She's never done a hard day's work. My grandfather poured money over her to make up for her mother – *your* mother – rejecting her, but he never seemed to love her . . . I suppose I shouldn't say that. Anyway, Hannah's not married but she has a son called Jack who's a pain in the arse. Who else is there? Great Aunt Marjorie. Apart from Stratton money, she married a plutocrat who did the decent thing by dying fairly early. No children.' He considered. 'That's the lot.'

'What about Forsyth?' I asked

A shutter came down fast on his easy loquacity.

'Grandfather divided his seventy-five shares of Stratton Park among all of us,' he stated. 'Twenty-one shares each to his three sons, and three shares each to his four grandchildren. Forsyth gets his three like the rest of us.' He stopped, his expression carefully non-committal. 'Whatever Forsyth does isn't my business.' He left the clear implication that it wasn't mine, either.

'What will you all do,' I asked, 'about the racecourse?'

'Besides quarrel? In the short term, nothing, as that's what the great aunt is set on. Then we'll get some hopeless new stands at enormous cost, then we'll have to sell the land to pay for the stands. You may as well tear up your shares right away.'

'You don't seem unduly worried.'

His quick grin shone and vanished. 'To be honest, I don't give a toss. Even if I get myself disinherited by doing something diabolical, like voting to abolish hunting, I can't help but get richer as time goes by. Grandfather gave me millions nine years ago, for a start. And my father has his good points. He's already given me a chunk of his own fortune, and if he lives another three years it'll be clear of tax.' He stared at me, frowning. 'Why do I tell you that?'

'Do you want to impress me?'

'No, I don't. I don't care a bugger what you think.' He blinked a bit. 'I suppose that's not true.' He paused. 'I have irritating holes in my life.'

'Like what?'

'Too much money. No motivation. And I'm going bald.'

'Marry,' I said.

'That wouldn't grow hair.'

'It might stop you minding.'

'*Nothing* stops you minding. And it's damned unfair. I go to doctors who say I can't do a bugger about it, it's in the genes, and how did it get *there*, I'd like to know? Father's OK and Grandfather had the full thatch, even though he was eighty-eight last birthday, and look at Keith with enough to brush back with his hands all the time like a ruddy girl. I hate that mannerism. And even Ivan has no bare patches, he's going thin all over but that's not as *bad*.' He looked balefully at my head. 'You're about my age, and yours is *thick*.'

'Try snake oil,' I suggested.

'That's typical. People like you have *no idea* what it's like to find hair all over the place. Washbasin. Pillow. Hairs which ought to stay growing in my scalp, dammit. How did you know I wasn't married, anyway? And don't give me the stock answer that I don't look worried. I *am* worried, dammit, about my hair.'

'You could try implants.'

'Yes. Don't laugh, I'm going to.'

'I'm not laughing.'

'I bet you are, inside. Everybody thinks it's hilarious, someone else going bald. But when it's you, it's tragic.'

There were irretrievable disasters, I saw, that could only get worse. Dart drank deep as if beer would irrigate the failing follicles and asked if I were married, myself.

'Do I look it?'

'You look stable.'

Surprised, I said yes, I was married.

'Children?'

'Six sons.'

'*Six!*' He seemed horrified. 'You're not old enough.'

'We married at nineteen, and my wife likes having babies.'

'Good Lord.' Other words failed him, and I thought back, as I did pretty often, to the heady student days when Amanda and I had taken to each other with excitement. Friends around us were pairing and living together: it was accepted behaviour.

'Let's get married,' I said impulsively. 'No one gets *married*,' Amanda said. 'Then let's be *different*,' I said.

So we married, giggling happily, and I paid no attention to my mother, who tried to tell me I was marrying Amanda with my eyes, marrying a half-grown woman I didn't really know. 'I married Keith Stratton for his beauty,' she told me, 'and it was a dreadful mistake. It's always a mistake.'

'But Amanda's lovely.'

'She's lovely to look at and she's kind and she clearly loves *you*, but you're both so young, you'll change as you grow older and so will she.'

'Mum, are you coming to the wedding?'

'Of course.'

I married Amanda for her long legs and her blonde hair and her name, Amanda, which I loved. It took ten years for me to face a long repressed recognition that my mother had been right about changes.

Neither Amanda nor I had known at nineteen that she would almost at once develop a hunger for babies. Neither of us could possibly have envisaged that she would ecstatically enjoy the actual birth process, or that she would plan the next pregnancy as soon as the last was accomplished.

Both Christopher and Toby had been born by the time I'd struggled through my qualifying exams, and feeding and housing the four of us had seemed an impossible task. It was then, in my first week out of college, that I'd gone to drown my sorrows in a depressing old pub and found the landlord weeping bankrupt tears into warm beer amid the crash of his own personal dream. The place had been condemned as unfit to live in, he owed money everywhere, his wife had left him and his licence to sell liquor would run out the next day.

We negotiated a rock-bottom price. I went to the council to get a stay of demolition. I begged and borrowed and mortgaged my soul, and Amanda, the two boys and I moved into our first ruin.

I began to make it habitable while I looked round for a job, and I found a lowly position in a large firm of architects, an existence I disliked but stuck to grimly for the pay packets.

Unlike Dart, I knew well what it was like to sweat at night over which bill to pay next, over how to pay *any* bill next, over which did I need most, electricity or a telephone (electricity) and do I pay the plumber (yes, but I learn his job) or do I pay first for roof tiles (yes) or new bricks (no).

I'd carted away free rubble and improvised and sanded old mortar off by the bucketful and given glamour to old stones and built a chimney that never smoked. The ruin came to life again, and I left the firm of architects and irrevocably grew and changed.

I hadn't known at nineteen that I would be unsuited to work as part of a team, or that my true *métier* was hands-on construction, not simply the drawing-board. Amanda hadn't imagined that life with an architect could mean dirt, upheaval and months without income; but to the extent that we'd settled for what we hadn't expected, she had coped with the ruins and I had agreed to the babies, and each of us had had what we needed for our own private fulfilment, even if we'd grown apart until even our sexual interest in each other had become perfunctory and sporadic, an effort, not a joy.

After Neil's birth, during a patch when nothing had seemed to go right, we had nearly split finally asunder, but the economics of feeding the nestlings had prevailed. I took to sleeping alone under the tarpaulins while the rest slept in the bus. I worked eighteen hours a day as a form of escape. After four increasingly prosperous but unhappy years, when neither of us had met anyone to supplant the other, we'd made a great effort to 'start again'. Jamie had been the result. He still kept Amanda happy and, even though the new start had slowly fizzled, we had, because of it, achieved a sort of tolerant to-our-mutual-advantage stand-off which I reckoned enough for the foreseeable future, at least until the boys were grown.

So where was free choice in all of that? I chose to marry to be different and to stick to what it brought me because of an inability to admit failure. I'd chosen to work alone because I hadn't the qualities needed for a team. Every choice a result of given factors. No free choice at all.

'I choose to be what I am,' I said.

Dart, startled, said, 'What?'

'Nothing. Only a theory. Was it inevitable that Conrad, Keith, Ivan and the rest of you should make the choices you all have about the future of the racecourse?'

He looked at his beer for answers and glanced up at me briefly. 'Too deep for me,' he said.

'Would you ever have expected your father to want to sell? Or Keith to potter along as things are?'

'Or Rebecca to love men?' He grinned. 'No, in all three cases, I wouldn't.'

'What do you yourself want for the racecourse?' I asked.

'You tell me,' he said amiably, 'you're the expert.'

I felt in him an encompassing lassitude. Not the sort of thing to say to a virtual stranger.

'Another half?' I suggested, indicating our almost empty glasses.

'No, don't bother. What about totally random choice? Pick a card, that sort of thing. What about rational choices? Like do I take an umbrella because it's raining.'

'Many people don't.'

'Because it isn't in their natures? Because they think it wimpish?'

'More or less.'

'How did we get into this?' He seemed to tire of the subject. 'Go back to the meeting. When you asked Father if he already had detailed plans of the new stands he's set on, was it because you're a builder?'

'Yes,' I nodded.

'Well . . . if you could see the proposals, would you have an opinion?'

'I might.'

He thought it over. 'I do know where you could see the plans, but no one will want you to, except me. If I get you a look at them, will you tell just *me* what you think of them? Then at least I'd have some idea of whether new stands are a good idea or not. I mean, I don't know *how* to vote about the future of the racecourse, because I don't really know the significance of the options. So yes, you're right, if I had to choose now it would be a gut reaction. I'd choose because of the way I am. Right?'

'Right.'

'How about taking a look-see at Conrad's pet architect's plans, then?'

'Yes,' I said.

He grinned. 'This choice game's a knock-out. Come on then, we'll do a bit of breaking and entering.' He stood up decisively and turned towards the door. 'Can you pick locks?'

'It depends on the lock. But given due warning and high need, possibly.'

'Good.'

'How long,' I asked, 'will it take?'

He paused, eyebrows rising. 'Half an hour, maybe.'

'OK.'

I followed him out of the Mayflower and into his runabout, and we set off with a jolt to a destination undisclosed.

'How about I choose not to go bald?' It amused him in a bitter sort of way.

'Not a choice.'

We were heading east, Swindon behind us, Wantage, according to the signposts, ahead. Long before we reached there, however, Dart put his foot on the brake and swerved in through some open gates set in a stone wall. Up a short driveway he came to a halt in front of a large house built of smooth grey bricks with bands of smooth pink bricks and inset patterns of smooth yellowish bricks, all in all (to me) an eyesore.

'I was brought up here,' Dart said encouragingly. 'What do you think of it?'

'Edwardian,' I said.

'Near enough. Last year of Victoria.'

'Solid, anyway.'

A turret. Big sash windows. A conservatory Affluent middle-class display.

'My parents rattle around in it now,' Dart said frankly. 'They're out, by the way. Father was going to meet Mother from the racecourse. They won't be back for hours.' He pulled a bunch of keys out of the ignition and stood up out of the car. 'We can get in round the back,' he said, sorting out one key. 'Come on.'

'No breaking and entering?'

'Later.'

At close quarters the walls were still repulsive and also slippery to the touch. The path round to the rear was edged with gloomy evergreen shrubs. At the back of the house, a red brick extension had been added to provide bathrooms: brown-painted drains zig-zagged over the exterior, an invitation to ice. Dart unlocked a brown-painted door and let us into the bowels (well, literally) of the house.

'This way,' he said, marching past a cloakroom and other plumbing, briefly glimpsed through half-open doors. 'Through here.' He pushed aside a swing door which led from utility to opulence; to the black-and-white tiled floor of a large entrance hall.

We made our way across this to a polished door and into a cluttered oak-panelled room whose chief eyecatchers were endless pictures of horses; some, in oil paintings, hanging thickly on the walls with individual lights on the frames, some in black-and-white photographs in silver frames standing on every surface, some on book jackets. Horse-head bookends supported leather-bound classics like *The Irish R.M.* and *Handley Cross*. A silver fox held down papers on a busy desk. Silver and gold coins were displayed in collections. A hunting crop lay casually coiled on a broken-springed chair. Copies of *Horse and Hound* and *Country Life* filled a magazine rack to overflowing.

'Father's sanctum,' Dart said unnecessarily. He strolled unconcernedly across the room, skirted the desk and the large chair behind it, and stopped beside a section of panelling which he said was a cupboard door always kept carefully locked by his parent.

'The racecourse plans are inside,' Dart said. 'How about opening it?'

'Your father wouldn't approve.'

'I dare say not. Don't tell me you're going all moral and starchy. You pretty well said you could do it.'

'This is too personal.'

I went round beside him, however, and bent to take a closer look at the lock. All that was to be seen from the outside was an inconspicuous keyhole: without Dart's knowledge of its existence the door itself would have remained more or less invisible, particularly as a painting of a meet with huntsman and foxhounds adhered on it, to make it indistinguishable from the walls around.

'Well?' Dart asked.

'What does its key look like?'

'How do you mean?'

'I mean, is it a small short key, or one with a longish narrow shaft with a clump of wards on the end?'

'A long shaft.'

I straightened up and gave him the bad news.

'I'll not touch it,' I said. 'Won't the key be somewhere in this room?'

'I tried to find it for years in my teens. No good at all. How about a bit of force?'

'Absolutely not.'

Dart fiddled around with things on the desk. 'What about this paper-knife? Or this?' He held up a long buttonhook. 'It isn't as if we're going to *steal* anything. Just to take a look.'

'Why does your father have the plans locked up?'

Dart shrugged. 'He's secretive by nature. It takes such a lot of *energy* to be secretive. I can never be bothered.'

The lock was an old and undoubtedly simple warded-bit key job, probably surface-mounted on the inside of the door. The keyhole itself was about an inch from top to bottom, a healthy size that made picking it a cinch. Failing a filed-down key, two wires would have been enough. I was not, however, going to undo it, on the grounds that Conrad would be legitimately furious if he found out, and also because my interest in seeing the plans was not uncontrollable.

'Wasted journey, then?' Dart asked.

'Sorry.'

'Oh, well.' It seemed his appetite for the enterprise had easily subsided, as if commonsense had somewhere raised its wiser head. He looked at me assessingly. 'I've a distinct feeling you *could*, but you won't.'

The trip had been an anticlimax. I looked at my watch and asked if he would mind taking me back to the racecourse. He agreed, seeming to feel the same deflation. I had not, it was clear, come up to his expectations.

We set off again in his car and I asked where he lived now, himself.

'Actually,' he said, 'in Stratton Hays.'

'Is that a village?'

'Lord, no.' He was amused. 'A house. Though, come to think of it, it's as big as a village. Grandfather's house. The old fellow was lonely when Gran died, so he asked me to stay

60

for a while. That was about ten years ago. Keith didn't like it, of course. He tried to get me out and himself in. He'd lived there a lot of his life, after all. He said it wasn't natural for a twenty-year-old boy to move in there, but Grandfather wouldn't have Keith back. I remember all the shouting. I used to get out of the way whenever Keith was around. That wasn't anything new, mind you. Anyway, I *liked* Grandfather, and we got on fine. We used to dine together every evening and I drove him most days round the estate and the racecourse. He ran the racecourse himself, really. That's to say, the colonel that Rebecca was complaining about, Colonel Gardner, he's the racecourse manager, he would do whatever Grandfather wanted. He's an excellent manager, whatever Rebecca says. Grandfather had a real knack of picking people to run things, like Colonel Gardner, and those two that I depend on, the farm manager and the land agent. Just as well, because to be frank we only ever had one genius in the family and that was the first baron, who was a merchant banker with a super-plus Midas touch.' His voice was light and self-deprecating, but there was a depth of feeling in his next statement. 'I miss the old man rotten, you know.'

We droned along until the woolly-head marchers were again in sight.

'Stratton Hays,' Dart said, 'is straight on past the gates. Not far. On the edge of the racecourse land. Do you want to see it? It's where your mother lived with Keith. Where she dumped Hannah.'

I looked at my watch, but curiosity prevailed over parental responsibility. I said I would be very interested, and on we went.

Stratton Hays was everything Conrad's house was not, an ancient homogenous pile in the manner of a smaller Hardwicke Hall. Early seventeenth-century stone and glass in light-hearted proportional harmony, built by the golden fortunes of the Elizabethan age, it looked exactly as it had done for almost four hundred years and certainly as it had forty years earlier when my mother had gone there as a bride.

She had spoken of 'the Stratton house' as a heartless heap,

projecting her own unhappiness into its walls, so that I was unprepared for its easy-going grandeur. It looked friendly to me, and welcoming.

'My great great grandfather bought it,' Dart said off-handedly, 'as being a suitable seat for a newly ennobled baron. The first baroness is on record as thinking it not aristocratic enough. She wanted Palladian pillars, pediments and porticos.'

As before, we went into the house via an unobtrusive side door, and as before found ourselves in a black-and-white hall, this time floored with marble. There was more space than furniture and no curtains at the high windows and, as my mother had said, it echoed with vanished generations.

'Keith used to have the west corridor,' Dart said, heading up a wide staircase. 'After he divorced your mother he got married again, and Grandfather made him and his new wife take Hannah and find somewhere else to live. Before I was born, of course. It seems Keith didn't want to go but Grandfather insisted.'

Dart headed across a large unfurnished area and turned a corner into a long wide corridor with a dark wood floor, a runner of crimson carpet and a tall window at the far end.

'West corridor,' Dart said. 'The doors are all unlocked. The rooms get dusted once a month. Browse around, if you like.'

I browsed, feeling uncomfortable. This was where my mother had suffered beatings and what was now called marital rape. Time had stood still in their bedroom. I shivered there.

A dressing room, a boudoir, a study and a sitting room, all with tall uncurtained windows, also opened onto the corridor. A Victorian bathroom and a twentieth-century kitchen had been fitted into what had probably once been another bedroom. No sign of a nursery.

I went back along the corridor and thanked Dart.

'Did these rooms never have curtains?' I asked.

'They rotted away,' Dart said. 'Grandfather got rid of them and wouldn't let Gran replace them.' He walked towards the stairs. 'Grandfather and Gran lived in the east corridor. It's the same architecturally but it's a proper home. Carpets, curtains, pretty. Gran chose everything there. It feels so empty, now, without either of them. I used to spend most evenings with Grandfather in their sitting room, but I don't go along there much any more.'

We went down the stairs.

'Where do you live, then?' I asked.

'This house is E-shaped,' he said. 'I have the ground floor of the south wing.' He pointed to a wide passage leading away from the main hall. 'Father has inherited this house but he and Mother don't want to live here. They say it's too big. I'm negotiating with Father to be allowed to stay here as a tenant. Keith wants me out and himself in, sod him.'

'It must cost a fortune to run,' I commented.

'There's no roof on the north wing,' he said. 'Ridiculous, but if part of the house is uninhabitable, they reduce the tax on it. The north wing needed a new roof, but it was more economical to take the roof right off and let the weather do its worst. The north wing's a ruin. The outside walls still look all right, but it's a shell.'

I would come back one day soon, I thought, and ask to see the ruin, but at the moment was concerned only to relieve the Gardners of their extended baby-sitting.

Dart obligingly drove me the mile back to the main gate, where our way in was barred by a large bearded man in a woolly hat who stepped into the path of our car. Dart, swearing, jolted to a stop, his only option.

'They were doing this earlier,' he said. 'They stopped Aunt Marjorie on her way to the shareholders' meeting. And Father, and Keith. They were furious.'

Owing to Roger Gardner having directed me to his house through a down-the-course entrance, I hadn't had to run the gauntlet myself. The boys, I knew, would have enjoyed it from the safe, high ground of the bus.

The large beard carried a red message on a placard – 'HORSES RIGHTS COME FIRST'. He stood without budging in front of the car while a sharp-faced woman rapped on Dart's window, signalling that he should lower it. Dart stolidly refused, which made her screech her message, which was that all persons to do with racing were murderers. Her thin intensity reminded me vividly of Rebecca, and I wondered which came to them both first, a leaning towards obsession or an activity worthy of it.

She carried a black-edged placard saying ominously 'DOOM TO RACEGOERS', and she was joined at the window by a jollier woman whose notice-on-a-stick read 'SET HORSES FREE'.

Someone rapped peremptorily on the window my side, and I turned my head and looked straight into the glaring eyes of a fanatical young man showing the blazing fervour of an evangelist.

He yelled 'Murderer' at me and shook for my attention a blown-up photograph of a horse lying dead beside white racecourse rails. 'Murderer', he repeated.

'They're potty,' Dart said, unconcerned.

'They're doing their thing.'

'Poor buggers.'

The proselytising group had now all gathered round the car, but were staring balefully rather than making overtly threatening movements. Their dedication to the cause stopped short of physically harming us. Their kicks would be a nice warm glow that evening at having expressed their caring natures. They would be unlikely, by themselves, to close down an industry that employed the sixth largest workforce in the country, but that probably made them feel all the safer in attacking it.

So far, I thought, looking at their angry committed faces, they hadn't been adopted by professional bully-boy saboteurs. A matter of time, perhaps.

Dart, having had enough, began edging his car forward. The bearded way-barrer leaned against the bonnet. Dart waved to the obstruction to remove itself. The obstruction shook its fist and continued leaning. Dart pushed his hand down irritably on the horn and the obstruction jumped to one side, galvanised. Dart rolled slowly ahead. The placard-bearer stalked beside us for several paces but stopped abruptly as we crossed through the gates themselves. Someone, it seemed, must have instructed them about trespass.

'Such a bore,' Dart said, accelerating. 'How long do you think they'll keep it up?'

'For your race meeting here next Monday,' I suggested, 'I would get a police cordon.'

CHAPTER 5

'Where's your car?' Dart asked. 'I'm going out the back way. I'm tired of those hate merchants. Where's your car?'

'I came in the back way,' I said. 'Drop me somewhere down there.'

His eyebrows rose, but all he said was 'Fine,' and he headed on the inner way past the grandstands and down the narrow private inconspicuous road to the racecourse manager's house.

'What's that monstrous bus doing there?' he demanded rhetorically when he saw it.

I said, 'It's mine,' but the words were lost in a sharp horrified exclamation from my driver who had seen, past the bus, the black parked shape of his great aunt's chauffeured Daimler.

'Aunt Marjorie! What the hell is *she* doing here?'

He braked his rusty runabout beside the gleaming ostentation and without much enthusiam decided to investigate. The view that presented itself as we rounded a corner of the manager's neat modern house had me helplessly laughing, even if I laughed alone.

Double garage doors stood open. Within the garage, empty space, swept clean. Out on the drive, the former contents lay untidily in clumps of gardening tools, cardboard boxes, spare roof tiles and rolls of netting for covering strawberry beds. To one side a discard section included a gutted refrigerator, a rotted baby buggy, battered metal trunk, mouse-eaten sofa and a heap of rusty wire.

Standing more or less to attention in a ragged row stood five young helpers deep in trouble, with Mrs Roger Gardner, sweet but threatened by authority, trying ineffectually to defend them.

Marjorie's penetrating voice was saying, 'It's all very well you boys carrying all that stuff out, but you're not to leave it there. Put everything back at once.'

Poor Mrs Gardner, wringing her hands, was saying, 'But Mrs Binsham, all I wanted was for them to empty the garage . . .'

'This mess is insupportable. Do as I tell you, boys. Put it all back.'

Christopher, looking desperately around, latched onto my arrival with Dart as if saved at the eleventh hour from the worst horror movie.

'Dad!' he said explosively. 'We cleared out the garage.'

'Yes, well done.'

Marjorie swivelled on one heel and directed her disapproval towards Dart and me, at which point my identification as the father of the workforce left her temporarily speechless.

'Mr Morris,' Roger Gardner's wife said hurriedly, 'your children have been great. Please believe me.'

It was courageous of her, I thought, considering her husband's vulnerability to the Stratton family's whims. I thanked her warmly for keeping the children employed while I'd attended the shareholders' meeting.

Marjorie Binsham stared at me piercingly but spoke to Dart, her displeasure a vibration in the air.

'What are you doing here with Mr Morris?'

Dart said with cowardice, 'He wanted to see Stratton Hays.'

'Did he, indeed? Stratton Hays is no business of his. This racecourse, however, is *yours*, or so I should have thought.

Yours and your father's. Yet what have either of you done to look after it? It is I who have had to drive round to see that everything is in order. Colonel Gardner and I, not you and your father, have made a thorough inspection of the course.'

I could see, as easily as she could, that it had never occurred to Dart that he had any responsibility for the state of the racecourse. It had never been his domain. He opened and closed his mouth a couple of times but came up with no protest or defence.

A frazzled looking Colonel drove up in a jeep and, springing out, assured Marjorie Binsham that he had already put in hand her requirement that spectators should be kept further away from the fences, to save them from injury henceforth.

'It isn't my job,' she complained to Dart. 'A few posts, and some rope, some instructions to stand back, that's all it takes. *You* should have thought of it. The racecourse has had too much bad publicity. We cannot afford another débâcle like last Saturday.'

No one mentioned that it had been the horses, not the spectators, which had caused the grief.

'Also,' Marjorie continued, 'you and your father must get rid of those people at the main gates. If you don't, they will attract extremists from all over the place, and the race crowds will stay away because of the aggravation. The racecourse will be killed off as quickly as by any of the crackpot schemes of Keith and your father. And as for Rebecca! If you notice, there's a woman just like her in that group at the gate. It's only a group now. Make sure it doesn't grow into a mob.'

'Yes, Aunt Marjorie,' Dart said. The task was beyond him, perhaps beyond anybody.

'Demonstrators don't want to succeed,' Marjorie pointed out. 'They want to *demonstrate*. Go and tell them to demonstrate for better conditions for stable lads. The horses are pampered enough. The lads are not.'

No one remarked that injured stable lads usually lived.

'You, Mr Morris,' she fixed me with a sharp gaze, 'I want to talk to *you*.' She pointed to her car. 'In there.'

'All right.'

'And you children, clear this mess up at once. Colonel, I don't know what you're thinking of. This place is a *tip*.'

She headed off vigorously towards her car and didn't look round to make sure I followed, which I did.

'Mark,' she told her chauffeur, who was sitting behind the steering wheel. 'Please take a walk.'

He touched his chauffeur's cap to her and obeyed her as if accustomed to the request, and his employer waited beside one of the rear doors until I opened it for her.

'Good,' she said, climbing into the spacious rear seat. 'Get in beside me and sit down.'

I sat where she pointed and closed the door.

'Stratton Hays,' she said, coming at once to the point, 'was where your mother lived with Keith.'

'Yes,' I acknowledged, surprised.

'Did you ask to see it?'

'Dart offered, very kindly. I accepted.'

She paused, inspecting me.

'I never saw Madeline again, after she left,' she said at length. 'I disapproved of her leaving. Did she tell you?'

'Yes, she told me, but after so many years she bore you no animosity. She said you had urged your brother to close family ranks against her, but she was fond of your brother.'

'It was a long time,' she said, 'before I found out what sort of a man Keith is. His second wife killed herself, did you know? When I said to my brother that Keith was an unlucky picker, he told me it wasn't bad luck, it was Keith's own nature. He told me your mother couldn't love or nurse the baby Hannah because of the way the child had been conceived. Your mother told my brother that touching the baby made her feel sick.'

'She didn't tell me that.'

Marjorie said, 'I am now offering you a formal apology for the way I behaved to your mother.'

I paused only briefly to check what my parent would have wanted. 'It's accepted,' I said.

'Thank you.'

I thought that that must conclude the conversation, but it seemed not.

'Keith's third wife left him and divorced him for irretrievable breakdown of marriage. He now has a fourth wife, Imogen, who spends half of the time drunk.'

'Why doesn't she leave him too?' I asked.

'She won't or can't admit she made a mistake.'

It was close enough to my own feelings to strike me dumb.

'Keith,' his aunt said, 'is the only Stratton short of money. Imogen told me. She can't keep her mouth shut after six glasses of vodka. Keith is in debt. That's why he's pushing to sell the racecourse. He needs the money.'

I looked at the appearance Marjorie presented to the world: the little old lady well into her eighties with wavy white hair, soft pink and white skin and hawk-like dark eyes. The pithy, forceful mind, and the sinewy vocabulary were, I imagined, the nearest in quality in the Stratton family to the financial genius who had founded them.

'I was furious with my brother for giving Madeline those shares,' she said. 'He could be obstinate sometimes. Now, all these years later, I'm glad that he did. I am glad,' she finished slowly, 'that someone outside the family can bring some sense of proportion into the Stratton hothouse.'

'I don't know that I can.'

'The point,' she said, 'is whether you want to. Or rather, how much you want to. If you hadn't been in the least bit interested, you wouldn't have turned up here today.'

'True.'

'You could oblige me,' she said, 'by finding out how much money Keith owes, and to whom. And by finding out what relationship Conrad has with the architect he's committed to, who Colonel Gardner tells me knows nothing about racing and is designing a monstrosity. The Colonel tells me we need an architect more like the one who built your own house, but that your architect only designs on a small scale.'

'The Colonel told you he'd visited me?'

'Most sensible thing he's done this year.'

'You amaze me.'

'I want you as an ally,' she said. 'Help me make the racecourse prosper.'

I tried to sort out my own jumbled responses, and it was out of the jumble and not from thought through reasons that I gave her my answer.

'All right, I'll try.'

She held out a small hand to formalise the agreement, and I shook on it, a binding commitment.

Marjorie was driven away without returning to the gutted garage, which was just as well as I found the mess unchanged and the boys, the Gardners and Dart all in the Gardners' kitchen with their attention on cake. Warm fragrant pale-coloured fruit cake, that minute baked. Christopher asked for the recipe 'so that Dad can make it in the bus'.

'Dad can cook?' Dart asked ironically.

'Dad can do anything,' Neil said, munching.

Dad, I thought to myself, had probably just impulsively set himself on a high road to failure.

'Colonel –' I started.

He interrupted. 'Call me Roger.'

'Roger,' I said, 'can I? . . . I mean, may the architect of my house come here tomorrow and make a thorough survey of the grandstands as they are at present? I'm sure you have professional advisers about the state of the fabric and so on, but could we take a fresh detached survey with a view to seeing whether new stands are or are not essential for a profitable future?'

Dart's cake came to a standstill in mid-chew and Roger Gardner's face lost some of its habitual gloom.

'Delighted,' he said, 'but not tomorrow. I've got the course-builders coming, and the full complement of groundsmen will be here getting everything in shape for next Monday's meeting.'

'Friday, then?'

He said doubtfully, 'That'll be Good Friday. Easter, of course. Perhaps your man won't want to work on Good Friday.'

'He'll do what I tell him,' I said. 'It's me.'

Both Dart and Roger were surprised.

'I am,' I said gently, 'a qualified architect. I did five arduous years at the Architectural Association, one of the most thorough schools in the world. I do choose houses in preference to high rises, but that's because horizontal lines that fit in with nature please me better. I'm a Frank Lloyd Wright disciple, not a Le Corbusier, if that means anything to you.'

'I've heard of them,' Dart said. 'Who hasn't?'

'Frank Lloyd Wright,' I said, 'developed the cantilever roof you see on all new grandstands everywhere.'

'We don't have a cantilever,' Roger said thoughtfully.

'No, but let's see what you *do* have, and what you can get away with not having.'

Dart's view of me had changed a little. 'You said you were a builder,' he accused.

'Yes, I am.'

Dart looked at the children. 'What does your father do?' he asked.

'Builds houses.'

'With his own hands, do you mean?'

'Well,' Edward amplified, 'with spades and trowels and a saw and everything.'

'Ruins,' Christopher explained. 'We're on a ruin hunt for our Easter holidays.'

Together they described the pattern of their lives to an ever more astonished audience. Their matter-of-fact acceptance of not every child's experience seemed especially to amaze.

'But we're going to keep the last one he did. Aren't we, Dad?'

'Yes.'

'*Promise.*'

I promised for roughly the twentieth time, which was an indication of the depth of their anxiety, as I'd always kept the promises I'd made them.

'You must all be so tired of moving on,' Mrs Gardner said sympathetically.

'It's not that,' Christopher told her, 'it's the house. It's brilliant.' Brilliant in his teenage vocabulary meant only the opposite of awful (pronounced *off*-al, ironically).

Roger nodded and agreed, however. 'Brilliant. Hell to heat, I should think, though, with all that space.'

'It has a hypocaust,' Neil said, licking his fingers.

The Gardners and Dart gazed at him.

'What,' Dart asked, giving in, 'is a hypocaust?'

'Central heating invented by the Romans,' said my seven-year-old composedly. 'You make hollow spaces and runways under a stone floor and drive hot air through, and the floor stays warm all the time. Dad thought it would work and it does. We ran about without shoes all winter.'

Roger turned his head my way.

'Come on Friday, then,' he said.

When I drove the bus back to the same spot on a sunny morning two days later, the ground outside the garage was cluttered not with the debris of decades but with horses.

My sons gazed out of their safe windows at a moving clutch of about six large quadrupeds and decided not to climb down among the hooves, even though every animal was controlled by a rider.

The horses, to my eyes, weren't fine-boned enough to be racehorses, nor were the riders as light as the average stable lad, and when I swung down from the cab Roger came hurrying across from his house, side stepping round massive hindquarters, to tell me these were Conrad's working hunters out for their morning exercise. They were supposed to be out on the road, Roger said, but they'd been practically attacked by the six or seven woollen hats still stubbornly picketing the main gates.

'Where do they come from?' I asked, looking around.

'The horses? Conrad keeps them here on the racecourse in a yard down near the back entrance, where you came in.'

I nodded. I'd seen the back of what could well have been the stables.

'They're trotting up and down the inner road instead,' Roger said. 'It's not ideal, but I won't let them out on the course, where they sometimes go, because everything is ready for Monday's meeting. Wouldn't your boys like to get out and see them?'

'I don't think so,' I said. 'Since the slaughter at the open ditch last Saturday they are a bit afraid of them. They were very shocked, you know, by that dead spectator's injuries.'

'I'd forgotten they'd seen him, poor man. Will they just stay in the bus, then, while you and I go over the stands? I've spread out some of the original drawings in my office. We'll look at those first, if you like.'

I suggested driving bus and boys as near to the office as possible, which resulted in our parking where the Stratton family's cars had been gathered two days earlier. The boys, relieved by the arrangement, asked if they could play a hide-and-seek game in the stands, if they promised not to do any damage.

Roger gave assent doubtfully. 'You'll find many of the doors are locked,' he told them. 'And the whole place was cleaned yesterday, ready for Monday, so don't make any mess.'

They promised not to. Roger and I left them beginning to draw up rules for their game and made our way to a low white-painted wooden building on the far side of the parade ring.

'Is it pirates again?' Roger asked, amused.

'I think it's storming the Bastille this time. That's to say, rescuing a prisoner without being captured yourself. Then the rescued prisoner has to hide and not be recaptured.'

I looked back as Roger unlocked his office door. The boys waved. I waved back and went in, and began to sort my way through ancient building plans that had been rolled up so long that straightening them out was like six bouts with an octopus.

I took off my jacket and hung it on the back of a chair, so as to come to grips with things more easily, and Roger made a comment about the warmth of the spring day and hoped the sunshine would last until Monday.

Most of the plans were in fact working drawings, which gave detailed specifications for every nut and bolt. They were thorough, complete and impressive, and I commented on it.

'The only problem is,' Roger said, with a twisting smile, 'that the builder didn't stick to the specs. Concrete that should be six inches thick with the reinforcing bars well covered has recently proved to be barely four and a half inches and we're having endless trouble with the private balcony boxes with water getting in through cracks and rusting the bars, which then of course expand because of the rust and crack the concrete more. *Crumble* the concrete, in some places.'

'Spalling,' I nodded. 'Can be dangerous.'

'And,' Roger went on, 'if you look at the overall design of the water inlets and outlets and sewer lines, the drawings make very good sense, but the water and drain pipes don't actually go where they should. We had one set of ladies' lavatories backing up for no reason we could think of and flooding the floor, but the drain seemed clear, and then we found we were checking the wrong drain, and the one from the lavatories went in an entirely different direction and was blocked solid.'

It was familiar territory. Builders had minds of their own and often ignored the architect's best instructions, either because they truly thought they knew better or because they could make a fatter profit by shaving the quality.

We uncurled a dozen more sheets and tried to hold them flat with pots of pens for paperweights, a losing battle. I acquired, all the same, an understanding of what should have been built, with some picture of stress points and weaknesses to look for. I'd studied ancient plans a great deal less trustworthy than these, and these grandstands weren't ruins after all: they'd withstood gales and rot for well over half a century.

Basically, the front of the stands, the viewing steps themselves, were of reinforced concrete supported by steel girders, which also held up the roof. Backing the concrete and steel, solid brick pillars formed the weight-bearers for the bars, dining rooms and private rooms for the owners and stewards. Centrally there was a stairway stretching upwards through five storeys giving access outwards and inwards throughout. A simple effective design, even if now out of date.

The door of the office was suddenly flung open, and Neil catapulted himself inside.

'Dad,' he said insistently, 'Dad . . .'

'I'm busy, Neil.'

'But it's urgent. Really really urgent.'

I let a set of drawings recurl by accident. 'How urgent?' I asked, trying to open them again.

'I found some white wires, Dad, going in and out of some walls.'

'What wires?'

'You know when they blew up the chimney?'

I left the plans to their own devices and paid full attention to my observant son. My heart jumped a beat. I did indeed remember the blowing up of the chimney.

'Where are the wires?' I asked, trying for calmness.

Neil said, 'Near that bar with the smelly floor.'

'What on earth is he talking about?' Roger demanded.

'Where are your brothers?' I said briefly.

'In the stands. Hiding. I don't know where.' Neil's eyes were wide. 'Don't let them be blown up, Dad.'

'No.' I turned to Roger. 'Can you switch on a public address system that can be heard everywhere in the stands?'

'What on earth –'

'*Can you?*' I felt my own panic rising: fought it down.

'But –'

'For God's sake,' I half yelled at him, quite unfairly. 'Neil's saying he's seen det cord and demolition charges in the stands.'

Roger's own face went taut. 'Are you *serious*?'

'Same as the factory chimney?' I asked Neil, checking.

'Yes, Dad. *Exactly* the same. Do come on.'

'Public address system,' I said with dreadful urgency to Roger. 'I have to get those children out of there at once.'

He gave me a dazed look but at last went into action, hurrying out of his office and half running across the parade ring towards the weighing room, sorting through his bunch of keys as he went. We came to a halt beside the door into Oliver Wells' office, the lair of the Clerk of the Course.

'We tested the system yesterday,' Roger said, fumbling slightly. 'Are you *sure*? This child's so young. I'm sure he's mistaken.'

'Don't risk it,' I said, practically ready to shake him.

He got the door open finally and went across to unlatch a metal panel which revealed banks of switches.

'This one,' he said, pressing down with a click. 'You can speak direct from here. Let me plug in the microphone.'

He brought an old-fashioned microphone from a drawer, fitted plug to socket, and handed me the instrument.

'Just speak,' he said.

I took a breath and tried to sound urgent but not utterly frightening, though utterly frightened was what I myself felt.

'This is Dad,' I said as slowly as I could, so they could hear clearly. 'Christopher, Toby, Edward, Alan, the grandstands are not safe. Wherever you're hiding, leave the stands and go to the gate in the rails where we went through and down the course last Saturday. Go out in front of the stands, and gather by that gate. The gate is the rallying point. Go *at once*. The Bastille game is over for now. It's *urgent* that you go at once to the gate where we went out onto the course. It's quite near the winning post. Go there *now*. The grandstands aren't safe. They might blow up at any moment.'

I switched off temporarily and said to Neil, 'Do you remember how to get to that gate?'

He nodded and told me how, correctly.

'Then you go there too, will you, so that the others can see you? And tell them what you saw.'

'Yes, Dad.'

I said to Roger, 'Have you the key to the gate?'

'Yes, but –'

'I'd be happier if they could go out through that gate and across to the winning post itself. Even that might not be far enough.'

'Surely you're exaggerating,' he protested.

'I hope to God I am.'

Neil hadn't waited. I watched his little figure run.

'We went to see an old factory chimney being blown up,' I

said to Roger. 'The boys were fascinated. They saw some charges being set. It was only three months ago.' I spoke again into the microphone. 'Boys, go down to the gate. It's very very urgent. The stands are unsafe. They might blow up. Just run.' I turned to Roger. 'Could you unlock the gate for them?'

He said, 'Why don't you?'

'I'd better check those wires, don't you think?'

'But –'

'Look, I've got to make sure Neil is right, haven't I? And we don't know *when* the charges are set for, do we? Maybe five minutes, maybe five hours, maybe after dark. Can't risk it for the boys, though. Have to get them out at once.'

Roger swallowed and made no more objections. Together we ran from his office round to the front of the stands, he taking the key with him, I wanting to check that all five were safe.

The little knot by the gate grew to four as Neil reached them. Four, not five.

Four. *Not Toby.*

I sprinted back to Oliver's office and picked up the microphone.

'Toby, this is *not* a game. Toby, get off the stands. The stands are not safe. Toby, for Christ's sake do what I say. *This is not a game.*'

I could hear my voice reverberating round and through the building and out in the paddocks. I repeated the urgent words once more and then ran round the stands again to check that Toby had heard and obeyed.

Four boys. Four boys and Roger, walking across the track to the winning post. Not running. If Toby were watching, he'd see no reason for haste.

'Come on, you little *bugger*,' I said under my breath. 'For once in your life, *be told*.'

I went back to the microphone and said it loud and baldly. 'There are demolition charges in the stands, Toby, are you listening? Remember the chimney? The stands can blow up too. Toby, get out of there quickly and join the others.'

I went back yet again to the front of the stands, and yet again Toby failed to appear.

I was not a demolitions expert. If I wanted to take a building down to its roots I usually did it brick by brick, salvaging everything useful. I'd have felt happier at that moment if I'd known more. The first priority, though, was obviously to look at what Neil had seen, and to do that I needed to enter and climb the central stairway, off which led the bar with the smelly floor; the members' bar which should have been much busier than it was.

It was the same staircase, I'd noticed, that on one landing led off through double-doors to the Strattons' carpeted and cosseted private rooms. According to the plans and also from what I myself remembered of it, that staircase was the central vertical artery feeding all floors of the grandstand; the central core of the whole major building.

At the top was a large windowed room like a control tower from where the Stewards with massive binoculars watched the races. A modern offshoot from there ran up yet again to an eyrie inhabited by race-callers, television equipment and the scribbling classes.

At other levels on its upward progress, the staircase branched off inwards to a members' lunch room and outwards to ranks of standing-only steps open to the elements. A corridor on the first floor led to a row of private balcony boxes where prim little light white wooden chairs gave respite to rich and elderly feet.

I went into the staircase from the open front of the stands and sprinted up to the level of the smelly members' bar. The door of the bar was locked, but along the white-painted landing wall outside, at about eighteen inches from the ground, ran a harmless looking thick white filament that looked like the sort of washing line used for drying laundry in back gardens.

At intervals along the wall the line ran into the wall itself and out again, and finally a hole had been drilled from the landing through into the bar, so that the white line ran into it, disappearing from view.

Neil had made no mistake. The white washing line look-alike was in fact itself an explosive known as 'det cord', short for detonating cord, along which detonation could travel at something like 18,000 metres a second, blowing apart everything it touched. At every spot where the cord went into the wall and out again there would be a compressed cache of plastic explosive. All explosives did more damage when compressed.

Det cord was not like old fuses spluttering slowly towards a bomb marked 'BOMB', as in comics and ancient westerns. Det cord *was* the explosive; and it seemed to be winding up and down through the walls of the stairwell for at least one floor above me and another below.

I yelled 'Toby' with full lungs and whatever power I could muster. I yelled 'Toby' up the staircase and I yelled 'Toby' down the staircase, and got no response at all.

'Toby, if you're here, this place is full of explosive.' I yelled it up the stairs, and down.

Nothing.

He had to be somewhere else, I thought. But where? *Where?* There could be det cord festooned throughout the length of all the buildings; throughout the Club, through the Tattersalls enclosure where on race days the bookies had their pitches, through the cheapest of three enclosures where there were almost more bars than viewing steps.

'Toby,' I yelled: and got silence.

There was no possibility that I could miraculously dismantle what looked like a thoroughly planned attack. I didn't know enough, nor where to start. My first priority, anyway, was the safety of my son, so with silence continuing, I turned to go back out into the open air, to run further down the sprawling complex and try again.

I'd already pivoted to run when I heard the tiniest noise, and it seemed to me it came from above, from somewhere up the stairs, over my head.

I sprinted up two levels, to the landing outside the Stewards' vantage point and yelled again. I tried the Stewards' room door, but like so much else, it was locked. He couldn't be in there, but I yelled anyway.

'Toby, if you're here, *please* come out. This place can blow up at any moment. Please, Toby. *Please.*'

Nothing. False alarm. I turned to go down again, to start searching somewhere else.

A wavery little voice said, 'Dad?'

I whirled. He was climbing with difficulty out of his perfect tiny hiding place, a small sideboard with spindly legs beside an empty row of pegs meant for the Stewards' hats and coats.

'Thank God,' I said briefly. 'Now come on.'

'I was the escaped prisoner,' he said, slithering out and standing up. 'If they'd found me they would have put me back in the Bastille.'

I hardly listened. I felt only urgency along with relief.

'Will it really blow up, Dad?'

'Let's just get out of here.'

I reached for his hand and tugged him with me towards the stairs, and there was a sort of *crrrump* from below us, and then a brilliant flash of light and a horrendous bang and a swaying all about us, and it was like what I imagine it must be like to be caught in an earthquake.

CHAPTER 6

In the fraction of time when thought was possible, both knowledge and instinct screamed that the stairs themselves, wreathed and tied with explosive like a parcel, were the embrace of death.

Enclosing Toby in my arms I spun on the heaving floor and hurled us with slipping feet and every labour-trained muscle back towards Toby's hiding-place cupboard beside the Stewards' box door.

The core of Stratton Park racecourse imploded, folding inwards. The staircase ripped and cracked and crashed as its walls collapsed into the well, splitting open into jagged caverns all the rooms alongside.

The Stewards' door blew open, its glass viewing walls splintering and flying in slicing spears. The terrifying noise deafened. The stands shrieked as they tore apart, wood against wood against brick against concrete against stone against steel.

With Toby beneath me, I fell forwards, scrabbling and seeking for footing so as not to slide back towards the gutted stairs; and the high precarious tower atop all else, the Press and television vantage point, came smashing down through the ceiling beams and plaster above us, plunging in sharp-edged pieces at crazy angles across my back and legs. I seemed to stop breathing. Sharp stabs of passing agony stapled me to the floor. Movement became impossible.

Billowing black smoke poured up from the stairs, lung-filling, choking, setting off convulsive coughing when there was no room to cough.

The thunderous noise gradually stopped. Far below, small creaks and intermittent crashes. Everywhere black smoke, grey dust. In me, pain.

'Dad,' Toby's voice said, 'you're squashing me.' He was coughing also. 'I can't breathe, Dad.'

I glanced vaguely down. The top of his head, brown-haired, came up as far as my chin. Inappropriately, but how can one help the things one thinks, I thought of his mother's once frequent complaint – 'Lee, you're squashing me' – and I would raise my weight off her by leaning on my elbows and I'd look into her gleaming laughing eyes and kiss her, and she'd say that I was too big and that one day I would collapse her lungs and break her ribs and suffocate her from love.

Collapse her lungs, snap her ribs, suffocate . . . dear God.

With a good deal of effort I levered my elbows up into the familiar supporting position and spoke to Amanda's twelve-year-old son.

'Wriggle out,' I said, coughing. 'Wriggle up this way, head first.'

'Dad . . . you're too heavy.'

'Come on,' I said, 'you can't lie there all day.' I meant, I didn't know for how long I could lift myself off him, so as not to kill him.

I felt like Atlas, only the world lay not on my shoulders, but beneath them.

Incongruously, sunlight fell all around us. Blue sky above, glimpsed through the hole in the roof. The black smoke funnelled up through there, slowly dispersing.

Toby made convulsive little heaves until his face came up level with mine. His brown eyes looked terrified and, uncharacteristically, he was crying.

I kissed his cheek, which normally he didn't like. This time he seemed not to notice and didn't wipe it away.

'It's all right,' I said. 'It's over. We're both all right. All we have to do is get out. Keep on wriggling. You're doing fine.'

He inched out with difficulty, pushing bits of masonry out of his way. There were some sobs but no complaints. He made it onto his knees by my right shoulder, panting quietly, coughing now and then.

'Well done,' I said. I let my chest relax onto the floor. Not an enormous relief, except for my elbows.

'Dad, you're bleeding.'

'Never mind.'

A few more sobs.

'Don't cry,' I said.

'That man,' he said, 'the horse kicked his eyes out.'

I moved my shirt-sleeved right forearm in his direction. 'Hold my hand,' I said. His own fingers slid slowly across my palm. 'Look,' I said, gripping lightly, 'dreadful things do happen. There's never going to be a time in your whole life when you won't remember that man's face. But you'll remember it less and less often, not all the time, like now. And you'll remember us being here, with all the stands blown inwards. A lot of people's memories are full of truly awful things. Any time you want to talk about that man, I'll listen.'

He squeezed my hand fiercely, and let it go.

'We can't just sit here for ever,' he said.

Despite our fairly disadvantaged state, I was smiling.

'It's quite likely,' I remarked, 'that your brothers and Colonel Gardner will have noticed the stands have been re-arranged. People will come.'

'I could go and wave out of those broken windows, to tell them where we are —'

'Stay right here,' I said sharply. 'Any floor might collapse.'

'Not this one, Dad.' He looked around wildly. 'Not this one, that we're on, will it, Dad?'

'It'll be all right,' I said, hoping I spoke the truth. The whole landing, however, now sloped towards where the stairs had been, and I wouldn't have cared to jump up and down on it with abandon.

The pressures of the chunks of ceiling, roof and Press tower were unremitting across my back and legs, pinning me comprehensively. I could, though, move my toes inside my shoes, and I could certainly feel. Unless the building subsided more from accumulated internal stress, it looked possible I might escape with a clear head, an intact spinal cord, both hands and feet and an undamaged son. Not bad, considering. I hoped, all the same, that rescuers would hurry.

'Dad?'

'Mm?'

'Don't shut your eyes.'

I opened them, and kept them open.

'When will people come?' he asked.

'Soon.'

'It wasn't my fault the stands exploded.'

'Of course not.'

After a pause, he said, 'I thought you were kidding.'

'Yep.'

'It's not my fault you're hurt, is it?'

'No.' He wasn't, I saw, reassured. I said, 'If you hadn't been hiding right up here I could have been lower down the stairs when the explosion happened, and would now very likely be dead.'

'Are you sure?'

'Yes.'

It seemed very quiet. Almost as if nothing had happened. If I tried to move, different story . . .

'How did you know the stands would explode?' Toby said.

I told him about Neil seeing the det cord. 'It's thanks to him,' I said, 'that all five of you weren't killed.'

'I didn't notice any cord.'

'No, but you know what Neil's like.'

'He *sees* things.'

'Yes.'

In the distance, at what seemed long last, we could hear sirens. One, at first, then several, then a whole wailing orchestra.

Toby wanted to move but again I told him to stay still, and before very long there were voices on the racecourse side, outside and below, calling my name.

'Tell them we're here,' I told Toby, and he shouted with his high voice, 'We're here. We're up here.'

After a brief silence a man's voice yelled, 'Where?'

'Tell them beside the Stewards' box,' I said.

Toby shouted the information and got another question in return.

'Is your father with you?'

'Yes.'

'Is he talking?'

'Yes.' Toby looked at me and spontaneously gave them more news. 'He can't move. Some roof fell in.'

'Stay there.'

'OK?' I said to Toby. 'I told you they would come.'

We listened to clanging and banging and businesslike shouting, all far away and outside. Toby was shivering, not with cold, as the midday sun still warmed us, but with accumulated shock.

'They won't be long,' I said.

'What are they *doing?*'

'Putting up some sort of scaffolding, I should think.'

They came up from the racecourse side, where the reinforced concrete viewing steps on the steel girders had, it transpired, survived the onslaught pretty well unscathed. A fireman in a big hard hat and a bright yellow jacket suddenly appeared outside the broken windows of the Stewards' box and peered inwards.

'Anyone home?' he cheerfully called.

'Yes.' Toby stood up joyfully and I told him abruptly to stay still.

'But, Dad —'

'*Stay still.*'

'You stay there, young 'un. We'll have you out in no time,' the fireman told him, and vanished as quickly as he'd come. Returning, he brought with him a colleague and a secure metal walkway for Toby to cross on to the window, and almost in no time, as he'd promised, he'd picked the boy out of the window and out of danger. As Toby disappeared from my view, I felt weak. I trembled from relief. A lot of strength seemed to drain away.

The colleague, a moment later, stepped through the window and crossed the walkway in reverse, stopping at the end of it, some several feet from where I lay.

'Lee Morris?' he asked. Dr Livingstone, I presume.

'Yes,' I said.

'It won't be long.'

They came in personal harnesses with jacks and cantilevers and slings and cutting equipment and a mini-crane, and they knew what they were doing, but the whole area where I was lying proved wickedly unstable, and at one point another big section of the Press box came crashing through the roof and, missing my feet by millimetres, bounced and plummeted down the five-storey hole where the stairs were meant to be. One could hear it colliding with wrecked walls all the way down until it reached the bottom with a reverberating disintegrating thud.

The firemen sweated and put jacks from floor to ceiling wherever they could.

There were three men working, moving circumspectly, taking no sudden unpremeditated steps. One of them, I slowly realised, seemed to be operating a video camera, of all things. The whirring came and went. I twisted my head round to check and found the busy lens pointing straight at my face, which I found deeply embarrassing but could do nothing about. A fourth man arrived, again in yellow, again with a rope to his waist, and he too brought a camera. Too much, I thought. He asked the first three for a progress report and I read his identification – 'Police' – in black on his yellow chest.

The building *creaked*.

The men all stopped moving, waiting. The sounds ceased and the firemen with extreme caution moved again, cursing, dedicated, brave, prosaically taking risks.

I lay gratefully inert on my stomach and thought I hadn't had a bad life, if this should prove to be the end of it. The firemen had no intention of letting me come to the end of it. They brought up and slid a harness under my chest and fastened it round my arms and across my shoulders so that if I slid I wouldn't go down the gaping hole and, bit by bit, they levered the extensive chunks of brick and plaster slightly off me and freed me from splintered beams until, by pulling on the harness, they could move me a couple of feet up the sloping floor towards the threshold of the Stewards' box. The footing was more solid there, they said.

I wasn't of much help to them. I'd lain squashed for so long that my muscles wouldn't move properly on demand. Many of them developed pins and needles and then throbbed as if released from tourniquets, which I didn't much mind. The cuts caused by spears of wood felt worse.

A man in a fluorescent green jacket came through the window, crossed the safe walkway and, pointing to the information lettered in black across his chest, told me he was a doctor.

Dr Livingstone? No, Dr Jones. Oh, well.

He bent down by my head, which I'd tired of holding up.

'Can you squeeze my hand?' he asked.

I squeezed his hand obligingly and told him I wasn't much hurt.

'Good.'

He went away.

It wasn't until much later, when I watched one of the video tapes, that I learned he hadn't totally believed me because, except for the collar and sleeves, my white shirt showed scarlet and had been ripped here and there like bits of skin underneath. In any case, when he returned it wasn't to expect me to stand up and walk out: instead he brought what looked to me like a sled, not a flat stretcher that one could easily fall off, but with raised rails down the sides, better for carrying.

One way or another, with one of the fireman levering the last chunk of timber off my legs and the other two pulling me forwards by the harness, with me tugging myself forward handhold by handhold, I slithered along face down onto the offered transport. When my centre of gravity was more or less onto the safe walkway, and I was supported from the thighs up, the ominous creaking started again in the building, this time worse, this time with tremors.

The fireman behind my feet said 'Christ' and leaped onto

the walkway, edging past me with infectious urgency. As if rehearsed, he and the others abandoned slow care, caught hold of the side rails of my sled-stretcher and yanked it with me hanging on like a limpet across the narrow path to the windows.

The building shuddered and shook. The rest of the Press room – by far the largest part – toppled up high, broke loose, smashed down lethally through what was left of the ceiling right onto the place where I'd been lying, and with its weight tore the whole landing away from its walls and, roaring and thundering, plunged horribly downwards. Grit, dust, bricks, chunks of splintered plaster and slivers of glass fog-filled the air. Mesmerised, I glanced back over my shoulder and saw Toby's hiding place, the small sideboard, topple over forwards and slide to oblivion. The floor of the Stewards' box subsided and left the cantilevered safe walkway protruding inward from the sill of the window, life-saving still but now with nothing beneath. My legs, from above the knees, stuck out over space.

Incredibly, the policeman, now just outside the window, went on filming.

I gripped the rails of the stretcher, my hands fierce with the elemental fear of falling. The firemen clutched the harness round my shoulders, lifted the stretcher, hurled themselves and me towards safety, and the whole lot of us popped out into sunshine, an untidy group, disorganised, coughing from dust, but alive.

Nothing even then proved simple. The concrete viewing steps of the stands reached only as far as a storey below the Stewards' box, and to bring the rescue equipment up the last nine or ten feet had demanded many struts ingeniously bolted together. Below near the racecourse rails, where crowds on race days cheered the finishes, the asphalt and grass viewing areas were packed with vehicles – fire appliances, police cars, ambulances – and, worst, a television station's van.

I said that it would be much easier and less embarrassing if I simply stood up and walked down, and no one paid any attention. The doctor reappeared talking about internal injuries and not giving me any chance to make things worse, so rather against my will I got covered with a dressing or two and a blanket and was secured to the stretcher with straps and slowly carried step by careful step to the ground and across to where the emergency vehicles waited. I thanked the firemen. They grinned.

At the end of the journey five boys stood in a row, frightened and terribly strained.

I said, 'I'm fine, chaps,' but they seemed unconvinced.

I said to the doctor, 'They're my children. Tell them I'm OK.'

He glanced at me and at their young distressed faces.

'Your father,' he said with commonsense, 'is a big strong fellow and he's quite all right. He has some bruises and cuts which we'll stick a few plasters on. You don't need to worry.'

They read the word 'Doctor' on the front of his bright green jacket and they decided, provisionally, to believe him.

'We're taking him to the hospital,' the man in green said, indicating a waiting ambulance, 'but he'll be back with you soon.'

Roger appeared beside the boys and said he and his wife would look after them. 'Don't worry,' he said.

Ambulance men began feeding me feet first into their vehicle.

I said to Christopher, 'Do you want your mother to come and take you home?'

He shook his head. 'We want to stay in the bus.'

The others nodded silently.

'I'll phone her,' I said.

Toby said urgently, 'No, Dad. We want to stay in the bus.' His anxiety level, I saw, was still far too high. Anything that would reduce it had to be right.

'Play marooned, then,' I said.

They all nodded, Toby, looking relieved, included.

The doctor, writing notes to give the ambulance men to take with me asked, 'What's play marooned?'

'Making do on their own for a bit.'

He smiled over his notes. 'Lord of the Flies?'

'I never let it get that far.'

He gave the notes to one of the ambulance men and glanced back at the boys. 'Good kids.'

'I'll look after them,' Roger said again. 'Be glad to.'

'I'll phone you,' I said. 'And thanks.'

The busy ambulance men shut the door on me, and Mrs Gardner, I found later, made fruit cake for the boys until they couldn't face another slice.

Judged solely as a medical casualty I was fairly low in priority in the hospital's emergency department but all too high on the local media's attention list. The airwaves were buzzing, it seemed, with 'terrorist bombing of racecourse'. I begged the use of a telephone from some half-cross, half-riveted nurses and got through to my wife.

'What the *hell's* going on?' she demanded, her voice high. 'Some ruddy newspaper just phoned me to ask if I knew my husband and sons had been blown up. Can you *believe* it?'

'Amanda . . .'

'You obviously *haven't* been blown up.'

'Which paper?'

'What does it matter? I can't remember.'

'I'll complain. Anyway, just listen. Someone with a grudge put some explosive in Stratton Park racecourse, and yes, the stands did slightly blow up –'

She interrupted. 'The *boys*. Are they all right?'

'Unharmed. Totally all right. Only Toby was anywhere near, and some fireman carried him out. I promise you, none of them has a scratch.'

'Where are you now?'

'The boys are with the racecourse manager and his wife –'

'Aren't they with *you*? Why aren't they with you?'

'I've just . . . um. I'll be back with them in no time. I've got a couple of grazes that the local hospital's putting stuff on, then I'm going back to them. Christopher will phone you.'

Every evening, from the mobile phone in the bus, the boys talked to their mother; family routine on expeditions.

Amanda took a bit of placating as well as reassuring. It was obviously my fault, she said, that the children had been put in danger. I didn't deny it. I asked her if she wanted them home.

'What? No, I didn't say that. You know I've a lot of things planned this weekend. They'd better stay with you. Just take more care of them, that's all.'

'Yes.'

'So what do I say if any other newspapers ring up?'

'Say you talked to me and everything's fine. You might see something about it on television, there were news cameras on the racecourse.'

'Do take more *care*, Lee.'

'Yes.'

'And don't phone this evening. I'm taking Jamie over to Shelly's for the night. It's her birthday dinner, remember?'

Shelly was her sister. 'Right,' I said.

We said goodbye; always polite. Acid, by effort, diluted.

The variety of gashes and grazes that I had minimised as much as possible eventually got uncovered and tut-tutted over. Dust and rubble got washed out, impressive splinters were removed with tweezers and rows of clips got inserted with local anaesthetic.

'You'll be sore when this wears off,' the stitcher cheerfully told me. 'Some of these wounds are deceptively deep. Are you *sure* you won't stay here overnight? I'm certain we can find a bed for you.'

'Thanks,' I said, 'but no thanks.'

'Lie on your stomach for a few days then. Come back in a week and we'll take the clips out. You should be healed by then.'

'Thanks a lot,' I said.

'Keep on taking the antibiotics.'

The hospital dredged up an ambulance to take me back to Roger Gardner's house (by the back road, at my insistence) and with a bit of help from a borrowed walking frame and dressed in a blue dressing gown/robe from the hospital shop, I made the end of the journey upright.

The bus, I gratefully noted, had been driven down and parked outside the tidied garage. Its five younger inhabitants were in the Gardners' sitting room watching television.

'*Dad!*' they exclaimed, springing up, then, at the sight of the walking aid to the elderly, falling uncertainly silent.

'Yes,' I said, 'we will have no giggles about this, OK? A lot of bricks and ceiling fell on my back and legs and made a few cuts, which have now been stitched up. Some cuts were on my back and quite a lot on my legs and one cut is straight across my bottom so that I can't very easily sit down, and we will *not laugh* about that.'

They did, of course, chiefly from relief, which was fine.

Mrs Gardner offered sympathy.

'What can I get you?' she asked. 'Hot cup of tea?'

'Treble scotch?'

Her sweet face creased. She poured the hard stuff generously and told me Roger had been busy all day along at the stands and was worn out by the police and by the news people and by most of the Stratton family, who had flocked to the place in fury.

The boys and Mrs Gardner were, it appeared, waiting for the television news to start, which presently happened, with the bombing of Stratton Park racecourse prominently featured. Various shots showed the rear of the stands, from where the central column of damage couldn't be missed. A five-second interview with Conrad revealed his innermost thoughts ('shocked and angry'). 'Fortunately only one minor casualty' said a voice over a shot of myself (luckily unrecognisable) being carried down the steps.

'That's you, Dad,' Neil told me excitedly.

A brief shot of Toby walking down hand in hand with a fireman had the boys cheering. Next, ten seconds of Roger – 'Colonel Gardner, racecourse manager' – saying the Stratton family promised the Monday race meeting would be held as scheduled. 'Important not to give in to terror tactics.' Finally a shot of the woolly hats with their placards at the gates, leaving viewers with an unspoken but sinister implication. Unfair, I thought.

When the news slid away into a plethora of politicians, I told Mrs Gardner and the boys that I would go and put some clothes on, and I limped slowly with the frame over to the bus and winced without it up the steps, and although I'd meant to get dressed I lay down instead on the long sofa that was also my bed, and felt shivery and ill, and finally admitted to myself that I was a good deal more injured than I wanted to be.

After a while the outer door opened and I expected a child, but it was in fact Roger who had come.

He sat on the other long sofa opposite and looked weary.

'Are you all right?' he asked.

'Yes,' I said, not moving.

'My wife says you look grey.'

'You don't look too rosy yourself.'

He smiled briefly and massaged his nose with a finger and thumb; a lean, neat, disciplined soldier allowing himself a gesture of tiredness after a long day's manoeuvres.

'The police and all the safety-first people came out like bloodhounds. Oliver dealt with them – I phoned him at once to get over here – and he's bloody marvellous with those sort of people, always. He had them agreeing immediately that, taking precautions, we could hold the races on Monday. Silver-tongued magician, he is.' He paused. 'The police have driven off to the hospital to interview you. Surely there was a bed for you there, in your state?'

'I didn't want to stay.'

'But I told you we would look after your boys.'

'I know. One or two might have been all right, but not five.'

'They're easy children,' he protested.

'They're subdued, today. It was best I came back.'

He made no more demur but, as if unready yet to talk of the things uppermost in his thoughts, asked which was which. 'To get them straight in my mind,' he said.

I answered him in much the same way, postponing for a breathing space the questions that would have to be asked and answered.

'Christopher, the tall fair one, he's fourteen. Like most oldest children, he looks after the others. Toby, the one with me today in the stands, he's twelve. Edward's ten. He's the quiet one. Any time you can't find him, he's sitting in a corner somewhere reading a book. Then there's Alan –'

'Freckles and a grin,' Roger said, nodding.

'Freckles and a grin,' I agreed, 'and a deficient sense of danger. He's nine. Leaps first. Oops after.'

'And Neil,' Roger said. 'Little bright-eyed Neil.'

'He's seven. And Jamie, the baby, ten months.'

'We have two daughters,' Roger said. 'Both grown and gone and too busy to marry.'

He fell silent, and I also. The respite from gritty life slowly evaporated. I shifted with sharp discomfort on the sofa and Roger noted it but made no comment.

I said, 'The stands were cleaned yesterday.'

Roger sighed. 'They were cleaned. They were clean. No explosives. Certainly no det cord running round that staircase. I walked everywhere myself, checking. I make rounds continually.'

'But not on Good Friday morning.'

'Late yesterday afternoon. Five o'clock. Went round with my foreman.'

'It wasn't a matter of killing people,' I said.

'No,' he agreed. 'It was to kill one main grandstand, on one of the very few weekdays in the year when there are no race meetings anywhere in Britain. Precisely *not* to kill people, in fact.'

'I expect you have a night watchman,' I said.

'Yes, we do.' He shook his head frustratedly. 'He makes his rounds with a dog. He says he heard nothing. He didn't hear people drilling holes in the walls. He saw no lights moving in the stands. He clocked out at seven this morning and went home.'

'The police asked him?'

'The police asked him. I asked him. Conrad asked him. The poor man was brought back here soggy with sleep and bombarded with accusing questions. He's not ultra-bright at the best of times. He just blinked and looked stupid. Conrad blames me for employing a thicko.'

'Blame will be scattered like confetti,' I said.

He nodded. 'The air's dense with it already. Mostly everything's my fault.'

'Which Strattons came?' I asked.

'Which didn't?' He sighed. 'All of them except Rebecca that were here for the shareholders' meeting, plus Conrad's wife, Victoria, plus Keith's wife Imogen who was squinting drunk, plus Hannah's layabout son Jack, plus Ivan's mousy wife, Dolly. Marjorie Binsham used her tongue like a whip. Conrad can't stand up to her. She had the police pulverised. She wanted to know why you, particularly, hadn't stopped the stands blowing up once your infant child had done the trouble-spotting for you.'

'Dear Marjorie!'

'Someone told her you'd damn nearly been killed and she said it served you right.' He shook his head. 'Sometimes I think the whole family's unhinged.'

'There's some Scotch and glasses in that cupboard above your head,' I said.

He loosened into a smile and poured into two tumblers. 'It won't make you feel better,' he observed, placing one on the built-in table with drawers under it that marked the end of my bed. 'And where did you get this splendid bus? I've never seen anything like it. When I drove it down here with the boys on board they showed me all round it. They seemed to think you built the interior with your own hands. I reckon you had a yacht designer.'

'Both right.'

He tossed off his drink neat in two gulps, army fashion, and put down the glass.

'We can't give your boys beds, not enough room, but we could do food.'

'Thanks, Roger. I'm grateful. But there's enough food in this bus for a battalion, and the battalion's had a good deal of practice in do-it-yourself.'

Despite his assurances I could see his relief. He was indeed, if anything, more exhausted than myself.

I said, 'Do me a favour, though?'

'If I can.'

'Be vague about my whereabouts tonight? If, say, the police or the Strattons should ask.'

'Somewhere to the left of Mars do you?'

'One day,' I said, 'I'll repay you.'

The real world, as Toby would have said, had a go in the morning.

Travelling uncomfortably, I went along with Roger in his jeep to his office beside the parade ring, having left the five boys washing the outside of the bus with buckets of detergent, long-handled brushes and mops and the borrowed use of the Gardners' outdoor tap and garden hose.

Such mammoth splashy activity terminated always in five contentedly soaked children (they loved water-clown acts in circuses) and an at least half-clean bus. I'd advised Mrs Gardner to go indoors and close her eyes and windows, and after the first bucketful of suds had missed the windscreen and landed on Alan, she'd given me a wild look and taken my advice.

'Don't you mind their getting wet?' Roger asked as we left the scene of potential devastation.

'They've a lot of compressed steam to get rid of,' I said.

'You're an extraordinary father.'

'I don't feel it.'

'How are the cuts?'

'Ghastly.'

He chuckled, stopped beside the office door and handed me the walking frame once I was on my feet. I would have preferred not to have needed it, but the only strength left anywhere, it seemed, was in my arms.

Although it was barely eight-thirty, the first car-load of trouble drew up on the tarmac before Roger had finished unlocking his office door. He looked over his shoulder to see who had come, and said a heartfelt *'Bugger!'* as he recognised the transport. 'Bloody Keith.'

Bloody Keith had not come alone. Bloody Keith had brought with him his Hannah, and Hannah, it transpired, had brought with her her son Jack. The three of them climbed out of Keith's car and began striding purposefully round to Roger's office.

He finished unlocking, opened the door, and said to me abruptly, 'Come inside.'

At walking-frame pace I willingly followed him round towards the far side of his desk where, as it happened, my jacket still hung over the back of his chair, abandoned since the previous morning. A lifetime, almost a deathtime, ago.

Keith, Hannah and Jack crowded in through the door, all three faces angry. Keith had reacted to the sight of me as if to an allergy, and Hannah wouldn't have admired her own shrewish expression. Jack, a loose-lipped teenager, mirrored his grandfather too thoroughly: handsome and mean.

Keith said, 'Gardner, get that damned man out of here! And you're sacked. You're incompetent. I'm taking over your job, and you can clear out. As for you . . .' he turned his glare fully my way, 'your bloody children had no right to be anyway near the grandstands, and if you're thinking of suing us because you were stupid enough to get yourself blown up you've another think coming.'

I hadn't thought of it at all, actually. 'You've given me ideas,' I said rashly.

Roger, too late, made a warning movement with his hand, telling me to cool it, not stir. I had myself seen the speed with which Keith's violence had risen in him at the shareholders' meeting, and I remembered the complacency with which I'd reflected that he'd have no physical chance against Madeline's thirty-five-year-old son.

Things had changed slightly since then. I now needed a walking frame if I were to stay upright. And besides, there were three of them.

CHAPTER 7

Roger said '*Hell*' under his breath.

I muttered to him similarly, 'Get out of here.'

'No.'

'Yes. Keep your job.'

Roger stayed.

Keith kicked the office door shut and though he, for a second or two, seemed to hesitate, Hannah had no doubts or restraints. I was, to her, the hated symbol of every resentment she'd fed and festered on for forty years. Keith, who could and should have soothed from childhood her hurt feelings, had no doubt encouraged them. Hannah's loathing was beyond her control. A dagger between the shoulder blades . . . it was there in her eyes.

She came towards me fast in the same leonine stride I'd seen in Rebecca and used her full weight to thrust me back against the wall while at the same time aiming with sharp-clawed fingernails to rip my face.

Roger tried civilised protest. 'Miss Stratton –'

The stalking cat pounced, oblivious.

I'd have liked to have punched her hard at the base of the sternum and to have slapped her into concussion, but hindering taboos bristled in my subconscious, and maybe I couldn't floor that particular woman because of Keith's hitting my mother. My mother, Hannah's mother. A jumble. In any case, I tried merely to grasp my wretched half-sister's wrists, which involved taking both my hands off the walking frame, and this gave Keith an opportunity he had no qualms in seizing.

He tweaked up the frame, barged Hannah out of the way and delivered a damaging clout in my direction in the shape of sturdy chromium tubing with black rubber-tipped feet. Not good. On the clipped-shut cuts, rotten.

Roger held onto Keith's arm to prevent a second strike and I held Hannah's wrists and tried to avoid her spitting in my face. All in all it had developed into a poorish Saturday morning.

It got worse.

Keith lashed out at Roger with the frame. Roger ducked. Keith swung the tubes round my way and again connected and, what with Hannah tugging furiously to get free and Keith crowding in with the four black-tipped legs aimed roughly now at my stomach, my legs inefficiently decided against continued support and to all intents buckled, so that I wavered and wobbled and in the end folded up ignominiously onto the floor.

Hannah yanked her wrists out of my grasp and put her boot in. Her son, who didn't even know me, stepped into the fracas and kicked me twice with equal venom, but also without considering any consequences to himself. I grabbed the foot coming forward for a third time and jerked hard, and with a yell of surprise he overbalanced, falling down within my reach.

His bad luck. I grabbed him and hit him crunchingly in the face and banged his head on the floor, which set Hannah screeching over us like a banshee. Her shoes, I learned, had sharp toes and spikes for heels.

I was aware that Roger, somewhere above, was trying to stop the fray, but what the Colonel really needed was a gun.

Keith took his heavy feet to me, stamping and kicking. There were deep shudders in my body under his weight and his savagery. Roger, to his credit, did his best to pull him off, and roughly at that time, and not a moment too soon, the outer door opened again, bringing a welcome interruption.

'I say,' a man's voice bleated, 'what's going on here?'

Keith, shaking off Roger's clutch and undeterred, said, 'Go away, Ivan. It's none of your business.'

Ivan, I supposed, might have done as he was told, but on his heels came a much tougher proposition.

Marjorie's imperious voice rose above the general noise of battle.

'Keith! Hannah! What on earth do you think you're doing? Colonel, call the police. Call the police this minute.'

The threat worked instantaneously. Hannah stopped kicking and screeching. Keith, panting, stepped back. Jack slithered away from me on all fours. Roger put the walking frame next to me and stretched out a hand to haul me to my feet. It took him more effort than he'd expected, but by martial perseverance he succeeded. I propped myself upright on the frame by force of arms and leaned wearily against the wall, and found that not only Ivan and Marjorie had arrived, but also Conrad and Dart.

For a moment of speechlessness Marjorie took stock of things, noting the still scorching fury in Hannah's manner, the brutish force unspent in Keith and the sullen nose-bleeding vindictiveness of Jack. She glanced at Roger and lastly flicked her gaze over me, head to foot, coming to rest on my face.

'Disgraceful,' she said accusingly. 'Fighting like animals. You ought to know better.'

'He shouldn't be here,' Keith said thickly, and added, lying easily, 'He punched me. He started it.'

'He's broken my nose,' Jack complained.

'Don't tell me he attacked all three of you,' Dart mocked. 'Serves you right.'

'You shut up,' Hannah told him with bile.

Conrad gave his opinion. 'He must have done *something* to start all this. I mean, it's obvious.' He became the examining magistrate, the heavyweight of the proceedings, the accuser; pompous.

'Well, Mr Morris, why precisely did you punch my brother and attack his family? What have you to say?'

Time, I thought, for the prisoner at the bar to defend himself. I swallowed. I felt weak. Also angry enough not to give in to the weakness, or to let them all see it and enjoy it.

When I could trust my voice not to come out as a croak, I said neutrally, 'I didn't punch your brother. I did nothing. They had a go at me for being who I am.'

'That doesn't make sense,' Conrad said. 'People don't get attacked just for being who they are.'

'Tell that to the Jews,' Dart said.

It shocked them all, but not much.

Marjorie Binsham said, 'Go outside, the lot of you. *I* will deal with Mr Morris, in here.' She turned her head to Roger. 'You too, Colonel. Out.'

Conrad said, 'It's not safe –'

'Rubbish!' Marjorie interrupted. 'Off you go.'

They obeyed her, shuffling out without looking at each other, losing face.

'Close the door,' she commanded, and Roger, last out, closed it.

She sat down composedly, wearing that day a narrow tailored navy blue overcoat with a white band of collar again showing beneath. The waved white hair, the fragile looking complexion and the piercing hawk eyes, all those were as before.

She inspected me critically. She said, 'You got yourself blown up yesterday and trampled today. Not very clever, are you?'

'No.'

'And get off the wall. You're bleeding on it.'

'I'll paint it, later.'

'From where, exactly, are you bleeding?'

I explained about the multitude of bruises, cuts and clips. 'Some of those,' I said, 'feel as if they've popped open.'

'I see.'

She seemed for a few moments undecided, not her usual force. Then she said, 'I will free you, if you like, from our agreement.'

'Oh?' I was surprised. 'No, the agreement stands.'

'I did not expect you to be hurt.'

I briefly considered things. Hurt, even if grievous, was in some ways immaterial. I ignored it as best I could. Concentrated on anything else.

'Do you know,' I asked, 'who set the explosive?'

'No, I don't.'

'Which Strattons could have the knowledge?'

'None of them.'

'What about Forsyth?'

Shutters came down in her, too.

'Whatever Forsyth is or isn't,' she said, 'he is not expert in blowing things up.'

'Does he have a motive for getting someone else to do it?'

After a pause, she said, 'I don't think so.'

My forehead was sweating. I put a hand up automatically to wipe it and started swaying, and regripped the walking frame urgently, fighting to regain balance and not to fall down. Too many crushed muscles, too many cut fibres, too much damned battering overall. I stood quietly, breathing deeply, crisis over, my weight on my arms.

'Sit down,' Marjorie commanded.

'That might be worse.'

She stared. I smiled. 'My children think it funny.'

'But not.'

'Not very.'

She said slowly, 'Are you going to charge Keith with assault? Hannah also?'

I shook my head.

'Why not? They were kicking you. I saw them.'

'And would you say so in court?'

She hesitated. She had used the police as a threat to end the fight, but that was all it had been, a threat.

I thought of the pact my mother had made with Lord Stratton, to keep quiet about Keith's violent behaviour. I had hugely benefited from that silence. My unthought-out instinct was to do the same as my mother.

I said, 'I will even things one day, with Keith. But not by embroiling you against your family in public. It will be a private matter, between him and me.'

With evident relief and formality, she said, 'I wish you well.'

There was a brief single wail of a siren outside the window, more an announcement of arrival than of hurry.

The police had arrived anyway. Marjorie Binsham looked not enchanted and I felt very tired, and presently the office door opened to let in far more people than the space had been designed for.

Keith was making abortive attempts to persuade the law that I had caused actual bodily harm to his grandson, Jack.

'Jack,' observed Roger calmly, 'shouldn't try to kick people when they're down.'

'And you,' Keith said to him viciously, 'you can clear out. I told you. You're sacked.'

'Don't be ridiculous,' Marjorie snapped. 'Colonel, you are *not* sacked. We need you. Please stay here. Only by a majority vote of the board can you be asked to leave, and there will be no such majority.'

'One of these days, Marjorie,' Keith said, his voice heavy and shaking with humiliation, 'I will get rid of you.'

'Look here, Keith –' Conrad began.

'And you shut up,' Keith said with hatred. 'It was you or your blackmailing architect that put paid to the stands.'

Into the shocked silence, which left all Stratton mouths dropping open, the police with bathos consulted a notebook full of pre-arranged agenda and asked which of the family normally drove a dark green six-year-old Granada with rusted near wings.

'What's that got to do with anything?' Dart demanded.

Without answering that question the police presence repeated their own.

'I do, then,' Dart said. 'So what?'

'And did you drive that car through the main gates of the racecourse at eight-twenty yesterday morning, and did you oblige Mr Harold Quest to leap out of your path to avoid serious injury, and did you make an obscene gesture to him when he protested?'

Dart nearly laughed, and prudently thought better of it at the last moment.

'No, I didn't,' he said.

'Didn't do what, sir? Didn't drive through the gates? Didn't make Mr Quest leap out of the way? Didn't make an obscene gesture?'

Dart said unworriedly, 'I didn't drive through the main gates at twenty past eight yesterday morning.'

'But you identified the car, sir . . .'

'I wasn't driving it at eight-twenty yesterday morning. Not through the main gates, here. Not anywhere.'

The police asked the inevitable question, politely.

'I was in my bathroom, since you ask,' Dart said, and left his actual activity there to the collective imagination.

I asked, 'Is Mr Quest a large man with a beard, a knitted hat and a placard reading "HORSES RIGHTS COME FIRST"?'

The policeman admitted, 'He does answer to that description, yes, sir.'

'That man!' exclaimed Marjorie.

'Should be shot,' Conrad said.

'He walks straight out in front of one's car,' Marjorie told the policemen severely. 'He will, no doubt, achieve his aim in the end.'

'Which is, madam?'

'To be knocked down, of course. To fall down artistically at the slightest contact. To suffer for the cause. One has to be frightfully careful with that sort of man.'

I asked, 'Are you sure that Mr Quest was actually outside the gates himself at twenty past eight yesterday morning?'

'He insisted that he was,' said the policeman.

'On Good Friday? It's a day when no one goes to racecourses.'

'He said he was there.'

I left it. Lack of energy. Dart and the car had gone in and out of the gates often enough for every picketer to be able to describe it down to its tattered rear bumper-sticker, which read, 'If you can read this, drop back'. Dart had annoyed big beard the day I'd been with him. Big beard, Harold Quest, felt compelled to make trouble. Where lay the truth?

'And you, Mr Morris . . .' The notebook's pages were

flipped over and were consulted. 'We were told you were to be detained in hospital but when we went to interview you they said you had discharged yourself. They hadn't officially released you.'

'Such punitive words!' I said.

'What?'

'Detained and released. As in prison.'

'We couldn't find you,' he complained. 'No one seemed to know where you'd gone.'

'Well, I'm here now.'

'And ... er ... Mr Jack Stratton alleges that at approximately eight-fifty this morning you attacked him and broke his nose.'

'Jack Stratton alleges nothing of the sort,' Marjorie said with certainty. 'Jack, speak up.'

The sullen young man, dabbing his face with a handkerchief, took note of Marjorie's piercing displeasure and mumbled he might have walked into a door, like. Despite Keith's and Hannah's protestations, the policeman resignedly drew a line across the entry in his notebook and said his superiors wanted information from me on the whereabouts of the explosive charges 'prior to detonation'. Where, they asked, could I be found?

'When?' I asked.

'This morning, sir.'

'Then ... here, I suppose.'

Conrad, looking at his watch, announced that he had summoned a demolitions expert and an inspector from the local council to come to advise how best to remove the old stands and clear the area ready for rebuilding.

Keith, in a rage, said, 'You've no right to do that. It's my racecourse just as much as yours, and I want to sell it, and if we sell to a developer *he* will clear away the stands at no expense to us. We are *not* rebuilding.'

Marjorie, fierce eyed, said they needed an expert opinion on whether or not the stands could be restored as they had been, and whether the racecourse insurance would cover any other course of action.

'Add the insurance to the profit from selling, and we will all benefit,' Keith obstinately said.

The policemen, uninterested, retired to their car outside and could be seen talking on their private phone line, consulting their superiors, one supposed.

I said doubtfully to Roger, '*Can* the stands be restored?'

He answered with caution. 'Too soon to say.'

'Of course, they can.' Marjorie was positive. 'Anything can be restored, if one insists on it.'

Replaced as before, or copied, she meant. A mistake, I thought it would be, for Stratton Park's racing future.

The family went on quarrelling. They had all turned up early, it appeared, precisely to prevent any unilateral decision-making. They left the office in an arguing mass, bound together by fears of what any one could do on his own. Roger watched them go, his expression exasperated.

'What a way to run a business! And neither Oliver nor I have been paid since before Lord Stratton died. He used to sign our cheques personally. The only person empowered to pay us since then is Mrs Binsham. I explained it to her when we were walking round the course last Wednesday, and she said she understood, but when I asked her again yesterday after the stands blew up, when she came here with all the others, she told me not to bother her at such a time.' He sighed heavily. 'It's all very well, but it's over two months now since we had any salary.'

'Who pays the racecourse staff?' I asked.

'I do. Lord Stratton arranged it. Keith disapproves. He says it's an invitation to fraud. Judges me by himself, of course. Anyway, the only pay cheques I can't sign are Oliver's and my own.'

'Have you made them out ready?'

'My secretary did.'

'Give them to me, then.'

'To you?'

'I'll get the old bird to sign them.'

He didn't ask how. He merely opened a desk drawer, took out an envelope and held it towards me.

'Put it in my jacket,' I said.

He looked at the walking frame, shook his head at his thoughts, and tucked the cheques into my jacket pocket.

'Are the stands,' I asked, 'a total loss?'

'You'd better see for yourself. Mind you, no one can get close. The police have cordoned everything off.'

From the office window, little damage was visible. One could see the end wall, the roof, and an oblique side view of the open steps.

'I'd rather see the holes unaccompanied by Strattons,' I said.

Roger almost grinned. 'They're all afraid to let the others out of their sight.'

'I thought so too.'

'I suppose you do know you're bleeding.'

'Staining the wall, Marjorie said.' I nodded. 'It's stopped by now, I should think.'

'But . . .' He fell silent.

'I'll go back for running repairs,' I promised. 'Though God knows when. They keep one waiting so long.'

He said diffidently, 'One of the racecourse doctors would be quicker. I could ask him for you, if you like. He's very obliging.'

'Yes,' I said tersely.

Roger reached for his telephone and reassured the doctor that racing was still going ahead as planned on Monday. Meanwhile, as a favour, could a casualty be stitched? When? At once, preferably. Thanks very much.

'Come on, then,' he said to me, replacing the receiver. 'Can you still walk?'

I could and did, pretty slowly. The police protested at my vanishing again. Back in an hour or so, Roger said soothingly. The Strattons were nowhere in sight, though their cars were still parked. Roger aimed his jeep towards the main gates, and Mr Harold Quest refrained from planting his obsessions in our path.

The doctor was the one who had attended the fallers at the open ditch, businesslike and calm. When he saw what he was being asked to do, he didn't want to.

'GPs don't do this sort of thing any more,' he told Roger. 'They refer people to hospitals. He should be in a hospital. This level of pain is ridiculous.'

'It comes and goes,' I said. 'And suppose we were out in the Sahara Desert?'

'Swindon is not the Sahara.'

'All life's a desert.'

He muttered under his breath and stuck me together again with what looked like adhesive tape.

'Haven't I seen you before?' he asked, puzzled, finishing.

I explained about the fence.

'The man with the children!' He shook his head regretfully. 'They saw a horror, I'm afraid.'

Roger thanked him for his services to me, and I also. The doctor told Roger that the racing authorities had received a complaint from Rebecca Stratton about his professional competency, or lack of it. They wanted a full report on his decision to recommend that she should be stood down for concussion.

'She's a bitch,' Roger said, with feeling.

The doctor glanced my way uneasily.

'He's safe,' Roger assured him. 'Say what you like.'

'How long have you known him?'

'Long enough. And it was Strattons that kicked his wounds open again.'

It had to be hellish, I thought, being in even the smallest way reliant on the Strattons for employment. Roger truly lived on the edge of an abyss: and out of his job would mean out of his home.

He drove us carefully back to the racecourse, forbearing from lecturing me about the hand I clamped over my face, or my drooping head. As far as he was concerned, what I chose to do about my troubles was my own affair. I developed strong feelings of friendship and gratitude.

Big-beard stepped in front of the jeep. I wondered if his name was really Quest, or if he'd made it up. Not a tactful question to ask at that time. He barred our way through the main gates peremptorily, and Roger, to my surprise, smartly backed away from him, swung the jeep round and drove off down the road, continuing our journey.

'It just occurred to me,' he said judiciously, 'that if we go in by the back road we not only avoid words with that maniac, but you could call at your bus for clean clothes.'

'I'm running out of them.'

He glanced across doubtfully. 'Mine aren't really big enough.'

'No. It's OK.'

I was down to a choice between well-worn working jeans and race going tidiness. I opted for the jeans and a lumberjack-type wool checked shirt and dumped the morning's bloodied garments in a washing locker already filled with sopping smaller clothes.

The boys had finished sluicing both the bus and themselves. The bus looked definitely cleaner. The boys must be dry, even though nowhere in sight. I descended slowly to the ground again and found Roger walking round the home-from-home, interested but reticent, as ever.

'It used to be a long-distance touring coach,' I said. 'I bought it when the bus company replaced its cosy old fleet with modern glass-walled crowd-pleasers.'

'How . . . I mean, how do you manage the latrines?'

I smiled at the army parlance. 'There were huge spaces for suitcases, underneath. I replaced some of them with water and sewage tanks. Every rural authority runs pump-out tankers for emptying far-flung cesspits. And there are boatyards. It's easy to get a pump-out, if you know who to ask.'

'Amazing.' He patted the clean coffee-coloured paintwork, giving himself another interval, I saw again, before having to go back to the distasteful present.

He sighed. 'I suppose . . .'

I nodded.

We climbed back into the jeep and returned to the grandstands, where, leaning again on the walking frame, I took my first objective look at the previous day's destructive mayhem. We stood prudently outside the police tapes, but movement had ceased in the pile.

First thought: *incredible* that Toby and I had come out of that mess alive.

The building had been centrally disembowelled, its guts spilling out in a monstrous cascade. The weighing room, changing rooms and Oliver Wells's office, which jutted forward from the main structure, had been crushed flat under the spreading weight of the collapsing floors above. The long unyielding steel and concrete mass of the course-facing viewing steps had meant that all the explosive force had been directed one way, into the softer resistance of the brick, wood and plaster of dining rooms, bars and staircase.

Above the solidly impacted rubble, a hollow column of space rose through the upper floors like an exclamation mark, topped with a few stark remaining fingers of the Stewards' viewing box pointing skyward.

I said slowly, under my breath, 'Jesus Christ.'

After a while, Roger asked, 'What do you think?'

'Chiefly,' I said, 'how the hell are you going to hold a race meeting here the day after tomorrow?'

He rolled his eyes in frustration. 'It's Easter weekend. More weddings today than on any other day of the year. Monday, horse shows, dog shows, you name it, all over the place. I spent all yesterday afternoon trying to get hire firms to bring marquees. *Any* sort of tent. But every scrap of canvas is already out in service. We're shutting off the whole of this end of the stands, of course, and are having to move everyone and everything along into Tattersalls, but so far I've only managed a promise of a couple of Portakabins for the changing rooms and it looks as if we're going to have to have the scales out in the open air, as they used to do at point-to-points. And as for food and extra bars . . .' He shrugged helplessly. 'We've told the caterers to make their own arrangements and they say they're stretched already. God help us if it rains, we'll be working under umbrellas.'

'Where were you planning to put tents?' I asked.

'In the members' car park.' He sounded disconsolate. 'The Easter Monday holiday meeting is our biggest money-spinner of the year. We can't afford to cancel it. And both Marjorie

Binsham and Conrad are adamant that we go ahead. We've told all the trainers to send their runners for the races. The stables are all right. We'll still comply with all the regulations such as six security boxes, and so on. The saddling stalls are fine. The parade ring's OK. Oliver can use my office.'

He turned away from his gloomy contemplation of the ruined grandstand and we began a slow traverse towards his telephone. He had to confirm some electrical plans, he said.

His office was full of Strattons. Conrad sat in Roger's chair behind the desk. Conrad was talking on Roger's telephone, taking charge.

Conrad was saying, 'Yes, I know you told my manager that all your tents were out, but this is Lord Stratton himself speaking, and I'm telling you to dismantle and bring in a suitable marquee from anywhere at all, and put it up here tomorrow. I don't care where you get it from, just get it.'

I touched Roger's arm before he could make any protest, and waved to him to retreat. Outside the office, ignored by all the Strattons, I suggested he drive us both back to the bus.

'I've a telephone in it,' I explained. 'No interruptions.'

'Did you hear what Conrad was saying?'

'Yes, I did. Will he be successful?'

'If he is, my job's gone.'

'Drive down to the bus.'

Roger drove and, to save having to get in and out of the bus again, I told him where to find the mobile phone and asked him to bring it out, along with a book of private phone numbers he would find beneath it. When he climbed down the steps with the necessary, I looked up a number and made a call.

'Henry? Lee Morris. How goes it?'

'Emergency? Crisis? The roof's fallen in?'

'How did you guess?'

'Yes, but Lee, my usual big top is out as an indoor pony school. Little girls in hard hats. They've got it for the year.'

'What about the huge one that takes so much moving?'

A resigned sigh came down the wire. Henry, long-time pal, general large-scale junk dealer, had acquired two big tops from a bankrupt travelling circus and would rent them out to me from time to time to enclose any thoroughly gutted ruin I wanted to shield from the weather.

I explained to him what was needed and why, and I explained to Roger who he was going to be talking to, and I leaned peacefully on the walking frame while they discussed floor space, budget and transport. When they seemed to be reaching agreement I said to Roger, 'Tell him to bring all the flags.'

Roger, mystified, relayed the message and got a reply that made him laugh. 'Fine,' he said, 'I'll phone back to confirm.'

We took the telephone and the numbers book with us in the jeep and returned to the office. Conrad was still shouting down the phone there but, judging from the impatience now manifest in the Stratton herd, was achieving nil results.

'You're on,' I murmured to Roger. 'Say *you* found the tent.'

It didn't come naturally to him to take another man's credit, but he could see the point in it. The Strattons could perversely turn down any suggestion of mine, even if it were to their own advantage to adopt it.

Roger walked over to his desk as Conrad slammed down the receiver in fury.

'I . . . er . . . I've located a tent,' he said firmly.

'About time!' Conrad said.

'Where?' Keith demanded, annoyed.

'A man in Hertfordshire has one. He can ship it here by tomorrow morning, and he'll send a crew to erect it.'

Conrad was grudgingly pleased but wouldn't admit it.

'The only thing is,' Roger continued, 'that he doesn't supply this tent on short leases. We would need to keep it for a minimum of three months. However,' he hurried on, sensing interruptions, 'that condition could be to our advantage, as the grandstands will be out of operation for much longer than that. We could keep the tent for as long as we need. And this tent has a firm floor and versatile dividing partitions and sounds stronger than a normal marquee.'

'Too expensive,' Keith objected.

'Less expensive, actually,' Roger said, 'than erecting tents separately for each meeting.'

Marjorie Binsham's gaze by-passed both Roger and her family and fastened on me.

'Any ideas?' she asked.

'Ignore him,' Keith insisted.

I said neutrally, 'All four directors are here. Hold a board meeting and decide.'

A smile, quickly hidden, tugged at Marjorie's lips. Dart, though, grinned openly.

'Give us the details,' Marjorie commanded Roger, and he, consulting his notes, told them the space and price involved, and said the insurance from non-availability of the stands would easily cover it.

'Who arranged that insurance?' Marjorie asked.

'Lord Stratton and I and the insurance brokers.'

'Very well,' Marjorie said crisply, 'I put forward a motion that the Colonel arranges a contract for the tent on the terms proposed. And Ivan will second it.'

Ivan, galvanised, said vaguely, 'Oh? Yes, rather.'

'Conrad?' Marjorie challenged him.

'Well . . . I suppose so.'

'Carried,' Marjorie said.

'I object,' Keith seethed.

'Your objection is noted,' Marjorie said. 'Colonel, summon the tent.'

Roger turned the leaves of my phone book and spoke to Henry.

'Very well done, Colonel!' Marjorie congratulated him warmly when all was arranged. 'This place could not function without you.'

Conrad looked defeated; Ivan, bewildered; and Keith, murderous.

Jack, Hannah and Dart, minor players, put no thoughts into words.

The brief ensuing pause in the proceedings came to an end with the arrival of two more cars, one containing, it transpired, two senior policemen with an explosives expert, and the other, Conrad's demolition man and a heavily moustached manifestation of local authority.

The Strattons, as a flock, migrated into the open air.

Roger wiped a hand over his face and said service in Northern Ireland had been less of a strain.

'Do you think we had an Irish bomb here?' I said.

He looked startled but shook his head. 'The Irish boast of it. No one so far has done any crowing. And this one wasn't aimed at people, don't forget. The Irish bombers aim to maim.'

'So who?'

'Crucial question. I don't know. And you don't need to say it . . . this may not be the end.'

'What about guards?'

'I've press ganged my groundsmen. There are relays of them in pairs patrolling the place.' He patted the walkie-talkie clipped to his belt. 'They're reporting all the time to my foreman. If anything looks wrong, he'll report it to me.'

The newly-arrived policemen came into the office and introduced themselves as a detective chief inspector and a detective sergeant. An accompanying intense looking young man was vaguely and anonymously introduced as an explosives expert, a defuser of bombs. It was he who asked most of the questions.

I answered him simply, describing where the det cord had been and how it had looked.

'You and your young son both knew at once what it was?'

'We'd both seen it before.'

'And how close to each other were the charges in the walls?'

'About three feet apart. In some places, less.'

'And how extensive or widespread?'

'All round the stairwell and the landing walls on at least two floors. Perhaps more.'

'We understand you're a builder. How long, do you think, it would have taken you personally to drill the holes for the charges?'

'Each hole? Some of the walls were brick, some were composition, like breeze-block, all of them plastered and painted. Thick and load bearing, but soft, really. You'd hardly need a hammer-drill, even. The holes would probably have to be five inches deep, about an inch in diameter – given a wide drill bit and electricity, I could do perhaps two a minute if I was in a hurry.' I paused. 'Threading the holes with det cord and packing them with explosives obviously takes longer. I've been told you need to compress and tamp it all in very carefully with something wooden, no sparks, like a broom handle.'

'Who told you?'

'Demolitions people.'

The chief inspector asked, 'How are you so sure the walls were made of brick and breeze-block? How could you possibly tell, if they were plastered and painted?'

I thought back. 'On the floor beneath each charge there was a small pile of dust caused by drilling the hole. Some piles were pink brick dust, others were grey.'

'You had time to see that?'

'I remember it. At the time, it just made it certain that there was a good deal of explosive rammed into those walls.'

The expert said, 'Did you look to see where the circuit began or ended?'

I shook my head. 'I was trying to find my son.'

'And did you see anyone else at all in the vicinity of the stands near that time?'

'No. No one.'

They asked me and Roger to walk with them as far as the safety cordon, so that we could explain to the expert where the staircase and walls had been before the explosion. The expert, it seemed, would then put on a protective suit and a hard hat and go in wherever he could to take a look from the inside.

'Rather you than me,' I commented.

They watched the best I could do at walking with them. When we reached the point of maximum visual bad news, the bomb-defusing expert looked upwards to the fingers of the Stewards' box and down to my walking frame. He put on his large head-sheltering hat and gave me a twisting self-mocking smile.

'I'm old in my profession,' he said.

'How old?'

'Twenty-eight.'

I said, 'All of a sudden, I can't feel a thing.'

His smile broadened. 'People sometimes get lucky.'

'Good luck, then,' I said.

CHAPTER 8

'You know what?' Roger said to me.

'What?'

We were standing on the tarmac a little apart from the policemen but still looking at the rubble.

'I'd think our demolitionist got more bang for his bucks than he intended.'

'How do you mean?'

He said, 'High explosives are funny things. Unpredictable, often. They weren't my speciality in the army, but of course most soldiers learn about them. There's always a tendency to use too much explosive for the job in hand, just to make sure of effective results.' He smiled briefly. 'A colleague of mine had to blow up a bridge, once. Just to blow a hole in it, to put it out of action. He over-estimated how much explosive it would take, and the whole thing totally disintegrated into invisible dust which was carried away in the river below. Not a thing left. Everyone thought he'd done a brilliant job, but he was laughing about it in private. *I* wouldn't have known how much to use to cause this much damage here in the grandstands. And I've been thinking that whoever did it probably meant only to put the stairway out of action. I mean . . . setting all those careful charges rounds its walls . . . if he'd meant to destroy the whole stand, why not use one single large bomb? Much easier. Less chance of being spotted setting it up. See what I mean?'

'Yes, I do.'

He glanced directly at my face. 'Look,' he said awkwardly, 'I know it's not my business, but wouldn't you be better lying down in your bus?'

'I'll go if I have to.'

He nodded.

'Otherwise,' I said, 'it's better to have other things to think about.'

He was happy with that. 'Just say, then.'

'Yes. Thanks.'

The Strattons were suddenly all round us. Dart said in my ear, 'Conrad's architect has come. Now for some fireworks!' I looked at his impish enjoyment. 'Did Keith really *kick* you?' he asked. 'Ivan says I missed a real pretty sight by a few seconds.'

'Too bad. Where's the architect?'

'That man beside Conrad.'

'And is he a blackmailer?'

'God knows. Ask Keith.'

He knew as well as I did that I wouldn't ask Keith anything.

'I reckon Keith made that up,' Dart said. 'He's a terrible liar. He can't tell the truth.'

'And Conrad? Does he lie?'

'My father?' Dart showed no anger at the possible slur. 'My father tells the truth on principle. Or else from lack of imagination. Take your pick.'

'The twins at the fork in the road,' I said.

'What the heck are you talking about?'

'Tell you later.'

Marjorie was saying formidably, 'We do *not* need an architect.'

'Face facts,' Conrad pleaded. 'Look at this radical destruction. It's a heaven-sent opportunity to build something meaningful.'

Build something meaningful. The words vibrated in memory. Build something meaningful had been one of the precepts repeated *ad nauseam* by a lecturer at college.

I looked carefully at Conrad's architect, turning the inward eye back more than sixteen years. Conrad's architect, I slowly realised, had been a student like myself at the Architectural Association School of Architecture: senior to me, one of the élite, a disciple of the future. I remembered his face and his glittering prospects, and I'd forgotten his name.

Roger left my side and went across to put in a presence at the Marjorie–Conrad conflict, a hopeless position for a manager. Conrad's architect nodded to him coolly, seeing Roger as critic, not ally.

Dart, waving a hand towards the rubble, asked me, 'What do you think they should do?'

'I, personally?'

'Yes.'

'They don't care what I think.'

'But I'm curious.'

'I think they should spend their time finding out who did it, and why.'

'But the police will do that.'

'Are you saying that the family doesn't want to find out?'

Dart said, alarmed, 'Can you see through brick?'

'Why don't they want to know? I wouldn't think it safe not to.'

'Marjorie will do anything to keep family affairs private,' Dart said. 'She's worse than Grandfather, and he would pay the earth to keep the Stratton name clean.'

Keith must have cost them a packet, I thought, from my own mother onwards; and I wondered fleetingly again what Forsyth could have done to cause them such angst.

Dart looked at his watch. 'Twenty to twelve,' he said. 'I'm fed up with all this. What do you say to the Mayflower?'

On reflection I said yes to the Mayflower, and without fanfare retreated with him to the green six-year-old Granada with rusted near wings. Harold Quest, it seemed, never interfered with exits. We made an unhindered passage to imitation AD 1620, where Dart accepted a half-pint and I also ordered fifteen fat rounds of cheese, tomato, ham and lettuce home-made sandwiches and a quart tub of ice cream.

'You can't be *that* hungry!' Dart exclaimed.

'I've five beaks to fill.'

'Good God! I'd forgotten.'

We drank the beer while waiting for the sandwiches, and then he good-naturedly drove us down through the back entrance to park outside Roger's house, near the bus.

Beside the main door into the bus, in a small outside compartment, I'd long ago installed a chuck-wagon-type bell. Dart watched in amusement when I extended it on its arm outwards, and set it clanging with vigour.

The cowboys came in from the prairie, hungry, dry and virtuous, and sat around on boxes and logs for their open-air lunch. I stood with the walking frame. Getting used to it, the boys took it for granted.

They had built a stockade from sticks, they said. Inside the fort were the United States cavalry (Christopher and Toby) and outside were the Indians (the rest). The Indians were (of course) the Good Guys, who hoped to overrun the stockade and take a few scalps. Sneaky tactics were needed, Chief Edward said. Alan Redfeather was his trusty spy.

Dart, eating a sandwich, said he thought Neil's lurid warpaint (Mrs Gardner's lipstick) a triumph for political correctness.

None of them knew what he meant. I saw Neil storing the words away, mouthing them silently, ready to ask later.

Locust-like, they mopped up the Mayflower's food and, as it seemed a good time for it, I said to them, 'Ask Dart the riddle of the pilgrim. He'll find it interesting.'

Christopher obligingly began, 'A pilgrim came to a fork in the road. One road led to safety, and the other to death. In each fork stood a guardian.'

'They were twins,' Edward said.

Christopher, nodding, went on, 'One twin always spoke the truth and the other always lied.'

Dart turned his head and stared at me.

'It's a very *old* riddle,' Edward said apologetically.

'The pilgrim was allowed only one question,' Toby said. 'Only one. And to save his life he had to find out which road led to safety. So what did he ask?'

'He asked which way was safe,' Dart said reasonably.

Christopher said, 'Which twin did he ask?'

'The one who spoke the truth.'

'But how did he know which one spoke the truth? They both looked the same. They were twins.'

'Conrad and Keith aren't identical,' Dart said.

The children, not understanding, pressed on. Toby asked again, 'What question did the pilgrim ask?'

'Haven't the foggiest.'

'*Think,*' Edward commanded.

Dart turned my way. 'Save me!' he said.

'*That's* not what the pilgrim said,' Neil informed him with relish.

'Do you all know?'

Five heads nodded. 'Dad told us.'

'Then Dad had better tell *me.*'

It was Christopher, however, who explained. 'The pilgrim could only ask one question, so he went to one of the twins and he asked, "If I ask your brother which way leads to safety, which way will he tell me to go?"'

Christopher stopped. Dart looked flummoxed. 'Is that all?' he asked.

'That's all. So what did the pilgrim do?'

'Well . . . he . . . I give in. What did he do?'

They wouldn't tell him the answer.

'You're *devils*,' Dart said.

'One of the twins was a devil,' Edward said, 'and the other was an angel.'

'You just made that up,' Toby accused him.

'So what? It makes it more interesting.'

They all tired abruptly of the riddle and trooped off, as was their habit, back to their make-believe game.

'For Christ's sake!' Dart exclaimed. 'That's not bloody fair.'

I laughed in my throat.

'So what did the pilgrim do?'

'Work it out.'

'You're as bad as your children.'

Dart and I got back into his car. He put the walking frame onto the back seat and observed, 'Keith really hurt you, didn't he?'

'No, it was the explosion. Bits of roof fell in.'

'Fell in on you. Yes, I heard.'

'From the shoulder blades down,' I agreed. 'Could have been worse.'

'Oh, sure.' He started the engine and drove up the private inner road. 'What did the pilgrim do, then?'

I smiled. 'Whichever road either twin told him was safe, he went down the other one. Both twins would have pointed to the road leading to death.'

He thought very briefly. 'How come?'

'If the pilgrim asked the truthful twin which way his brother would send him to safety, the truthful twin, knowing his brother would lie, would point to the road to death.'

'You've lost me.'

I explained over again. 'And,' I said, 'if the pilgrim happened to ask the lying twin which way his brother would send someone to safety, the lying twin, though knowing his brother would speak the truth, lied about what he would say. So the lying twin also would point to the road to death.'

Dart relapsed into silence. When he spoke he said, 'Do your boys understand it?'

'Yes. They acted it out.'

'Don't they ever quarrel?'

'Of course, they do. But they've been moved around so much that they've made few outside friendships. They rely on each other.' I sighed. 'They'll grow out of it, shortly. Christopher's already too old for half their games.'

'A pity.'

'Life goes on.'

Dart braked his rusty car gently to a halt in the impromptu car park outside Roger's office.

I said diffidently, 'Did you, in fact, drive here yesterday morning in this car, as Harold Quest said?'

'No, I didn't.' Dart took no offence. 'And what's more, I *was* in my bathroom from eight to eight-thirty, and don't bloody laugh, I'm not telling anyone else, but I've got a new scalp vibrator thing that's supposed to stop hair falling out.'

'Snake oil,' I said.

'Bugger you, I said don't laugh.'

'I'm not laughing.'

'Your face muscles are *twitching*.'

'I do believe, anyway,' I said, 'that because of your hair you didn't arrive at the racecourse at eight-twenty yesterday morning with your old jalopy bulging with detonating cord and plastic explosive.'

'Thanks a bunch.'

'The thing is, could anyone have borrowed your car without you knowing? And would you mind very much if the bomb expert or the police tested this car for the presence of nitrates?'

He looked aghast. 'You can't mean it!'

'Someone,' I pointed out, 'brought explosives to the stairs in the grandstands yesterday. It's probably fair to say it was plugged into the walls after the night watchman went home at seven. It was fully light by then. There was no one else about because of its being Good Friday. There was only Harold Quest and his pals at the gate, and I don't know how much one can trust him.'

'The lying twins,' Dart said.

'Maybe.'

I tried to imagine easy-going Dart, with his thickening frame and his thinning hair, his ironic cast of mind and his core of idleness, ever caring enough about anything to blow up a grandstand. Impossible. But to lend his car? To lend his car casually for an unspecified purpose, yes, certainly. To lend it knowing it would be used for a crime? I hoped not. Yet he would have let me open the locked cupboard in his father's study. Had taken me there and given me every illegal chance. Hadn't cared a jot when I'd backed off.

A sloppy sense of right and wrong, or a deep alienation that he habitually hid?

I liked Dart; he lifted one's spirits. Among the Strattons, he was the nearest to normal. The nearest, one should perhaps say, to a rose among nettles.

I said neutrally, 'Where's your sister Rebecca today? I'd have thought she'd have been here, practically purring.'

'She's racing at Towcester,' he said briefly. 'I looked in the newspaper. No doubt she's thrilled the stands have had it, but I haven't spoken to her since Wednesday. She's talked to Father, I think. She's riding one of his horses here on Monday. It's got a good chance of winning, so no way would she have put the meeting in jeopardy, with dynamite shenanigans, if that's what you're thinking.'

'Where does she live?' I asked.

'Lambourn. Ten miles away, roughly.'

'Horse country.'

'She lives and breathes horses. Quite mad.'

I lived and breathed building. I got fulfilment from putting brick on brick, stone on stone: from bringing a dead thing to life. I understood a single-minded encompassing drive. Not much in the world, for good or for evil, gets done without it.

The rest of the Strattons came round from the racecourse side of the grandstands, bringing Conrad's architect with them. The police and the bomb expert seemed to be sifting carefully through the edges of the rubble. The moustached local authority was scratching his head.

Roger came over to Dart's car and asked where we'd been.

'Feeding the children,' I said.

'Oh! Well, the Honourable Marjorie wants to demolish you. Er . . .' He went on more prudently in the presence of Dart, 'Mrs Binsham wants to see you in my office.'

I clambered stiffly onto the tarmac and plodded that way. Roger came along beside me.

'Don't let her eat you,' he said.

'No. Don't worry. Do you happen to know that architect's name?'

'What?'

'Conrad's architect.'

'It's Wilson Yarrow. Conrad calls him Yarrow.'

'Thanks.'

I stopped walking abruptly.

Roger said, 'What's the matter? Is it worse?'

'No.' I looked at him vaguely, to his visible alarm. I asked, 'Did you tell any of the Strattons that I'm an architect?'

He was perplexed. 'Only Dart. You told him yourself, remember? Why? Why does it matter?'

'Don't tell them,' I said. I did a one-eighty back towards Dart, who got out of his car and came to meet us.

'What's the matter?' he said.

'Nothing much. Look ... did you happen to mention to any of your family that I'm a qualified architect?'

He thought back, frowning. Roger, reaching us, looked thoroughly mystified. 'What does it matter?' he asked.

'Yes,' Dart echoed, 'what does it matter?'

'I don't want Conrad to know.'

Roger protested. 'But Lee, why ever not?'

'That man he's brought here, Wilson Yarrow, he and I were trained at the same school. There's something about him ...' I dried up, thinking hard.

'What's odd about him?' Roger demanded.

'That's the trouble, I can't quite remember. But I can easily find out. I'd just rather find out without his knowing about it.'

'Do you mean,' Dart asked, 'that he blew up the stands to get the commission to build the new ones?'

'God,' Roger said. 'You do jump to conclusions.'

'Keith thinks so. He said so.'

'I think they just know you're a builder,' Roger said to me thoughtfully, 'and, to be honest, at the moment that's just what you look like.'

I glanced down at my loose checked shirt and my baggy faded working jeans and acknowledged the convenient truth of it.

'Won't he know *you*,' Roger asked, 'if you trained at the same place?'

'No. I was at least three years behind him and not very noticeable. He was one of the flashing stars. Different firmament to me. I don't think we ever spoke. People like that are too wrapped up in their own affairs to learn the faces and names of junior intakes. And it wasn't last week. It's seventeen years now since I enrolled there.'

When two architects met, the most normal opening gambit between them was, 'Where were you taught?' And one took preconceived ideas from the answer.

To have learned architecture at Cambridge, for instance, indicated a likelihood of cautious conservation; at Bath, of anatomy before beauty; and at the Mackintosh in Glasgow, of partisan Scottishness. People who'd been to any of them knew how their fellows had been influenced. One understood a stranger because of the experiences shared.

The Architectural Association, alma mater of both Yarrow and myself, tended to turn out innovative ultra-modernists who saw into the future and built people-coercive edifices cleverly of glass. The spirit of Le Corbusier reigned, even though the school itself stood physically in Bedford Square in London, in a beautifully proportioned Georgian terraced mansion often at odds with the lectures within.

The library windows shone out, brightly lit always, into the night shadows of the square, celebrating distinction of knowledge, and if a certain arrogance crept into self-satisfied star students, perhaps the supreme excellence and thoroughness of the tuition excused it.

The Association was mostly outside the state education system, which meant few student grants, which in turn meant that chiefly paying students went there, the intake having consequently changed slowly over the years from a preponderance of indigenous bohemian English to the offspring of wealthy Greeks, Nigerians, Americans, Iranians and Hong Kong Chinese, and I reckoned I'd learned a good deal and made unexpected friends from the mixture.

I myself had emerged from the exhaustively practical, and sometimes metaphysical, teaching with Le Corbusier technology and humanist tendencies, and would never be revered in the halls that had nurtured me: restoring old ruins carved no fame for posterity.

Dart asked curiously, 'Do you have letters after your name?'

I hesitated. 'What? Yes, I do. They're AADipl, which stands for Architectural Association Diploma. It may not mean much to the outside world generally, but to other architects, and to Yarrow, it's pretty revealing.'

'Sounds like Alcoholics Anonymous Dipsomaniac,' Dart said.

Roger laughed.

'Keep that joke under wraps,' I begged, and Dart said maybe he would.

Mark, Marjorie's chauffeur, joined us and told us disapprovingly that I was keeping Mrs Binsham waiting. She was sitting in the office tapping her foot.

'Tell her I'll come instantly,' I said, and Mark went off with the message.

'That brave man deserves the Victoria Cross,' Dart grinned, 'for conspicuous valour.' I set off in Mark's wake. 'So do you,' Dart shouted.

Marjorie, stiff backed, was indeed displeased but, it transpired, not with Mark or myself. The chauffeur had been told to go for a walk. As for myself, I was invited to sit.

'I'd rather stand, really.'

'Oh, yes, I forgot.' She gave me a short shirt-by-jeans inspection, as if uncertain how to categorise me because of my changing appearance.

'I believe you're a builder by trade,' she began.

'Yes.'

'Well, as a builder, now that you've had a good look at the extent of the damage to the grandstand, what do you think?'

'About restoring things as they were?'

'Certainly.'

I said, 'As much as I understand that that's what you'd like, I frankly think it would be a mistake.'

She was obstinate. 'But could it be done?'

I said, 'The whole structure may prove to be unsafe. The

building's old, though well built, I grant you. But there may be fractures that can't be seen yet, and undoubtedly there are new stresses. Once the rubble is removed, more of the building could fall in. It would all need shoring up. I'm really sorry, but my advice would be to take it down and rebuild it from scratch.'

'I don't want to hear that.'

'I know.'

'But could it be done so it was the same as before?'

'Certainly. All the original plans and drawings are here, in this office.' I paused. 'But it would be a lost opportunity.'

'Don't tell me you side with Conrad!'

'I don't side with anyone. I'm just telling you honestly that you could improve the old stands enormously for modern comfort if you redesigned them.'

'I don't like the architect that Conrad's thrusting down our throats. I don't understand half of what he says, and the man's *condescending*, can you believe?'

I could certainly believe it. 'He'll find out his mistake,' I said, smiling. 'And, incidentally, if in the end you decide to modify the stands, it would be sensible to announce a competition in magazines architects read, asking for drawings to be submitted to a jury which you could appoint. Then you'd have a choice. You wouldn't be in a take-it-or-leave-it situation with Wilson Yarrow who, the Colonel assures me, doesn't know a jot about racing. One wouldn't choose even a chair without sitting in it. The stands need to be comfortable as well as good looking.'

She nodded thoughtfully. 'You were going to look into this Yarrow's background. Have you done it?'

'It's in hand.'

'And about Keith's debts?'

'Working on it.'

She made a 'Hmph' noise of disbelief, justifiably. 'I suppose,' she added, trying to be fair, 'you're finding it difficult to get about.'

I shrugged. 'It's a holiday weekend, that's another of the problems.' I thought briefly. 'Where does Keith live?'

'Above his expectations.'

I laughed. Marjorie primly smiled at her own wit.

She said, 'He lives in the Dower House on the estate. It was built for the widow of the first baron and, as she had a taste for ostentation, it is large. Keith pretends he owns it, but he doesn't, he rents it. Since my brother has died, ownership passes to Conrad, of course.'

I asked tentatively, 'And . . . Keith's source of income?'

Marjorie disapproved of the question but on reflection answered: it was she, after all, who'd set me in motion.

'His mother left him provided for. He was a beautiful looking little boy and young man, and she doted on him. Forgave him anything. Conrad and Ivan were always clumsy and plain and never made her laugh. She died ten years ago, I suppose. Keith inherited his money then, and I'd say he's lost it.'

I thought a bit, and asked, 'Who is Jack's father?'

'That's none of your business.'

'Not relevant?'

'Certainly not.'

'Does Keith gamble on horses? Or anything? Cards? Backgammon?'

'Perhaps you'll find out,' she said. 'He will never, of course, tell me anything.'

I could think of only one way of getting a window into Keith's affairs, and even that was problematical. I would have to borrow a car and drive it, for a start, when it was hard enough to walk. Give it two or three days, I thought. Say Tuesday.

'What does Keith do with his time?' I asked.

'He says he has a job in the City. He may have had once, but I'm sure he's lying about it now. He does lie, of course. He's sixty-five, anyway. Retiring age, I'm told.' She more or less sniffed. 'If one has obligations, my brother used to say, one *never* retires.'

Retiring wasn't always one's own choice, but why argue? Not everyone was a hereditary baron with dependent Honourables and a paternal nature. Not everyone had wealth enough to oil wheels and calm storms. My non-grandfather, I thought, must have been a nice man, whatever his faults; and my mother had liked him, and Dart also.

'How about Ivan?' I asked.

'Ivan?' Her eyebrows rose. 'What do you mean?'

'He has a garden centre?'

She nodded. 'My brother made over to him fifty acres of the estate. Years ago, that was, when Ivan was young. He's good at growing things.' She paused, and went on, 'One doesn't need to be intellectual to lead a contented and harmless life.'

'One needs to be lucky.'

She considered me, and nodded.

I asked her, as it seemed she had run out of inquisition, if she would sign Roger's and Oliver's pay cheques.

'What? Yes, I said I would. Tell the Colonel to remind me some time again.'

'They're here,' I said, picking the envelope out of my still chair-draping jacket. 'Do you have a pen with you?'

She resignedly rummaged in a large handbag for a pen, took the cheques out of the envelope and wrote her name with precision, no flourish, on the lines provided.

I said diffidently, 'To save you the trouble in future, you directors could enable Conrad or Ivan or Dart to sign cheques. It only needs to have their signatures registered with the bank. There are bound to be many things, and not only salary cheques, needing signatures in the future. The Colonel has to have authorisations, in order to run things.'

'You seem to know a lot about it!'

'I know about business. I have a limited company.'

She frowned. 'Very well. All three of them. Will that do?'

'Make it any two of the four of you. Then you will have safeguards, and the Colonel's honesty will be beyond being queried by Keith or Rebecca.'

She didn't know whether to be annoyed or amused. 'It's taken you no time at all, has it, to lay bare our Stratton souls?'

Without warning, and before I could answer, the office door opened fast and Keith and Hannah came in. Ignoring my presence they complained loudly to Marjorie that Conrad was talking to his architect as if the new plans would definitely be agreed.

'He's saying *when*,' Keith griped, 'not *if*. I'm wholly against this ridiculous project and you've got to stop it.'

'Stop it yourself,' his aunt told him tartly. 'You make a lot of noise, Keith, but you don't get things done. You want to get rid of me one minute, and you ask me to fight battles for you the next. And as you and Hannah are both here, you can apologise to Mr Morris for attacking him.'

Keith and Hannah gave me matching looks of malevolence from between narrowed eyelids. From their point of view, I understood, their ultimate purpose had been frustrated by Marjorie and Ivan's fortuitous arrival. I was still present, still standing, still and for ever the symbol of their having been detested and rejected unbearably. That their hatred was irrational made no difference. Irrational hatred, the world over, set the furrows flooding with an impure blood – though it was only France that actively encouraged massacre in its patriotic war cry, the Marseillaise still glorifying the sentiments of 1792.

The impure blood at that time had been Austrian. Two hundred or so years later, blood-hatred flourished around the globe. Blood-hatred could almost be smelled in the manager's office of Stratton Park. I had by my presence there already activated responses beyond Keith and Hannah's control, and felt no confidence whatever that we'd come to the end of it.

Only Marjorie, at that moment, stood between me and a continuation of what they'd intended to do earlier that morning. I thought wryly that every big and usually powerful weakling should have a staunch octogenarian bodyguard.

Marjorie waited only briefly for the apology that would never come: and I could happily dispense for ever with apologies, I thought, if they would clearly see that no amount of Stratton money could cancel charges of manslaughter.

Or half-brother slaughter. Or ex-wife's son's slaughter. Whatever.

Amoeba-like, Strattons followed Strattons as if components

of one organic mass, and Conrad with Jack and Ivan joined the company, also swelled by the foreign substance of Wilson Yarrow and completed by Dart, looking mischievously entertained, and Roger, trying to be inconspicuous. The crowd again was too big for the space.

Wilson Yarrow didn't know me. I gave him a flicking glance only, but he'd accorded me barely that. His attention was chiefly engaged by Conrad, whose suspicions had been aroused by Keith's talking to Marjorie behind a closed door.

Physically, Wilson Yarrow was remarkable not so much for his actual features as for his posture. His reddish brown hair, tall narrow-shouldered body, and square heavy jaw made no indelible statement. The way he held his head back, so that he could look down his nose, was unforgettable.

Condescending, Marjorie had said of him. Convinced of his own superiority, I thought, and without modesty to cloak it.

Conrad said, 'Wilson Yarrow is of the opinion we should clear the site and start rebuilding immediately, and I've agreed to that proposal.'

'My dear Conrad,' Marjorie said in her stop-the-world voice, 'you may *not* make such a decision. Your father had the right to make such decisions because he owned the racecourse. It now belongs to us all, and before anything is done, a majority of our board must agree to it.'

Conrad looked affronted and Wilson Yarrow impatient, obviously thinking the old lady a no-account interruption.

'It is clear,' Marjorie went on in her crystal diction, 'that we have to have a new grandstand.'

'No!' Keith interrupted. 'We sell!'

Marjorie paid him no attention. 'I am sure Mr Yarrow is a highly competent architect, but for something as important as new stands I propose we put an advertisement in a magazine read by architects, inviting any who are interested to send us plans and proposals in a competition so that we could study various possibilities and then make a choice.'

Conrad's consternation was matched by Yarrow's.

'But Marjorie –' Conrad began.

'It would be the normal course of activity, wouldn't it?' she asked with open-eyed simplicity. 'I mean, one wouldn't buy even a chair without considering several for comfort and appearance and usefulness, would one?'

She gave me a short, expressionless, passing glance. Double bravo, I thought.

'As a director,' Marjorie said, 'I put forward a motion that we seek a variety of suggestions for a grandstand, and of course we will welcome Mr Yarrow's among them.'

Dead silence.

'Second the motion, Ivan?' Marjorie suggested.

'Oh! Yes. Sensible. Very sensible.'

'Conrad?'

'Now look here, Marjorie . . .'

'Use commonsense, Conrad,' she urged.

Conrad squirmed. Yarrow looked furious.

Keith unexpectedly said, 'I agree with you, Marjorie. You have my vote.'

She looked surprised, but although she may have reckoned, as I did, that Keith's motive was solely to impede the rebuilding, she pragmatically accepted his help.

'Carried,' she said without triumph. 'Colonel, could you possibly find a suitable publication for an advertisement?'

Roger said he was certain he could, and would see to it.

'Splendid.' Marjorie levelled a limpid gaze on the discomfited personage who'd made the error of condescension. 'When you have your plans ready, Mr Yarrow, we'd be delighted to see them.'

He said with clenched teeth, 'Lord Stratton has a set.'

'Really?' Conrad squirmed further under a similar gaze. 'Then, Conrad, we'd all like to see them, wouldn't we?'

Stratton heads nodded with various graduations of urgency.

'They're in my house,' Conrad informed her grudgingly. 'I suppose I could bring them to you sometime.'

Marjorie nodded. 'This afternoon, shall we say? Four o'clock.' She looked at her watch. 'My goodness! We're all terribly late for lunch. Such a busy morning.' She rose to her small feet. 'Colonel, as our private dining room in the stands is, as I suppose, out of action, perhaps you could arrange somewhere suitable for us on Monday? Most of us, I imagine, will be attending.'

Roger said again, faintly, that he would see to it.

Marjorie, nodding benignly, made a *grande dame* exit and, surrendering herself to Mark's solicitous care, was driven away.

More or less speechlessly, the others followed, Conrad taking an angry Yarrow, leaving Roger and myself in quiet occupancy of the combat zone.

'The old battleaxe!' Roger said with admiration.

I handed him his pay cheques. He looked at the signature.

'How did you do that?' he said.

CHAPTER 9

Roger spent the afternoon with the racecourse's consultant electrician, whose men by-passed the main grandstand while restoring power to everywhere else. Circuits that hadn't fused by themselves had been disconnected prudently by Roger, it seemed. 'Fire,' he explained, 'is the last thing we need.'

A heavy-duty cable in an insulating tube was run underground by a trenching machine to the Members' car park, for lights, power and refrigerators in the big top. 'Never forget champagne on a racecourse,' Roger said, not joking.

The investigators in the ruins had multiplied and had brought in scaffolding and cutters. At one point they erected and bolted together a long six-foot-high fence, replacing the cordoning tape. 'We could lose priceless clues to souvenir hunters,' one told me. 'Monday's crowd, left alone, could put piranhas to shame.'

I said to one of the bombfinders, 'If you'd been drilling upwards of thirty holes into the walls of a stairway, would you have posted a look-out?'

'Christ, yes.' He thought for a bit. 'Course, you know, when you have someone drilling, you mostly can't tell where the noise is coming from. Drilling's deceptive, like. You can think it's next door and it's a hundred yards away; and the other way round. If anyone heard the drilling, is what I'm trying to say, one, they wouldn't know where it was happening, and two, they wouldn't think nothing of it, not in a place this big.'

Only Roger, I thought, would have known drilling was wrong: and Roger had been in his house half a mile out of earshot.

I used my mobile phone, still in Roger's jeep, to try to locate friends and staff from my student days to ask about Yarrow, but almost no one answered. I raised one wife, who said she would give Carteret my number but, sorry, he was busy in St Petersburg, and I spoke also to a very young daughter who told me Daddy didn't live with them any more. This sort of thing, I thought ruefully, didn't happen to the best private eyes.

In the office, Roger and I drew up plans for the positioning of the big top and of the two Portakabins he'd been promised. Male jockeys were to change in one, with the scales and attendant officials given housing in the other. We placed both structures near the parade ring within a few steps of Roger's office, and agreed that if his men took down the fence between the paddock and the Members' car park, the access to the big top would be unhampered for the public. It meant re-routing the horses round the big top to get them out onto the course, but all, Roger promised, could be accomplished.

'Rebecca!' he exclaimed at one point, clapping palm to aghast forehead. 'Women jockeys! Where do we put them?'

'How many of them?'

'Two or three. Six, max.'

I phoned Henry, got an answering machine, and left a message begging for side tents of any description. 'Also send anything pretty,' I added. 'Send Sleeping Beauty's castle. We need to cheer people up.'

'This is a racecourse, not a fairground,' Roger said, a touch disapprovingly, as I finished the call.

'This is Easter Bank Holiday,' I reminded him. 'This is restore-confidence day. This is ignore-bombs day, feel-more-secure day, have-a-good-time day. On Monday people coming here are going to forget there's a frightening disaster lying behind that new fence.' I paused. 'And we're going to have lights over the whole area tonight and tomorrow night, and as many people patrolling the stables and Tattersalls and the cheap rings as you can possibly press gang.'

'But the expense!' he said.

'Make a success of Monday, and Marjorie will pay for the guards.'

'You're infectious, you know that?' He gave me an almost lighthearted smile and was about to hurry back to his electricians when the telephone rang.

Roger said, 'Hallo,' and 'Yes, Mrs Binsham,' and 'At once, of course,' and put down the receiver.

He relayed the news. 'She says Conrad and Yarrow are with her, and they've shown her his plans, and she wants a copy made here on the office copier.'

'And did Conrad agree?' I asked with surprise.

'It seems so, as long as we lock the copy in the office safe.'

'She's amazing,' I said.

'She's got Conrad in some sort of hammer-lock. I've noticed before. When she applies pressure, he folds.'

'They all blackmail each other!'

He nodded. 'Too many secrets, paid for and hushed up.'

'That's what Dart says, more or less.'

Roger pointed to the door of his secretary's office. 'Both the copier and the safe are in there. Conrad and Yarrow are coming straight over.'

'In that case, I'll vanish,' I said. 'I'll wait in your jeep.'

'And when they've gone – back to your bus?'

'If you don't mind.'

'Long after time,' he said briefly, and opened the door for my clip-clomping progress outwards.

I sprawled sideways in the jeep and watched Conrad and Wilson Yarrow arrive with a large sized folder and later leave, both of them striding stiff-legged in annoyance.

When they'd gone, Roger brought the new copies over to the jeep and we looked at them together.

He said the plans had been on three large sheets, with blue

lines on pale grey paper, but owing to the size of the office machine, the copies came on smaller sheets with black lines. One set of copies laid out a ground floor plan. One set showed elevations of all four sides. The third looked a maze of thin threadlike lines forming a three-dimensional viewpoint, but hollow, without substance.

'What's *that*?' Roger asked, as I frowned over it. 'I've never seen anything like that.'

'It's an axonometric drawing.'

'A what?'

'An axonometric projection is a method of representing a building in three dimensions that is easier than fiddling about with true perspectives. You rotate the plan of the building to whatever angle you like and project verticals upwards ... Well,' I apologised, 'you did ask.'

Roger was more at home with the elevations. 'It's just one big slab of glass,' he protested.

'It's not all that bad. Incomplete, but not bad.'

'Lee!'

'Sorry,' I said. 'Anyway, I wouldn't build it in Stratton Park, and probably not anywhere in England. It's crying out for tropical weather, vast air-conditioning and million-aire members. And even those aren't going to be ultra-comfortable.'

'That's better,' he said, relieved.

I looked at the top left-hand corner of each set of copies. All three were inscribed simply 'Club Grandstands', 'Wilson Yarrow, AADipl.' A lone job. No partners, no firm.

'The best racing grandstands ever built,' I said, 'are at Arlington Park, near Chicago.'

'I thought you didn't go racing much,' Roger said.

'I haven't been there. I've seen pictures and prints of the plans.'

He laughed. 'Can we afford stands like that?'

'You could adapt their ideas.'

'Dream on,' he said, shuffling the copies into order. 'Wait while I tuck these into the safe.' He went off on the short errand and returned to drive the scant half-mile to his house, which was quiet and empty: no children, no wife.

We found them all in the bus. The boys had invited Mrs Gardner to tea (tuna sandwiches with crusts on, crisps and chocolate wafer biscuits) and they were all watching the football results unwaveringly on television.

When the guest of honour and her husband had gone, Christopher gave her the highest of accolades, 'She understands even the off-side rule!'

Football coverage went on. I claimed my own bed, dislodging a viewer or two, and lay on my stomach to watch the proceedings. After the last possible report had been made (*ad infinitum* re-runs of every goal that afternoon), Christopher made supper for everyone of tinned spaghetti on toast. The boys then chose a video from the half dozen or so I'd rented for the ruin-hunt journey and settled down to watch that. I lay feeling that it had been a pretty long day and, somewhere during the film, went to sleep.

I awoke at about three in the morning, still face down, fully dressed.

The bus was dark and quiet, the boys asleep in their bunks. I found that they had put a blanket over me instead of waking me up.

On the table by my head stood a full glass of water.

I looked at it with grateful amazement, with a lump in the throat.

The evening before, when I'd stood a glass there, Toby, to whom, since the explosion, anything out of routine was a cause of quivering anxiety, had asked what it was for.

'The hospital,' I explained, 'gave me some pills to take if I woke up in the night and the cuts started hurting.'

'Oh. Where are the pills?'

'Under my pillow.'

They'd nodded over the information. I hadn't slept much and I had taken the pills, which they'd commented on in the morning.

So now, tonight, the glass of water was back, standing ready, put there by my sons. I took the pills, drinking, and I lay in the dark feeling grindingly sore and remarkably happy.

In the morning, a fine one, the boys opened all the windows to air out the bus, and I gave them the Easter presents Amanda had packed into the locker under my bed. Each boy received a chocolate Easter egg, a paperback book and a small hand-held computer game, and all spoke to their mother to thank her.

'She wants to talk to you, Dad,' Alan said, handing me the telephone, and I said, 'Hi,' and 'Happy Easter,' and 'How's Jamie?'

'He's fine. Are you feeding the boys properly, Lee? Sandwiches and tinned spaghetti aren't enough. I asked Christopher . . . he says you didn't buy fruit yesterday.'

'They've had bananas and cornflakes for breakfast today.'

'Fruit and fresh vegetables,' she said.

'OK.'

'And can you stay out a bit longer? Say Wednesday or Thursday?'

'If you like.'

'Yes. And take their clothes to a launderette, won't you?'

'Sure.'

'Have you found a good ruin yet?'

'I'll keep looking.'

'We're living on savings,' she said.

'Yes, I know. The boys need new trainers.'

'You could get them.'

'All right.'

Conversation, as usual, confined itself mostly to child-care. I said, trying my best, 'How did your sister's party go?'

'Why?' She sounded almost, for a moment, wary: then she said, 'Great, fine. She sends you her love.'

'Thanks.'

'Take care of the boys, Lee.'

'Yes,' I said, and 'Happy Easter,' and 'Goodbye, Amanda.'

'She asked us to phone her tomorrow night,' Christopher said.

'She cares about you. She wants us to go on hunting ruins for another day or two.'

None of them objected, surprisingly. They were eyes-down, of course, to their bleep-bleeping flickering games.

There was a bang on the door, which was opened without pause by Roger, who stuck his head in while still standing outside.

'Your pal Henry,' he told me, 'has himself arrived with a crane on a low-loader and brought the big top on about six vast lorries and he won't unload a thing without talking to you first.'

'Henry's big top!' Christopher exclaimed. 'The one we had over the pub, before you built our house?'

'That's right.'

The boys shut the windows instantly and presented themselves fast in the driveway, looking hopeful. Roger resignedly gestured towards the jeep and they all packed into the back, jostling and fighting for their favourite seats.

'Sit down or get out,' Roger commanded in his best parade-ground bark and, subdued, they sat down.

'I'll swop you the boys for Marjorie,' I suggested.

'Done.' He careered in battle fashion up the private road, did a flourish of a four-wheel drift stop outside his office, and informed my progeny that any sign of disobedience would incur immediate banishment to the bus for the rest of the day. The troops, very impressed, took the warning respectfully, but ran off to greet Henry with out-of-school whoops.

Henry, huge, bearded, always made me feel short. He lifted Neil effortlessly to sit on his shoulders and beamed in my direction, walking frame and all.

'Nearly got yourself squelched, then?' he said.

'Yeah. Careless.'

He gestured with a huge hand to his heavily laden monster trucks, currently cluttering the tarmac.

'I brought the whole razzmatazz,' he said, pleased with it.

'Yes, but, look here –' Roger began.

Henry looked down on him kindly. 'You trust Lee, here,' he said. 'He knows what people like. He's a bloody wizard, is Lee. You let him and me set you up here for tomorrow, and six weeks from now, when you've got another Bank Holiday meeting – I looked it up, so I know – you won't have enough room in the car parks. Word of mouth, see? Now, do you want crowds here, or don't you?'

'Er . . . yes.'

'Say no more.'

Roger said to me despairingly, 'Marjorie . . .'

'She'll love it. She wants the racecourse to prosper, above all.'

'Are you sure?'

'Hundred per cent. Mind you, she'll take five seconds to get over the shock.'

'Let's hope it takes longer for her to drop down dead from a heart attack.'

'Did you get those electrical cables laid?' Henry asked him. 'Heavy duty?'

'As you specified,' Roger said.

'Good. Then . . . site plans?'

'In the office.'

For most of the day Roger directed his groundsmen to help where they could and himself stood in long spells of wonderment as Henry and his crew built before his eyes a revolutionary vision of grandstand comfort.

First, they erected four pylon-like towers in crane-lifted sections, towers strong enough, Henry told Roger, for trapeze artists to swing from: then with thick wire cables and heavy electric winches they raised tons of strong white canvas and spread them wide. The final height and the acreage matched those of the old stands, and easily outdid them for splendour.

Henry and I discussed crowd movement, racegoers' behaviour, provision for rain. We set out the essentials, rubbed out the bottlenecks, made pleasure a priority, gave owners their due, allocated prime space for Strattons, for Stewards, for trainers' bars. Throughout the big top we planned solid-seeming flooring, with a wide centre aisle, firm partition walls, and tented ceilings in each 'room' of pale peach-coloured thin pleated silk-like material. 'I buy it by the mile,' Henry assured a disbelieving Roger. 'Lee told me sunlight shining through canvas and peach was more flattering to old faces than yellow, and it's seniors who pay the bills, mostly. I used to use yellow. Never again. Lee says the right light is more important than the food.'

'And what Lee says is gospel?'

'Have you ever seen anyone transform a derelict no-customer pub into a human beehive? He's done it twice before my eyes, and more times before that, so I'm told. He knows what *attracts* people, see? They don't know exactly *what* attracts them. They just feel attracted. But Lee knows, you bet your sweet life he knows.'

'Just what attracts people?' Roger asked me curiously.

'A long story,' I said.

'But *how* do you know?'

'For years I asked hundreds, literally hundreds of people, why they'd bought the old houses they lived in. What was the decider, however irrational, that made them choose that house and no other? Sometimes they said bits of trellis, sometimes hidden winding secondary staircases, sometimes Cotswold stone fireplaces, or mill wheels, or sometimes split levels and galleries. I asked them also what they disliked, and would change. I simply grew to know how to rebuild near-ruins so that people hunger to live in them.'

Roger said slowly, 'Like your own house.'

'Well, yes.'

'And pubs?'

'I'll show you one day. But with pubs, it's not just rebuilding. It's good food, good prices, fast service and a warm welcome. It's essential to learn the customers' faces and greet them as friends.'

'But you always move on?'

'Once they're up and running,' I nodded. 'I'm a builder, not a restaurateur.'

To Henry's men, many of them circus people themselves and accustomed to raising magic from an empty field overnight, twenty-four hours to gate-opening time was a luxury. They heaved on ropes, they swung mallets, they sweated. Henry bought a barrel of beer from the Mayflower for his 'good lads'.

Henry had brought not only the big top but a large amount of the iron piping and planking that, bolted together, had formed the basis of the tiered seating round the circus ring.

'Thought you might need it,' he said.

'Grandstands!' I breathed. 'You broth of a boy.'

Henry beamed.

Roger couldn't believe it. His own workmen, under Henry's circus men's direction, erected all the steps not round a ring but in the open air alongside the rails of the track, their backs to the big top and their slanting faces towards the action, with a wide strip of grass for access between the bottom step and the racecourse rails.

'We could do better given more time,' Henry said, 'but at least some of the customers will be able to see the races from here, without all squeezing onto the Tattersalls' steps.'

'We probably need planning permission,' Roger said faintly. 'Safety officers. Heaven knows what.'

Henry waved a couple of licences under his nose. 'I'm a licensed contractor. This is a temporary structure. Get who you like. Get them on Tuesday. Everything I do is safe and legal. I'll show you.'

Grinning, he waved a huge hand and hey-prestoed an army of fire extinguishers from one of the trucks.

'Happier?' he asked Roger.

'Speechless.'

Henry at one point drew me aside. 'Who are those arseholes blocking the gates? We as near as buggery knocked one of them over when we came across with the beer. He walked straight out. Raving lunatic.'

I explained about Mr Harold Quest, his followers and their quest to get steeplechasing banned. 'Weren't they here when you first arrived?' I asked.

'No, they weren't. Do you want them shifted?'

'You mean physically shifted?'

'What other way is there?'

'Persuasion?' I suggested.

'Come off it.'

'If you stamp on one wasp, fifty come to the funeral.'

He nodded. 'See what you mean.' He rubbed his beard. 'What do we do, then?'

'Put up with them.'

'That's pathetic.'

'You could tell them that banning steeplechasing would mean hundreds of horses being killed, once there was no use for them. Not just one horse would die occasionally, but all of them within a year. Tell Harold Quest he's advocating equine massacre and turning horses into an endangered species.'

'Right.' He looked as if he would do it immediately.

'But,' I said, 'quite likely he's not really fussed about the horses. Quite likely he's looking for a way to stop people enjoying themselves. *He's* enjoying himself, that's his main aim. He's been trying for days to get knocked down gently. Tomorrow he may manage to get himself arrested. If he does, he'll be ecstatic.'

'All fanatics are nutters,' he said.

'What about suffragettes and the twelve apostles?'

'Want a beer?' he said. 'I'm not arguing with *you*.'

'What we really want is a counter demonstration,' I suggested. 'People marching alongside Harold Quest with placards saying, "ADD TO UNEMPLOYMENT". "PUT STABLELADS OUT OF WORK". "SEND ALL STEEPLECHASE HORSES TO THE GLUE FACTORY". "PUT BLACKSMITHS ON THE DOLE".'

'Farriers,' Henry said.

'What?'

'Farriers shoe horses. Blacksmiths make wrought-iron gates.'

'Let's have that beer,' I said.

Beer got postponed however by the arrival of two cars, both driven by boiling tempers as a result of near-contact with Harold Quest.

Stuck behind the leading bumper came the torn remains of a placard saying 'BAN CRUELTY' but as so often in such confrontations, a bossy platitudinous admonition had evoked an opposite response.

In the driver, Oliver Wells, the veneer of gentlemanly affability had rawly peeled to disclose a darker, heavier authority; and I was seeing, I thought, the equivalent of the ramming force of the pistons usually hidden within a smooth-running engine. More power, more relentlessness than on display to the world. Cruelty, in this unveiling of the man, could be considered a possibility.

His long nose and sticking-out ears quivering with the strength of his anger, he gave me a brief dismissive glance and demanded, 'Where's Roger?'

'In his office,' I said.

Oliver strode towards the office door, seemingly oblivious to the hammering activity all around him. The second car, a scarlet Ferrari, arrived to park beside his with a burning of tyres and from it, self-ejecting, came the scowling fury of Rebecca.

She was, it briefly occurred to me, the first Stratton of the day, infinitely less welcome to me than her hair-fixated brother.

Rebecca, too, in well-cut fawn trousers and brilliant scarlet sweater, resonated hotly with maximum outrage.

'I'll kill that verminous cretin,' she told the world. 'He's begging to be run down, and I'll do it, I swear it, if he dares to call me "ducky" again.'

I had difficulty swallowing the inappropriate laugh. Henry, having no inhibitions and sizing up the bristling feminism instantly, simply guffawed.

She half lowered her expressive eyelids and delivered a look of whole-hearted venom which left Henry unmoved.

'Where's Oliver?' Her voice, like her manner, conveyed uncontrolled arrogance. 'The man who drove in ahead of me?'

'In that office,' Henry said, pointing; and I swear the word 'ducky' got as far as his teeth.

He watched her pantherish gait as she set off away from us and for comment raised comical eyebrows, a real dagger-between-the-shoulders invitation if she'd chanced to turn round.

'She's good looking and brave,' I said. 'Pity about the rest.'

'Who is she?'

'The Honourable Rebecca Stratton, steeplechase jockey.'

Henry lowered his eyebrows and shrugged her out of his immediate attention.

'Beer,' he announced.

Another car again frustrated him; a small black Porsche this time, coasting up like a shadow from the private inner road and coming to an inconspicuous halt half hidden by one of Henry's trucks. No driver emerged. The tinted side windows obstructed identification.

Henry frowned in the newcomer's direction. 'Who's that skulking behind my lorries?'

'Don't know,' I said. 'Go and see.'

He padded over, inspected briefly, padded back.

'He's thin, young, looks like Ducky. He's sitting in there with the doors locked. He wouldn't speak to me.' Henry leered. 'He made an Italian truck drivers' gesture! Are you any the wiser?'

'He just might be Forsyth Stratton. Ducky's cousin. He looks very like her.'

Henry shrugged, his interest waning. 'What do you want done with the empties in the bars?'

'The caterers will deal with them.'

'Beer, then.'

'Beer.'

We finally lifted the elbows, discussing things as yet undone. His crew would work to midnight or later, he promised. They would sleep in the cabs of the trucks, as they often did, and would finish setting up early in the morning. His trucks would be gone by nine-thirty, all except the smallest, his own personal travelling workshop, which contained everything for maintenance and urgent repairs.

'I'll stay for the races,' he said. 'Can't miss them, after all this.'

Roger joined us, a lot of strain showing.

'Oliver's in one of his vilest tempers,' he reported. 'And as for Rebecca . . .'

Rebecca herself came fast on his heels but by-passed our group and tried to find a way through the bolted together fence that hid the gutted grandstand. Failing, she powered back to Roger and said forcefully, 'Let me through that fence. I want to see how much damage has been done.'

'I'm not in charge of the fence,' Roger said with restraint. 'Perhaps you should ask the police.'

'Where are the police?'

'On the other side of the fence.'

She narrowed her eyelids. 'Fetch me a ladder, then.'

When Roger failed to move fast to obey her, she turned instead to a passing workman. 'Fetch me a step-ladder,' she told him. She gave him no 'please', nor 'thank you' when he brought one. She merely told him where to place it and gave him the slightest nod of ungracious approval when he stepped back to let her climb.

She went up the steps with assured liquid movement and looked for a long time at what the fence hid.

Henry and Roger sloped off fast like wily old soldiers and left me alone to benefit from Rebecca's scalpel-sharp opinions. She descended the steps with the same athletic grace, cast a disparaging look at my still useful walking frame and told me to leave the racecourse at once, as I had no right to be there. I had also had no right to be in the stands two days earlier, on Friday morning, and if I were thinking of suing the Strattons for damages because of my injuries, the Strattons would sue me for trespass.

'OK,' I said.

She blinked. 'OK what?'

'Have you been talking to Keith?'

'That's none of your business, and I'm telling you to leave.'

'The prosperity of this racecourse is my business,' I said, unmoving. 'I own eight hundredths of it. You, after probate, will own three hundredths. So who has the better right to be here?'

She narrowed the brilliant eyes, impatiently ducking the majority-of-interest issue but targeting the truly significant. 'What do you mean, after probate? Those shares are mine, in the will.'

'Under English law,' I said, having discovered it in settling my mother's affairs, 'no one actually owns what has been bequeathed to them until the will has been proved genuine, until taxes have been paid and a certificate of probate issued.'

'I don't believe you.'

'Doesn't alter the facts.'

'Do you mean,' she demanded, 'that my father and Keith and Ivan have no right to be directors? That all their stupid decisions are null and void?'

I dashed her awakening hopes. 'No, it doesn't. Directors don't have to be shareholders. Marjorie could have appointed anyone she liked, whether or not she was aware of it.'

'You know too damned much,' Rebecca said with resentment.

'Are you pleased,' I asked, 'that the main stands are now rubble?'

She said defiantly, 'Yes, I am.'

'And what would you want done?'

'New stands, of course. Modern. Glass walled. New everything. Get rid of bloody Oliver and fuddy duddy Roger.'

'And run things yourself?' I said it without seriousness, but she seized on it fervently.

'I don't see why not! Grandfather did. We need change, now. New ideas. But this place should be run by a Stratton.' Her zeal shone out like a vision. 'There's no one else in the family who knows a rabbet from a raceway. Father has to leave Stratton Hays to his heir, but the racecourse land is not entailed. He can leave his racecourse shares to *me*.'

'He's only sixty-five,' I murmured, wondering what galvanising effect this conversation would have had on Marjorie and Dart, not to mention Roger and Oliver, and Keith.

'I can wait. I want to ride for at least two more seasons. It's time a woman reached the top five on the jockeys' list, and I'm going to do that this year, bar falls and bloody stand-downs by stupid doctors. After that, I'll manage the place.'

I listened to her confidence, not sure whether she were self-deluded or, in fact, capable.

'The directors would have to appoint you,' I said prosaically.

She sharpened her gaze on me assessingly. 'So they would,' she said slowly. 'And I've two whole years to make sure that they do.' She paused. 'Whoever they are, by then.'

Deciding abruptly that she'd given me enough of her time she prowled back to her scarlet car, casting hungry looks left and right at the domain she aimed to rule. Marjorie, of course, would frustrate her: but couldn't for ever, in consequence of the difference in decades. Rebecca had had that in mind.

Henry and Roger cravenly returned as Rebecca's exhaust pipe roared towards the exit.

'What was she saying to you?' Roger asked curiously. 'She looked almost human.'

'I think she wants to take charge here, like her grandfather.'

'Rubbish!' He began a laugh which turned uneasily into a frown. 'The family won't let her.'

'No, they won't.' Not this year, I thought, nor next year: but thereafter?

Roger shrugged away the untenable thought. 'Don't tell Oliver,' he said. 'He'd strangle her first.'

A policeman and the twenty-eight-year-old bomb expert came through a section of the fence, swinging it partly open, revealing the slow sifting activity of others within.

Roger and I walked to meet them and looked curiously at what they were carrying.

'Remains of an alarm clock,' the expert said cheerfully, holding up a cog wheel. 'One nearly always comes across pieces of timing devices. Nothing actually vaporises with this type of explosive.'

'What type?' I asked.

'P.E.4. Not Semtex. Not fertiliser and diesel oil. Not do-it-yourself terrorism. I'd say we're handling regular army here, not Irish Republican.'

Roger, the colonel, said stiffly, 'The army keeps strict control of detonators. P.E.4 is pussy-cat stuff without detonators.'

The expert nodded. 'You can pat it and mould it like marzipan. I wouldn't hit it with a hammer, though. But detonators under lock and key? Don't make me laugh. My life would be easier if it were true. But the army's been known to mislay tanks. What's a little fulminate of mercury between friends?'

'Everyone is very careful about detonators,' Roger insisted.

'Oh, sure.' The expert grinned wolfishly. 'Old soldiers

could liberate a field-gun from under your nose. And – you know what they say – there's nothing as good as a fire.'

From the look on Roger's face, the saying was all too familiar.

'When a certain large depot the size of five football pitches went up in flames a few years ago,' the expert enlarged to me with unholy relish, 'enough stuff was reported lost to fill double the space. The army produced tons of constructive paperwork to prove that all sorts of things had been sent to the depot during the week before the fire. Things that had earlier gone missing, and might have had to be accounted for, were all reported as having been "sent to the depot". Things were reported to have been "sent to the depot" that had, after the fire, marched out of their home bases by the suitcaseful to much nearer destinations. A good fire is a godsend, right, Colonel?'

Roger said formally, 'You don't expect me to agree.'

'Of course not, Colonel. But don't tell me it's impossible for a caseful of detonators to fail to be counted.' He shook his head. 'I'll grant you no one but a fool or an expert would handle them, but a word here, a word there, and there's a market for anything under the sun.'

CHAPTER 10

The work went on.

Electric cables snaked everywhere and were gradually assimilated invisibly into the canvas. Lighting grew, looking as if it belonged there anyway. White silently whirling fans hung beneath roof vents, to get rid of smells and used air. Henry himself understood tent management and crowd comfort in a way that sweltering guests in sunbaked marquees had never imagined, and as I too put climate control near the top of all living priorities, the Stratton Park racegoers were going to breathe easily without knowing why.

The nineteenth-century chimney-born updraughts in houses had created a boom then in footstools, winged chairs and screens; twentieth-century wind tunnels meant gale-ridden city street corners.

Air pressure, air movement, air temperature; dust removal, mite reduction, dehumidification: all were not just a matter of soft self-indulgence indoors, but of positive no-allergy health and the deterrence of rot, rust, fungus and mildew. The Lazarus act on old buildings began, in my no doubt obsessional mind, with the provision of clean dry air, unobtrusively circulating.

We fed everyone from the Mayflower's kitchen. My sons

fetched and carried, acted as waiters, willingly collected rubbish and generally behaved as they never did normally unless bullied.

Roger and I consulted the racecourse's water-main maps, and his men laid a branch pipe to the side-tents' catering areas, with a twiglet off to the female jockeys' changing room especially for Rebecca. Cold water, of course, but perhaps better than none. Persistent telephoning finally wrung out a promise of one Portaloo van and, from Ivan, Roger bravely cajoled a truckload of garden centre potplants.

'He says it's one of the top selling days in his year,' Roger commented, putting down the receiver. 'He says the racecourse must pay for what he sends.'

'Charming.'

We discussed a few more arrangements before Roger bustled away, leaving me in the office. I'd begun in the past hour to find walking easier but on the other hand I felt weary across the shoulders and glad of a chance to perch a rump on the desk, avoiding the worst winces but resting arms and legs. I thought of the admonition card back home in my workshop, given me in happier times by Amanda, which read, 'If everything is going well you have obviously overlooked something', and idly wondered what hadn't occurred to Roger and Henry and me that could become a hopeless disaster on the morrow.

The door opened abruptly to reveal Forsyth Stratton striding over the threshold. None of the Strattons seemed capable of entering a room slowly.

'What are you doing in here?' he demanded.

'Thinking,' I said. Thinking in fact that I was not pleased to see him, particularly if he had similar ideas to Hannah and Keith. It appeared, however, and somewhat to my relief, that his attack would be verbal, not physical.

He said with rage, 'You've no right to take charge here.'

'The Colonel's in charge,' I replied mildly.

'The Colonel consults you before he does anything.' His dark eyes glittered in the same way as Rebecca's, and I wondered fleetingly whether either or both of them wore contact lenses. 'And that huge man whose staff are putting up tents, he asks the Colonel for decisions, then they come and ask *you*, or he by-passes the Colonel and comes to you first. You're much younger than them, but whatever *you* say, that's what they do. I've been sitting for hours watching and getting angrier and angrier, so don't tell me I don't know what I'm talking about. None of us want you here . . . just who the hell do you think you are?'

I said dryly, 'A builder.'

'A sodding builder shouldn't be running our racecourse.'

'A shareholder then. A part owner.'

'Sod that! I'm a *Stratton*.'

'Bad luck,' I said briefly.

He was furiously affronted. His voice rose a couple of octaves and, with a vindictive twist to his mouth, he practically shouted, 'Your sodding mother had no right to those shares. Keith should have given her a good hiding instead. And Jack says that's just what you got from Keith yourself yesterday only not enough and you've a sodding nerve to stick your snout into our affairs and if you're thinking of screwing money out of us you can piss in the wind.'

The incoherence of his speech only added to the bile pouring out of him. As far as I was concerned I'd taken one insult too many from the Strattons and it annoyed me into a brutality I seldom felt. I said, with intention to wound, '*You* don't have an ounce of authority in your own family. They ignore you. They won't even look at you. What have you done?'

His hands rose fast, closing into fists. He took a fierce step forward. I stood up straight, not looking (I hoped) the pushover I actually was and, regardless of the threat, and with hot blood, I taunted him, 'I'd guess it's cost them a fortune to keep you free, walking about and out of prison.'

He yelled, 'Shut up, shut up. I'll complain to Aunt Marjorie.' One of his fists made a pass near my chin.

'Complain,' I said. I strove unsuccessfully to regain the tatters of my temper, but even to my own ears, my words came out hurtful and rough. 'You're a fool, Forsyth, and no doubt also a knave, and Marjorie despises you enough already, without you snivelling to her to have your pitiful nose wiped. And if you could see the ugly mess hate's making of your face, you'd run a mile and hide.'

That last childish jibe pierced him keenly. He clearly liked his own good looks. The spiteful facial contortions slackened, the lips lost their rigidity and covered the teeth and his sallow skin reddened.

'You *shit*!' He shook with humiliations past and present. The fists unclenched and fell away. He unravelled fast into a pathetic failure, all sound and posture, no substance.

I abruptly felt ashamed of myself. Oh great, I thought, unleashing the artillery on the least of the Strattons. Where were my brave words yesterday when I'd been faced with Keith?

'I make a better ally than enemy,' I said, cooling down. 'Why don't you try me?'

He looked confused besides defeated: softened enough maybe to answer a few questions.

I said, 'Was it Keith who told you I'd come here to screw money out of your family?'

'Of course.' He nodded weakly. 'Why else would you come?'

I did not say, 'Because your grandfather's money paid for my schooling.' I did not say, 'Perhaps to avenge my mother.' I said, 'Did he say it before or after the stands blew up?'

'What?'

I didn't repeat the question. He stared sullenly for a bit and finally answered, 'After, I suppose.'

'When exactly?'

'Friday. The day before yesterday. In the afternoon. A lot of us came here when we heard about the explosion. They'd taken you off to hospital. Keith said you'd be exaggerating a few grazes far more than their worth. Bound to, he said.'

'Which you naturally believed?'

'Of course.'

'All of you?'

He shrugged. 'Conrad said we'd have to be prepared to buy you off and Keith said they couldn't afford it, not after ...' His voice stopped suddenly, his confusion worsening.

'Not after what?' I asked.

He shook his head miserably.

'Not after,' I guessed, 'what it had cost them to get *you* out of trouble?'

'I'm not listening,' he said, and like a child put his hands over his ears. 'Shut up.'

He was twenty-something, I thought. Unintelligent, unemployed and apparently unloved. Also, primarily, a Stratton. Buying people off had become standard Stratton behaviour, but from the way the others had behaved to Forsyth at the Wednesday Board meeting, he had cost them too much. If they had had any affection for him earlier, by that meeting it had turned to resentment.

Within the family there were levers and coercions: I could see they existed, couldn't know what they were. Forsyth's actual sin was probably not as important to them as the expense of it on one hand, and the power gained over him on the other. If the threat of disclosure could still be applied to him, he would now do, I reckoned, whatever the family told him.

Roger had said that Marjorie held Conrad in some sort of hammer-lock; that he would always give in to her when she demanded it.

I myself had agreed, without realising the possible significance of it, to try to find out for her how much Keith owed and to whom, and also to discover what pressure was being put on Conrad by the would-be architect of the new stands, who had proved to be Wilson Yarrow, of whom I knew something but had forgotten more.

Was I, I wondered, being used by Marjorie to seek out facts for her chiefly to give her more leverage for ruling her family? Had she shrewdly guessed I would help her if she engaged my interest in the prosperity of the racecourse? Was she that clever, and was I that dumb? Probably, yes.

I still did believe, though, that she genuinely did want the racecourse to prosper, even if she'd intended to use me as a tool in the achievement of her no-change policy.

Marjorie herself would not, and could not, have blown the

grandstand apart. If, through me or in any other way, she found out who had, or who had arranged it, and if it should turn out to be one of themselves, she would not necessarily, I now thought, seek any public or law-driven retribution. There would be no trial or conviction or official penal sentence for the culprit. The Stratton family, and Marjorie above all, would assimilate one more secret into the family pool, and use it for internal family blackmail.

I said to Forsyth, 'When you were at school, did you join a cadet corps?'

He stared. 'No, of course not.'

'Why "of course"?'

He said impatiently, 'Only a fool wants to march around in uniform being shouted at.'

'Field Marshals begin that way.'

He sneered, 'Power-hungry cretins.'

I tired of him. It was unlikely he'd ever handled det cord or explosives himself: boys in the cadet forces might have done. Forsyth didn't seem even to understand the drift of my question.

Christopher, Toby and Edward all came into the office, close together as if for strength, looking anxious.

'What's the matter?' I asked.

'Nothing, Dad.' Christopher relaxed slightly, his gaze on Forsyth. 'The Colonel asked us to bring you over to position the taps for the water.'

'You *see*?' Forsyth said bitterly.

Still using the walking frame, I went past Forsyth and out of the door with my boys and, though I could hear Forsyth coming behind me, I neither expected nor received any more trouble from that quarter. Trouble enough manifested itself irritatingly in a bunch of the Strattons issuing from the big top's main entrance like a posse intent on intercepting me mid-way on the tarmac. My three sons stopped walking, too young, too inexperienced for this sort of thing.

I took one step past them and stopped also. The Strattons formed a semi-circle in front of me; Conrad on my left, then a woman I didn't know, then Dart, Ivan, Jack with a bruised swollen face, then Hannah and Keith. Keith, on my right, stood just out of my peripheral vision, to me an unsatisfying state of affairs. I took a half-pace backwards so that I could see if he made any unwelcome movement; a step that the Strattons seemed to interpret as a general retreat. They all, in fact, took an equal step forward, crowding a shade closer, with Keith again behind my vision unless I turned my head his way.

Christopher, Toby and Edward hesitated, wavered and separated from each other behind me. I could sense their fright and dismay. They sidled off and round into my view, backing away behind the Strattons, then frankly turning and running off, disappearing into the big top. I didn't blame them: felt like running myself.

'No Marjorie?' I asked flippantly of Dart. And where, I might have added, was my bodyguard when I might need her?

'We went to church,' Dart said unexpectedly. 'Marjorie, Father, Mother and I. Easter Sunday, and all that.' He grinned insouciantly. 'Marjorie gave us lunch afterwards. She didn't want to come here with us. She didn't say why.'

No one bothered with introductions, but I gathered that the woman between Conrad and Dart was Dart's mother, Lady Stratton, Victoria. She was thin, cool, well-groomed and looked as if she would rather be anywhere else. She regarded me with full-blown Stratton disdain, and I wondered fleetingly if Ivan's wife Dolly and Keith's fourth victim, Imogen, fitted as seamlessly into the family ethos.

Forsyth came to a halt on my left, beside Conrad, who paid him not the slightest attention.

Across the tarmac Roger appeared briefly in the big top entrance, took note of the Stratton formation, and went back inside.

I surveyed the half-circle of disapproving faces and hard eyes and decided on attack. Better one shot than none, I supposed.

'Which of you,' I said flatly, 'blew up the stands?'

Conrad said, 'Don't be ridiculous.'

Talking to Conrad meant turning too much of my back

towards Keith, but though the skin on my neck might creep with alarm, it was Conrad, I reckoned, who might deter Keith from action.

I said to him, 'One of you did it, or otherwise arranged it. Blowing up the stands was Stratton work. Not outside terrorism. Homegrown.'

'Rubbish.'

'The real reason you want to be rid of me is fear that I'll find out who did it. You're afraid because I saw how the explosive charges looked before they were set off.'

'No!' The strength of Conrad's denial was in itself an admission.

'And fear that if I find out who did it, I'll offer silence for money.'

None of them uttered.

'Which you can't easily afford,' I went on, 'after Forsyth's adventure.'

They looked furiously at Forsyth.

'I didn't tell him,' he begged desperately. 'I didn't say *anything*. He guessed.' He summoned a flash of healthier rage. 'He guessed because you've all been so *beastly* to me, so serve you all right.'

'Shut up, Forsyth,' Hannah said viciously.

I said to Conrad, 'How do you like your tent grandstand?'

For half a second Conrad looked instinctively, genuinely pleased, but Keith said violently behind my right ear, 'It won't stop us selling the land.'

Conrad gave him a glance of disgusted dislike and told him that, without the tents now, disgruntled racegoers would stay away in droves in the future, the course would go bust and be left with huge debts that would cut deep into anything the land could be sold for.

Keith fumed. Dart smiled secretly. Ivan said judiciously, 'The tents are *essential*. We're lucky to have them.'

All except Keith nodded agreement. Keith growled in his throat, much too close to my shoulder. I could feel his intent.

I said with fierceness to Conrad, 'Keep your brother off me.'

'What?'

'If he,' I said, 'or any of you lays another finger on me, the big top comes down.'

Conrad stared.

I leaned on the walking frame. I said, 'Your brother knows he can still knock me over. I'm telling you that if he or Hannah or Jack has any idea of continuing what they were stopped from doing yesterday, tomorrow morning you'll find an empty field over there.' I nodded towards the canvas.

Hannah sneered, 'Don't be stupid.'

Conrad said to me, 'You can't do that. It isn't in your power.'

'Want to bet?'

Henry came out of the big top, all my boys with him. They stood near the entrance, watching, awaiting events. Conrad followed the direction of my gaze and looked back at me thoughtfully.

'Henry,' I told him, 'that giant of a man, he brought the big top here to help you out because I asked him to. He's a friend of mine.'

Conrad protested, 'The Colonel found the tent.'

'I told him where to look. If I get one more threat, one more bruise from you lot, Henry takes everything home.'

Conrad knew the truth when it battered his eardrums. He was, moreover, a realist when it came to being persuaded by a threat he knew could be carried out. He turned away, breaking the alarming half-circle, taking his wife and Dart with him. Dart, looking back, gave me a gleam from his teeth. The crown of his head showed pink under the thinning fuzz, which he would not like to know.

I turned towards Keith, who still stood with hunched shoulders, head sticking forward, jaw prominent, eyes angry; a picture overall of unstable aggression.

I had nothing to say. I simply stood there, not daring him, just trying to convey that I expected nothing at all: not any onslaught, not a backing down, no loss of face on his part or on mine.

Forsyth, from behind me, said meanly, 'Go on, Keith, give

it to him. What are you waiting for? Kick him again, while you can.'

The spiteful urging had the opposite effect. Keith said as if automatically, 'Keep your stupid mouth shut, Forsyth,' and shook with frustration as much as rage, the dangerous moment defusing into a more general state of continuing hatred.

I found my son Alan appearing at my side, holding onto the walking frame and watching Keith apprehensively, and a moment later Neil joined us, on my other side, giving Keith a wide perplexed stare. Keith, for all his bullying years, looked slightly unnerved at being opposed by children.

'Come on, Dad,' Alan said, tugging at the frame, 'Henry wants you.'

I said, 'Right,' with decisiveness and began moving forward, with Hannah and Jack straight ahead in my way. Uncertainly, they parted to let me go by: no lack of ill will in their faces, but not the unstoppable boiling fury of the previous morning.

The other three boys trickled across and crowded round also, so that I reached Henry finally as if guarded by a young human hedge.

'You saw them off, then,' he said.

'Your size was the ultimate deterrent.'

He laughed.

'Also I told them that you would pack up the big top and go home if there were any more messing about, and they can't afford that.'

'Right little raver, aren't you?' he said.

'I'm not keen on their sort of football.'

He nodded. 'The Colonel told me about that. Why the heck do you bother to help them?'

'Cussedness.'

Christopher said unhappily, 'We left you, Dad.'

'We went to get help,' Edward assured me, believing it.

Toby, whispering as much to himself as to me, said, 'We were frightened. We just . . . ran away.'

'You came into the office to fetch me,' I pointed out, 'and that was brave.'

'But afterwards . . .' Toby said.

'In the real world,' I said mildly, 'no one's a total hero day in and day out. No one expects it. You can't do it.'

'But Dad . . .'

'I was glad you went to find the Colonel, so forget it.'

Christopher and Edward sensibly believed me, but Toby looked doubtful. There were too many things, that Easter school holidays, that he would never forget.

Roger and Oliver Wells came out of the big top chatting amicably. The fireball of Oliver's temper had been extinguished that morning by a conducted tour of the emerging arrangements inside the tents. Who cared about Harold Quest, he finally said. Henry's work was miraculous: all would be well. He and Roger had planned in detail how best to distribute racecards to all, and entry badges to the Club customers. At Oliver's insistence, a separate viewing stand for the Stewards was being bolted together directly behind the winning post on the inside of the course. It was imperative, he said, that since that high-up box was no more, the Stewards should have an unimpeded all-round view of every race. Roger had found a sign-painter who'd agreed to forfeit his afternoon's television viewing in favour of 'Stewards Only', 'Club Enclosure', 'Private Dining Room', 'Women Jockeys' Changing Room' and 'Members' Bar'.

Roger and Oliver crossed to Roger's jeep, started the engine and set off on an unspecified errand. They'd gone barely twenty yards in the direction of the private road, however, when they smartly reversed, did a U-turn and pulled up beside me and the boys.

Roger stuck his head out and also a hand, which grasped my mobile phone.

'This rang,' he said. 'I answered it. Someone called Carteret wants to speak to you. Are you at home?'

'Carteret! Fantastic!'

Roger handed me the instrument, and went on his way.

'Carteret?' I enquired of the phone. 'Is it you? Are you in Russia?'

'No, dammit,' a long-familiar voice spoke in my ear. 'I'm here in London. My wife says you told her it was urgent.

After years of nothing, not even Christmas cards, everything's urgent! So what gives?'

'Er ... what gives is that I need a bit of help from your long-term memory.'

'What the hell are you talking about?' He sounded pressed and not over pleased.

'Remember Bedford Square?'

'Who could forget?'

'I've come across an odd situation, and I wondered ... do you by any chance remember a student called Wilson Yarrow?'

'Who?'

'Wilson Yarrow.'

After a pause Carteret's voice said indecisively, 'Was he the one three years or so ahead of us?'

'That's right.'

'Something not right about him.'

'Yes. Do you remember what, exactly?'

'Hell, it was too long ago.'

I sighed. I'd hoped Carteret, with his oft-proven retentive memory, would come out snapping with answers.

'Is that all?' Carteret asked. 'Look, sorry, mate, but I'm up to my eyes in things here.'

Without much hope, I said, 'Do you still have all those diaries you wrote at college?'

'I suppose so, well, yes, somewhere.'

'Could you just look at them and see if you wrote anything about Wilson Yarrow?'

'Lee, have you *any* idea what you're asking?'

'I've seen him again,' I said. 'Yesterday. I *know* there's something I ought to remember about him. Honestly, it might be important. I want to know if I should ... perhaps ... *warn* some people I know.'

A few moments of silence ended with, 'I got back from St Petersburg this morning. I've tried the number you gave my wife several times without success. Nearly gave up. Tomorrow I'm taking my family to Euro Disney for six days. After that, I'll look in the diaries. Failing that, come to think of it, if you're in more of a hurry, you could come over here, tonight, and take a quick look yourself. Would that do? You *are* in London, I suppose?'

'No. Near Swindon, actually.'

'Sorry, then.'

I thought briefly and said, 'What if I came up to Paddington by train? Will you be at home?'

'Sure. All evening. Unpacking and packing. Will you come? It'll be good to see you, after all this time.' He sounded warmer, as if he suddenly meant it.

'Yes. Great. I'd like to see you, too.'

'All right then.' He gave me directions for coming by bus from Paddington Station and clicked himself off. Henry and the children gave me blank stares of disbelief.

'Did I hear right?' Henry said. 'You hang onto a walking frame with one hand and plan to catch a train to London with the other?'

'Maybe,' I said reasonably, 'Roger could lend me a stick.'

'What about us, Dad?' Toby said.

I glanced at Henry who nodded resignedly. 'I'll see they come to no harm.'

'I'll be back by their bedtime, with a bit of luck.'

I phoned Swindon railway station and asked about timetables. If I ran, it seemed, I could catch a train in five minutes. Otherwise, yes, possibly I could get to London even on the reduced Sunday service and be back in Swindon by bedtime. Just. With luck.

Roger, returning from his errand, offered not one but two walking sticks, plus, at my cajoling, a copy of Yarrow's grandstand plans ('You'll get me *shot*'), plus a ride to the station, though as we set off he said he doubted my sanity.

'Do you want to know if Wilson Yarrow can be trusted?' I asked.

'I'd be happy to know he can't be.'

'Well, then.'

'Yes, but . . .'

'I'm healing,' I said briefly.

'I'll say no more.'

I paid for my ticket by credit card, tottered onto the train, took a taxi from Paddington and arrived without incident on Carteret's doorstep near Shepherd's Bush. (Bay-windowed terrace built for genteel but impoverished Edwardians.)

He opened the door himself and we took stock of each other, the years of no contact sliding away. He was still small, rounded, bespectacled and black haired, an odd genetic mixture of Celt and Thai, though born and educated in England. We had paired as strangers to share digs together temporarily during our first year in architectural school and had gone through the whole course helping each other where necessary.

'You look just the same,' I said.

'So do you.' He eyed my height, curly hair and brown eyes; raised his eyebrows not at the working clothes but at the sticks I leaned on.

'Nothing serious,' I said. 'I'll tell you about it.'

'How's Amanda?' he asked, leading me in. 'Are you still married?'

'Yes, we are.'

'I never thought it would last,' he said frankly. 'And how are the boys? Three, was it?'

'We have six, now.'

'Six! You never did anything by halves.'

I met his wife, busy, and his two children, excited about going to meet Mickey Mouse. I told him, in his untidy, much lived-in sitting room, about the present and possible future of Stratton Park racecourse. I explained a good deal.

We drank beer. He said he hadn't remembered anything else about Wilson Yarrow except that he had been one of the precious élite tipped for immortality.

'And then . . . what happened?' he asked. 'Rumours. A cover-up of some sort. It didn't affect us, personally, and we were always working so hard ourselves. I remember his name. If he'd been called Tom Johnson or something, I'd have forgotten that too.'

I nodded. I felt the same. I asked if I could look at his diaries.

'I did find them for you,' he said. 'They were in a box in the attic. Do you seriously think I'd have written anything about Wilson Yarrow?'

'I hope you did. You wrote about most things.'

He smiled. 'Waste of time, really. I used to think my life would go by and I'd forget it, if I didn't write it down.'

'You were probably right.'

He shook his head. 'One remembers the great things anyway, and all the dreadful things. The rest doesn't matter.'

'My diaries are balance sheets,' I said. 'I look at the old ones and remember what I was doing, when.'

'Did you go on with rebuilding old wrecks?'

'Yeah.'

'I couldn't do that.'

'I couldn't work in an office. I tried it.'

We smiled ruefully at each other, old improbable friends, unalike in everything except knowledge.

'I brought an envelope,' I said, having clutched its large brown shape awkwardly along with one of the walking sticks during the journey. 'While I read the diaries, you look at the way Wilson Yarrow thinks a grandstand should be built. Tell me your thoughts.'

'All right.'

A sensible plan, but no good in the performance. I looked with dismay as he brought out his diaries and piled them on his coffee table. There were perhaps twenty large spiral-bound notebooks, eight inches by ten and a half, literally thousands of pages filled with his neat cramped handwriting; a task of days, not half an hour.

'I didn't realise,' I said weakly. 'I didn't remember . . .'

'I told you you didn't know what you were asking.'

'Could you . . . I mean, *would* you, lend them to me?'

'To take away, do you mean?'

'You'd get them back.'

'You swear?' he said doubtfully.

'On my diploma.'

His face lightened. 'All right.' He opened the brown envelope and took a look at the contents, pausing with raised eyebrows at the axonometric drawing. 'That's showing off!' he said.

'Yeah. Not necessary.'

Carteret looked at the elevations and floor plans. He made no comment about the amount of glass: building in difficult ways with glass was typical Architectural Association doctrine. We'd been taught to regard glass as avant-garde, as the pushing back of design frontiers. When I'd murmured that surely building with glass had been old hat since Joseph Paxton stuck together the old Crystal Palace in Hyde Park in 1851, I'd been reviled as an iconoclast, if not ruthlessly expelled for heresy. In any case, glass was acceptable to Carteret in futuristic ways that I found clever for the sake of cleverness, not for grace or utility. Glass for its own sake was pointless to me: except as a source of daylight, it was normally what one could see through it that mattered.

'Where are the rest of the plans?' Carteret asked.

'This is all Yarrow showed the Strattons.'

'How does he get crowds up five storeys?'

I smiled. 'Presumably they walk, like they did in the old grandstand that exploded . . .'

'No lifts. No escalators in the floor plan.' He looked up. 'No client would buy this, not in this day and age.'

'I'd guess,' I said, 'that Conrad Stratton has committed himself and the racecourse to whatever Yarrow produced.'

'Signed a contract, do you mean?'

'I don't know. If he did, it's not binding, as he hadn't the power to.'

He frowned. 'Bit of a mess, though.'

'Not if Wilson Yarrow's disqualified himself in some way.'

'Literally? Do you mean disbarred? Struck off?'

'More like dishonest.'

'Well, good luck with the diaries. I don't remember anything like that.'

'But . . . something?'

'Yes.'

I looked at my watch. 'Do you have a number I could ring for a taxi?'

'Sure. It's in the kitchen. I'll do it for you.' He went away on the errand and presently returned, carrying a carrier bag and followed by his wife, who hovered in the doorway.

'Take the diaries in this,' he said, beginning to transfer them to the carrier, 'and my wife says I must drive you to Paddington myself. She says you're in pain.'

Disconcerted, I glanced at his wife and rubbed a hand over my face while I sought for a response.

'She's a nurse,' Carteret said. 'She thought you had arthritis until I explained about the roof falling in. She says you're forcing yourself to move and you need to rest a bit.'

'Haven't time.'

He cheerfully nodded. 'Like, I may have a roaring temperature today but I can't fit in flu until, let's say, next Tuesday?'

'Quite right.'

'So I will drive you to Paddington.'

'I'm truly grateful.'

He nodded, satisfied that I meant it.

'Anyway,' I said, 'I thought the current medical theory was "get up and go".'

Carteret's wife gave me a sweetly indulgent smile and went away, and Carteret himself put the carrierful of diaries in his car and on arrival at Paddington Station drove round the back taxi road to park close between platforms, among the trains.

On the way there I said, 'Stratton Park racecourse will be advertising for proposals for its new stands. Why don't you ask your firm to put in for the competition?'

'I don't know anything about grandstands.'

'I do,' I said. 'I could tell you what's needed.'

'Why don't you do it yourself?'

I shook my head. 'Not my sort of thing.'

'I'll see what my firm says,' he remarked doubtfully.

'Tell them to write and express interest and ask for how large a crowd the stands are envisaged to cater for. You can't even begin to design stands until you've an idea of the size needed. Someone must have told Yarrow, because he got that about right.'

'My firm can but try, I suppose,' Carteret said. 'There are fifteen thousand architects in Britain currently out of work. People don't think they *need* architects. They don't want to pay the fees, then they complain if they knock down a wall and the bedrooms fall into the basement.'

'Life's rotten,' I said dryly.

'Still the same cynic, I see.'

He carried the diaries to the train and stored them and me into a seat. 'I'll phone you when I get back from Disney. Where will you be?'

I gave him my home number. 'Amanda may answer. She'll take a message.'

'Don't let's leave it another ten years,' he said. 'OK?'

Swaying towards Swindon I dipped into the diaries and finally drowned in nostalgia. How young we'd been! How unformed and trusting! How serious and certain.

I came to a deep thrust of the knife.

Carteret had written:

> Lee and Amanda got married today in church, the whole bit, like she wanted. They're both nineteen. I think he's a fool but have to admit they looked very pleased with themselves. She's dreamy. Trust Lee. Her father, ultra pukkah, he paid for it all. Her young sister Shelly was bridesmaid, a bit spotty. Lee's mother came. Madeline. A knockout. Fancied her rotten. She says I'm too young. Went to Amanda's folks' house after, for champagne and cake etc. About forty people. Amanda's cousins, girl friends, old uncles, that sort of thing. I had to toast the bridesmaid. Who'd be a best man? Lee says they'll live on air. Must say they were walking on it. They went off to practise being Mr and Mrs in Paris for three days. Amanda's parents gave it to them for a wedding present.

God, I thought, I remembered that wedding day in every tiny detail. I'd been positive we'd be blissful for ever and ever. Sad, sad illusion.

On the next page, Carteret had written:

> Lee and Amanda's party last night. Most of our year came. A rave up. Bit different from last week's wedding!! They still look ecstatic. Beer and pizza this time. Lee was paying. I went to bed at six and slept through old Hammond's lecture this morning. I miss Lee in our lodgings. Didn't realise what I'd got. Better start looking for a replacement, can't afford this place on my own, bleak though it is.

Watching lights flash by in the dark countryside outside the train's windows, I wondered what Amanda was doing at that moment. Was she quietly alone at home with Jamie? Or was she, as I couldn't help speculating, embarking on an adventure of her own; had she met a new man at her sister's party? Had she *been* to her sister's party? Why did she want me and the boys to stay away for two more days?

I wondered how I would deal with it if she had finally, after all these years, fallen seriously in love with someone else.

For all the fragile state of our marriage, I desperately wanted it to continue. Perhaps because I myself hadn't been engulfed by an irresistible new passion, I still saw only advantages in staying, even unsatisfactorily, together; and top of that list came stability for six young lives. My whole mind skittered away from the thought of breaking everything up, from division of property, loss of sons, uncertainty, unhappiness, loneliness, acrimony. That sort of pain would disintegrate me into uselessness as nothing physical could.

Let Amanda have a lover, I thought: let her light up with excitement, go off on trips, even bear a child not mine; but, dear God, let her stay.

I would find out, I thought, when we went home on Thursday. I would see, then. I would know. I didn't want Thursday to come.

With an effort I turned back to dipping into Carteret's diaries for the rest of the journey, but Wilson Yarrow might never have existed for all I found of him.

It was after ten o'clock when I directed the Swindon taxi to drive into the racecourse by the back road and stop at the bus.

The boys were all there, drowsily watching a video, Neil fast asleep. Christopher, relieved, went off, as he'd promised, to tell the Gardners I'd come safely back. I lay down gratefully myself with an intense feeling that *this* was home, this bus, these children. Never regret that unwise wedding day, this had grown out of it. Now, keeping it together was all that mattered.

Sleep enfolded us all, peacefully; but there was a fire in the night.

CHAPTER 11

The boys and I surveyed the smoking ruins of the fence at the open ditch. Black, scorched to stumps and ash, it stretched across the course, smelling healthily of garden bonfire, thirty feet long by three feet wide.

Roger was there, unworried, with three groundsmen who had apparently dowsed the flames earlier and were now waiting with spades and a truck for the embers to cool to dismantling point.

'Harold Quest?' I asked Roger.

He shrugged resignedly. 'His sort of thing, I suppose, but he left no signature. I'd have expected a "BAN CRUELTY" poster, at the least.'

'Will you doll off the fence?' I asked.

'Lord, no. Once we get this mess cleared away, we'll rebuild it. No problem. It's just a nuisance, not a calamity.'

'No one saw who set it alight?'

''Fraid not. The night watchman spotted the flames from the stands at about dawn. He phoned me, woke me up, and of course I drove up here, but there was no one about. It would have been handy to catch someone with a can of petrol, but no dice. It was a pretty thorough job, as you see. Not a cigarette. The whole width of the fence burned at once. There isn't much wind. It had to be petrol.'

'Or firelighters,' Christopher said.

Roger looked interested. 'Yes. I didn't think of that.'

'Dad won't let us light fires with petrol,' my son explained. 'He says we could easily light ourselves.'

'Firelighters,' Roger said thoughtfully.

All the boys nodded.

'Lots of twigs,' Neil said.

'Birch,' Edward corrected.

Toby said, shuddering, 'I don't like this place.'

Roger and I both abruptly remembered that it was here that Toby had seen the racegoer with his eyes kicked out. Roger said briskly, 'Jump in the jeep, boys,' and as they tumbled to obey him, added to me, 'You *walked* up here from the bus!'

'It's not far,' I pointed out, 'and it's getting easier all the time.' I'd taken only one stick: felt stiff and creaky but definitely stronger.

Roger said, 'Good. Well, get in the jeep yourself. Henry's a genius!'

He drove up to the by now familiar roadway and parked outside his office and positively beamed at the sight before us.

The fine weather, though cooling, had lasted. The sky was a washed pale blue with a few streaky clouds slowly thinning and vanishing. The morning sun shone unhampered on strings of bright flags, which fluttered gently from the ridge lines of the big top's spreading roof right down to the ground in a blizzard of strings, arcading the whole huge tent like an arch of honour. Merrie Englande come again to gorgeous light-hearted life, uplifting the spirits, making one laugh.

I breathed, 'Oh, my boy,' and Roger said, 'There are your flags. Henry said he brought every last one. When his men unfurled them all less than an hour ago, and that big white spread of canvas blossomed like that . . . well, you'd have to have been a sneering misogynist not to have been moved.'

'Colonel, you're a sentimentalist!'

'Who's talking!'

'I'm a hard-headed businessman,' I said, only half truthfully. 'The flags make people ready to spend more. Don't ask for the psychology, it just happens.'

He said contentedly, 'That's the perfect squelch for possible cynics. Mind if I use it?'

'Be my guest.'

Henry's vast trucks had gone. Henry's own personal van, Roger said, was now parked out of sight at the far end of the big top. Henry was somewhere about.

Two Portakabins now stood, neatly aligned end to end, where Henry's trucks had been. Into one of them jockeys' valets were carrying saddles and hampers from their nearby vans, setting up the changing room for the male riders. Through the open door of the other could be seen an official weighing machine, borrowed from an obliging Midlands course.

A row of caterers' vans were drawn up outside the small feeder tents on the side of the big top furthest from the track, with busy hands carrying tables and trestles and folding chairs through the specially made passages into what would soon be fully-fledged dining rooms and bars.

'It's all working,' Roger said in wonderment. 'It's bloody amazing.'

'It's great.'

'And the stables, of course, are OK. Horses have been arriving as usual. The canteen for drivers and lads is open, serving hot food. The Press are here. The stable security staff say that for once everyone seems to be in a holiday mood. Like the Blitz, there's nothing like a bloody disaster to make the English good humoured.'

We climbed out of the jeep and went into the big top itself. Each 'room' now had a high-rising Moorish-looking tented ceiling of pleated peach 'silk' above white solid-seeming walls, some of which were in fact taut whitened canvas laced onto poles. The floor throughout was of brown matting glued onto wooden sections slotted levelly together, firm and easy to the feet. Lights shone everywhere, discreetly. The fans up by the high roof silently circled, changing the air. Each room had an identifying board at its entrance. It all looked spacious, organised and calm. A rebirth; marvellous.

'What have we forgotten?' I said.

'You're such a comfort.'

'Can I ask you something?'

'Of course.'

'You remember, a week or so ago, that you learned about the precise distribution of shares among the Strattons, that they wouldn't tell you before?'

He flicked a glance at me, mentally a fraction off balance.

'Yes,' he said slowly. 'You noticed.'

'Was it Forsyth who told you?'

'What does it matter?'

'Was it?' I asked.

'As a matter of fact, yes. Why did you think it was him?'

'He resents the way the others treat him, which makes him untrustworthy from their point of view. He knows he thoroughly earned the way they treat him. They think they control him, but they could compress him too far.'

'Like plastic explosive.'

'Yeah. Too close to home.'

Roger nodded. 'He told me in a moment of spite against them, and then said he was only guessing. He's not very bright.'

'Very unhappy, though.'

'I don't like him, don't trust him and, no, I really don't know what he did. When the Strattons hide something, they do a good job.'

We walked out of the big top and found a van and a car parked near the entrance. The van, green with white lettering, announced 'Stratton Garden Centre'. The car, door opening, disgorged Ivan.

He stood with his hands on his hips, head back, staring up in utter amazement at the sunlit splendour of flags. I waited for his disapproval, forgetting the little boy in him.

He looked at Roger, his eyes shiny with smiling.

'Colonel,' he said, 'what *fun*.' He transferred his gaze first to my walking stick and then up to my face. 'Would you mind,' he said awkwardly, 'if I reconsidered a bit?'

'In what way?'

'Actually,' he said, 'I think Keith's wrong about you, don't you know.' He turned away, embarrassed, and instructed his driver to get out of the cab and open the rear doors of the van. 'I talked it over with Dolly – that's my wife – last night,' he went on, 'and we thought it didn't make sense. If you were meaning to blackmail the family, why would you help us by getting this tent? And then, don't you know, you don't seem a bad fellow at all, and Hannah has had bees in her bonnet about her mother – *your* mother – all her life. So we decided I might just, don't you know, *apologise*, if the occasion arose.'

'Thank you,' I said.

His face lightened, his errand achieved. His men opened the van's rear doors and disclosed a packed blaze of colour inside. A whole army of flourishing pots.

'Superb!' Roger said, genuinely delighted.

'You see,' Ivan explained, pleased, 'when I saw the big top yesterday I understood why you'd asked me for plants, and this morning I went along to the centre myself and told my manager to load not just green stuff, but *flowers*. Lots of flowers. The least I could do, don't you know.'

'They're wonderful,' I assured him.

He beamed, a heavy-set man in his fifties, not clever, not charismatic, polished in a way, but at heart uncomplicated. He hadn't been much of an enemy and wouldn't be much of a friend, but any neutralised Stratton could, in my terms, be counted a blessing.

Under Ivan's happy direction, my children enthusiastically carried and positioned all the flowers. I guessed they would be missing when it became time to collect them up again, except that Ivan in good humour gave them a pound each for their labours, making anything possible.

'You don't *have* to,' Christopher told him earnestly, pocketing his coin, 'but thanks very much.'

'Forsyth,' Ivan told me wistfully, 'was a nice little boy.'

I watched Toby stagger by with a huge pot of hyacinths. I would give almost anything, I thought, to have my own problem son grow into a well-balanced man, but it had to come from within him. He would make his own choices, as Forsyth had, as everyone did.

The plants positioned, Ivan and his van drove away and Roger asked if I would like to see the burned fence rebuilt. I glanced down at Neil who happened to be holding my hand and Roger resignedly yelled 'Boys!' in his parade-ground voice and waited while they came running and piled into the jeep.

Toby refused to get out when he found where we'd got to, but I and the others watched the ultimate in prefabrication.

'It used to take days to put a new fence together,' Roger said. 'That was when we positioned poles as framework and filled the frame with bundle after bundle of birch, finally cutting the rough top edges into shape. Now we build fences in sections away in a separate area, take them to wherever's needed, and stake them into the ground. We can replace a whole fence or part of one at very short notice. Today's fire was at dawn and we don't race over this fence until two-thirty this afternoon. Piece of cake!'

His men, already having cleared the embers, were busy manhandling the first of the new sections into place.

'All our fences are built like this, now,' Roger said. 'They're good to jump but not as hard and unforgiving as the old sort.'

I asked, 'Did your men find any ... well, *clues* ... in the ashes to say who started the fire?'

Roger shook his head. 'We always have trouble with vandalism. It's hopeless bothering to find out who did it. It's nearly always teenagers, and the courts hardly give them a slap on the wrist. We simply write vandalism into the budget and find ways to minimise the nuisance.'

'How many people would know you could replace a fence this fast?' I asked.

'Trainers might,' he said judiciously. 'Jockeys, perhaps. Not many others, unless they worked here.'

Roger went to speak to his foreman who looked at his watch, nodded, and got on with the job.

'Right,' Roger said, returning and shepherding us back to his jeep. 'Now, boys, muster at the jeep up by my office at eleven-thirty, right? I'll drive you and your father down to the bus then, and go on to my house. We all change for racing. At noon precisely I drive you back to the paddock. Understand?'

The boys were near to saluting. Roger, the peak of his tweed cap well pulled down over his eyes like a guards officer was, with his clipped, very civilised voice and his spare decisive manner, the sort of senior soldier it was natural to obey. I could see I was never going to achieve such effortless mastery of my children's behaviour.

We returned to Roger's office to find a flourishing row in full progress out on the tarmac. All the protesters from outside the gate were now inside, all of them clustered round Henry who held Harold Quest's elbow in an unyielding grip. The fierce woman was using a placard saying 'ANIMAL RIGHTS' to belabour Henry as with a paddle. Four or five others howled verbal abuse with stretched ugly mouths and Henry shook Harold Quest without respect or mercy.

When he saw us Henry yelled, his voice as effortlessly rising above the screeching din as his height above everyone else, 'This fellow's an imposter! A bloody imposter. They all are. They're rubbish.'

He stretched out the hand not busy with shaking Quest and tweaked the placard away from the harpy attacking him.

'Madam,' he roared, 'go back to your kitchen.'

Henry stood eighteen inches above her. He towered over Quest. Henry's beard was bigger than Quest's, Henry's voice mightier, Henry's strength double, Henry's character – no contest.

Henry was laughing. Harold Quest, the scourge of entering vehicles, had met more than his match.

'This man,' Henry yelled, shaking Quest's elbow, 'do you know what he was doing? I went over to the Mayflower and when I came back I found him *eating a hamburger*.'

My sons stared at him in perplexity. Eating hamburgers came well within normal behaviour.

'Animal rights!' Henry shouted joyously. 'What about hamburgers' rights? This man was *eating an animal*.'

Harold Quest squirmed.

'*Three* of these dimwits,' Henry yelled, glancing at the screeching chorus, 'were *dripping* with hamburgers. Animal rights, my *arse*.'

My boys were fascinated. Roger was laughing. Oliver Wells came out of Roger's office primed to disapprove of the noise only to crease into a smile once he understood Quest's dilemma.

'This jacket he's wearing,' Henry yelled, 'feels like *leather*.'

'No.' Quest shook his head violently, tipping his woolly hat over one ear.

'And,' Henry yelled, 'when I accused him of eating an animal he put the hamburger in his *pocket*.'

Alan jumped up and down, loving it, his freckled face grinning.

Henry flung the 'ANIMAL RIGHTS' placard far and wide and plunged his hand into the pocket of Harold Quest's leather-like jacket. Out came a wrapper, a half-eaten bun, tomato ketchup and yellow oozing mustard and a half-moon of meat with the Quest bite marks all over it.

Out of the pocket, too, unexpectedly, fell a second ball of plastic wrapper which had never seen a short-order cook.

In the general mêlée, no one saw the significance of the second wrapper until Christopher, from some obscure urge to tidiness, picked it up. Even then it would have meant nothing to most people, but Christopher was different.

'Come on,' Henry yelled at his hapless captive, 'you're not a real protestor. What are you doing here?'

Harold Quest didn't answer.

'Dad,' Christopher said, pulling my sleeve, 'look at this. Smell it.'

I looked at the ball of wrapping material he'd picked up, and I smelled it. 'Give it,' I said, 'to the Colonel.'

Roger, hearing my tone of voice, glanced at my face and took the crumbled ball from Christopher.

There were two brown transparent wrappers scrunched together, with scarlet and yellow printing on them. Roger smoothed one of them out and looked up at Henry who, no slouch on the uptake, saw that more had been revealed than a hamburger.

'Bring him into the office,' Roger told Henry.

Henry, receiving the message, roared at Quest's followers,

'You lot, clear off before you get prosecuted for being a nuisance on the highway. You with the leather shoes, you with the hamburgers, next time get your act right. Shove off, the lot of you.'

He turned his back on them, marching Quest effortlessly towards the office door, the rest of us interestedly watching while Quest's noisy flock collapsed and deserted him, straggling off silently towards the way out.

The office filled up again: Oliver, Roger, myself, five boys trying to look unobtrusive, Harold Quest and, above all, Henry who needed the space of three.

'Could you,' Roger said to Henry, 'search his other pockets?'

'Sure.'

He must have loosened his grip a little in order to oblige because Quest suddenly wrenched himself free and made a dash for the door. Henry plucked him back casually by the collar and swung his arm before leaving go. With anyone else's strength it wouldn't have much mattered, but under Henry's easy force Quest staggered across the room and crashed backwards against the wall. A certain amount of self-pity formed moisture round his eyes.

'Take the jacket *off*,' Henry commanded, and Quest, fumbling, obeyed.

Roger took the jacket, searched the pockets and laid the booty out on the desk beside the blotter where Henry had parked the half-eaten hamburger. Apart from a meagre wallet with a return bus ticket to London, there were a cigarette lighter, a box of matches and three further dark brown transparent wrappers with scarlet and yellow overprinting.

Roger smoothed out one of these flat on the desk and read the writing aloud.

'"Sure Fire",' he announced. '"Clean. Non-toxic. Long-burning. Infallible. A fire every time. Twenty sticks."' He did brief sums. 'Five empty wrappers; that means one hundred firelighters. Now what would anyone want with one hundred firelighters on a racecourse?'

Harold Quest glowered.

Henry stood over him, a threat simply by size.

'As you're *unreal*,' he boomed, 'what were you up to?'

'Nothing,' Quest weakly said, mopping his face with his hand.

Henry's loud voice beleaguered him, 'People who burn fences can blow up grandstands. We're turning you over to the force.'

'I never blew up the grandstand,' said Quest, freshly agitated.

'Oh really? You were here, Friday morning. You admitted it.'

'I never . . . I wasn't here then.'

'You definitely *were*,' I said. 'You told the police you saw Dart Stratton's car drive in through the gates between eight and eight-thirty in the morning.'

Harold Quest looked baffled.

'And it was *pointless*,' Roger added, 'to be picketing the gates of a racecourse at that hour on a day none of the public would come.'

'A day the TV cameras came, though,' I said, 'after the explosion.'

'We saw you,' Christopher said vehemently. 'They said on the telly you'd done it. You nearly got my brother killed and you hurt my dad badly.'

'I *didn't!*'

'Who did, then?' Henry roared. 'You did it! You've been a bloody nuisance, you're not a real protestor, you've destroyed racecourse property and you're heading for jail. Colonel, fetch the police, they're here already poking around behind that fence. Tell them we've caught their terrorist.'

'*No!*' Quest squealed.

'Then *give*,' Henry commanded. 'We're listening.'

'All right then. All right. I did burn the fence.' Quest was not confessing, but pleading. 'But I never touched the grandstand. I didn't, as God's my witness.'

'As to God, that's one thing. You've got to convince *us*.'

'*Why* did you burn the fence?' Roger demanded.

'Why?' Quest looked around desperately as if the answer might be written on the walls.

'*Why?*' Henry bellowed. 'Why? Why? Why? And don't give us any shit about animal rights. We know that's all crap as far as you're concerned.' He waved a hand at the hamburger relics. 'So *why* did you do it? You're in dead trouble unless you come up with the goods.'

Quest saw hope. 'If I tell you, then, will that be the end of it?'

'It depends,' Henry said. 'Tell us first.'

Quest looked up at the big man and at all of us staring at him with sharp hostile eyes and at the wrappers and the hamburger on the desk and, from one second to the next, lost his nerve.

He sweated. 'I got paid for it,' he said.

We met this announcement with silence.

Quest cast an intimidated look round the accusing faces and sweated some more.

'I'm an actor,' he pleaded.

More silence.

Quest's desperation level rose with the pitch of his voice. 'You don't know what it's like, waiting and waiting for jobs and sitting by the telephone *forever* and living on *crumbs* . . . you take *anything*, anything . . .'

Silence.

He went on miserably. 'I'm a good actor . . .'

I thought that none of us, probably, would refute that.

'. . . but you have to be *lucky*. You have to *know* people . . .'

He pulled off his askew woolly hat and began to look more credibly like Harold Quest, out-of-work actor, and less like Harold Quest, psyched-up fanatic.

He said, 'I got this phone call from someone who'd seen me play a hunt saboteur in a TV film . . . only a bit part, no dialogue, just screaming abuse, but my name was there in the credits, hunt saboteur leader, Harold Quest.'

Extraordinarily, he was proud of it: his name in the credits.

'So this phone caller said would I demonstrate for real, for money? And I wouldn't have to pay any agents' fees as he'd looked me up in the phone directory and just tried my number on the off-chance . . .'

He stopped, searching our faces, begging for understanding but not getting much.

'Well,' he said weakly, 'I was being evicted from my flat for non-payment of rent and I'd nowhere to go and I lived rough on the streets once before and anything's better than that.'

Something in this recital, some tinge in the self-pity, reminded me sharply that this was an actor, a good one, and that the sob-stuff couldn't be trusted. Still, I thought, let him run on. There might be truth in him somewhere.

He realised himself that the piteousness wasn't achieving an over-sympathetic response and reacted with a more business-like explanation.

'I asked what was wanted, and they said to come here and make a bloody intolerable nuisance of myself . . .'

'They?' Roger asked.

'He, then. *He* said to try to get some real demonstrators together and persuade them to come here and rant and rave a bit, so I went to a fox hunt and got that loud-mouthed bitch Paula to bring some of her friends . . . and I tell you, I've spent nearly a week with them and they get on my wick something chronic . . .'

'But you've been paid?' I suggested. 'You've taken the money?'

'Well . . .' grudgingly, 'some up front. Some every day. Yes.'

'*Every day?*' I repeated, incredulously.

He nodded.

'And for burning the fence?'

He began to squirm again and to look mulishly sullen. 'He didn't say anything about burning the fence, not to begin with.'

'Who,' Roger asked without threat, 'is *he*?'

'He didn't tell me his name.'

'Do you mean,' Roger said in the same reasonable voice, 'that you mounted a threatening demonstration here for someone unknown?'

'For *money*. Like I said.'

'And you just trusted you'd get paid?'

'Well, I *was*.' His air of defiance was of no help to him;

much the reverse. 'If I *hadn't* been paid, all I'd have laid out was the bus fare from London, but he promised me, and he kept his promise. And every day that I caused trouble, I got more.'

'Describe him,' I said.

Quest shook his head, rear-guarding.

'Not good enough,' Roger said crisply. 'The racecourse will lay charges against you for wilful destruction of property, namely burning down the fence at the open ditch.'

'But you *said* . . .' began Quest, impotently protesting.

'We promised nothing. If you withhold the identity of your, er, *procurer*, we fetch the police across here immediately.'

Quest, looking hunted, caved in.

'He told me,' he said, seeking to persuade us, 'to stop every car and be as much nuisance as I could, and one of the cars would be *his*, and he would wind down the window and tell me my telephone number, and I would know it was *him*, and I would put my hand into the car and he would put money into my hand, and I was not to ask questions or speak to him – as God's my judge.'

'Your judge will be a damn sight nearer than God,' Henry bellowed, 'if you're not telling us straight.'

'As God's my . . .' Quest began, and collapsed into speechlessness, unable to deal with so many accusers, with such complete disbelief.

'All right,' Roger told him prosaically, 'you may not have wanted to look at him in the face, to be able to identify him, but there's one thing you do now know, which you can tell us.'

Quest simply looked nervous.

'*Which car?*' Roger said. 'Describe it. Tell us its number.'

'Well . . . I . . .'

'After the first payment,' Roger said, 'you'd have been looking out for that car.'

I suppose that rabbits might look at snakes as Quest looked at Roger.

'*Which car?*' Henry yelled in Quest's ear.

'A Jaguar XJ6. Sort of silver.' He mumbled the number.

Roger, slightly aghast but not disbelieving, said to me succinctly, 'Keith's'.

He and I digested the news. Henry raised his eyebrows our way. Roger flapped a hand, nodding. Henry, perceiving that the really essential piece of information had surfaced, looked more benignly upon his demoralised captive.

'Well, now,' he said, at only medium fortissimo, 'when did you get hold of the firelighters?'

After a moment, meekly, Quest said, 'I bought them.'

'When?' Roger asked.

'Saturday.'

'On *his* instructions?'

Quest said feebly, 'There was a piece of paper in with the money. He said to burn the open ditch fence, where a horse had been killed on the Saturday. He said dowse it with petrol, to make sure.'

'But you didn't.'

'I'm not *daft*.'

'Not far off it,' Henry told him.

'Where do I get petrol?' Quest asked rhetorically. 'Buy a can from a garage, buy five gallons of petrol, then burn a fence down? I ask you! He took me for daft.'

'Eating a hamburger was daft,' Henry said.

'Do you still have the paper with the instructions?' I asked.

'The paper said to burn the instructions.'

'And you did?'

He nodded. 'Of course.'

'Silly,' I said. 'You're not much of a villain. Who's going to believe you, without those instructions?'

'But,' he spluttered, 'I mean, but . . .'

'How did you actually do it?' I asked. 'I mean, how did you position the firelighters?'

He said matter of factly, 'I pushed them into the fence in bunches. Then I lit a roll of newspaper and went along lighting the bunches all at once.' He almost smiled. 'It was easy.'

He should have burned the wrappers as well, I thought, but then people were fools, especially actors who weren't practised criminals.

'I think,' I said to Roger and Henry and Oliver, 'that we might do a spot of Strattoning here.'

'How do you mean, exactly?'

'Could I borrow your typewriter?'

'Of course,' Roger said, pointing to the inner office. 'In there.'

I went through to the machine, switched on the electricity and typed a short statement:

> I, Harold Quest, actor, agreed that in return for money I would mount nuisance demonstrations at the main gates of Stratton Park racecourse, ostensibly but not actually in support of a movement to discredit the sport of steeplechasing. For this service I received payments on several occasions from a man driving a silver Jaguar XJ6, registration number as follows,   To comply with instructions received from this driver I also bought one hundred 'Sure Fire' firelighters and, using them, burned to the ground the birch fence at the open ditch in the straight, at approximately six a.m. Monday, Easter Bank Holiday.

Roger, Oliver and Henry read it and presented it to Quest for signing. He was predictably reluctant. We told him to add the date and his address.

'You might as well,' I said, when he shrank from it, 'as you're in the phone book and we can find you any time, I should think, if your photo's in *Spotlight* with the name of your agent.'

'But this is an admission of guilt,' he protested, not disputing our ability to track him down, as one could with any actor, through their professional publication.

'Of course,' I said, 'but if you sign it, you can buzz off now, at once, and use your return bus ticket, and with luck we won't give your confession to the police.'

Quest searched our faces, not finding much to reassure or comfort him; but he did sign the paper. He did, in his own handwriting, fill in the car registration (verified by Roger), and also his address and the date.

The others scrutinised the pages.

'Is that everything?' Roger asked me.

'I'd think so.'

Roger said to Henry, 'Let him go,' and Henry opened the office door to freedom and jerked his thumb in that direction, giving Quest a last order, 'Out!'

Quest, an amalgam of relief and anxiety, didn't wait for a change of heart on our part but took himself off at the double.

Henry looked at the abandoned bits of hamburger and said disgustedly, 'We should have rubbed the little shit's nose in that mustard.'

I said with mock seriousness, 'Quest's not all bad. Remember, he did call Rebecca "ducky".'

Henry guffawed. 'So he did.'

Roger picked up the signed confession. 'What do we do with this, then? Do we, in fact, give it to the police?'

'No,' I said, 'we give it to Marjorie Binsham.'

CHAPTER 12

Notwithstanding our threats to Quest, the police presence behind the partitioning wall had by that morning fallen to two constables, both there more to prevent the public from entering and hurting themselves in the unstable building than to investigate further for evidence.

As far as Roger and Oliver had been able to discover the previous afternoon, after I'd left, the higher ranks and the bomb expert had completed their work with the discovery and reassembling of a blown-apart clock face, and had said their further enquiries would be conducted 'elsewhere', unspecified.

'They don't know who did it,' Roger baldly interpreted.

In front of the boring and forbidding partition fence there now rose an inflated Sleeping Beauty's Bouncing Castle, complete with fairytale towers and a child-minder in the shape of Henry's one remaining maintenance man.

Ivan, in a flush of generosity, had returned with a second vanload of (free) plants, this time young bushy trees in pots, which he spread out on each side of the castle, making the fence in consequence a tamer, even decorative, part of the scenery.

By the time Roger drove us towards his house at eleven-thirty, neither he nor I nor Henry could think of any improvements that could be managed in time for that afternoon, though many that could be achieved afterwards, before the next meeting.

The boys changed into tidy clothes with only medium grumbles. I changed from navvy to gentleman and with my walking stick clumsily managed to knock to the floor the pile of Carteret's diaries that had been on the table by my bed. Edward obligingly picked them up for me, but held one awkwardly open, its pages tearing halfway along from the spiral wire binding.

'Hey, careful!' I said, taking it from him. 'You'll get me shot.'

I concentrated on closing the book to minimise the damage, and there, leaping out at me from the page, was the name I'd sought for unsuccessfully on the train.

Wilson Yarrow.

'Wilson Yarrow,' Carteret had written, 'that paragon we've had stuffed down our throats, they say he's a fraud!'

The next paragraph didn't explain anything but merely consisted of remarks about a lecture on miniaturisation of space.

I groaned. 'They says he's a fraud' got me no further. I flicked forward a few pages and came to:

> There's a rumour going round that Wilson Yarrow won the Epsilon Prize last year with a design he pinched from someone else! Red faces on the staff! They're refusing to discuss it, but perhaps we'll hear less about the *brilliant* Wilson Yarrow from now on.

The Epsilon Prize, I remotely remembered, had been given each year for the most innovative design of a building by a senior student. I hadn't won it. Nor had Carteret. I couldn't remember ever having submitted an entry.

Roger banged on the bus door, stuck his head in and said, 'Ready?' and the Morris family, dressed to impress, trooped out for his inspection.

'Very good,' he approved. He gave us all racecards, entry badges and lunch tickets out of an attaché case.

'I don't want to go to the races,' Toby said, suddenly frowning. 'I want to stay here and watch football.'

Roger left the decision to me.

'OK,' I said to my son peaceably. 'Get yourself some lunch, and if you change your mind, walk up later to the office.'

Toby's worried frown turned to a more carefree expression. 'Thanks, Dad,' he said.

'Will he be all right by himself?' Roger asked, driving away with the rest of us, and Edward assured him, 'Tobe *likes* being by himself. He hides from us often.'

'He goes off on bike rides,' Christopher said.

Roger's mind switched to the day ahead. 'We've done all we could,' he said dubiously.

'Don't worry so much,' I told him. 'Do you know a rabbet from a raceway?'

'What on earth are you talking about?'

'Testing a theory.'

'Is it a riddle, Dad?' Neil asked.

'Sort of. But don't ask, it hasn't an answer.'

Roger parked the jeep at the end of the office building, where it would be ready if he needed to drive round the course. The boys paired off, Neil with Christopher, Edward and Alan together, with a rallying point near the office door for after the first, third and fifth races.

People were coming: a bus-load of Tote operators, the St John's Ambulance people, the squad of policemen for traffic control and the general prevention of fights in the betting rings, the bookies with their soap boxes and chalk boards, the gate-men, the racecard sellers; and then the jockeys, the sponsors of the races, the Stewards, the trainers, the Strattons and, finally, the racegoers with all bets still to lose.

I stood near the main entrance, watching the faces, seeing on almost all of them the holiday pleasure we'd aimed for. Even the TV crew, invited by Oliver, seemed visibly impressed, cameras whirring outside the big top and within.

Mark drove the Daimler right up to the gate into the paddock so that Marjorie wouldn't have to walk from the car park. She saw me standing not far away, and beckoned as one seldom refused.

Without comment she watched me limp, with the stick, to her side.

'*Flags*,' she said dubiously.

'Watch the faces.'

She was sold, as I'd thought she would be, by the smiles, the chatter, the hum of excitement. A fairground it might be, but something to talk about, something to give Stratton Park races a more positive face than a bomb-blasted grandstand.

She said, 'The Colonel promised us *lunch* . . .'

I showed her the way to the Strattons' own dining room, where she was greeted by the same butler and waitresses who always served her at the races, and obviously she felt instantly at home. She looked around carefully at everything, at the table the caterers had brought and laid with linen and silver, and up at the shimmering tent-ceiling with its soft oblique lighting and hidden air-vents.

'Conrad told me,' she said slowly. 'He said . . . a miracle. A miracle is saving us. He didn't say it was *beautiful*.' She stopped suddenly, swallowing, unable to go on.

'There's champagne for you, I think,' I said, and her butler was already bringing her a glass on a salver and pulling out a chair for her to sit down – a collapsible plastic-seated chair at base, covered now, as were ten round the table, with flowery material tied with neat bows.

Since pleasing Marjorie herself would mean the success of the whole enterprise, nothing we could think of that would make her comfortable had been left undone.

She sat primly, sipping. After a while she said, 'Sit down, Lee. That is, if you can.'

I sat beside her, able by now to do it without openly wincing.

Lee. No longer Mr Morris. Progress.

'Mrs Binsham . . .'

'You can call me Marjorie . . . if you like.'

My great old girl, I thought, feeling enormous relief. 'I'm honoured,' I said.

She nodded, agreeing with my assessment.

'Two days ago,' she said, 'my family treated you shamefully. I can hardly speak of it. Then you do this for us.' She gestured to the room. 'Why did you do it?'

After a pause I said, 'Probably you know why. You're probably the only person who does know.'

She thought. 'My brother,' she said, 'once showed me a letter you wrote to him, after Madeline died. You said his money had paid for your education. You thanked him. You did all this for *him*, didn't you? To repay him?'

'I suppose so.'

'Yes. Well. He would be pleased.'

She put down her glass, opened her handbag, took out a small white handkerchief and gently blew her nose. 'I miss him,' she said. She sniffed a little, put the handkerchief away and made an effort towards gaiety.

'Well, now,' she said. 'Flags. Happy faces. A lovely sunny spring day. Even those horrid people at the gate seem to have gone home.'

'Ah,' I said, 'I've something to show you.'

I took Harold Quest's confession from my pocket and, handing it over, explained about Henry and the out-of-character hamburger.

She searched for spectacles and read the page, soon putting a hand over her heart as if to still it.

'*Keith*,' she said, looking up. 'That's Keith's car.'

'Yes.'

'Did you give a copy of this to the police?'

'No,' I said. 'That's a copy too, incidentally. The original is in the safe in the Colonel's office.' I paused and went on. 'I don't think I can find out how much money Keith owes, or to whom, but I did think this might do for you as a lever instead.'

She gave me a long inspection.

'You understand me.' She sounded not pleased, nor displeased, but surprised, and accepting.

'It took me a while.'

A small smile. 'You met me last Wednesday.'

A long five days, I thought.

A woman appeared in the entrance to the dining room, with a younger woman hidden behind her.

'Excuse me,' she said, 'I was told I could find Lee Morris in here.'

I stood up in my unsprightly fashion.

'I'm Lee Morris,' I said.

She was plump, large-bosomed, friendly-looking, about sixty, with large blue eyes and short greyish-blonde curly hair. She wore layers of blue and beige clothes with brown low-heeled shoes, and had an untidy multicoloured silk square scarf tied in a bunched knot round her neck. Under her arm she carried a large brown handbag with its gold shoulder-chain dangling down, and there was altogether about her an air of being at home with herself: no mental insecurity or awkwardness.

Her gaze casually slid past me and fell on Marjorie, and there was a moment of extraordinary stillness, of suspension, in both women. Their eyes held the same wideness, their mouths the same open-lipped wonder. I thought in a flash of enlightenment that each knew the identity of the other, even though they showed no overt recognition nor made any attempt at polite speech.

'I want to talk to you,' the newcomer said to me, removing her gaze from Marjorie but continuing to be tinglingly aware of her presence. 'Not here, if you don't mind.'

I said to Marjorie, 'Will you excuse me?'

She could have said no. If she'd wanted to, she would have done. She cast an enigmatic glance at the newcomer, thought things over, and gave me a positive 'Yes. Go and talk.'

The newcomer backed out into the central aisle of the big top, with me following.

'I'm Perdita Faulds,' the newcomer said, once outside. 'And this,' she added, stepping to her right and fully revealing her companion, 'is my daughter, Penelope.'

It was like being hit twice very fast with a hammer; no time to take in the first bit of news before being stunned by the second.

Penelope Faulds was tall, slender, fair-haired, long-necked and almost the double of Amanda: the young Amanda I'd fallen in love with, the nineteen-year-old marvellous girl with grey smiling eyes going laughingly to her immature marriage.

I was no longer nineteen. I felt as breathless, however, as if I still were. I said, 'How do you do,' and it sounded ridiculous.

'Is there a bar in here?' Mrs Faulds asked, looking round. 'Someone outside told me there was.'

'Er . . . yes,' I said. 'Over here.'

I took her into one of the largest 'rooms' in the big top, the members' bar, where a few early customers were sitting at small tables with sandwiches and drinks.

Perdita Faulds took easy charge. 'Was it champagne that Mrs Binsham was drinking? I think we should have some.'

Faintly bemused, I turned towards the bar to do her bidding.

'My treat,' she said, opening her handbag and providing the funds. 'Three glasses.'

Penelope followed me to the bar. 'I'll carry the glasses,' she said. 'Can you manage the bottle?'

My pulse quickened. Stupid. I had six sons. I was too old.

The bar staff popped the cork and took the money. Mrs Faulds watched in good-natured enjoyment while I poured her bubbles.

'Do you know who I am?' she demanded.

'You own seven shares in this racecourse.'

She nodded. 'And you own eight. Your mother's. I knew your mother quite well at one time.'

I paused with the drinks. 'Did you really?'

'Yes. Do get on. I'm thirsty.'

I filled her glass, which she emptied fast. 'And how well,' I asked, refilling it, 'do you know Marjorie Binsham?'

'I don't exactly know her. I met her once, years ago. I know who she is. She knows who I am. You noticed, didn't you?'

'Yes.'

I watched Penelope. Her skin looked smooth and enticing in the softly diffused peach light. I wanted to touch her cheek, stroke it, to kiss it, as I had with Amanda. For God's sake, I told myself astringently, take a grip on things. Grow up, you fool.

'I've never been here before,' Mrs Faulds said. 'We saw on the television about the grandstand being bombed, didn't we, Pen? I got all curious. Then it was in Saturday's papers of course, with your name and everything, and they said the races would go on as planned. They said you'd been in the stands when they blew up, and that you were a shareholder, and in hospital.' She looked at the walking stick. 'They got that wrong, obviously. Anyway, I phoned the office here to ask where you were and they said you'd be here today, and I thought I'd like to meet you, Madeline's son, after all these years. So I told Pen I had some old shares in this place and asked if she would like to come with me, and here we are.'

I thought vaguely that there was much she'd left out, but Penelope held most of my attention.

'Pen, darling,' her mother said kindly. 'This must be pretty boring for you, Mr Morris and I talking about old times, so why don't you buzz off for a look at the horses?'

I said, 'It's too early for there to be any horses in the parade ring yet.'

'Hop off, Pen,' her mother said, 'there's a love.'

Penelope gave a resigned conspiratorial smile, sucked her glass dry, and amicably departed.

'She's a darling,' her mother said. 'My one and only. I was forty-two when I had her.'

'Er . . . lucky,' I murmured.

Perdita Faulds laughed. 'Do I embarrass you? Pen says I'm embarrassing. She says I tell total strangers things I should never tell anyone. I do like to shock people a bit, to be honest. There are so many tight-lipped fuddy-duddies about. But secrets, they're different.'

'What secrets?'

'What secret do you want to know?' she bantered.

'How you came by seven shares,' I said.

She put down her glass and regarded me with eyes that were suddenly shrewd, besides being benign.

'Now, there's a question!' She didn't answer it at once. She said, 'A couple of weeks ago the papers were saying the Strattons were rowing over the future of this racecourse.'

'Yes, I read that too.'

'Is that why you're here?'

'Basically, I guess so, yes.'

She said, 'I was brought up here, you know. Not here on the racecourse, but on the estate.'

I said, puzzled, 'But the Strattons – except Marjorie – say they don't know you.'

'No, silly, they don't. Years ago, my father was Lord Stratton's barber.'

She smiled at the surprise I hadn't hidden.

'You don't think I look like a barber's daughter?'

'Well, no, but then I don't know any barbers' daughters.'

'My father rented a cottage on the estate,' she explained, 'and he had shops in Swindon, and Oxford and Newbury, but he used to go to Stratton Hays himself to cut Lord Stratton's hair. We moved before I was fifteen and lived near the Oxford shop, but my father still went to Stratton Hays once a month.'

'Do go on,' I said. 'Did Lord Stratton give your father the shares?'

She finished the pale liquid in her glass. I poured some more.

'No, it wasn't like that.' She considered a little, but continued. 'My father died and left me the barber business. You see, by that time I'd learned the whole beauty trade, got diplomas, everything. Lord Stratton just strolled into the Oxford shop one day when he was passing, to see how I was getting on without my father, and he stayed to have a manicure.'

She smiled. She drank. I asked no more.

'Your mother used to come into the Swindon shop to have her hair done,' she said. 'I could have told her not to marry that vicious swine, Keith, but she'd done it by then. She used to come into the shop with bruises on her face and ask me personally to style her hair to hide them. I used to take her into a private cubicle, and she'd cling to me sometimes, and just cry. We were about the same age, you see, and we liked each other.'

'I'm glad she had someone,' I said.

'Funny, isn't it, what happens? I never thought I'd be sitting here talking to *you*.'

'You know about me?'

'Lord Stratton told me. During manicures.'

'How long did you . . . look after his hands?'

'Until he died,' she said simply. 'But things changed, of course. I met my husband and had Penelope, and William – I mean, Lord Stratton, of course – he got *older* and couldn't . . . well . . . but he still liked to have his nails done, and we would *talk*. Like old, old friends, you see?'

I saw.

'He gave me the shares at the same time he gave them to your mother. He gave them to his solicitors to look after for me. He said they might be worth something one day. It wasn't a great big deal. Just a present. A loving present. Better than money. I didn't ever want money from him. He knew that.'

'He was a lucky man,' I said.

'Oh, you *dear*. You're as nice as Madeline was.'

I rubbed a hand over my face, finding no answer.

'Does Penelope know,' I asked, 'about you and Lord Stratton?'

'Pen's a *child*!' she replied. 'She's eighteen. Of course she doesn't know. Nor does her father. I never told anyone. Nor did William . . . Lord Stratton. He wouldn't hurt his wife, and I didn't want him to.'

'But Marjorie guesses.'

She nodded. 'She's known all these years. She came to see me in the Oxford shop. She made a special appointment. I think it was just to see what I was like. We just talked a bit, not about anything much. She never said anything afterwards. She loved William, as I did. She wouldn't have given him away. She didn't, anyway. She still hasn't, has she?'

'No, she hasn't.'

After a pause, Perdita changed gears with her voice, shedding nostalgia, taking on business, saying crisply, 'So what are we going to do now, about William's racecourse?'

'If the course is sold for development,' I said, 'you'll make a nice little capital gain.'

'How much?'

'You can do sums as well as anyone. Seventy thousand pounds for every million the land raises, give or take a little capital gain.'

'And you?' she asked frankly. 'Would you sell?'

'You can't say it's not tempting. Keith's pushing for it. He's actually trying to put people off coming here, so that there's no profit in the course staying open.'

'That puts me off selling, for a start.'

I smiled. 'Me, too.'

'So?'

'So if we get a brilliant new stand built – and by brilliant, I don't mean huge, but clever, so that the crowds like to come here – our shares should pay us more regular dividends than they have in the past.'

'You think, then, that horse racing as such will go on?'

'It's lasted in England so far for more than three hundred years. It's survived scandals and frauds and all sorts of accidental disasters. Horses are beautiful and betting's an addiction. I'd build a new stand.'

'You're romantic!' she teased.

'I'm not deeply in debt,' I said, 'and Keith may be.'

'William told me Keith was the biggest disappointment of his life.'

I looked at her in sudden speculation, fifty questions rising like sharp rays of light; but before I could do anything constructive, a racecourse official came to my side and said Colonel Gardner would like me to go urgently to the office.

'Don't go away without telling me how to find you,' I begged Perdita Faulds.

'I'll be here all afternoon,' she reassured me. 'If I miss you, this is the phone number of my Oxford shop. That'll reach me.' She gave me a business card. 'And how do I find *you*?'

I wrote my mobile phone number and the Sussex house number on the back of another of her cards, and left her contentedly continuing with her champagne while I went to find out what crisis had overcome us.

The trouble, essentially, was the state of Rebecca's nerves. She was pacing up and down outside the office and gave me an angry stare as I went past her and through the door, and I'd never seen her look more unstable.

Roger and Oliver were inside, steaming and grinding their teeth.

'You are not going to believe this,' Roger said tautly, when he saw me. 'We have all the normal sort of troubles – we've caught a would-be nobbler in the stables, the lights on the Tote board have fused and there's a man down in Tattersalls having a heart attack – and we also have Rebecca creating the father and mother of a stink because there are no hangers in the women jockeys' changing tent.'

'*Hangers?*' I said blankly.

'Hangers. She says they can't be expected to hang their clothes and colours up on the floor. We gave her a table, a bench, a mirror, a basin, running water and a drain. And she's creating about *hangers.*'

'Er ...' I said helplessly. 'How about a rope, for their clothes?'

Roger handed me a bunch of keys. 'I wondered if you'd take the jeep down to my house – it's locked, my wife's somewhere here but I can't find her – and bring back some hangers. Take the clothes off them. It's madness, but do you mind? Can you do it? Will your legs be up to it?'

'Sure,' I said, relieved. 'I thought it was serious, when you sent for me.'

'She's riding Conrad's horse in the first race. It would be serious enough for him – and for all of us – if she went completely off her rocker.'

'OK.'

Outside, I found Dart trying without success to pacify his sister. He gave it up when he saw me and walked with me to the jeep, asking where I was going. When I said to fetch some hangers he was at first incredulous and then offered to help, so I drove both of us on the errand.

'She gets into states,' Dart said, excusing her.

'Yes.'

'I suppose it's a strain, risking your life every day.'

'Perhaps she should stop.'

'She's just blowing off steam.'

We disunited Roger's clothes from a whole lot of hangers and on the way back called at the bus, where I opened the door and stuck my head into a football roar, maximum decibels.

'Toby,' I yelled, 'are you all right?'

'Yes, Dad.' He turned the volume down slightly. 'Dad, they had Stratton Park on the telly! They showed all the flags and the bouncing castle and everything. They said people should come here, the racing was going ahead and it was a real Bank Holiday day out.'

'*Great!*' I said. 'Do you want to come up to the paddock?'

'No, thanks.'

'OK, see you later.'

I told Dart about the television coverage. 'That was Oliver's doing,' he said. 'I heard him screwing the arms off those camera guys to get them rolling. I must say, he and Roger and you, you've done a fantastic job here.'

'And Henry.'

'Father says the family got you wrong. He says they shouldn't have listened to Keith.'

'Good.'

'He's worried about Rebecca, though.'

So would I be, I thought, if she were my daughter.

Dart gave the hangers to his sister who stalked off with them, tight mouthed. He also, to save my legs, he said, took the jeep's keys back into the office and told Roger and Oliver the big top had been news. Finally he suggested a beer and a sandwich in the bar so that he could skip the Stratton lunch. 'Keith, Hannah, Jack and Imogen,' he said. 'Yuk.' Then, 'Did you know the police took my old wheels away for testing?'

'No,' I said, looking for signs of worry on Dart's face, and finding none. 'I didn't know.'

'It's a bloody nuisance,' he said. 'I've had to rent a car. I told the police I would send them the bill and they just sneered. I'm fed up with this bomb thing.' He grinned at my walking stick. 'You must be, too.'

Perdita Faulds had left the bar and was nowhere in sight when we reached it. Dart and I drank and munched and I told him I'd read a recipe once for curing falling hair.

He looked at me suspiciously. 'You're taking the mickey.'

'Well,' I said judiciously, 'it might be on a par with tearing off tree barks to cure malaria, or using mould growing on jelly to cure blood poisoning.'

'Quinine,' he said, nodding, 'and penicillin.'

'Right. So this cure for baldness came from a Mexican medicine-man's handbook written in 1552.'

'I'll try *anything*,' he said.

'You grind up some soap plant,' I said, 'and you boil it in dog's urine, and you throw in a tree frog or two and some caterpillars . . .'

'You're a *shit*,' he said bitterly.

'That's what the book says.'

'You're a bloody liar.'

'The Aztecs swore by it.'

'I'll throw you to Keith,' he said. 'I'll stamp on you myself.'

'The book's called *The Barberini Codex*. It was all serious medicine five hundred years ago.'

'What is soap plant, then?'

'I don't know.'

'I wonder,' he said thoughtfully, 'if it works.'

We leaned on the parade ring rails before the first race, Dart and I, watching his father and mother, Conrad and Victoria, talking to their jockey-daughter, Rebecca, in a concerned little group that also included the horse's trainer. Other concerned little groups similarly eyed their four-legged performers stalking patiently around them, and hid their wild hopes under judicious appraisals.

'He won last time out,' Dart said, appraising judiciously from his own sidelines. 'She can ride well, you know, Rebecca.'

'She must do, to get so high on the list.'

'She's two years younger than me, and I can't remember

when she wasn't besotted by ponies. I got kicked by one once, and that was enough for me, thanks very much, but Rebecca . . .' his voice held the familiar mix of exasperation and respect, 'she's broken her bones as if they were fingernails. I can't imagine *ever* wanting *anything* as much as she wants to win.'

'I think,' I said, 'that all top achievers are like that, at least for a while.'

He turned his head, assessing me. 'Are you?'

'Afraid not.'

'Nor am I.'

'So we stand here,' I said, 'watching your sister.'

Dart said, 'You have such a *damned* clear way of looking at things.'

The signal was given for the jockeys to mount. Rebecca, wearing the distinctive Stratton colours of green and blue checks on the body with mismatched orange and scarlet sleeves and cap, swung her thin lithe shape into the saddle as softly as thistledown landing. The excessive strain brought on by the trivial annoyance of a lack of hangers had vanished: she looked cool, concentrated, a star on her stage, in command of her performance.

Dart watched her with all his ambivalent feelings showing; the female sibling whose prowess outshone him, whom he admired and resented, understood but couldn't love.

Conrad's runner, Tempestexi, a chestnut gelding, looked, by comparison with some of the others in the ring, to have a long back and short legs. The two-mile hurdle race, according to the card, was for horses that hadn't won a hurdle race before January 1st. Tempestexi, who had won one since, carried a 7lb penalty for doing so, but had, all the same, been made favourite.

I asked Dart how many racehorses his father had in training and he said five, he thought, though they came and went a bit, he said, according to their legs.

'Tendons,' he said succinctly. 'Horses' tendons are as temperamental as violin strings. Tempestexi is Father's current white-hot hope. No leg problems, so far.'

'Does Conrad bet?'

'No. Mother does. And Keith. He'd have put the Dower House on this one, if he'd owned it – the Dower House, that is. He'll have bet anything he can lay his hands on. If Rebecca doesn't win, Keith will kill her.'

'That wouldn't help.'

Dart laughed. 'You of all people must know that logic never interferes with instinct, in Keith.'

The horses streamed out of the parade ring on their way to the course, and Dart and I went to watch the race from the makeshift stands Henry had bolted together from the circus tiers.

The steps were packed to the point that I hoped Henry's boast of infallible safety would hold up. Crowds, in fact, had poured through the gates like a river during the past hour and had spread over the tarmac and into the big top and down to the betting rings in chattering thousands. The dining rooms were full, with customers waiting. There were crushes in all the bars and long lines at the Tote, and the booths by the entrance had sold out of regular racecards. The big office copier was churning out paper substitutes and running red-hot. Oliver, glimpsed briefly, sweated ecstatically.

'The television did it,' he said, gasping.

'Yes, your work, well done.'

Waiting for the race to start I said to Dart, 'Perdita Faulds is here at the races.'

'Oh? Who is she?'

'The other non-Stratton shareholder.'

He showed minimal interest. 'Didn't someone mention her at the family board meeting the other day? Why did she come?'

'Like me, to see what was happening about her investment.'

Dart cast it out of his mind. 'They're off!' he said. 'Now, come on, Rebecca.'

It looked an uneventful race from the stands, though no doubt not from the saddle. The runners stayed bunched throughout the first circuit, clattered safely over the flights of hurdles, swept in an overlapping ribbon past the winning post for the first time and set off again into the country.

Down the far side the less fit, the less speedy, fell back, leaving Rebecca in third place round the last bend. Dart's genuine wish for his sister to win couldn't be doubted. He made scrubbing, encouraging movements with his whole body, and when she reached second place coming towards the last flight he raised his voice like the rest and yelled to her to win.

She did. She won by less than a length, accelerating, a thin streak of neat rhythmic muscle against an opponent who flapped his elbows and his whip but couldn't hang onto his lead.

The crowd cheered her. Dart oozed reflected glory. Everyone streamed down towards the winner's unsaddling enclosure where Dart joined his parents and Marjorie in a kissing and back-slapping orgy. Rebecca, pulling off the saddle, ducked the sentiment and dived purposefully into the Portakabin weighing room to sit on the scales. Very professional, fairly withdrawn; rapt in her own private world of risk, effort, metaphysics and, this time, success.

I took myself over to the office door and found four boys faithfully reporting there.

'Did you have lunch OK?' I asked.

They nodded. 'Good job we went early. There were no tables left, pretty soon.'

'Did you see Rebecca Stratton win that race?'

Christopher said reproachfully, 'Even though she called us brats, we wanted to back her with you, but we couldn't find you.'

I reflected. 'I'll pay you whatever the Tote pays on a minimum bet.'

Four grins rewarded me. 'Don't lose it,' I said.

Perdita Faulds and Penelope, passing, stopped by my side, and I introduced the children.

'All yours?' Perdita asked. 'You don't look old enough.'

'Started young.'

The boys were staring at Penelope, wide-eyed.

'What's the matter?' she asked. 'Have I got mud on my nose?'

'No,' Alan said frankly, 'you look like Mummy.'

'Like your mother?'

They all nodded, and they moved off with her, as if it were natural, to go and look at the horses walking round for the next race.

'Like your wife, is she, my Pen?' Perdita said.

I dragged my gaze back. Heart thudded. Idiotic.

'Like she was then,' I said.

'And now?'

I swallowed. 'Yes, like now, too.'

Perdita gave me a look born of long, knowing experience. 'You can never go back,' she said.

I would do it again, I thought helplessly. I'd marry with my eyes and find an unsuspected stranger inside the package. Did one never grow up?

I wrenched my mind away from it and said to Perdita, 'Did Lord Stratton happen to know – and tell you – what it was that Forsyth Stratton did that has tied the whole family into knots?'

Her generous red mouth formed an O of amused surprise.

'You don't mess about, do you? Why should I tell you?'

'Because if we're going to save his racecourse, we have to unravel the strings that work the family. They all know things about each other that they use as threats. They blackmail each other to make them do – or not do – what they want.'

Perdita nodded.

'And as a part of that,' I said, 'they pay people off, to keep the Stratton name clean.'

'Yes, they do.'

'Starting with my own mother,' I said.

'No, before that.'

'So you *do* know!'

'William liked to talk,' she said. 'I told you.'

'And . . . Forsyth?'

Penelope and the boys were on their way back. Perdita said, 'If you come to see me in my Swindon shop tomorrow morning, I'll tell you about Forsyth . . . and about the others, if you think up the questions.'

CHAPTER 13

Keith's rage, when he discovered that the runners in the second race would be jumping the open ditch as scheduled, verged on the spectacular.

Henry and I happened to be walking along behind the caterers' tents when the eruption occurred (Henry having had to deal with a leak in the new water main) and we hurried down a caterer's passage towards the source of vocal bellowing and crockery-smashing noises; into the Strattons' private dining room.

The whole family had clearly returned, after their victory, to finish their lunch and toast the winner, and typically, but perhaps luckily, had invited no outsiders to join them.

Keith, legs astride, shoulders back, mane of hair flying, had flung the entire dining table over and swept an arm along the line of bottles and glasses on the serving sideboard. Tablecloths, knives, plates, cheese, champagne, coffee, whipped-cream puddings, lay in a mess on the floor. Wine poured out of opened bottles. The waitresses pressed their hands to their mouths and various Strattons grabbed napkins and tried to clean debris from laps, trousers, legs.

'Keith!' screeched Conrad, equally furious, quivering on his feet, thunderous as a bull before charging. 'You *lout*.'

Victoria's cream silk suit ran with coffee and Bordeaux. 'I'm presenting the Cup,' she yelled, wailing, 'and *look* at me.'

Marjorie sat calm, unspattered, icily furious. Ivan, beside her, said, 'I say, Keith, I say . . .'

Hannah, trifle dripping down her legs, used unfilial language to her father and also to her son, who turned ineffectively to help her. The thin woman who sat beyond Ivan, unconcernedly continuing a relationship with a large snifter of brandy, I provisionally guessed to be Imogen Dart wasn't there. Forsyth, sullenly seeming to be relieved that someone other then he was the focus of family obloquy, made his way to the doorway into the main passage, where we'd arranged a flap of canvas that could be fastened across to give privacy.

People were pulling the flap aside, trying to see in, to find out the cause of the commotion. Forsyth shouldered his way out, telling people rudely to mind their own business which, of course, they didn't.

The whole scene was laughable but, not far below the farcical surface, as each family member uneasily knew, lay the real cause of destructive violence, the melt-down in Keith that had so far gained most expression in hitting his wives and taking a belt at Lee Morris, but would one day go too far for containment.

Marjorie was holding in plain sight the copy of Harold Quest's confession; the cause of the débâcle.

Keith suddenly seized it out of her hand, snatched the brandy glass rudely from his wife, poured the alcohol over the letter, threw down the glass and with economic speed produced a lighter from his pocket and put a flame to the paper. Harold Quest's confession flared brightly and curled to ash and was dropped and stamped on, Keith triumphant.

'It was only a copy,' Marjorie said primly, intentionally goading.

'I'll kill you,' Keith said to her, his lower jaw rigid. His gaze rose over her and fastened on me. The animosity intensified, found a more possible, a more preferred target. 'I *will* kill *you*,' he said.

In the small following silence I turned and went out the

back way with Henry, leaving the poor waitresses to clear up the garbage.

'That was only half funny,' Henry said thoughtfully.

'Yes.'

'You want to be careful. He might just kill you next time. And *why*? *You* didn't bring Harold Quest here. *You* didn't suss out the hamburger.'

'No,' I sighed. 'My pal Dart Stratton says logic never interferes with instinct, in Keith. But then, half the world's like that.'

'Including murderers,' Henry said.

'How inflammable,' I asked, 'is the big top?'

Henry stopped walking. 'You don't think he'd try –? He's pretty handy with that lighter. And burning the fence . . .' Henry looked angry but after a moment shook his head.

'This big top won't go on fire,' he said positively. 'Everything I brought here is flame-retardant, flame-resistant or can't burn, like all the metal poles and the pylons. There were disasters in circuses in the past. The regs now are stringent. This big top won't burn by accident. Arson . . . well, I don't know. But we've got extinguishers all over the place, as you know, and I ran a bit of water main up to the roof in a sort of elementary sprinkler system.' He took me along to see. 'That bit of rising main,' he pointed, 'the pressure's pretty good in it. I fed a pipe up and connected it to a garden hose running along inside, below the ridge. The hose has small holes in it. The water squirts out OK.'

'Henry! You're a genius.'

'I had a bit of time yesterday, when you went off to London, and I reckoned the racecourse couldn't afford another calamity like the stands. A good precaution's never wasted, I thought, so I rigged up this very basic sprinkler. Don't know how long it would work. If ever flames got that high, they could melt the hose.' He laughed. 'Also, I, or someone who knows, has to be around to turn the tap on. I had to stick tape and those labels all over it, saying, "DO NOT TOUCH THIS" in case someone turned it on while all the crowds were inside tucking into their smoked salmon sandwiches.'

'My God!'

'Roger knows about it and Oliver, and now you.'

'Not the Strattons?'

'Not the Strattons, I don't trust them.'

Keith, definitely, would have soaked the paying customers to ruin their day.

Henry went on, trying to reassure me. 'But Keith won't actually try to kill you, not after he said in public that he was going to.'

'That wasn't public. That was the Stratton family.'

'But I heard him, and the waitresses did.'

'They would pay off the waitresses and swear you misheard.'

'Do you mean it?'

'I'm certain they've done that sort of thing often. Maybe not for murder, but other crimes, certainly.'

'But . . . what about newspapers?'

'The Strattons are rich,' I said briefly. 'Money will and does buy more than you'd think. Money's for using to get what you want.'

'Well, obviously.'

'The Strattons don't want scandal.'

'But they can't bribe the Press!'

'How about the sources that speak to the Press? How about suddenly blind waitresses with healthy bank balances?'

'Not these days,' he protested. 'Not with our insatiable tabloids.'

'I never thought I'd feel older than you, Henry. The Strattons can outbid the tabloids.'

Henry's mind I knew to be agile, practical, inventive and straight, but of his homelife and background I knew nothing. Henry the giant and I had worked together in harmony over a stretch of years, never intimate, always appreciative; on my part, at least. Henry's junk dealings had found me a whole untouched Adam room once, and dozens of antique fireplaces and door frames. Henry and I did business by telephone – 'Can you find me . . .' or 'I've come across this . . .' These Stratton Park days were the first I'd spent so much in his company and they would, I thought contentedly, lead to a positive friendship.

We rounded the far end of the big top and watched the runners for the second race walk by on their way out onto the track. I found I was liking more and more to watch them, having given them little thought for most of my life. Imagine the world without them, I thought: history itself would have been totally different. Land transport wouldn't have existed. Mediaeval battles wouldn't have been fought. No six hundred to ride into a valley of death. No Napoleon. The seafarers, Vikings and Greeks, might still rule the world.

Horses, fleet, strong, tamable, had been just the right size. I watched the way their muscles moved under the groomed coats; no architect anywhere could have designed anything as functional, economical, supremely proportioned.

Rebecca rode by, adjusting her stirrup leathers, her attentions inward on the contest ahead. I had never wanted to ride, but at that moment I envied her: envied her skill, her obsession, her absolute commitment to a physical – animal – partnership with a phenomenal creature.

People could bet; they could own, train, breed, paint, admire, write about thoroughbreds: the primaeval urge to be first, in both runner and rider, was where the whole industry started. Rebecca on horseback became for me the quintessence of racing.

Henry and I stood on the ex-circus stands and watched the race together. The whole field jumped the restored open ditch without faltering. Rebecca finished well back, not taking part in the finish.

Henry said racing didn't grab him like rugger and went away to patrol his defences.

The afternoon passed. 'There were the usual disasters,' Roger said, dashing about.

I came across the racecourse doctor taking a breather between casualties. 'Come to see me on Thursday,' he suggested. 'I'll take all those clips out. Save you waiting around in the hospital.'

'Great.'

Oliver, in the office, dealt with enquiries and wrathful trainers and arranged for a Stewards' enquiry into an objection to the winner to take place in the inner office among the computers, copier and coffee machine.

On the whole, the pros whose business was everyone else's pleasure made allowances for the stop-gap provisions, though it was interesting, as the day wore on, that they took the truly remarkable conjured-up arrangements more and more for granted and began to complain about the cramped weighing room and the inadequate view from the improvised stands.

'You give them a man-made miracle,' Roger complained, 'and they want the divine.'

'Human nature.'

'Sod them.'

I spent some of the time with Perdita and Penelope, feeling disjointedly crazy, and some with my sons, thrust back into adulthood and paternity; but no more, thankfully, being told I was for the fairly immediate chop.

I did speak to Marjorie, who stood in for Victoria in the Cup-presenting ceremony, her neat upright little figure being protected through the throng by the solicitous bulks of Conrad and Ivan. Photographs flashed, a hand-held microphone produced fuzzy noises; the winning owners floated, the trainer looked relieved, the jockey prosaic (his tenth pair of cufflinks) and the horse, excited. A regular prizewinning; irregular day.

'Lee,' Marjorie said, beginning to make her way back to the big top but pausing when she saw me nearby. 'A cup of tea?'

I went with her obediently, though the tea idea was quickly abandoned in favour of vintage Pol Roger from Stratton Hays' cellars. Dismissing Conrad and Ivan, she took me alone into the tidied up dining room, where the trusting staff had righted the table and laid it freshly with crustless cucumber sandwiches and small coffee eclairs.

Marjorie sat on one of the chairs and came straight to the point.

'How much is this all costing?' she peremptorily enquired.

'What is it worth?'

'Sit down, sit down.' She waited while I sat. 'It is worth, as you well know, almost anything your huge friend asks. We have been *flooded* with compliments all afternoon. People love this tent. The future of the racecourse, no less, has been saved. We may not make a cash profit on the day, but we have banked priceless goodwill.'

I smiled at her business metaphor.

'I have told Conrad,' she said collectedly, 'not to quibble about the bills. Oliver Wells is so busy, I'm giving you this message for him instead. I've called for a family meeting on Wednesday, the day after tomorrow. Can you and Oliver and the Colonel draw up a list of costs and expenses for me before then?'

'Probably.'

'Do it,' she said, but more with persuasion than bossiness. 'I've told Conrad to instruct our accountants to present an up-to-date realistic audit of the racecourse as soon as possible and not to wait for the end of its financial year. We need a survey of our present position, and it's imperative we sort out what we intend to do next.' The clear voice paused briefly. 'You have shown us today that we should not rebuild the old stand as it was before. You have shown us that people respond to a fresh and unusual environment. We must build some *light-hearted* stands.'

I listened in awe. Eighty-four, was she? Eighty-five? A delicate-looking tough-minded old lady with a touch of tycoon.

'Will you come to the meeting?' she asked, far from sure.

'I expect so.'

'Will Mrs Faulds?'

I looked at her dryly. 'She said you recognised her.'

'Yes. What did she say to you?'

'Not a great deal. She said chiefly that if the racecourse can be run prosperously, she won't press for the land to be sold.'

'Good.' Marjorie's interior relief surfaced in a subtle loosening of several facial muscles that I hadn't realised were tight.

'I don't think she'll want to come to the meeting,' I added. 'She had read about the family disputes in the newspapers. She just wanted to know how things stood.'

'The newspapers!' Marjorie shook her head in disgust. 'I don't know how they heard of our arguments. Those reports were disgraceful. We cannot *afford* any more discord. What's more, we cannot afford *Keith*.'

'Perhaps,' I said tentatively, 'you should just let him ... sink.'

'Oh, no,' she said at once. 'The family name ...'

The dilemma remained, age old; unresolvable, from their point of view.

At the end of the day the crowds straggled off, leaving litter in tons. The big top emptied. The caterers packed their tables and chairs and departed. The afternoon sun waned in deep yellow on the horizon, and Henry, Oliver, Roger and I sat on upturned plastic crates in the deserted expanse of the members' bar, drinking beer from cans and holding anti-climactic post-mortems.

The five boys roamed around scavenging, Toby having joined them belatedly. The Strattons had left. Outside, horseboxes were loading the last winner and losers. The urgency was over, and the striving, and the glories. The incredible weekend was folding its wings.

'And for our next act ...' I declaimed like a ringmaster, waving an arm.

'We go home to bed,' Roger said.

He drove me and the boys good-naturedly down to the bus, but in fact he himself returned to the buildings and the tents to oversee the clearing up, the locking, and the security arrangements for the night.

The boys ate supper and squabbled over a video. I read Carteret's diaries, yawning. We all phoned Amanda.

Carteret wrote:

> Lee persuaded me to go to an evening lecture on the effects of bombing on buildings. (The I.R.A. work, more than air-strikes.) Boring, really. Lee said sorry for wasting my time. He's got a thing about tumbledown buildings. I

tell him it won't get him bonus points here. He says
there's life after college . . .

'Dad,' Neil said, interrupting.

'Yes?'

'I asked Henry the riddle.'

'What riddle?'

'Do you know a rabbit from a raceway?'

I gazed in awe at my super-retentive small son. 'What did
he say?'

'He said who wanted to know. I said you did, and he just
laughed. He said if anyone knew the answer, you did.'

I said, smiling, 'It's like the Mad Hatter's riddle in *Alice in
Wonderland*: "What's the difference between a raven and a
writing desk?" There's no answer at all.'

'That's a silly riddle.'

'I agree. I always thought so.'

Neil, whose taste for Pinocchio had won the video fight (for
perhaps the tenth time) returned his attention to the nose that
grew longer with lying. Keith's nose, I reckoned, would in
that line of fantasy make Cyrano de Bergerac a non-starter.

Carteret's diary:

> The 'great' Wilson Yarrow was there, asking questions to
> show off his own brilliance. Why the staff think he's so
> marvellous is a mystery. He sucks up to them all the
> time. Lee will get himself chucked out for heresy if the
> staff hear his comments on Gropius. Better stop writing
> this and get on with my essay on political space.

Pages and pages followed in a mixture of social events and
progress on our courses: no more about Yarrow. I fast-
forwarded in time to the partially ripped note-book and read
onwards from the exclamation marks about the Epsilon prize.
There seemed, for all my searching, to be only one further
comment, though it was damning enough in its way.

Carteret wrote:

> More rumours about Wilson Yarrow. He's being allowed
> to complete his diploma! They're saying someone else's

design was entered in his name for the Epsilon prize *by mistake*!! Then old Hammond says a brilliant talent like that shouldn't be extinguished for one little lapse! How's that for giving the game away? Discussed it with Lee. He says choice comes from inside. If someone chooses to cheat once, they'll do it again. What about consequences, I asked? He said Wilson Yarrow hadn't considered consequences because he'd acted on a belief that he would get away with it. No one seems to know – or they're not telling – how the 'mistake' was spotted. The Epsilon has been declared void for this year. Why didn't they give it to whoever's design it was that won it?

* Just heard a red hot rumour. The design was by Mies!!! Designed in 1925, but never built. *Some* mistake!!!

I read on until my eyes ached over his handwriting but nowhere had Carteret confirmed or squashed the red-hot rumour.

One long ago and disputed bit of cheating might be interesting, but even Marjorie wouldn't consider Carteret's old diaries a sufficient lever, all these years later, especially as no action had been taken at the time. To call Wilson Yarrow a cheat now would sail too close to slander.

I couldn't see any way that a dead ancient scandal, even if it were true, could have been used by Yarrow to persuade or coerce Conrad into giving him, alone, the commission for new stands.

Sighing, I returned the diaries to their carrier bag, watched the last five minutes of *Pinocchio* and settled my brood for the night.

On Tuesday morning, with pressing errands of their own to see to, the Gardners took me and the boys with them to Swindon, dumping us outside the launderette and arranging a rendezvous later at a hairdressing salon called Smiths.

While almost our entire stock of clothes circled around washing and drying, we made forays to buy five pairs of trainers (difficult – and expensive as, for the boys, the colours and shapes of the decorative flashing had to be *right*, though to my eyes the 'Yuk, Dad' shoes looked much the same), and after that (making a brief stop to buy a large bag of apples), I marched them relentlessly towards haircuts.

Their total opposition to this plan vanished like fruit cake the second they stepped over the threshold of Smiths, as the person who greeted us first there was Penelope Faulds. Blonde, tall, young Penelope, slapping hands with my children and deconstructing my every vestige of maturity.

Smiths, which I had expected somehow to be quiet and old fashioned because of its age, proved to have skipped a couple of generations and now presented a unisex front of street cred, blow-dries and rap music. Hair-styles in photographs on the walls looked like topiary. Chrome and multiple mirrors abounded. Young men in pigtails talked like Eastenders. I felt old there, and my children loved it.

Penelope herself cut their hair, consulting with me first about Christopher's instructions to have his head almost shaved, leaving only a bunch of his natural curls falling over his forehead. 'Compromise,' I begged her, 'or his mother will slay me. It's she who normally gets their hair cut.'

She smiled deliciously. I desired her so radically that the pain made a nonsense of falling-in roofs. She cut Christopher's hair short enough to please him, too short to my eyes. It was *his hair*, he said. Tell that to your mother, I told him.

Toby, interestingly, asked for his cut to be 'ordinary': no statement of rebellion. Vaguely pleased, I watched Penelope fasten a gown round his throat and asked if her mother were anywhere about.

'Upstairs,' she said, pointing. 'Go up. She said she was expecting you.' She smiled. Hop, skip and jump, heart. 'I won't make your kids look freaks,' she promised. 'They've got lovely shaped heads.'

I went upstairs reluctantly to find Perdita, and it was there, out of sight, that the old order persisted: the ladies with their hair in rollers, sitting under driers reading *Good Housekeeping*.

Perdita, vibrant in black trousers, a bright pink shirt and a long rope of pearls, led me past the grandmotherly customers who watched a large man with a walking stick go by as if he'd come from a different species.

'Never mind my old loves,' Perdita teased me, beckoning me into a sheltered be-chintzed sanctum on the far side of the beautification. 'Tanqueray do you?'

I agreed a little faintly that it would, and she pressed into my hand a large glass holding lavish gin and little tonic with tinkling ice and a thick slice of lemon. Eleven-fifteen on a Tuesday morning. Ah, well.

She closed the door between us and the old loves. 'They have ears like bats for gossip,' she said blithely. 'What do you want to know?'

I said tentatively, 'Forsyth . . .?'

'Sit down, dear,' she commanded, sinking into a rose-printed armchair and waving me into its pair.

She said, 'I've thought all night about whether I should tell you these things. Well, half the night. Several hours. William always trusted me not to repeat what he told me, and I never have. But now . . . I don't really know if he would say I should be silent for ever, but things are different now. Someone blew up his beloved racecourse, and you saved the race meeting yesterday and I think . . . I really do think that, like you said, you can't finish the job for him unless you know what you're up against, so, well, I don't think he'd mind.' She drank some gin. 'I'll tell you about Forsyth first, and then we'll see.'

'All right,' I said.

She sighed deeply and began, gathering ease and momentum gradually as she went along.

'Forsyth,' she said, 'set out to defraud an insurance company, and the family had to come up with the whole pay-off or visit him behind bars for God knows how many years.'

'I thought,' I said slowly, 'it might be something like that.'

'William said . . .' She paused, still a little inhibited; uncertain, despite her decision. 'It seems odd to be telling you these things.'

I nodded.

'I wouldn't say a word if he were alive, but I don't care so much for his family. I often told him he ought to let them suffer properly for their criminal actions, but he wouldn't hear of it. Keeping the Stratton name clean . . . a sort of obsession.'

'Yes.'

'Well,' she took a deep breath, 'about a year ago, Forsyth borrowed a fortune from the bank, guaranteed by Ivan – his father – on the security of the garden centre, and he started buying and selling radio-controlled lawn mowers. Ivan's no great businessman, but at least he listens to his manager and goes to Conrad or William . . . used to go, poor lamb . . . for advice, and has proper audits . . . but that know-it-all Forsyth, he went his own way and wouldn't listen to anybody and he bought a huge warehouse on a mortgage and thousands of lawn mowers that were supposed to cut the grass while you sat and watched, but they were already going out-of-date when he signed a contract for them, and also they kept breaking down. The people who sold them to him must have been laughing themselves sick, William said. William said Forsyth talked about "cornering the market", which no one can ever do, William said, in anything. It's a short cut to bankruptcy. So there is Forsyth with this vast stock he has contracted to buy but can't sell, paying a huge mortgage he can't afford, with the bank bouncing his cheques and Ivan facing having to cover this enormous bank loan . . . and you can guess what happened.' She paid attention to her drink.

'A little fire?' I suggested, swirling the ice round in my own glass.

'*Little!* Half an acre of it. Warehouse, mowers, radio controls, all cinders. William said everyone took it for granted it was arson. The insurance company sent investigators. The police were all over the place. Forsyth went to pieces and confessed to William in private.'

She paused, sighing.

'So, what happened?' I asked.

'Nothing.'

'*Nothing?*'

'No. It's not a crime to set fire to your own property. William paid it all off. He didn't claim the insurance. He paid off the warehouse mortgage with penalties and sold the land it had stood on. Paid off all the contracts for the rotten mowers, to avoid lawsuits. Repaid the money the bank had lent, plus all the interest, to save Ivan losing the garden centre to the guarantee. It all cost an *enormous* amount. William told all the family that they would each inherit a good deal less from him because of Forsyth's business venture and criminal folly. None of them would speak to Forsyth after that. He whined to William about it and William told him it was Coventry or jail, and to be grateful. Forsyth said Keith had told him to burn the warehouse. Keith said Forsyth was lying. But William told me it was probably true. He said Keith always said you could get rid of things by burning them.'

Like fences at open ditches, I thought. And grandstands, by blowing them up?

'There!' she said, as if surprised at herself for the ease of the telling, 'I've told you! I can't feel William standing at my shoulder telling me to shut up. In fact . . . it's the other way round. I think he *approves*, dear, wherever he is.'

I wasn't going to question that feeling. I said, 'At least Forsyth's was a straightforward fraud. No rapes or drugs involved.'

'Yes, dear, *much* harder to cover those up.'

Some nuance in her voice, a quiet amusement, made me ask, 'But not impossible?'

'You're encouraging me to be wicked!'

Once started, however, she'd been enjoying the saga.

'I won't tell them,' I said. 'I'll be like you, with William's secrets.'

I don't know if she believed me. I don't know that I meant what I said. It encouraged her, all the same, to go on.

'Well . . . there was Hannah . . .'

'What about her?' I prompted, when she paused.

'She grew up so bitter.'

'Yes, I know.'

'No self-esteem, you see, dear.'

'No.'

'Keith never let her forget she'd been abandoned by her mother. By Madeline, poor dear. Madeline used to cry and tell me she'd give anything for a miscarriage, but we were both young then and we didn't know how to get her an abortion . . . you had to *know* someone in those days as you'd never get a family doctor to help you. No one would ever help a young married woman get rid of her first child. Keith got to hear she'd been *asking* about it and he flew into a terrible rage and knocked two of her teeth out.' She drank deeply of gin at the memory. 'William told me that Keith told Hannah her mother had wanted to abort her. Can you believe it? Keith had always been cruel, but saying that to your own daughter! He wanted Hannah to hate Madeline, and she did. William said he tried for Madeline's sake to love Hannah and bring her up properly, but Keith was there, poisoning her mind, and she was never a sweet little girl, William said, but always sullen and spiteful.'

'Poor Hannah.'

'Anyway, she grew up very pretty in a sharp sort of way, but William said young men were put off when they got to know her and she felt more and more rejected and hated everybody, and then she fell for this gypsy and let him have sex with her.' Perdita shrugged, sighing. 'William said he wasn't even a proper Romany, just a rough wanderer with a police record for thieving. William said he couldn't understand Hannah, but it was low self-esteem, dear. Low self-esteem.'

'Yes.'

'Well, she got pregnant, of course. And this gypsy, he knew a good thing when it was shoved under his nose. He turned up on Keith's doorstep demanding money, else he'd go round the village telling everyone how he'd got Keith's posh daughter in the family way, and Keith knocked him down and kicked him and burst one of his kidneys.'

Hell, I thought, I'd been lucky.

'Keith told William. Those three boys always loaded their troubles onto their father. William paid off the gypsy, and it cost ten times as much as the gypsy had been asking from Keith in the first place.'

'Dire,' I said.

'So Jack was born, and he didn't have much chance either of growing up decent. Hannah dotes on him. William, of course, paid and paid for his upbringing.'

'William told you all this?'

'Oh yes, dear. Not all at once, like I told you. In little bits. Sort of squeezed out of him, over the years. He would come to me very tired of them all, and unburden some of his thoughts, and we'd have a little gin and – if he felt like it, well, *you know*, dear – and he'd say he felt better, and go off home . . .'

She sighed deeply for times past.

'Conrad,' she said surprisingly, 'years ago, he got addicted to heroin.'

'Can't believe it!'

Perdita nodded. 'When he was young. Kids nowadays, they know they face terrible dangers all the time from drugs. When Conrad was twenty, he thought it a great adventure, William said. He was at university. He was with another young man, both of them injecting themselves, and his friend had too much, and died. William said there was a terrible stink, but he got Conrad out and hushed it all up and sent him to a very private and expensive clinic for treatment. He got Conrad to write him a letter describing his drug experiences, what he felt and saw when he was high. William didn't show me what Conrad wrote, but he still had the letter. He said Conrad had been cured, and he was proud of him. Conrad didn't go back to university, though. William kept him at home on the estate.'

Ah, I thought, *that* was Marjorie's hammer-lock. Even after so many years, Conrad wouldn't want his youthful indiscretion made public.

Perdita finished her gin and poured some more. 'Freshen your glass?' she asked me.

'No, I'm fine. Do go on, I'm riveted.'

She laughed, talking easily now. 'When Keith was about that age, when he was young and handsome and before all these really bad things, he spanked the daughter of one of the farm workers. Pulled down her knickers and spanked her. She hadn't done anything wrong. He said he wanted to know what it felt like. William paid her father a fortune – for those days – to keep him from going to the police. It wasn't a case of rape, though.'

'Bad enough.'

'Keith learned his lesson, William said. After that he only beat and raped his wives. You couldn't get done for it, then.'

The fun went out of her face abruptly, and no doubt out of mine.

'Sorry, dear,' she said. 'I loved Madeline, but it was all forty years ago. And she did get out, and marry again and have you. William said Keith never forgave her for despising him.'

Perhaps because I couldn't help having it on my mind, I said, 'Keith said yesterday that he's going to kill me. Forty years on, he's trying to get even.'

She stared. 'Did he mean it?'

'He meant it when he said it.'

'But dear, you have to take him seriously. He's a violent man. What are you going to do about it?'

I saw that she was basically more interested than anxious, but then it wasn't her life or death problem.

'It's the sight of me that enrages him,' I said. 'I could simply go away. Go home. Trust to luck he wouldn't follow me.'

'I must say, dear, you take it very calmly.'

I'd spent my own semi-wakeful night thinking about it, but I answered her casually. 'It's probably because it seems so unreal. I mean, it's not exactly routine to be discussing the possibility of one's own murder.'

'I do see that,' she agreed. 'So . . . are you going?'

I couldn't answer her, because I still didn't know. I had the five children to consider, and for their sakes I thought I should avoid any further confrontations as much as possible. The manic quality of Keith's hatred for me had been all too evident in the ferocity of his kicks and now he also had the justification for an attack – in his eyes – because of my involvement in the uncovering of Harold Quest and the delivery of Quest's confession to Marjorie. I had thrown him at her feet: he would kill me for it. I did deep down believe he would try and, although I didn't want to, I feared him.

I could probably ensure the boys a live father by leaving the arena.

I could . . . run away.

It was unrealistic, as I'd told Toby, to expect to be steadfast every day of the week. It would be *prudent* to go.

The trouble was that though I might long to, the part of me that ultimately decided things *couldn't* go.

'I wish,' I said fervently, 'that I were able to do as the Strattons do, and *blackmail* Keith into leaving me alone.'

'What a thought, dear!'

'No chance, though.'

She put her head on one side, looking at my face and thinking on my behalf.

'I don't know if it's of much help, dear,' she said slowly, 'but Conrad might have something like that.'

'What sort of thing? What do you mean?'

'I never knew exactly what it was,' she said, 'but William did have a way of keeping Keith in order during the past few years. Only, for once he didn't tell me everything. I'd have said he was too *ashamed* of Keith, that time. He sort of winced away from his name, even. Then one day he said there were things he didn't want people to know, not even after he died, and he thought he would have to give the knowledge to Conrad, his *heir*, you see, dear, so that Conrad could use it if he had to. I'd never seen him so troubled as he was that day. I asked him about it the next time he came to see me, but he still didn't want to talk about it much. He just said he would give a sealed packet to Conrad with very strict instructions about when or if ever it should be opened, and he said he had always done the best he could for his family. The very best.'

She stopped, overcome. 'He was such a *dear*, you know.'

'Yes.'

The secrets were out. Perdita wept a few tears of fondness and felt clearly at peace. I stood up, kissed her cheek, and went downstairs to collect my newly-shorn children.

They looked great. Penelope's pleased professionalism liquified my senses. The boys laughed with her, loving her easily, and I, who ached for her body, paid for their haircuts (despite her protestations) and thanked her, and took my sons painfully away.

'Can we go back there, Dad?' they asked.

I promised, 'Yes, one day,' and wondered 'Why not?' and 'Perhaps she would love me' and thought that the children liked her anyway, and fell into a hopeless jumble of self-justification, and was ready to dump my unsatisfactory marriage, which so recently, on the train, I had prayed to preserve.

The Gardners picked us up and took the clean clothes, the apples, the new trainers and the haircuts back to the racecourse and ordinary life.

In the evening we telephoned Amanda. At eight o'clock, she sounded languorously sleepy.

I spent a long night unhappily, thinking both of my own obligations and desires, but also of Keith and whatever he might be plotting. I searched for ways to defeat him. I thought of fear and the need for courage, and felt unready and inadequate.

CHAPTER 14

By Wednesday morning Henry had gone home in his last truck, leaving everything so far accomplished ready for next time, and promising future improvements.

On Tuesday the flags over the big top had been furled into storage bags by ropes and pulleys and winches. The lights and the fans were switched off. The caterers' side-tents were laced tight, giving no casual access. The fire extinguishers remained in place, scarlet sentinels, unused. Henry's man and some of the groundsmen had scrubbed the tramp of a few thousand feet off the flooring with brooms and hoses.

On Wednesday morning Roger and I walked down the centre aisle, desultorily checking the big empty rooms to each side. No chairs, no tables; a few plastic crates. The only light was daylight from outside, filtering through canvas and the peach roofing, and changing from dull to bright and to dull again as slow clouds crossed the sun.

'Quiet, isn't it?' Roger said.

A flap of canvas somewhere rattled in the wind but all else was silent.

'Hard to believe,' I agreed, 'how it all looked on Monday.'

'We had the final gate figures yesterday afternoon,' Roger said. 'The attendance was eleven per cent up on last year.

Eleven per cent! And in spite of the stands being wrecked.'

'Because of them,' I said. 'Because of the television coverage.'

'Yes, I suppose so.' He was cheerful. 'Did you see the papers yesterday? 'Plucky Stratton Park.' Goo like that. Couldn't be better!'

'The Strattons,' I said, 'said they were holding a meeting this morning. Do you know where?'

'Not here, as far as I've heard. There's only the office,' he said doubtfully, 'and it's really too small. Surely they'll tell you where, if they're meeting.'

'I wouldn't bet on it.'

We walked slowly back towards the office, unusually idle; and Dart in his beaten-up car drove onto the tarmac.

'Hello,' he said easily, climbing out, 'am I the first?'

Roger explained about his lack of instructions.

Dart's eyebrows rose. 'When Marjorie said meeting, I took it for granted she meant here.'

The three of us continued towards the office, amicably.

Dart said, 'The police gave me my wheels back, as you see, but it's a wonder I'm not in the slammer. A matter of time, I dare say. They've decided I blew up the stands.'

Roger paused briefly in mid-stride, astounded. '*You?*'

'Like, my car came up positive for HIV, hashish, mad cow disease, dirty finger-nails, you name it. Their dogs and their test-tubes went mad. Alarm bells all over the place.'

'Nitrates,' I interpreted.

'You've got it. The stuff that blew up the stands came to the racecourse in my car. Eight to eight-thirty, Good Friday morning. That's what they say.'

'They can't mean it,' Roger protested.

'Yesterday afternoon they gave me a bloody rough time.' For all his bright manner, it was clear he'd been shaken. 'They hammered away at where did I get the stuff, this P.E.4 or whatever. My accomplices, they kept saying. Who were they? I just goggled at them. Made a weak joke or two. They said it was no laughing matter.' He made a comic-rueful face. 'They accused me of having been in the army cadet corps at school.

Half a lifetime ago! I ask you! I said so what, it was no secret. I marched up and down for a year or two to please my grandfather, but a soldier by inclination I am definitely *not*. Sorry, Colonel.'

Roger waved away the apology. We all went into the office, standing around, discussing things.

Dart went on. 'They said I would have handled explosives in the cadets. Not me, I said. Let others play at silly buggers. All I really remembered vividly of the cadets is crawling all over a tank once and having nightmares afterwards about falling in front of it. The *speed* it could go! Anyway, I said, talk to Jack, he's in the cadets for the same reason as I was, and he's still at school and hates it, and why didn't they ask *him* where you could get boom boom bang bangs, and they practically clicked on the handcuffs.'

I said, when he paused, 'Do you usually lock your car? I mean, who else could drive it at eight-thirty on a Good Friday morning?'

'Don't you believe me?' he demanded, affronted.

'Yes, I do believe you. I positively do. But if *you* weren't driving it, who was?'

'There *can't* have been explosives in my car.'

'You'll have to face that there were.'

He said obstinately, 'I don't know anything about it.'

'Well . . . er . . . *do* you lock your car?'

'Not often, no. Not when it's outside my own door. I told the police that. I said it was just sitting there and yes, probably I'd left the key in it. I said *anyone* could have taken it.'

Roger and I both looked away from Dart, not wanting to be accusatory. 'Outside his own door' wasn't exactly in plain view of the general car-stealing public. Outside his own door was beside the back entrance of the family pile, Stratton Hays.

'What if it were Keith that took your car?' I asked. 'Would your family loyalty stretch to *him*?'

Dart was startled. 'I don't know what you're talking about. I don't know who took my car.'

'And you don't want to find out.'

He grinned a shade uneasily. 'What sort of pal are you, anyway?'

228

Roger said neutrally, 'Keith swore to Lee only the day before yesterday that he would kill him. There's no doubt he meant it. You can't blame Lee for wanting to know if Keith blew up the stands.'

Dart gave me a long look. I smiled with my eyes.

'I don't think it was Keith,' Dart said finally.

'I search under my bus,' I said to him. 'I won't let my children get into it before I'm as sure as I can be that it's safe.'

'*Lee!*' It was a word full of shock. 'No, he *wouldn't*. Not even Keith. I swear to you . . .' He stopped dead. He had, anyway, told me what I wanted to know. A fragment of truth, even if not whole knowledge.

'From family feeling,' I said, aiming at lightness, 'would you consider helping me find a way of preventing Keith from carrying out his unpleasant threat? To save him and all of you, one might say, from the consequences?'

'Well, of course.'

'Great.'

'But I don't see what I can do.'

'I'll tell you a bit later. At the moment, where is your meeting?'

'Holy hell, yes.'

He picked up the office telephone and got through, it was evident, to his parents' home, where he talked to a cleaner who didn't know where either Lord or Lady Stratton could be found.

'Damn,' Dart said, trying another number. 'Ivan? Where's this bloody meeting? In *your* house? Who's there? Well, tell them I'm late.' He put the receiver down and gave Roger and me the old carefree grin. 'My parents are there, so are Rebecca and Hannah, Imogen and Jack, and they're waiting for Aunt Marjorie. I could hear Keith shouting already. Tell you the truth, I'm not keen to go.'

'Don't then,' I said.

'It's a three-line whip, Ivan says. The whole family. That means I have to.'

Carpe diem, they say. Seize the day. Seize the moment. I'd been handed an opportunity I had been wondering how to achieve.

'How about,' I said, 'if you drive me to your parents' house, tell the cleaner I'm a friend of the family, and leave me there while you go to the meeting?'

He said, puzzled, 'What ever for?'

'For luck,' I said.

'Lee . . .'

'OK. For that look at the grandstand plans that I backed away from last time.'

Roger made the beginnings of a gesture to remind me I'd already seen the plans, and then, to my relief, subsided.

Dart said with furrowed brow, 'I don't honestly understand . . .'

As I didn't *want* him to understand I said confusingly, 'It's for the sake of your family. Like I said, if you're not keen for Keith to bump me off, just trust me.'

He trusted me more than anyone else in his family did, and his easy-going nature won the day.

'If that's what you want,' he agreed, still not understanding – as how could he? 'Do you mean *now*?'

'Absolutely. Except, do you mind going down the back road, as I'd better tell my boys I'll be off the racecourse for a while.'

'You're extraordinary,' Dart said.

'They feel safer if they know.'

Dart looked at Roger, who nodded resignedly. 'Christopher, the eldest, told me that when they're away from home, in that bus, they don't mind their father leaving them, as long as they knows he's gone, and roughly when he'll be back. They look after themselves then without worrying. It does seem to work.'

Dart rolled his eyes comically at the vagaries of my domestic arrangements but accompanied me out to his car. Lying on the front seat, when I went round there, was a large glossy magazine entitled *American Hair Club*, with a young well-thatched model-type man smiling broadly on the cover.

Dart, removing it to the door pocket beside him, said defensively, 'It's all about bonding hair on with polymers. It does seem to be a good idea.'

'Follow it up,' I suggested.

'Don't laugh at me.'

'I'm not.'

He gave me a suspicious look, but drove me down amiably enough to report to my sons, who proved not to be in the bus, where I called to pick up a small tool or two, but to be elbow-deep in flour in Mrs Gardner's kitchen, making her perfect pale fruit cake and eating most of it raw. She gave me a flashing smile and a kiss and said, 'I'm having such *fun* here. Don't hurry back.'

'Where do you find a wife who'll give you five sons?' Dart asked moodily, driving away. 'Who the hell wants a podgy going bald thirty-year-old with no talents?'

'Who wants a good-natured easy-going nice guy not ridden by demons?'

'Me, do you mean?' He was surprised.

'Yes.'

'No girls really want me.'

'Have you asked any?'

'I've *slept* with some, but they all seem to have their sights on huge old Stratton Hays, and they tell me how great it would be for parties there, and one even talked about our daughter's coming-out *ball* . . .'

'And it frightens you?'

'They want to marry a *house*.'

'When I go home,' I said, 'you can come and stay, and I'll see you meet people who've never heard of Stratton Hays, and don't know about your father's title or your own millions, and you can be Bill Darlington, or whatever name you like, and see how you go.'

'Are you *serious*?'

'Yes, I am.' I thought for a moment and said, 'What will happen in your family when Marjorie dies?'

'I don't think about it.'

'You should be married by then. You'll be the head of the family one day, and the others should take that for granted, and respect you and your wife, and look ahead to a good well-rooted future.'

'God,' he protested, 'you don't ask much!'

'You're the best of the Strattons,' I said.

He swallowed; reddened; fell silent. He drove between the gateposts of his parents' ugly striped house and parked, and we walked round to the rear as before.

The back door was unlocked. We went past the plumbing and through into the black-and-white-floored hall, and Dart shouted out loudly, 'Mrs Chinchee? Mrs Chinchee!'

A small middle-aged woman in a pink overall appeared at the top of a long flight of stairs saying, 'Mr Dart, I'm up here.'

'Mrs Chinchee,' Dart called up to her, 'this friend and I will be in the house for a while, but just carry on with the cleaning.'

'Yes, sir. Thank you, sir.'

Dart turned away and Mrs Chinchee retreated towards her upstairs tasks, any awkward curiosity well neutralised.

'Right,' Dart said. 'Now what? I'm not going off to that meeting. You might need me here.'

'OK,' I said, vaguely relieved. 'Now you go out to your car, and if either of your parents should come back sooner than we expect from the meeting, you put your palm on the horn and you give five or six urgent blasts to warn me.'

'You mean . . . I'm just a look-out?'

'If your parents come back, blow the horn, then tell them you've lent me the phone, or the bathroom, or something.'

'I don't like it,' he frowned. 'Suppose they find you looking at the plans?'

'You didn't mind before. You encouraged me, in fact.'

He sighed. 'Yes, I did. I didn't know you so well, then, or care. Look, don't be too long.'

'No.'

Still hesitantly he turned away and went back towards the rear door, and I went on into Conrad's private room where horse pictures crowded the walls and endless shiny bric-à-brac suggested a magpie disposition. Miniature silver horses, antique gold coins on a tray, a tiny gold hunting scene; every surface held treasures.

Without wasting time, I skirted the large cluttered desk and attended to the illegal act of picking someone else's lock, the keyhole fortunately living up to the promise of easy access. The small flat tool I'd brought with me slid obligingly past the ward that guarded the simple works and moved the tongue back from the socket. For picking simple locks, any flat filed-down narrow version of an ordinary key will do the job; the simpler, the better.

The panelled door, so like the walls, pushed easily open, revealing a cupboard large enough to walk into. Leaving the walking stick lying on the desk I limped into the cupboard and pressed a light switch I found there, activating an overhead bulb in a simple shade.

Inside, the walls were lined throughout by shelves, on which stood endless boxes, all of different sizes, colours and shapes, and all unhelpfully unlabelled.

The drawings for the proposed new stands were in clear view, the large folder that Conrad and Wilson Yarrow had taken to Roger's office standing on the floor, leaning against one of the shelf-walls. Untying the pink tape bow that held the folder shut, I took out the drawings, laying them flat, outside, on Conrad's desk.

They were, I had to confess, a sort of window-dressing in case Dart came to find me, as the drawings were those I had already seen, without any additions.

The chief object of my risky enterprise had been to try to find the packet that Perdita had said William, Lord Stratton, third baron, had intended to entrust to Conrad, fourth baron; the packet containing enough dirt on Keith to keep him controlled. If I could but find it, I thought, I could use it perhaps to preserve my own life, promising for instance that if I should die violently, the packet's contents would become public knowledge inexorably.

Faced with the actual array of random containers, I had to re-think. Finding any particular packet in those could take hours, not minutes, particularly as I'd been given no clear description of what sort of packet I was looking for.

I took the lid off a box straight ahead. The box was the size of a large shoe box, made of stiff decorative cardboard in a mottled maroon colour; the sort of box my mother had stored photographs in.

This box held no photographs and no mysterious packets, but only mementoes of social events to do with the hunt of which Conrad was joint master; stiff gilt-edged invitations, menus, order of speeches. A longer box next to it held dozens of loose clippings from newspapers and magazines, all showing either future hunting programmes or accounts of past sport.

Box after box contained the same sort of thing: Conrad was not so much secretive, as Dart had described him, as a compulsive collector of the minutiae of his life, far outdoing Carteret's diaries or my balance-sheet memories as a proof of existence.

I tried to think my way into Conrad's mind, to imagine just where he would have stowed the most sensitive knowledge: and baulked at wondering if I should simply be searching his desk or the bookshelves. If the packet's existence had been enough to worry William Stratton into passing it on, Conrad wouldn't leave it anywhere where an unsuspecting person could open it accidentally. Given the hidden cupboard, for all that its lock was child's play, Conrad would use it.

I hurried along the rows, tipping open the lids, turning over reams of irrelevant papers, finding nothing worth the risk. It was in an ordinary shoe box that I finally came across a gem that I'd been hoping for, though not the ultimate jackpot.

I found myself looking at a black and white glossy photograph of Rebecca: not by any means a portrait, but a picture of her in ordinary clothes, not jockey's colours, holding out her hand and receiving a wad of what looked like banknotes from a man whose back was to the camera, but who wore a trilby hat with hair curling from beneath the brim and a jacket cut from a distinctive check cloth. The background, a shade out of focus, was nevertheless identifiable as a racecourse.

I turned the photograph over: no notes, no provenance, nothing.

In the same box, where the photograph had been lying, lay a recording tape. Apart from those two objects, the box was empty.

The tape, ordinary looking, bore no information as to what it carried.

Even without believing in extra-sensory perception, I felt an unusual frisson over the juxtaposition of photograph and tape, and their sole occupancy of a box. I took them out and put them on Conrad's desk, meaning to look around for a tape-recorder; but meanwhile I returned to the cupboard, still obstinately seeking a packet that was quite likely not there to be found.

Old out-of-date lists of hounds. Years old estate accounts. Boxes packed with Dart's school reports. On the maxim thieves work by, that everyone hides valuable things at the *bottom* of drawers, and that the quickest way of finding profit is to empty the drawer out onto the floor, I began, not emptying exactly, but tipping up all the contents to look at the bottom-most in each box, and it was by doing that that I finally came across an ordinary brown envelope with the single word 'Conrad' written on it.

I drew it out from under a pile of similar envelopes holding ancient insurance policies, long out of date. The 'Conrad' envelope had been slit open. I looked inside without excitement, having by then concluded I'd been clutching at straws, that anything of critical importance would be somewhere else after all. Sighing, I drew out a single sheet of paper with a short note handwritten on it. It said:

Conrad
This is the envelope I told you of. Take care with it.
Knowledge is dangerous.

S.

I looked into the brown envelope further. Inside it lay another brown envelope, this one smaller and unopened, but fatter, with more sheets than one or two inside.

Either it was what I was looking for, or it wasn't. In either case, I was taking it with me, and so as to conceal my pilfering even from Dart, I hid the outer envelope, with letter and unopened envelope inside it, in my clothes: in, to be exact, my close-fitting underpants, against the skin of my abdomen.

Looking round to make sure that all the boxes were closed and appeared undisturbed, I went out to Conrad's desk to put the grandstand plans back in their folder, to prop them where they had been, to relock the cupboard door and beat an undiscovered retreat.

The photograph of Rebecca and the tape lay on top of the plans. Frowning, I unzipped my trousers again and put the photograph face down against my stomach, where the glossy surface stuck to me, the brown envelope outside it, both of them held snugly, too large and flat to slide out down my legs.

It was at that point that I heard voices out in the hall, near, coming nearer.

'But, Father,' Dart's voice reached me loudly, desperately, 'I want you to come and look at the fence along the five-acre covert –'

'Not now, Dart,' Conrad's voice said. 'And why were you not at the meeting?'

Bloody hell, I thought. I snatched up the tape and stuck it into my trousers pocket, and leaned over the set of grandstand plans as if they were the only interest in my life.

Conrad pushed open the door of the room, his until-then friendly expression becoming rapidly surprised and then thunderous, as anyone's would on seeing their most private heartland invaded.

Worse; behind him came Keith.

Conrad looked at his open cupboard with the light shining within, and at me by his desk. His bullish features darkened, his heavy eyebrows lowered, his mouth hardened implacably.

'Explain yourself!' he demanded, his voice harsh and scathing.

'I'm very sorry,' I said awkwardly. I put the plans into the folder and closed it. 'I can't excuse myself. I can only apologise. I do, very sincerely, apologise.'

'It's not good enough!' His anger was deep and all the worse for being alien to his everyday nature, which was not quick to violence, like Keith's. 'That cupboard was locked. I *always* lock it. How did you open it?'

I didn't answer him. The shaved key I'd used was still in the keyhole. I felt appallingly embarrassed, which no doubt he could see.

In an access of real rage he snatched up my walking stick, which lay on his desk, and raised it as if he would strike me.

'Oh no, Conrad,' I said. 'Don't.'

He hesitated, his arm high. 'Why not? Why bloody not? You deserve it.'

'It's not your sort of thing.'

'It's mine,' Keith said loudly. He tugged the walking stick unceremoniously from his unprotesting twin and took a quick slash at my head.

I put an arm up in a reflex parrying action, caught the stick in my hand and, with more force than he'd envisaged, pulled it vigorously towards me. He held on long enough to overbalance, his weight coming forward, and he let go only in order to put both hands on the desk to steady himself.

All three of them, Conrad, Keith and Dart, looked stunned, but in truth that morning I'd felt some of my old strength returning like an incoming, welcome and familiar tide. They'd grown used to my weakness: had been unprepared for anything else.

I leaned on the stick, nevertheless; and Keith straightened himself, and in his eyes promised me death.

I said to Conrad, 'I wanted to look at the plans.'

'But why?'

'He's an architect,' Dart said, defending me, though I wished he hadn't.

'A builder,' contradicted his father.

'Both,' I said briefly. 'I'm very sorry. Very. I should have asked you to give me a sight of them, and not broken in here. I'm humbled . . . mortified . . .' And so I was, but not repentant nor truly ashamed.

Conrad interrupted my grovelling, saying, 'How did you know where the plans were?' He turned to Dart. 'How did he know? He couldn't have found that cupboard by himself. It's practically invisible.'

Dart, looking as uncomfortable as I felt, came round the desk and stopped a pace behind my left shoulder, almost as if sheltering from the parental ire brewing in Conrad.

'You told him where to look,' Conrad accused his son indignantly. 'You *showed* him.'

Dart said weakly, 'I didn't think it would matter. What's the big deal?'

Conrad gaped at him. 'How can I explain if you can't see? But *you*,' he turned to me, 'I'd just begun to think we might trust you.' He shrugged defeatedly. 'Get out, both of you. You disgust me.'

'No,' Keith protested, 'how do you know he's not stolen anything?' He looked round the room. 'You have all these silver and gold pieces in here. He's a *thief*.'

Damn bloody Keith, I thought, smothering panic. I'd stolen better than gold, and intended to keep what I'd taken. Stronger I might be, but couldn't yet swear to the outcome of a straightforward brawl, one against two. *Guile*, I told myself: all I had in the locker.

I raised my chin, until then tucked down in abashment. I looked as unworried as I could manage. I propped the walking stick against the desk, unzipped the front of the easy jacket which had spent several days earlier draped over the chair in Roger's office, slid my arms out of it and threw it to Conrad.

'Search it,' I said.

He caught the bunched cloth. Keith seized the jacket and went through the pockets. No silver or gold. Nothing stolen.

I was wearing my loose wool checked shirt. I unbuttoned the cuffs and undid the front buttons, tugged off the shirt and threw it too to Conrad.

I stood bare to the waist. I smiled. I unzipped my fly and began to unbuckle my belt.

'Trousers next?' I asked Conrad lightly. 'Shoes? Socks? Anything else?'

'No. No.' He was confused. He made an upzipping gesture. 'Put your shirt on again.' He threw the shirt back to me. 'You may be untrustworthy – I'm disappointed, I admit – but not a petty thief.' He turned to Keith. 'Let him go, Keith. Pick your fight somewhere else. Not in this room.'

I put my shirt on and did up the buttons, but left the tails hanging down, like a coat.

Dart said abjectly, 'Father, I'm sorry.'

Conrad made a dismissive gesture. Dart edged round the desk, looking warily at Keith, who still held my jacket.

I followed Dart, limping slowly, the walking stick both a prop and a defence.

Conrad said mordantly, 'I don't want to see you again, Mr Morris.'

I ducked my head, acknowledging fault.

Keith clung onto my jacket.

I was not going to ask for it back. Don't push your luck, I thought: the slightest quiver could erupt the volcano. I was glad simply to reach the door unmolested and to creep through into the hall, and scuttle across it ignominiously, as low in Conrad's esteem as a cockroach.

I held my breath until we were out of the house, but no angry yells stopped us. Dart scurried into his car, now flanked by Keith's Jaguar, and waited impatiently during my slower progress.

He let out an agonised 'Whew' of relief as his engine fired and we sped to the road. 'My God, he was angry.'

'You're a bloody lousy look-out,' I said bitterly. 'Where was my warning?'

'Yes, well, look, *sorry*.'

'Were you asleep?'

'No . . . no . . . I was reading.'

Comprehension arrived. 'You were reading that damned magazine about hair loss!'

'Well . . . I . . .' He grinned, shamefacedly, admitting it.

There was nothing to be done about it. The toots on the horn would have given me time to transfer from Conrad's sanctum to the innocence of the bathroom near the rear entrance. Being caught with my hand in the till, so to speak, had not only been a rotten experience but might set Conrad checking the contents of the boxes. The consequences could be utterly disastrous.

'You took such a long time,' Dart complained. 'What kept you so long?'

'Just looking around.'

'And it was *Keith's* car they came back in,' Dart said, excusing himself. 'I was on the look-out for Father's.'

'Not much of a look-out.'

'You looked terribly guilty,' Dart said accusingly, shifting the blame.

'Yes, I felt it.'

'But as for Keith thinking you'd steal ...' He paused. 'When you took your shirt off ... I mean, I knew parts of the stands fell on you, but all those stitches and bruises ... they must *hurt*.'

'Not any more,' I sighed. I'd forgotten, in the urgency of the moment, that he'd been standing behind me. 'It's the cuts on my legs that have made walking difficult, but they're all getting better.'

'You gave Keith a shock, catching that walking stick.'

I had made him more careful, I thought ruefully, which might not be a good thing, from my point of view.

'Where are we going?' Dart asked. He'd turned out of the gates in the direction of the racecourse, automatically. 'Back to the Gardners?'

I tried to think, to pull together a few scattered wits.

I asked, 'Is Rebecca racing today, do you know?'

He answered as if bewildered, 'No, I don't think so. She was at the meeting, of course.'

'I need to talk to Marjorie,' I said. 'And to go to Stratton Hays.'

'I don't follow you.'

'No, but will you *take* me?'

He laughed. 'I'm your chauffeur, now?'

'You're a better chauffeur than look-out.'

'Thanks very much.'

'Or lend me your car,' I suggested.

'No,' he said. 'I'll drive you. Life's never boring, with you around.'

'The Gardners first, then.'

'Yes, *sir*.'

In the Gardners' kitchen Mrs Gardner greeted my return with friendly dismay, saying I'd lent her the five cooks for less

240

than an hour, not long enough. I offered their services for another few hours. Accepted, she said.

'Tell me if I'm leaving them with you too much,' I begged her.

'Don't be silly. I love it. And besides, Roger says that but for you he'd be halfway out of his job and we'd be sick with worry.'

'Does he think so?'

'He knows it.'

Grateful and partially comforted I left Dart in the kitchen and went over to the bus, and there in the privacy of the cab fed the tape I'd stolen into the tape-playing slot of the radio.

It proved to be a recording of a telephone call made on a cellular phone: the sort of spying that was diabolically easy if one listened on a scanner close to the transmitting and receiving cell.

I'd always had misgivings about the randomness of overheard conversations that had come to public light: what sort of person listened in to other people's privacy day in and day out *and taped it all*, hoping to overhear marketable secrets? Someone apparently had, in this case.

The conversation was between a voice provisionally identifiable as Rebecca's and a man speaking in a south-east accent, not cockney, but all glottal stops where 'd's, 't's or 'c's occurred in the centre of words. Stratton came out as 'Stra-on'. Rebecca as 'Rebe-ah'.

'Rebe-ah Stra-on?' said the man's voice.

'Yes.'

'What have you got for me, darlin'?'

'How much is it worth?'

'Same as usual.'

After a short pause, speaking quietly, she said, 'I'm riding Soapstone in the fifth, it's got no chance, it's only half fit. Lay off all you can on Catch-as-Catch, it's jumping out of its skin and they're putting a bundle on it.'

'That's the lot?'

'Yes.'

'Thanks, darlin'.'

'I'll see you at the races.'

'Same place,' the man agreed. 'Before the first.'

The tape clicked and fell silent. I ejected it grimly and returned it to my pocket and, climbing back into the body of the bus, unzipped my trousers and retrieved the glossy photograph and also the packet of dangerous knowledge.

From that I took out the interior, fatter brown envelope and slit it open with a knife. Inside were yet another envelope, white this time, and another short letter from William Stratton, third baron, to his son Conrad, fourth.

It read:

> Conrad,
> This grieves me beyond measure. Remember always that Keith, to my despair, tells lies. I sought out knowledge, and now I don't know how to use it. You must decide. But take care.
> S.

Apprehensively, I slit open the white envelope and read its lengthier contents and by the end found my hands trembling.

My non-grandfather had shown me a way, once and for all, of dealing with Keith.

I reassembled the packet in its original order and, finding some sticky-tape, sealed the outside brown envelope so that no one could open it by chance. Then I sat for a while with my head in my hands, realising that if Keith knew what I'd got he would kill me immediately, and also that saving myself from him posed a dilemma I'd never imagined.

Dangerous knowledge. Not dangerous: deadly.

CHAPTER 15

Dart drove me to Stratton Hays. On the way, using my own mobile phone (anyone listening?) I got through to Marjorie's house and found her at home, forthrightly displeased.

'You didn't come to the meeting!'

'No. Very sorry.'

'It was a shambles,' she said crossly. 'Waste of time. Keith shouted continually and nothing got done. He couldn't ignore the gate receipts, which were *excellent*, but he's fanatical about selling. Are you *sure* you cannot uncover his debts?'

'Does Imogen know them?' I asked.

'*Imogen?*'

'If I got her paralytically drunk, would she know anything at all of her husband's affairs?'

'You're disgraceful!'

'I'm afraid so.'

'I wish she did. But don't try it, because if Keith caught you at it . . .' She paused, then said without pressure, 'Do you take his threats seriously?'

'I have to.'

'Have you thought of . . . retreat?'

'Yes, I have. Are you busy? I need to tell you a few things.'

She said if I gave her an hour I could come to her house, to which I agreed. Dart and I continued to Stratton Hays, where he parked in the same place as on my first visit and as usual left the key in the ignition.

The great graceful pile, full of forgotten lives and quiet ghosts, stood peacefully in the mottled sunlight, a house built for hundreds, lived in by one.

'What now?' the one said; Darlington Stratton, fifth baron to be.

'We've got almost an hour. Can we look at the north wing?'

'But it's a ruin. I told you.'

'Ruins are my business.'

'I forgot. Well, OK.' He unlocked the rear door and took me again across the vast unfurnished, uncurtained front hall and along a wide windowed passage proportioned like a picture gallery, but with bare walls.

At the end of it we came to a heavy door, unpanelled, unpolished and modern, fastened by bolts. Dart wrestled with the bolts and creaked open the door, and we walked into the sort of desolation I went looking for: rotting wood, heaps of debris, saplings growing.

'They took the roof off sixty or more years ago,' Dart said glumly, looking upwards to the sky. 'All those years of rain and snow ... the upper floor just rotted and fell in. Grandfather asked the National Trust and the Heritage people ... I think they said the only thing to do was to demolish this wing and save the rest.' He sighed. 'Grandfather didn't like change. He just let time run on and nothing got done.'

I clambered with difficulty over a hillock of weathered grey beams and looked along a wide storm-struck landscape flanked by high, still standing, but unbuttressed stone walls.

'Do be careful,' Dart warned. 'No one's supposed to come in here without hard hats.'

The space gave me no creative excitement, no desire to restore it. All it did give me, in its majestic proportions, and its undignified death, was an interval of respite, of nerve-calming patience, a deep breath-taking perception of life passing, a drawing-in of the faith and industry that had designed and built here four hundred years earlier.

'OK,' I said, stirring and rejoining Dart in the open doorway. 'Thanks.'

'What do you think?'

'Your grandfather was given good advice.'

'I was afraid so.'

He rebolted the heavy door and we returned across the great hall to the rear entrance.

'Can I borrow your bathroom?' I asked.

'Sure.'

He continued on past the door, heading towards his own personal quarters, the ground floor of the south wing.

Here, present life went on very comfortably with carpets, curtains, antique furniture and a fresh polished smell. He led me to the door of his bathroom, a mixture of ancient and modern, a room converted from perhaps a sitting room, with a large free-standing Victorian bath and two new-looking washbasins built into a marble-topped fitment. The surface of the fitment was covered with bottles of shampoo and conditioner, and every variety of snake oil.

Sympathetically I went over to the window, which was curtained in lace, and looked out. Away to the left, Dart's car stood in the driveway. Ahead, lawns and trees. To the right, open gardens.

'What is it?' he said, as I stood there. After a moment, when I didn't move, he came over to stand beside me, to see what I was looking at.

He came, and he saw. He switched his gaze to my face, searching, and without trouble read my thoughts.

'*Shit*,' he said.

An appropriate word for a bathroom. I said nothing, however, but walked back the way we had come.

'How did you know?' Dart asked, following.

'Guessed.'

'So what now?'

'Go to Marjorie's house.'

'I mean . . . what about *me*?'

'Oh, nothing,' I said. 'It's not up to me.'

'But . . .'

245

'You were in the bathroom seeing to your hair,' I said. 'And through the window you saw who took your car on Good Friday morning. No one's going to put you to the torture to find out who it was. Just pretend you saw nothing, as you've been doing so far.'

'Do you know . . . who?'

I half smiled. 'Let's go and see Marjorie.'

'*Lee*.'

'Come and listen.'

Dart drove us to Marjorie's house, which proved to be unadulterated early Georgian, as well-bred and trim as she was herself. Set four-square in weedless grounds at one end of Stratton village, it had sash windows in disciplined rows, a central front door and a circular driveway reached past gateposts with urns on.

Dart parked near the front door and as usual left the key in the ignition.

'Don't you *ever* lock it?' I asked.

'Why bother? I wouldn't mind an excuse to get a new car.'

'Why not just buy one?'

'One day,' he said.

'Like your grandfather.'

'What? Oh, yes. I suppose I'm like him, a bit. One day. Maybe.'

Marjorie's front door was opened to us by a manservant ('She lives in the past,' murmured Dart) who pleasantly guided us across a hall to her drawing room. As expected, faultless taste there in time-stands-still land, gentle colours overall in dim pinks, green and gold. The window embrasures still held the original shutters, but there were floor-length curtains as well, and swagged valances, and a view of sunlit spring gardens beyond.

Marjorie sat in a wide armchair that commanded the room, very much and always the person in charge. She wore, as often, dark blue with white at the neck, looking doll-like and exquisite and temporarily hiding the tough cookie.

'Sit down,' she commanded, and Dart and I sat near her, I on a small sofa, Dart on a spindly chair – Hepplewhite, probably.

'Things to tell me,' she began. 'That's what you said, Lee.'

'Mm,' I said. 'Well, you asked me to find out two things.'

'And on the subject of Keith's finances, you've failed,' she nodded decisively. 'You've already told me.'

'Yes. But . . . as regards your other assignment . . .'

'Go *on*,' she said, as I stopped. 'I remember exactly. I asked you to find out what pressure that wretched architect was putting on Conrad to get his new stands built.'

Dart looked surprised. '*Assignment?*' he asked.

'Yes, yes.' His great aunt was impatient. 'Lee and I had an agreement. We shook hands on it. Didn't we?' She turned her head to me. 'An agreement you did not want to break.'

'That's right,' I said.

'Aunt Marjorie!' Dart looked flummoxed. 'You've had Lee working for *you*?'

'And what's wrong with that? It was for the ultimate good of the family. How can we proceed, if we don't know the facts?'

The world's politicians could learn from her, I thought with admiration. The clearest of brains under the waved white hair.

'Along the way,' I said, 'I learned about Forsyth and the lawn mowers.'

Dart gasped. Marjorie's eyes widened.

'Also,' I went on, 'I heard about Hannah's bit of rough trade, and its results.'

'What are you talking about?' Dart asked me, lost.

Marjorie enlightened him. 'Hannah went off into the bushes with a gypsy and got herself pregnant, the silly ninny. Keith assaulted the gypsy, who demanded money, of course. My brother paid him off.'

'Do you mean . . .' Dart worked it out, 'that Jack's father was a *gypsy*?'

'Near enough. Not even a Romany. A good-for-nothing tramp,' Marjorie said.

'Oh, my God,' Dart said, weakly.

'And don't speak of it again,' Marjorie commanded severely. 'Hannah tells Jack his father was a foreign aristocrat who would have been ruined by the scandal.'

'Yes,' Dart's voice sounded faint. 'Jack told me that himself.'

'And let him believe it. I hope, Lee,' she said to me, 'that that's all.'

The telephone rang on the small table beside her chair. She picked up the receiver and listened.

'Yes . . . when? Dart is here. So is Lee. Yes.' She put the receiver down and said to Dart, 'That was your father. He says he is coming here. He sounds incredibly angry. What have you done?'

'Is Keith with him?' My words came out with a jerk, which she pounced on.

'You're afraid of Keith!'

'Not unreasonably.'

'Conrad said Keith told him to come here, but I don't know if Keith was with him or not. Do you wish to leave now, at once?'

Yes, I did, and no, I didn't. I thought of murder in her quiet drawing room and hoped she wouldn't allow it.

I said, 'I brought a photograph to show you. It's in Dart's car. I'll just fetch it.'

I stood up and walked to the door.

'Don't drive off and leave me here,' Dart said, only half joking.

The temptation bit deep, but where would I go? I picked the photograph, in an envelope, out of the door pocket, where I'd placed it, and returned to the drawing room.

Marjorie took out the photograph and looked at it uncomprehendingly. 'What does it mean?'

'I'll explain,' I said, 'but if Conrad's coming, I'll wait until he gets here.'

The distance from Conrad's house to Marjorie's was short. He came very soon and, to my relief, without Keith. He came armed, though, carrying a shotgun, the landowner's friend. He carried it not broken open, over his arm, as one should, but straightened, and ready.

He brushed past the manservant, who had opened the door for him and was saying, 'Lord Stratton, madam,' punctiliously, and strode across Marjorie's pale Chinese carpet, coming to a halt in front of me with the twin barrels pointing my way.

I rose to my feet. Barely three paces lay between us.

He held the gun not as if aiming at flying birds but down at his waist, easily familiar with shots from the hip. At that distance he couldn't miss a mosquito.

'You're a liar and a thief.' He was growling with fury, his fingers frighteningly unsteady in the region of the trigger.

I didn't deny the charge. I looked past him and his gun to the photograph Marjorie held, and he followed my gaze. He recognised the picture and the look he gave me was as murderous as any of Keith's. The barrels aimed straight at my chest.

'Conrad,' Marjorie said sharply, 'calm down.'

'Calm down? *Calm down?* This *despicable* person broke into my private cupboard and stole from me.'

'However, you may *not* shoot him in my house.'

In a way it was funny, but farce was too close to tragedy always. Even Dart didn't laugh.

I said to Conrad, 'I'll free you from blackmail.'

'*What?*'

'What are you talking about?' Marjorie demanded.

'I'm talking about Wilson Yarrow blackmailing Conrad into giving him the go-ahead for the new grandstand.'

Marjorie exclaimed, 'So you *did* find out!'

'Is that gun loaded?' I asked Conrad.

'Yes, of course.'

'Would you mind . . . uh . . . pointing it somewhere else?'

He stood four-square, bullish, unwavering: unmoving.

'Father,' Dart protested.

'You shut up,' his father said grittily. 'You abetted him.'

I said, risking things, 'Wilson Yarrow told you that if he didn't get the commission for the stands, he would see that Rebecca was warned off as a jockey.'

Dart goggled. Marjorie said, 'That's ridiculous.'

'No. Not ridiculous. That photograph is a picture of Rebecca receiving a wad of money on a racecourse from a man who might be a bookmaker.'

I tried to work saliva into my mouth. I'd never before had a loaded gun pointed at me in anger. Even though I clung to the belief that Conrad's inner restraints existed where Keith's didn't, I could feel my scalp sweating.

'I listened to the tape,' I said.

'You *stole* it.'

'Yes,' I agreed. 'I stole it. It's damning.'

'So now it's *you* who'll blackmail me.' His trigger hand tightened.

'Oh for Christ's sake, Conrad,' I said, almost exasperated. 'Use some sense. I'll not blackmail you. I'll see that Yarrow doesn't.'

'*How?*'

'If you'll put that bloody gun down, I'll tell you.'

'What tape?' Dart asked.

'The tape you helped him steal from my cupboard.'

Dart looked blank.

'Dart didn't know,' I said. 'He was outside in his car.'

'But Keith searched your jacket,' Dart protested.

I put my hand into my trousers pocket and brought out the tape. Conrad flicked a glance at it and went on scaring me silly.

'This tape,' I told Marjorie, 'is a recording of a telephone call of Rebecca selling information about the horses she would be riding. It's the worst of racing crimes. Sending it and that photograph to the racing authorities would end her career. She'd be warned off. The Stratton name would be mud.'

'But she *wouldn't* do that,' Dart wailed.

Conrad said, as if the words hurt his tongue, 'She admitted it.'

'No!' Dart moaned.

'I challenged her,' Conrad said. 'I played her the tape. She can be so hard. She listened like stone. She said I wouldn't let Yarrow use it.' Conrad swallowed. 'And . . . she was right.'

'Put the gun down,' I said.

He didn't.

I threw the tape to Dart, who fumbled it, dropped it and picked it up again.

'Give it to Marjorie,' I said and, blinking, he obeyed.

'If you'll unload the gun and put it against the wall,' I said to Conrad, 'I'll tell you how to get rid of Yarrow, but I'm not doing it with your hand on the trigger.'

'Conrad,' Marjorie said crisply, 'you're not going to shoot him. So put the gun down in case you do it by accident.'

Blessed bodyguard. Conrad woke to realities as if in a cold shower, looking down indecisively at his hands. He undoubtedly would have laid down his fire power were it not that Rebecca, at that moment, swept in like a whirlwind, having outrun the manservant altogether.

'What's going on here?' she demanded. 'I've a right to know!'

Marjorie stared at her with her customary disfavour. 'Considering what you've done, you've no right to *anything*.'

Rebecca looked at the photograph of herself and the tape in Marjorie's hand, and at the shotgun in her father's, and at me, threatened.

'Keith told me that this . . . this . . .' she pointed at me, not finding words bad enough, 'stole enough to get me warned off . . .'

I said fiercely to Conrad, 'That tape is a *fake*.'

The effect on Rebecca was an increase in fury. While the rest of the family tried to understand what I'd said, she snatched the gun from her father, swung it round at shoulder height, took a quick aim at me and without pause pulled the trigger.

I saw the intention in her eyes and flung myself sideways full length onto the carpet, rolling onto my stomach, missing the ball of fizzing pellets by fractions, conscious of *two* barrels, two cartridges, and no way of escaping a shot in the back.

The room had filled with a thunderous cracking noise, with flame and smoke, with the acrid smell of cordite at close quarters. *Jesus*, I thought. God almighty. Not Keith, but Rebecca.

The second shot didn't come. I cringed on the floor – no other word for it. There was the smell, the ringing echo, and beyond that . . . silence.

I stirred, turned my head, saw her shoes, crawled my gaze upwards as far as her hands.

She was *not* pointing the second of the barrel holes at me.

Her hands were empty.

Eyes slowly right . . . Conrad himself held his gun.

Dart came down on his knees by my head, saying, 'Lee,' helplessly.

I said thickly, 'She missed me.'

'God, Lee.'

I felt breathless, but I couldn't stay there for ever. I rolled into a sitting position; felt too shaken to stand.

The shot had shocked them all, even Rebecca.

Marjorie, straightbacked, looked over-white, her mouth open, fixed, animation suspended. Conrad's eyes stared darkly at a bloody mess too narrowly averted. I couldn't . . . yet . . . look straight at Rebecca.

'She didn't mean to,' Conrad said.

But she had indeed meant it; an act beyond caution.

I coughed once, convulsively. I said again, 'The tape is a fake.' And this time, no one tried to kill me for it.

Conrad said, 'I don't understand.'

I breathed deeply, slowly, trying to steady the racket of my pulse.

'She *couldn't* have done it,' I said. 'Wouldn't have. She wouldn't put in jeopardy the . . . the *citadel* of her most inner self.'

Conrad said, in perplexity, 'I don't really follow.'

I looked at last at Rebecca. She stared back, her face hard and expressionless.

'I saw you race,' I said. 'You exalt in it. And the other day, I listened to you say you would be in the top five this year on the jockeys' list. You were passionate about it. You're a Stratton, you're infinitely proud, and you're rich and don't need the money. There's no way you're ever going to sell sleazy information that could bring you unbearable disgrace.'

Rebecca's eyes slitted narrowly under lowered eyelids, her face rigid.

'But she confirmed it was true!' Conrad said again.

I said regretfully, 'She made the tape herself to put pressure on you to get new stands built, and she tried to shoot me to stop me telling you.'

'Rebecca!' Conrad couldn't believe it. 'This man's lying. Tell me he's lying.'

Rebecca said nothing.

'You've been showing all the signs of intolerable strain,' I said to her. 'I would think it seemed a good idea to you to begin with, to let your father believe he was being blackmailed to save you from being warned off, but once you'd done it, and he had in fact allowed himself to be blackmailed, I'd guess you regretted it sorely. But you didn't confess *that* to him. You went straight on with your obsessive and drastic plan to modernise Stratton Park radically, and it's been tearing you apart for weeks and making you . . . lose balance.'

'The hangers!' Dart said.

'But *why*, Rebecca?' Conrad begged, intensely disturbed. 'I'd have done anything for you . . .'

'You might not have agreed,' I said, 'to build new stands at all, let alone have Wilson Yarrow design them. And it was he, wasn't it, who came to you and said, "I have the dirt on your daughter, and all you have to do to save her honour is give me this commission"?'

Conrad didn't answer directly, but he broke open his shotgun and with unsteady fingers pulled out both cartridges, the spent one, blackened and empty, and the unfired one, orange and bright. He put them both in his pocket and stood the gun by the wall.

As he did so there was a quiet tap on the door. Conrad went to open it and found Marjorie's manservant there, worried. 'Nothing wrong,' Conrad assured him fruitily. 'Gun went off by accident. Bit of a nuisance to clear up, I'm afraid. We'll see to it later.'

'Yes, my lord.'

The door closed. I noticed for the first time that the spreading shot had smashed a mirror on the wall and torn pieces of gold silk upholstery from chairs. Much too damned close.

I reached for the walking stick I'd laid beside the small sofa where I'd been sitting and, with its help, returned to my feet.

'You must have said something to Keith about blackmail,' I

told Conrad. 'He used that word in connection with Yarrow. You all heard him.'

Conrad made a helpless gesture. 'Keith went on and on at me to abandon the idea of new stands and I said I *couldn't*.' He paused. 'But *how* did you find all this out?'

'A lot of small things,' I said. 'For example, I went to the same school of architecture as Wilson Yarrow.'

'*Architecture!*' Marjorie interrupted.

'Yes. When I saw him ... heard his name ... I knew there was something wrong about him. I only vaguely remembered, so I looked up a man I was at architectural school with, that I hadn't heard from for ten years, and asked him. He kept a diary all those years ago and he'd written down a rumour he'd heard, that Wilson Yarrow had won a prestigious prize with an architectural design he'd sent in, while knowing that it wasn't his own. The school took the prize away and hushed it all up a bit, but the stigma of cheating remained, and there must be several hundred architects, like me, who associate that name of Yarrow with something not right. The word goes around in professional circles, and memories are long – and better than mine – and the brilliant career once expected of Yarrow has not come to pass. There was his name alone on the plans he drew for you, which means he's probably not employed in a firm. He may very well be unemployed altogether, and there's a glut of architects now, with the schools every year training more than the market can absorb. I'd guess he saw the prestige of building new stands at Stratton Park as a way back into esteem. I think he was *desperate* to get that commission.'

They listened, even Rebecca, as if spellbound.

I said, 'Before I ever came to Stratton Park, Roger Gardner told me there was an architect designing new stands who knew nothing about racing and didn't understand crowd behaviour, and that as he wouldn't listen to advice he would be the death of the racecourse, but that you, Conrad, wouldn't be deflected from him.'

I paused. No one said anything.

'So,' I went on, 'I came to your shareholders' meeting last

Wednesday, and met you all, and listened. I learned what you all wanted for the racecourse. Marjorie wanted things to remain as they were. You, Conrad, wanted new stands, actually to save Rebecca from ruin, though I didn't know that then. Keith wanted to sell, for the money. Rebecca, of course, wanted a clean sweep, as she said; new stands, new manager, new Clerk of the Course, a new image for old-fashioned Stratton Park. Marjorie managed that meeting in a way that would have had superpowers kneeling in admiration, and she manipulated you all so that she got *her* way, which was for Stratton Park to continue in its old manner for the foreseeable future.'

Dart cast an admiring glance at his great aunt, the grin very nearly appearing.

I said, 'That was not good enough for Rebecca, nor for Keith. Keith had already enlisted the actor, Harold Quest, to make a nuisance of himself demonstrating against steeplechasing outside the main gates, so that people would be put off going to the races at Stratton Park and the course would lose its attraction and its income, and go bankrupt as a business so that you would have to sell its big asset, the land. He also got Harold Quest to burn a fence – the open ditch; symbolically the open ditch, as it was there that a horse had been killed at the last meeting – but that ploy was a dud, as you know. Keith isn't bright. But Rebecca . . .'

I hesitated. There were things that had to be said: I wished there were someone else . . . anyone else . . . to say them.

'In the Stratton family, as it is now,' I resumed, approaching things sideways, 'there are two good-natured harmless fellows, Ivan and Dart. There's one very clever person, Marjorie. There's Conrad, more powerful in appearance than fact. There's a strain of ruthlessness and violence in everyone else of Stratton blood, which has cost you all fortunes. When you ally those traits with stupidity and arrogance, you get Forsyth and his mowers. There is in many of the Strattons, as in him, a belief that you'll never be found out, and if you should be, you believe the family will use its money and muscle to save you, as it always has done in the past.'

'And will again,' Marjorie said firmly.

'And will again,' I acknowledged, 'if you can. You'll need all your skills soon, though, in damage control.'

Surprisingly, they went on listening, not trying to make me stop.

I said carefully, 'In Rebecca, that violence is chiefly controlled and comes out as a consuming competitiveness in a testing sport. In her, there's splendid courage and will-to-win. There's also a tremendous overpowering urge to get her own way. When Marjorie blocked her first plan for achieving new stands, she hit on a simple solution – get rid of the old ones.'

This time, Conrad protested incredulously, and Marjorie also, but not Rebecca or Dart.

'I'd guess,' I said to Rebecca, 'that you told Wilson Yarrow to do it, as, if he didn't, he could kiss the commission goodbye.'

She glared at me unblinkingly, a tigress untamed.

I said, 'Wilson Yarrow was in deep already with that blackmailing attempt. He saw, as you did, that destroying a part of the main grandstand would mean new ones had to be built. He knew those old grandstands and, as an architect, he saw how maximum damage could be achieved for minimum effort. The staircase in the centre was the main artery of the building. Collapse that core, and the rooms round it would cave in.'

'I had nothing to do with it,' Rebecca yelled suddenly.

Conrad jumped. Conrad . . . aghast.

'I saw those charges before they exploded,' I said to Rebecca. 'I saw how they were laid. Very professional. I could have done it myself. And I know other dealers, not as responsible as my giant friend Henry, who'll sell you anything, few questions asked. But it's difficult, even for people whose whole job is demolition, to get right the amount of explosive needed. Every structure has its own strengths and weaknesses. There's pressure to use too much rather than too little. The amount Yarrow used tore half the building apart.'

'No,' Rebecca said.

'Yes,' I contradicted her. 'Between you, you decided it

should be done early on Good Friday morning, when there would be no one about.'

'No.'

'Wilson Yarrow drilled the holes and set the charges, with you acting as look-out.'

'No!'

'He couldn't do it without a look-out. If you go in for crime, it's much best to post a look-out you can trust.'

Dart squirmed. Then he grinned. Irrepressible.

'You sat on watch in Dart's car,' I said.

Rebecca's eyes opened wide, abruptly. The 'no' she produced lacked the fire of the other denials.

'You thought,' I said, 'that if you went in your own bright scarlet Ferrari, and any stray groundsman, perhaps, saw it on the racecourse on that non-racing day, he would remember it and report it after the stands had exploded. So you drove to Stratton Hays, and parked your car there, and took Dart's, which always has the keys left in, and you drove that car into the racecourse, because Dart's car is so familiar there as to be practically invisible. But you didn't reckon with Harold Quest, actor and busybody, who wouldn't have been at the gates there anyway on that day if he'd been a genuine protestor, and you must have been shattered when he said Dart's car had been there, and described it to the police. But not as shattered as you would have been if Harold Quest had reported your Ferrari.'

'I don't believe all this,' Conrad said faintly; but he did.

'I imagine,' I said to Rebecca, 'that somewhere you picked up Yarrow and took him and the explosive to the racecourse, because the police tested the car and found traces of nitrates.'

Rebecca said nothing.

I said, 'Dart has known all along that it was you – or you and Yarrow – who blew up the stands.'

'Dart told you!' Rebecca shouted, furiously turning to Dart, who looked staggered and hurt. 'You gave me away to this ... this ...'

'No, he didn't,' I said fiercely. 'Dart was unswervingly loyal to you. He went through a considerable grilling from the police yesterday and didn't say a word. They accused him of setting the explosives himself, and he's still their chief suspect, and they'll question him again. But he won't tell them about you. He's proud of you, he has mixed feelings, he thinks you're crack-brained, but he's a Stratton and he won't give you away.'

'How do you *know*?' Dart wailed, agonised.

'I stood next to you when she won on Tempestexi.'

'But . . . you couldn't tell from *that*.'

'I've lived and breathed Strattons for a week.'

'*How* did you know?' Rebecca demanded of her brother.

'I saw your Ferrari from my bathroom, parked where my old car was supposed to be.'

She said helplessly, 'It was there for less than an hour.'

Conrad's shoulders sagged.

'I was back in Lambourn long before the explosion,' Rebecca said crossly. 'And Yarrow was putting himself about in London by then.'

'I want to know,' Marjorie said to me, after a silence, 'what made you first suspect Rebecca?'

'Such small things.'

'Tell them.'

'Well,' I said, 'she fanatically wanted things changed.'

'And?' Marjorie prompted, when I stopped.

'She mentioned new stands made of glass. There are stands in Britain with glassed-in sections, aren't there, but not sheeted altogether in glass, as Yarrow's plans are, and I wondered if she had *seen* the plans, which Conrad had locked away so secretively. And then . . .'

'Then what?'

'Rebecca said she was the only one in the family who knew a rabbet from a raceway.'

They all, except Rebecca, looked uncomprehending.

'I don't follow,' Marjorie said.

'It's not a racing term,' I explained. 'It meant nothing to Roger Gardner.'

'Nor to me,' Conrad interposed, 'and I've owned and ridden horses all my life.'

'It's clear to an architect,' I said, 'and to a builder, to a carpenter, to an engineer. Not, I wouldn't have expected, to a jockey. So I wondered, but not very conclusively at that point, if she'd been talking a good deal to an architect, and if that architect might not be Yarrow. Just a vague passing speculation, but that sort of thing sticks in your brain.'

'So what *are* a rabbit and a raceway?' Dart asked.

'A rabbet, with an 'e', is a tongue and groove joint, mostly in wood, to enable you to slot boards, say, together, as in a fence, or floorboards, without using nails. Like the floor in the big top, in fact.'

Marjorie looked bewildered, Conrad not.

'And a raceway?' she asked. 'Not a racecourse?'

'I suppose it could be. But otherwise it's either a sort of gully for draining fast-flowing fluids, or it could be a sort of collar that houses ball-bearings. In either case, it's not common racecourse parlance.'

'A rabbet from a raceway,' Dart said thoughtfully. 'Wasn't your youngest son chanting that?'

'Quite likely.'

'I should have killed you when I had the chance,' Rebecca said to me bitterly.

'I thought you were going to,' I agreed.

'She was aiming straight at you,' Dart said. 'Father snatched the gun away from her. If you ask him, he'll probably say that shooting you once in the chest might have been passed off as an accident, but putting a second shot into your back couldn't be anything but murder.'

'Dart!' Marjorie remonstrated severely; but there was no doubt he'd got it right. Dart was one of them. He knew.

Conrad had a question for his daughter. 'Where did you meet Yarrow in the first place? How did you get to know him?'

She shrugged. 'At a party. He was doing stupid imitations in the accent you heard on the tape. Rebe-ah Stra-on, darlin'. Someone told me he was an exceptionally good architect, but flat broke. I wanted new stands. He wanted a job badly and he wasn't fussy how he got it. We did a deal.'

'But you don't usually like men.'

'I didn't like him,' she said brutally. 'I *used* him. I despise him, as a matter of fact. He's in a blue funk now, predictably.'

'So ... what next?' Conrad asked me wretchedly. 'The police?'

I looked at Marjorie. 'You,' I said, 'are the one who pulls the levers in the family. You've ruled them all for forty years. You ruled even your own brother, in the gentlest of ways.'

'How?' Dart said, avid.

Marjorie beseeched me with wide open eyes, but it was for Perdita Faulds' sake that I said to Dart, 'Your grandfather's secret was his alone, and died with him. I can't tell you it.'

'Won't,' Dart said.

'Won't,' I agreed. 'Anyway, to go to the police or not must be Marjorie's decision, not mine. My brief was to give her a lever against Yarrow, and she has it. That's where I finish.' I paused. 'I'm sure,' I said, 'for what it's worth, that the police haven't got, and won't find, enough for a prosecution against you, Dart. Just go on knowing nothing, and you'll be all right.'

'What about Yarrow, though?' Dart asked.

'Marjorie must decide,' I said. 'But if you prosecute Yarrow, you give away Rebecca's schemes and your own involvement. I can't see her doing it.'

'But Keith?' Marjorie said, not dodging the burden I'd placed on her. 'What about *him*?'

Keith.

I turned to Conrad. 'Did you tell Marjorie that *Keith* sent you here?'

'I did, yes.'

'Sent you ... with a gun?'

He looked faintly shamefaced. 'You can't really blame me. I mean, after you and Dart had gone, Keith and I were standing in my room talking about you breaking into my cupboard, and we found that key sort of thing of yours in the lock and I was saying what a risk you'd taken just for a look at some plans ... and it simply flashed into my mind that you'd been so *involved* in things, and although I couldn't believe you'd been searching for anything else, or that you knew *enough*, I went into the cupboard and looked into the box where I'd put the photograph and the tape, and I was so devastated that Keith asked what was the matter, and I told him. He said – we both thought – you would of course blackmail me.'

'Oh, of course.'

'Yes, but . . .'

'You all do it to each other; you think no one's capable of anything else.'

Conrad shrugged his heavy shoulders as if he believed that to be self evident. 'Anyway,' he said, 'Keith asked me to give him the envelope our father had entrusted to me shortly before he died. I told Keith I couldn't do that. We had a bit of an argument, but Father had given me very explicit instructions about not letting anyone else see it. Keith asked me if I knew what was in it, but I don't, and I said so. He said he had to have it. He began opening the boxes and tipping everything out. I tried to stop him, but you know what he's like. Then he came to the box where I thought I'd put that letter but when he tipped everything out it didn't seem to be there . . . but how could you have taken it when you couldn't have known it existed? In the end, I helped him look for it. Everything's out on the floor, it's a terrible mess and I'll never put it straight . . .'

'But you did find the envelope?' Marjorie asked anxiously.

'No, we didn't.' He turned to me, insisting, 'I *know* it was in there, in one special box, under a pile of out-of-date *insurance policies*. Keith told me to bring the gun and kill you . . .'

'But he knew you wouldn't,' I said positively.

Dart asked, 'Why are you so sure?'

'One twin,' I said, 'would kill the pilgrim. The other wouldn't. They can't change their natures.'

'The fork in the road! You . . . you *subtle* bastard.'

Marjorie looked at me forthrightly, not understanding or caring what Dart had said. 'Did you take that envelope?'

'Yes, I did,' I said.

'Did you open it? Did you see what was inside?'

'Yes.'

'Then give it to me.'

'No.' I shook my head. 'This one . . .' I took a breath, 'this one I have to do alone.'

The telephone shrilled beside Marjorie. Mouth tightening with annoyance at the interruption, she lifted the receiver.

'Yes,' she said, her face going blank. 'Yes, he's here.'

She held out the receiver to me. 'It's Keith,' she said. 'He wants to talk to you.'

He knows, I thought, that I must have taken that letter; and he knows what is in it.

With foreboding, I said, 'Yes?'

He didn't speak at once, but he was there: I could hear him breathing.

Long seconds passed.

He said five words only before the line went dead. The worst five words in the language.

'Say goodbye to your children.'

CHAPTER 16

My brain went numb.

A flush of fear zipped from my heels to my scalp in one of those dreadful physical disturbances that come with perceived irretrievable disaster.

I stood immobile, trying to remember the Gardners' telephone number. Couldn't do it. Squeezed my eyes shut and let it come without struggling, let it come subliminally, known as a rhythm, not by sight. Pressed buttons and sweated.

Roger's wife answered.

'Where are the boys?' I asked her abruptly.

'They should be with you at any minute,' she said comfortingly. 'They set off . . . oh . . . say, fifteen minutes ago. They'll be with you directly.'

'With me . . . where?'

'Along at the big top, of course.' She was puzzled. 'Christopher got your message and they set off at once.'

'Did Roger drive them?'

'No. He's around the course somewhere, I'm not sure where. The boys set off on foot, Lee . . . is something wrong?'

'What message?' I said.

'A phone call, for Christopher . . .'

I threw the receiver to Marjorie and sprinted out of her

drawing room, across her calm hallway, and out of her front door and into Dart's car. Never mind that the sprint was a hobble, I'd never moved faster. Never mind that I knew I was heading for an ambush, for some thought-out fate. There was nothing to do but rush to it, hoping beyond hope that he'd be satisfied with me, that he would let the boys live . . .

I drove Dart's car like a madman through the village, but just when I could have done with a whole police posse, there was no police car to chase me for speeding.

In through the racecourse gates. Round onto the tarmac outside Roger's office. Keith's silver Jaguar was there. Nobody in sight . . . *Yes* . . . Christopher . . . and Edward . . . and Alan. All of them frightened to eye-staring terror. I scrambled out of the car, driven by demons.

'Dad!' Christopher's bottomless relief was not reassuring. 'Dad, hurry.'

'What's happening?'

'That man . . . in the big top.'

I turned that way.

'He's lit fires in there . . . and Neil . . . and Toby . . . and Neil's screaming.'

'Find Colonel Gardner,' I shouted to him, running. 'Tell him to turn on the sprinkler.'

'But . . .' Despair in Christopher's voice, 'we don't know where he is.'

'*Find him.*'

I could *hear* Neil screaming. Not words, nothing intelligible. High-pitched shrieks. *Screaming.*

How does one face such a thing?

I ran into the big top, into the centre aisle, looking for the fire extinguisher that ought to have been there at the entrance, and not seeing it, running on and finding Alan running beside me.

'Go back,' I yelled at him. 'Alan, go *back.*'

There was smoke in the tent and small bright fires here and there on the floor; scarlet, orange and gold flames leaping in rivers and pools. And beyond, standing like a colossus with his legs apart, his weight braced and his mouth stretched wide in gleeful enjoyment . . . *Keith.*

He held Neil by the wrist, easily clamping the small bones in a vice grip, and lifting him halfway into the air, holding my son at almost arm's length, the small body writhing and fighting to get free, but with only his toes touching the ground, giving no purchase.

'Let him go,' I yelled, beyond pride, into begging, into any craven grovelling needed.

'Come and get him, or I'll burn him.'

Beside Keith, in a tall decorative wrought-iron container, stood a long-handled torch flaring with a live naked flame, the sort designed for garden barbecues, for torchlight processions, for the evil firing of houses in raids; Neil on one side, torch on the other. In the centre, Keith held a plastic jerry can missing its cap.

'It's petrol, Dad,' Alan yelled beside me. 'He was pouring it on the floor and lighting it. We thought he might burn us . . . and we ran, but he caught Neil . . . don't let him burn Neil, Dad.'

'*Go back*,' I screamed at him, frantic, and he wavered and stopped in his tracks, tears on his cheeks.

I ran towards Keith, towards his terrible grin, towards my terrified son. I ran towards certain fire, ran as fast as I could, ran from instinct.

If Keith wants to get rid of something, he burns it . . .

I would overrun him, I thought. I would crash down with him. He would go with me . . . wherever I went.

He hadn't expected an onrush. He stepped back, looking less certain, and Neil went on screaming. One will do, I realised later, almost insane things in defence of one's children.

I was conscious then only of flames, of anger, of the raw smell of petrol, of a clear view of the outcome.

He would fling the petrol can at me and swing the torch, and to do that he would have to . . . *have* to let go of Neil. I would push him away beyond Neil, who would live and be safe.

Six paces away, running towards him, I gave up all hope of not burning. But Keith would burn too . . . and die . . . I would make sure of it.

A small dark figure launched itself in the shortening distance between us like a goblin from nowhere, all arms and legs, ungainly but fast. He banged into Keith and knocked him off balance, setting him reeling and windmilling backwards.

Toby . . . *Toby*.

Keith let go of Neil. I shoved my small son away from him in a frenzy. The petrol spilled out of the can and over Keith's legs in a glittering stream. Staggering, trying to evade the fuel, Keith knocked into the stand containing the torch. It rocked; rocked back and forwards and then overbalanced; started the flame falling in a deadly arc downwards.

I lunged forward, snatched up Toby with my right arm, scooped Neil into my left, lifted them both off their feet and turned in the same movement to escape.

There was a great whoosh at our backs and a blast of heat and sizzling fire as if the whole air were burning. I caught a split-second glimpse, looking over my shoulder, of Keith with his mouth open as if he, this time, would scream. He seemed to take a deep breath to yell and fire rushed into his open mouth as if drawn by bellows into his lungs, and he made no sound at all, but clutched at his chest, his eyes wide, with white showing all round, and he fell face down in an accelerating fireball.

The back of my own shirt was scorching from neck to waist, and Toby's hair was on fire. I ran with the boys in my arms, ran far enough down the aisle and tripped and fell over, dropping Neil, rolling onto my back and rubbing Toby's hair with my hands.

Desperate moments. Neil smelled of petrol, Toby also, and there were fires, a maze of fires, to traverse on the way out.

I lay momentarily panting for breath, collecting some strength, my left arm curving round Neil who was crying. I struggled to reassure Toby; and then from far above fell a blessed mist of drizzling drops of water, cooling, life-giving, spitting and sizzling on all the small fires around us, blackening the flames to extinction and turning to a smoking ruin the humped shape of Keith.

Toby leaned on my chest, staring into my face as if he couldn't bear to look anywhere else.

He said, 'He was going to set fire to you, wasn't he, Dad?'

'Yes, he was.'

'I thought so.'

'Where did you come from?' I asked.

'Out of the dining room, where we had lunch. I was hiding
. . .' His eyes were stretched. 'I was *scared*, Dad.' Water ran
through his singed hair and into his eyes.

'Anyone would be.' I rubbed my fist over his back, loving
him. 'You have the courage of ten thousand heroes.' I fought
for words. 'It isn't every boy who knows he saved his father's
life.'

I could see it wasn't enough for him. There had to be more,
something to give him a permanent feeling of self-worth, to
steady him, keep him always in command of himself.

I thought of his little figure launching itself at an impossibly
threatening target, arms and legs flying everywhere, but
achieving the aim.

I said, 'Would you like to learn karate, when we get home?'

His strained face split into a blazing smile. He wiped the
trickling water away from his mouth. 'Oh *yes*, Dad,' he said.

I sat up, still hugging both of them, and Christopher came
running, and the other two also, all of them staring beyond
me to the blackened and unimaginable horror.

'Don't go down there,' I said, pushing myself to my feet.
'Where's Colonel Gardner?'

'We couldn't find him,' Christopher said.

'But . . . the sprinkler?'

'I turned it on, Dad,' Christopher said. 'I saw Henry sticking
all those labels on, the day you went on the train. I knew
where the tap was.'

'*Brilliant*,' I said; but there weren't any words good enough.
'Well, let's get out of here, out of the rain.'

Neil wanted to be carried. I picked him up and he wound
his arms round my neck, clinging tightly, and all six of us,
soaking wet, made our slowish way out to the tarmac.

Roger drove up in his jeep, got out, and stared at us.

We must, I supposed, have looked odd. One tall boy, one
little boy, clinging, the three others close, all dripping.

I said to Christopher, 'Run and turn off the tap,' and to Roger, 'We had a fire in the big top. Bits of petrol-soaked matting and floorboards burned, but Henry was right, the canvas didn't.'

'A *fire*!' He turned towards the entrance, to go and see for himself.

'Better warn you,' I said. 'Keith's in there. He's dead.'

Roger paused for one stride and then went on. Christopher came back from the errand, and all of the boys and I began shivering, as much, I supposed, from shock and anxiety as from standing wet in the light April breeze, in air too cold for comfort.

'Get into the car,' I said, pointing at Dart's beaten up wheels. 'You need to get dry.'

'But Dad . . .'

'I'm coming with you.'

They piled in as Roger came out of the tent looking worried.

'Whatever's happened?' he said urgently. 'I'll have to get the police. Come into the office.'

I shook my head. 'First, I get the boys into dry clothes. I'll not have them catching pneumonia. I'll come back.'

'But Lee —'

'Keith tried to burn the big top,' I said. 'But . . .'

'But,' Roger finished, 'people who try to start fires with petrol can end up by burning themselves.'

I smiled faintly. 'Right.'

I walked over to Dart's car and drove the boys down to the bus, where everyone, myself emphatically included, showered and changed into dry clothes down to the skin. My check shirt, its back blackened as if pressed by a too-hot iron, went into the rubbish bin, not into a laundry bag. Underneath I felt as if sunburnt: a first-degree soreness, nothing worse. Dead lucky, I thought, that the shirt had been thick pure wool, not melting nylon.

When the boys were ready I marched them over to Mrs Gardner and begged her to give them hot sweet drinks and cake, if she had any.

'My *dears*,' she said, embracing them, 'come on in.'

'Don't leave us, Dad,' Edward said.

'I have to talk to the Colonel, but I won't be long.'

'Can I come with you?' Christopher asked.

I looked at his height, listened to the already deepening voice, saw the emerging man in the boy and his wish to leave childhood behind.

'Hop in the car,' I said and, deeply pleased, he sat beside me on the short return journey.

'When you went up to the big top,' I asked him, 'what did Keith Stratton say to you?'

'That man!' Christopher shuddered. 'It seemed all right at first. He told us to go into the big top. He said you would be coming.'

'So then?' I prompted, as he stopped.

'So we went in, and he came in behind us. He told us to go on ahead, and we did.'

'Yes.'

'Then . . .' he hesitated, 'it got *weird*, Dad. I mean, he picked up a can that was lying there and took the cap off, and we could *smell* it was petrol. Then he put the can down again and picked up that rod thing, and flicked his lighter, and the end of the rod lit up like those torches in Ku Klux Klan films.'

'Yeah.'

'Then he poured petrol onto the floor and trailed the torch into it and of course it went on fire, but just in one place.' He paused, remembering. 'We began to be scared, Dad. You've always told us never to put fire near petrol, and he had a big can of it in one hand and the torch in the other. He told us to go up further into the big top and he came along behind us and started another fire, and then another, and lots of them and we got really frightened, but all he said was that you would come soon. "Your father will come." He gave us the creeps, Dad. He didn't behave like a grown-up. He wasn't *sensible*, Dad.'

'No.'

'He told us to go on further in, past that sort of stand thing

269

that was there, and he put the torch into it so that it just burned *there*, and wasn't swinging about, and that was better, but we still didn't *like* it. But he put the petrol can down too, and then he just looked at us and *smiled*, and it was *awful*, I mean, I can't describe it.'

'You're doing well.'

'He frightened me rigid, Dad. We all wanted to be out of there. Then Alan darted past him suddenly and then Edward, and I did too, and he yelled at us and ran about to stop us and we dodged him and ran, I mean, *pelted*, Dad . . . and then Toby didn't come out after us, and Neil started screaming . . . and that's when you came.'

I stopped the car beside Roger's jeep. Keith's Jaguar stood beyond, and beyond that, a police car.

'And he didn't say anything else?' I asked.

'No, only something about not being blackmailed by *you*. I mean, it was silly, you wouldn't blackmail anyone.'

I smiled inwardly at his faith. Blackmail wasn't necessarily for money.

'No,' I said. 'All the same, don't repeat that bit, OK?'

'No, Dad, OK.'

Feeling curiously lightheaded, I walked across to the office with Christopher and told the police, when they asked, that I had no idea why Keith Stratton had behaved as irrationally as he had.

It was Friday before I left Stratton Park.

All Wednesday afternoon I replied 'I don't know' to relays of police questions, and agreed that I would return dutifully for an inquest.

I said nothing about rushing at Keith to overbalance him. It didn't sound sensible. I said nothing about Neil.

When asked, I said I hadn't used a fire extinguisher to try to save Keith's life, because I couldn't find one.

'Four of them were lying out of sight in the bar area,' Roger told me.

'Who put them there?' the police asked.

'I don't know,' I said.

Christopher told the law that Keith was a 'nutter'. They listened politely enough and decided he was too young to be called as an inquest witness, as he had anyway not himself been present at the moment of the accident.

The Press came; took photographs; asked questions, got the same answers.

A policewoman, in my presence, asked the younger boys later, down at the Gardners, what they'd seen, but in the manner of children with questioning strangers they clammed up into big-eyed silence, volunteering nothing and answering mainly in nods. Yes – nod – there had been fires in the tent. Yes – nod – Keith Stratton had lit them. Yes – nod – Toby's hair had got singed. Yes – nod – Christopher had turned on the sprinkler, and yes – nod – their father had looked after them.

The Strattons, I thought ironically at one point, had nothing on the Morris family when it came to keeping things quiet.

On Thursday the clips came out of my mostly-healed cuts and, with Dart chauffeuring, I took Toby to Swindon to see what Penelope could do with his unevenly burned hair.

I watched her laugh with him and tease him. Watched her wash the still lingering singe smell out, and cut and brush and blow-dry the very short remaining brown curls. Watched her give him confidence in his new appearance and light up his smile.

I spent the whole time wondering where and how I could get her into bed.

Perdita came downstairs behaving like a mother hen defending her chick against predators, as if reading my mind.

'I told you too much, dear, on Tuesday,' she said a shade anxiously.

'I won't give you away.'

'And Keith Stratton is dead!'

'So sad,' I agreed.

She laughed. 'You're a rogue. Did you kill him?'

'In a way.' With help from my twelve-year-old, I thought, whether he realised it or not. 'Self-defence, you might say.'

271

Her eyes smiled, but her voice was sober. She used only one word for an opinion. '*Good.*'

Penelope finished the twelve-year-old's hair. I paid her. She thanked me. She had no idea what I felt for her, nor gave any flicker of response. I was six boys' father, almost double her age. Perdita, seeing all, patted my shoulder. I kissed the cheek of the mother and still lusted for the daughter, and walked away, with Toby, feeling empty and old.

Dart returned Toby to his brothers at the Gardners and willingly took me on to see Marjorie.

The manservant, aplomb in place, let us in and announced us. Marjorie sat, as before, in her commanding armchair. The smashed looking glass had been removed, the torn chairs were missing. Rebecca's shot at me had left no permanent traces.

'I came to say goodbye,' I said.

'But you'll come back to Stratton Park.'

'Probably not.'

'But we need you!'

I shook my head. 'You have a great racecourse manager in Colonel Gardner. You'll have record crowds at the next meeting, with Oliver Wells's flair for publicity. You'll commission superb new stands – and what I will do, if you like, is make sure any firms submitting proposals to you are substantial and trustworthy. And beyond that, as regards your family, you have more power than ever to hold things together. You don't have Keith, so you don't need any way of restraining him. You have control of Rebecca, who aimed – probably still aims – to run the racecourse herself. She has probably done herself in there, as, even after you're gone, Conrad and Dart can both hold blackmail and attempted murder over her head, enough to out-vote her at Board meetings.'

Marjorie listened and came up with her own sort of solution.

'I want you,' she said, 'to be a director. Conrad and Ivan and I will vote for it. Unanimous decision of the Board.'

'Hear, hear,' Dart said, delighted.

'You don't need me,' I protested.

'Yes, we do.'

I wanted to disentangle myself from the Strattons. I did not want to step in any way into my non-grandfather's shoes. From beyond the grave his influence and way of doing things had sucked me into a web of duplicity, and three times in a week his family had nearly cost me my life. I'd paid my debt to him, I thought. I needed now to be free.

And yet . . .

'I'll think about it,' I said.

Marjorie nodded, satisfied. 'With you in charge,' she said, 'the racecourse will prosper.'

'I have to talk to Conrad,' I said.

He was alone in his holy of holies, sitting behind his desk.

I'd left Dart again outside in his car, reading about hair-loss, though not acting as look-out this time.

'With this American system,' he said, deep in before-and-after photographs, 'I would never worry again. You can go swimming – diving – your new hair is part of you. But I'd have to go to America every six weeks to two months to keep it right.'

'You can afford it,' I said.

'Yes, but . . .'

'Go for it,' I said.

He needed encouragement. 'Do you really think I should?'

'I think you should book your first ticket at once.'

'Yes. *Yes.* Well, yes, I *will.*'

Conrad stood up when I went in. His cupboard door was closed, but boxes stood higgledy-piggledy on his carpet, their contents stirred up.

He didn't offer his hand. He seemed to feel awkward, as I did myself.

'Marjorie telephoned,' he said. 'She says she wants you on the Board. She says I'm to persuade you.'

'It's your own wishes that matter.'

'I don't know . . .'

'No. Well, I didn't come to talk about that. I came to return what I stole from you yesterday.'

'Only yesterday! So much has happened.'

I put on his desk the outer brown envelope marked 'Conrad'. He picked it up, looking at the sticky-tape closure.

'Like I told you,' I said, 'I did look inside. Keith knew I would look. I don't think he could bear the thought of my using what I learned. I confess that I'm glad I don't have to, as he's dead, but I would have done, and you'd better know that. But I'll not tell Marjorie what's in there – it's evident she doesn't know – and I'll never tell anyone else.'

'I don't want to open it,' Conrad said, putting the envelope down.

'I can't say that you should.'

'But you think so.'

'Keith would have burned it,' I said.

'Burned.' He shuddered. 'What a death!'

'Anyway,' I said, 'the knowledge belongs here, whatever you do with it. Your father meant you to have it. So,' I sighed, 'read it or burn it, but don't leave it lying about.' I paused. 'I apologise again for breaking in here. I'll be leaving Stratton Park in the morning. I'm sorry,' I made a vague gesture, 'for everything.'

I turned regretfully and made for the door.

'Wait,' Conrad said.

I paused, half in, half out.

'I have to know what you know.' He looked wretched. 'He was my twin. I know he envied me . . . I know it wasn't fair that I had so much just for being twenty-five minutes older, I know he was violent and cruel and often dangerous, I know he beat your mother and all his wives. I know he nearly killed Hannah's gypsy. I saw him kick you abominably . . . I know all that and more, but he was my brother, my *twin*.'

'Yes.'

The Strattons, whatever their faults, had their own tight indestructible loyalty; a family, whatever their internal fights, that closed ranks against the ordinary world.

Conrad picked up the envelope and ripped off the tape.

He re-read the first letter, then drew out the second letter and the white inner envelope.

'Remember,' he murmured, reading, 'that Keith always tells lies . . .'

He removed the five folded sheets of paper from the white envelope and read the top one, yet another short note from his father.

It said:

> This lie of Keith's cost me a great deal of money, which I gave to Keith himself, too trustingly. It took me many years to suspect that he'd robbed me. A small matter, compared with the truth.

Conrad put the note down and looked at the next sheet, another letter, but in typescript.

'Arne Verity Laboratories?' Conrad said. 'Who are they?'

He read the letter, which was addressed to his father, and dated two years earlier.

In essence, it said that the laboratory had conducted the requested analyses. The detailed results of each separate analysis were appended but, summarising, the results were as follows:

> You sent us three hairs, labelled 'A', 'B', and 'C'.
> The results of DNA analysis are:
> 'A' is almost certainly the parent of 'B'
> and
> 'A' and 'B' are the parents of 'C'.

Conrad looked up. 'What does it mean?'

'It means there was no gypsy. Keith invented him.'

'But . . .'

'It means that Keith was the father of Jack.'

Conrad sat down and looked faint.

'I don't believe it,' he breathed. 'I can't. It's not true.'

'Jack doesn't look like a gypsy,' I said. 'He looks like Keith.'

'Oh dear God . . .'

'Hannah doesn't like the gypsy story. She tells Jack his

father was a foreign aristocrat who would have been ruined by the scandal. Apart from the foreign bit, that's more or less true.'

'Hannah!' He looked even more distressed. 'What are you going to do about *her*?'

'Nothing,' I said, surprised he should ask. 'With Keith dead, I don't need to use what I know. Hannah is safe from it ever leaking out through me.'

'But she attacked you!'

I sighed. 'She never had a chance, did she? She was conceived in rape, abandoned by her mother and impregnated by her father. She was rejected by young men and not loved by her grandfather but, whatever he may be, she has Jack, her son. I'll not spoil that for her. In the same way that Keith was your twin, Hannah, whether I like it or not, is my half-sister. Let her alone.'

Conrad sat without moving for a long minute, then he shovelled his father's letters and the laboratory reports into the outer brown envelope and held out the whole package in my direction.

'Take it,' he said succinctly, 'and burn it.'

'Yes, OK.'

I went back to the desk and, taking the envelope, set out again for the door.

'Come on the Board,' Conrad said. 'As usual, Marjorie has it right. We're going to need you.'

The boys and Mrs Gardner said farewells as lengthily as Romeo and Juliet, with many promises of meeting again. Roger and I, less effusively, were nonetheless pleased at the prospect of working together in the future. 'Such a lot to see to,' Roger said.

Dart produced a diary. He would come to stay, he said, *after* he had been to America. He had, he said, made bookings.

The boys piled into the bus and waved like maniacs through the windows, and I drove us all away, back home to the peaceful Surrey–Sussex border.

'Did you have a good time, my darlings?' Amanda asked, embracing the children. 'What did you find to do while your father was busy getting himself into the newspapers?'

They gazed at her. Bit by bit they would no doubt tell her, but at that moment the question struck them dumb.

Neil finally said, earnestly, 'We made brilliant fruit cakes.'

Amanda told me reproachfully, 'The phone here has been ringing non-stop.' She looked me over without much concern. 'I suppose you're all right?'

'Yes,' I said. 'Fine.'

'Good.'

She took the children indoors. I stood by the bus, its engine cooling, and after a while I went and climbed into the oak.

Other trees might be flushing into leaf, but the oak as always hung back, vying with the ash to be the last turning green. I sat in the cradle of the fuzzy boughs, feeling the residual aches and sorenesses in my body, stretching for quiet in my mind.

After a while Amanda came out of the house and crossed to the tree.

'What are you doing up there?' she asked.

'Considering things.'

'Come down. I want to talk to you.'

I climbed down, not wanting to hear.

I said, 'I was afraid I would return to an empty house. Afraid you and Jamie might have gone.'

Her eyes widened. 'You always know too damned much.'

'I was afraid you'd met someone else.'

'Yes, I have.'

She wasn't exactly defiant, but she had already thought out what she wanted to say. She still looked lovely. I wished things were different.

'I've decided,' she said, 'that a formal separation from you wouldn't be good for the children. Also ...' she slightly hesitated and then screwed up the courage, '. . . he is married, and feels the same about his own family. So we will see each other often. Take it or leave it, Lee.'

She waited.

Christopher, Toby, Edward, Alan, Neil and Jamie. Six reasons.

'I'll take it,' I said.

She nodded, making a pact of it, and returned to the house.

At bedtime she went up to our room an hour earlier than me, as always, but when I went up she was for once wide awake.

'Did you find a ruin?' she asked, as I undressed.

'No. I'll go looking once the boys are back at school. I'll go off for a while.'

'Good.'

It wasn't good. It was terrible.

Instead of lying the customary five feet away from her I went round to her side of the huge bed and climbed in beside her: and I made love to Penelope in Amanda, in a turmoil of lust, deprivation, hunger, passion and penetration. A wild, rough sexual action unlike anything before in our marriage.

She responded, after the briefest of protestations and withdrawal, with some of her original ardour, and lay afterwards apart from me, separate again, not full of recriminations but with her mouth curving in a secretive, cat-with-cream smile.

Two months later she said, 'I'm pregnant. Did you know?'

'I wondered,' I said. I screwed myself to the question. 'Is it mine . . . or *his*?'

'Oh, yours,' she said positively. 'He can't give me a child. He had a vasectomy too long ago.'

'Oh.'

'It might be a girl,' Amanda said coolly. 'You always wanted a daughter.'

In the fullness of time she gave rapturous birth to her seventh child.

A boy.

Fine by me.

HIGH STAKES

INTRODUCTION

It's impossible sometimes for an author to remember exactly what sight or sound kicked his imagination's starter-motor into life. I think that for *High Stakes* the basic idea arose simply from an abstract contemplation of the consequences of a betrayal of trust – in this case the blind trust of an enthusiastic but ignorant owner of racehorses in the friendship, good faith and honesty of his trainer.

I grafted on to this concept the all-too-common phenomenon of the sinner being seen as the victim in the public mind, while the real victim is cast as the sinner. I was much taken at that time by a bitter joke about a man who fell among thieves who robbed him, beat him and left him for dead in the gutter. Along came two social workers who looked at his wounds and said, 'The man who did this needs our help.'

My betrayed racehorse owner, victim cast as sinner, became Steven Scott, chief character of *High Stakes*. I gave him a mind that worked more comfortably in circles than in straight lines, and I made him an inventor of rotary gadgets and toys.

To defeat his enemies Scott gathered round him a circle of friends, and devised a circular conjuring trick with horses.

By this time thinking in circles myself, I borrowed the essentials of a belt-driven power system installed in my father-in-law's printing factory and translated them into a simplified version for Steven Scott's workshop.

On the ground floor of the factory, the thunder of the monster rollers on the huge printing presses made talking impossible. On the next floor came medium machines with, on the top floor, quietly clack-clacking contraptions that sorted, cut, glued and counted. All the machines on the two upper floors were driven by a weighty ground-floor engine that set heavy belts revolving on central spindles running the lengths of the upper-floor ceilings. Though nowadays no doubt every machine is individually powered by electricity, the centrally powered belt system ran economically for generations.

A man was killed in my father-in-law's factory. I used that, too, in *High Stakes*.

CHAPTER ONE

I looked at my friend and saw a man who had robbed me. Deeply disturbing. The ultimate in rejection.

Jody Leeds looked back at me, half smiling, still disbelieving.

'You're *what*?'

'Taking my horses away,' I said.

'But . . . I'm your *trainer*.' He sounded bewildered. Owners, his voice and expression protested, never deserted their trainers. It simply wasn't done. Only the eccentric or the ruthless shifted their horses from stable to stable, and I had shown no signs of being either.

We stood outside the weighing room of Sandown Park racecourse on a cold windy day with people scurrying past us carrying out saddles and number cloths for the next steeplechase. Jody hunched his shoulders inside his sheepskin coat and shook his bare head. The wind blew straight brown hair in streaks across his eyes and he pulled them impatiently away.

'Come on, Steven,' he said. 'You're kidding me.'

'No.'

Jody was short, stocky, twenty-eight, hardworking, clever, competent and popular. He had been my constant adviser since I had bought my first racehorses three years earlier, and right from the beginning he had robbed me round the clock and smiled while doing it.

'You're crazy,' he said. 'I've just won you a race.'

We stood, indeed, on the patch of turf where winners were unsaddled: where Energise, my newest and glossiest hurdler, had recently decanted his smiling jockey, had stamped and steamed and tossed his head with pride and accepted the crowd's applause as simply his due.

The race he had won had not been important, but the way he had won it had been in the star-making class. The sight of him sprinting up the hill to the winning post, a dark brown streak of rhythm, had given me a rare bursting feeling of admiration, of joy ... probably even of love. Energise was beautiful and courageous and chockfull of will to win and it was because he had won, and won in that fashion, that my hovering intention to break with Jody had hardened into action.

I should, I suppose, have chosen a better time and place.

'I picked out Energise for you at the Sales,' he said.

'I know.'

'And all your other winners.'

'Yes.'

'And I moved into bigger stables because of you.'

I nodded briefly.

'Well . . . You can't let me down now.'

Disbelief had given way to anger. His bright blue eyes sharpened to belligerence and the muscles tightened round his mouth.

'I'm taking the horses away,' I repeated. 'And we'll start with Energise. You can leave him here when you go home.'

'You're mad.'

'No.'

'Where's he going then?'

I actually had no idea. I said, 'I'll make all the arrangements. Just leave him in the stable here and go home without him.'

'You've no right to do this.' Full-scale anger blazed in his eyes. 'You're a bloody rotten *shit*.'

But I had every right. He knew it and I knew it. Every owner had the right at any time to withdraw his custom if he were dissatisfied with his trainer. The fact that the right was seldom exercised was beside the point.

Jody was rigid with fury. 'I am taking that horse home with me and nothing is going to stop me.'

His very intensity stoked up in me an answering determination that he should not. I shook my head decisively. I said, 'No, Jody. The horse stays here.'

'Over my dead body.'

His body, alive, quivered with pugnaciousness.

'As of this moment,' I said, 'I'm cancelling your authority to act on my behalf, and I'm going straight into the weighing room to make that clear to all the authorities who need to know.'

He glared. 'You owe me money,' he said. 'You can't take your horses away until you've paid.'

I paid my bills with him on the nail every month and owed him only for the current few weeks. I pulled my cheque book out of my pocket and unclipped my pen.

'I'll give you a cheque right now.'

'No you bloody well won't.'

He snatched the whole cheque book out of my hand and ripped it in two. Then in the same movement he threw the pieces over his shoulder, and all the loose halves of the cheques scattered in the wind. Faces turned our way in astonishment and the eyes of the Press came sharply to life. I couldn't have chosen anywhere more public for what was developing into a first class row.

Jody looked around him. Looked at the men with notebooks. Saw his allies.

His anger grew mean.

'You'll be sorry,' he said. 'I'll chew you into little bits.'

The face that five minutes earlier had smiled with cheerful decisive friendliness had gone for good. Even if I now retracted and apologised, the old relationship could not be re-established. Confidence, like Humpty Dumpty, couldn't be put together again.

His fierce opposition had driven me further than I

had originally meant. All the same I still had the same objective, even if I had to fight harder to achieve it.

'Whatever you do,' I said, 'you won't keep my horses.'

'You're ruining me,' Jody shouted.

The Press advanced a step or two.

Jody cast a quick eye at them. Maliciousness flooded through him and twisted his features with spite. 'You big rich bastards don't give a damn who you hurt.'

I turned abruptly away from him and went into the weighing room, and there carried out my promise to disown him officially as my trainer. I signed forms cancelling his authority to act for me, and for good measure also included a separate handwritten note to say that I had expressly forbidden him to remove Energise from Sandown Park. No one denied I had the right: there was just an element of coolness towards one who was so vehemently and precipitately ridding himself of the services of the man who had ten minutes ago given him a winner.

I didn't tell them that it had taken a very long time for the mug to face the fact that he was being conned. I didn't tell them how I had thrust the first suspicions away as disloyalty and had made every possible allowance before being reluctantly convinced.

I didn't tell them either that the reason for my determination now lay squarely in Jody's first reaction to my saying I was removing my horses.

Because he hadn't, not then or afterwards, asked the one natural question.

He hadn't asked *why*.

When I left the weighing room, both Jody and the Press had gone from the unsaddling enclosure. Racegoers were hurrying towards the stands to watch the imminent steeplechase, the richest event of the afternoon, and even the officials with whom I'd just been dealing were dashing off with the same intent.

I had no appetite for the race. Decided, instead, to go down to the racecourse stables and ask the gatekeeper there to make sure Energise didn't vanish in a puff of smoke. But as the gatekeeper was there to prevent villainous strangers walking *in*, not any bona fide racehorses walking *out*, I wasn't sure how much use he would be, even if he agreed to help.

He was sitting in his sentry box, a middle-aged sturdy figure in a navy blue serge uniform with brass buttons. Various lists on clip-boards hung on hooks on the walls, alongside an electric heater fighting a losing battle against the December chill.

'Excuse me,' I said. 'I want to ask you about my horse . . .'

'Can't come in here,' he interrupted bossily. 'No owners allowed in without trainers.'

'I know that,' I said. 'I just want to make sure my horse stays here.'

'What horse is that?'

He was adept at interrupting, like many people in small positions of power. He blew on his fingers and looked at me over them without politeness.

'Energise,' I said.

He screwed up his mouth and considered whether to answer. I supposed that he could find no reason against it except natural unhelpfulness, because in the end he said grudgingly, 'Would it be a black horse trained by Leeds?'

'It would.'

'Gone then,' he said.

'Gone?'

'S'right. Lad took him off, couple of minutes ago.' He jerked his head in the general direction of the path down to the area where the motor horseboxes were parked. 'Leeds was with him. Ask me, they'll have driven off by now.' The idea seemed to cheer him. He smiled.

I left him to his sour satisfaction and took the path at a run. It led down between bushes and opened abruptly straight on to the gravelled acre where dozens of horseboxes stood in haphazard rows.

Jody's box was fawn with scarlet panels along the sides: and Jody's box was already manoeuvring out of its slot and turning to go between two of the rows on its way to the gate.

I slid my binoculars to the ground and left them, and fairly sprinted. Ran in front of the first row of

7

boxes and raced round the end to find Jody's box completing its turn from between the rows about thirty yards away, and accelerating straight towards me.

I stood in its path and waved my arms for the driver to stop.

The driver knew me well enough. His name was Andy-Fred. He drove my horses regularly. I saw his face, looking horrified and strained, as he put his hand on the horn button and punched it urgently.

I ignored it, sure that he would stop. He was advancing between a high wooden fence on one side and the flanks of parked horseboxes on the other, and it wasn't until it became obvious that he didn't know what his brakes were for that it occurred to me that maybe Energise was about to leave over *my* dead body, not Jody's.

Anger, not fear, kept me rooted to the spot.

Andy-Fred's nerve broke first, thank God, but only just. He wrenched the wheel round savagely when the massive radiator grill was a bare six feet from my annihilation and the diesel throb was a roar in my ears.

He had left it too late for braking. The sudden swerve took him flatly into the side of the foremost of the parked boxes and with screeching and tearing sounds of metal the front corner of Jody's box ploughed forwards and inwards until the colliding doors of the cabs of both vehicles were locked in one crumpled mess. Glass smashed and tinkled and flew about with razor edges. The engine stalled and died.

The sharp bits on the front of Jody's box had missed me but the smooth wing caught me solidly as I leapt belatedly to get out of the way. I lay where I'd bounced, half against the wooden fence, and wholly winded.

Andy-Fred jumped down unhurt from the unsmashed side of his cab and advanced with a mixture of fear, fury and relief.

'What the bloody hell d'you think you're playing at?' he yelled.

'Why . . .' I said weakly, 'didn't . . . you . . . stop?'

I doubt if he heard me. In any case, he didn't answer. He turned instead to the exploding figure of Jody, who arrived at a run along the front of the boxes, the same way that I had come.

He practically danced when he saw the crushed cabs and rage poured from his mouth like fire.

'You stupid *bugger*,' he shouted at Andy-Fred. 'You stupid sodding effing . . .'

The burly box driver shouted straight back.

'He stood right in my way.'

'I told you not to stop.'

'I'd have killed him.'

'No you wouldn't.'

'I'm telling you. He stood there. Just stood there . . .'

'He'd have jumped if you'd kept on going. You stupid bugger. Just look what you've done. You stupid . . .'

Their voices rose, loud and acrimonious, into the wind. Further away the commentator's voice boomed over the tannoy system, broadcasting the progress of the steeplechase. On the other side of the high wooden fence the traffic pounded up and down the London to Guildford road. I gingerly picked myself off the cold gravel and leaned against the weathered planks.

Nothing broken. Breath coming back. Total damage, all the buttons missing from my overcoat. There was a row of small right-angled tears down the front where the buttons had been. I looked at them vaguely and knew I'd been lucky.

Andy-Fred was telling Jody at the top of a raucous voice that he wasn't killing anyone for Jody's sake, he was bloody well not.

'You're fired,' Jody yelled.

'Right.'

He took a step back, looked intensely at the mangled horseboxes, looked at me, and looked at Jody. He thrust his face close to Jody's and yelled at him again.

'*Right.*'

Then he stalked away in the direction of the stables and didn't bother to look back.

Jody's attention and fury veered sharply towards me. He took three or four purposeful steps and yelled, 'I'll sue you for this.'

I said, 'Why don't you find out if the horse is all right?'

He couldn't hear me for all the day's other noises.

'What?'

'Energise,' I said loudly. 'Is he all right?'

He gave me a sick hot look of loathing and scudded away round the side of the box. More slowly, I followed. Jody yanked open the groom's single door and hauled himself up inside and I went after him.

Energise was standing in his stall quivering from head to foot and staring wildly about with a lot of white round his eyes. Jody had packed him off still sweating from his race and in no state anyway to travel and the crash had clearly terrified him: but he was none the less on his feet and Jody's anxious search could find no obvious injury.

'No thanks to you,' Jody said bitterly.

'Nor to you.'

We faced each other in the confined space, a quiet oasis out of the wind.

'You've been stealing from me,' I said. 'I didn't want to believe it. But from now on . . . I'm not giving you the chance.'

'You won't be able to prove a thing.'

'Maybe not. Maybe I won't even try. Maybe I'll write off what I've lost as the cost of my rotten judgement in liking and trusting you.'

He said indignantly, 'I've done bloody well for you.'

'And out of me.'

'What do you expect? Trainers aren't in it for love, you know.'

'Trainers don't all do what you've done.'

A sudden speculative look came distinctly into his eyes. 'What have I done, then?' he demanded.

'You tell me,' I said. 'You haven't even pretended to deny you've been cheating me.'

'Look, Steven, you're so bloody unworldly. All right, so maybe I have added a bit on here and there. If you're talking about the time I charged you travelling expenses for Hermes to Haydock the day they abandoned for fog before the first . . . well, I know I didn't actually *send* the horse . . . he went lame that morning and couldn't go. But trainer's perks. Fair's fair. And you could afford it. You'd never miss thirty measly quid.'

'What else?' I said.

He seemed reassured. Confidence and a faint note of defensive wheedling seeped into his manner and voice.

'Well . . .' he said. 'If you ever disagreed with the totals of your bills, why didn't you query it with me? I'd have straightened things out at once. There was no need to bottle it all up and blow your top without warning.'

Ouch, I thought. I hadn't even checked that all the separate items on the monthly bills did add up to the totals I'd paid. Even when I was sure he was robbing me, I hadn't suspected it would be in any way so ridiculously simple.

'What else?' I said.

He looked away for a second, then decided that I couldn't after all know a great deal.

'Oh all right,' he said, as if making a magnanimous concession. 'It's Raymond, isn't it?'

'Among other things.'

Jody nodded ruefully. 'I guess I did pile it on a bit, charging you for him twice a week when some weeks he only came once.'

'And some weeks not at all.'

'Oh well . . .' said Jody deprecatingly. 'I suppose so, once or twice.'

Raymond Child rode all my jumpers in races and drove fifty miles some mornings to school them over fences on Jody's gallops. Jody gave him a fee and expenses for the service and added them to my account. The twice a week schooling session fees had turned up regularly for the whole of July, when in fact, as I had very recently and casually discovered, no horses had been schooled at all and Raymond himself had been holidaying in Spain.

'A tenner here or there,' Jody said persuasively. 'It's nothing to you.'

'A tenner plus expenses twice a week for July came to over a hundred quid.'

'Oh.' He tried a twisted smile. 'So you really have been checking up.'

'What did you expect?'

'You're so easy going. You've always paid up without question.'

'Not any more.'

'No ... Look, Steven, I'm sorry about all this. If I give you my word there'll be no more fiddling on your account ... If I promise every item will be strictly accurate ... why don't we go on as before? I've won a lot of races for you, after all.'

He looked earnest, sincere and repentant. Also totally confident that I would give him a second chance. A quick canter from confession to penitence, and a promise to reform, and all could proceed as before.

'It's too late,' I said.

He was not discouraged; just piled on a bit more of the ingratiating manner which announced 'I know I've been a bad bad boy but now I've been found out I'll be angelic.'

'I suppose having so much extra expense made me behave stupidly,' he said. 'The mortgage repayments on the new stables are absolutely bloody, and as you know I only moved there because I needed more room for all your horses.'

My fault, now, that he had had to steal.

I said, 'I offered to build more boxes at the old place.'

'Wouldn't have done,' he interrupted hastily: but the truth of it was that the old place had been on a plain and modest scale where the new one was frankly opulent. At the time of the move I had vaguely wondered how he could afford it. Now, all too well, I knew.

'So let's call this just a warning, eh?' Jody said cajolingly. 'I don't want to lose your horses, Steven. I'll say so frankly. I don't want to lose them. We've been good friends all this time, haven't we? If you'd just *said* . . . I mean, if you'd just said, "Jody, you bugger, you've been careless about a bill or two . . ." Well, I mean, we could have straightened it out in no time. But . . . well . . . When you blew off without warning, just said you were taking the horses away, straight after Energise won like that . . . well, I lost my temper real and proper. I'll admit I did. Said things I didn't mean. Like one does. Like everyone does when they lose their temper.'

He was smiling in a counterfeit of the old way, as if nothing at all had happened. As if Energise were not standing beside us sweating in a crashed horsebox. As if my overcoat were not torn and muddy from a too close brush with death.

'Steven, you know me,' he said. 'Got a temper like a bloody rocket.'

When I didn't answer at once he took my silence as acceptance of his explanations and apologies, and briskly turned to practical matters.

'Well now, we'll have to get this lad out of here.' He slapped Energise on the rump. 'And we can't get the ramp down until we get this box moved away from that other one.' He made a sucking sound through his teeth. 'Look, I'll try to back straight out again. Don't see why it shouldn't work.'

He jumped out of the back door and went round to

the front of the cab. Looking forward through the stalls I could see him climb into the driver's seat, check the gear lever, and press the starter: an intent, active, capable figure dealing with an awkward situation.

The diesel starter whirred and the engine roared to life. Jody settled himself, found reverse gear, and carefully let out the clutch. The horsebox shuddered and stood still. Jody put his foot down on the accelerator.

Through the windscreen I could see two or three men approaching, faces a mixture of surprise and anger. One of them began running and waving his arms about in the classic reaction of the chap who comes back to his parked car to find it dented.

Jody ignored him. The horsebox rocked, the crushed side of the cab screeched against its mangled neighbour, and Energise began to panic.

'Jody, stop,' I yelled.

He took no notice. He raced the engine harder, then took his foot off the accelerator, then jammed it on again. Off, on, repeatedly.

Inside the box it sounded as if the whole vehicle were being ripped in two. Energise began whinnying and straining backwards on his tethering rope and stamping about with sharp hooves. I didn't know how to begin to soothe him and could hardly get close enough for a pat, even if that would have made the slightest difference. My relationship with horses was along the lines of admiring them from a distance and giving them carrots while they were safely tied up. No one had briefed me about dealing with a hysterical animal at close quarters in a bucketing biscuit tin.

With a final horrendous crunch the two entwined cabs tore apart and Jody's box, released from friction, shot backwards. Energise slithered and went down for a moment on his hind-quarters and I too wound up on the floor. Jody slammed on the brakes, jumped out of the cab and was promptly clutched by the three newcomers, one now in a full state of apoplectic rage.

I stood up and picked bits of hay off my clothes and regarded my steaming, foam-flaked, terrified, four-footed property.

'All over, old fellow,' I said.

It sounded ridiculous. I smiled, cleared my throat, tried again.

'You can cool off, old lad. The worst is over.'

Energise showed no immediate signs of getting the message. I told him he was a great horse, he'd won a great race, he'd be king of the castle in no time and that I admired him very much. I told him he would soon be rugged up nice and quiet in a stable somewhere though I hadn't actually yet worked out exactly which one, and that doubtless someone would give him some excessively expensive hay and a bucket of nice cheap water and I dared say some oats and stuff like that. I told him I was sorry I hadn't a carrot in my pocket at that moment but I'd bring him one next time I saw him.

After a time this drivel seemed to calm him. I put

out a hand and gave his neck a small pat. His skin was wet and fiery hot. He shook his head fiercely and blew out vigorously through black moist nostrils, but the staring white no longer showed round his eye and he had stopped trembling. I began to grow interested in him in a way which had not before occurred to me: as a person who happened also to be a horse.

I realised I had never before been alone with a horse. Extraordinary, really, when Energise was the twelfth I'd owned. But racehorse owners mostly patted their horses in stables with lads and trainers in attendance, and in parade rings with all the world looking on, and in unsaddling enclosures with friends pressing round to congratulate. Owners who like me were not riders themselves and had nowhere of their own to turn horses out to grass seldom ever spent more than five consecutive minutes in a horse's company.

I spent longer with Energise in that box than in all the past five months since I'd bought him.

Outside, Jody was having troubles. One of the men had fetched a policeman who was writing purposefully in a notebook. I wondered with amusement just how Jody would lay the blame on my carelessness in walking in front of the box and giving the driver no choice but to swerve. If he thought he was keeping my horses, he would play it down. If he thought he was losing them, he'd be vitriolic. Smiling to myself I talked it over with Energise.

'You know,' I said, 'I don't know why I haven't told

him yet that I know about his other fraud, but as it turns out I'm damn glad I haven't. Do you know?' I said. 'All those little fiddles he confessed to, they're just froth.'

Energise was calm enough to start drooping with tiredness. I watched him sympathetically.

'It isn't just a few hundred quid he's pinched,' I said. 'It's upwards of thirty-five thousand.'

CHAPTER TWO

The owner of the crunched box accepted my apologies, remembered he was well insured and decided not to press charges. The policeman sighed, drew a line through his notes and departed. Jody let down the ramp of his box, brought out Energise and walked briskly away with him in the direction of the stables. And I returned to my binoculars, took off my battered coat and went thoughtfully back towards the weighing room.

The peace lasted for all of ten minutes – until Jody returned from the stables and found I had not cancelled my cancellation of his authority to act.

He sought me out among the small crowd standing around talking on the weighing room verandah.

'Look, Steven,' he said. 'You've forgotten to tell them I'm still training for you.'

He showed no anxiety, just slight exasperation at my oversight. I weakened for one second at the thought of the storm which would undoubtedly break out again and began to make all the old fatal allowances: he *was* a good trainer, and my horses *did* win, now and again.

20

And I could keep a sharp eye on the bills and let him know I was doing it. And as for the other thing . . . I could easily avoid being robbed in future.

I took a deep breath. It had to be now or never.

'I haven't forgotten,' I said slowly. 'I meant what I said. I'm taking the horses away.'

'*What?*'

'I am taking them away.'

The naked enmity that filled his face was shocking.

'You *bastard*,' he said.

Heads turned again in our direction.

Jody produced several further abusive epithets, all enunciated very clearly in a loud voice. The Press notebooks sprouted like mushrooms in little white blobs on the edge of my vision and I took the only way I knew to shut him up.

'I backed Energise today on the Tote,' I said.

Jody said 'So what?' very quickly in the second before the impact of what I meant hit him like a punch.

'I'm closing my account with Ganser Mays,' I said.

Jody looked absolutely murderous, but he didn't ask *why*. Instead he clamped his jaws together, cast a less welcoming glance at the attentive Press and said very quietly and with menace, 'If you say anything I'll sue you for libel.'

'Slander,' I said automatically.

'What?'

'Libel is written, slander is spoken.'

'I'll have you,' he said, 'if you say anything.'

'Some friendship,' I commented.

His eyes narrowed. 'It was a pleasure,' he said, 'to take you for every penny I could.'

A small silence developed. I felt that racing had gone thoroughly sour and that I would never get much fun from it again. Three years of uncomplicated enjoyment had crumbled to disillusionment.

In the end I simply said, 'Leave Energise here. I'll fix his transport,' and Jody turned on his heel with a stony face and plunged in through the weighing room door.

The transport proved no problem. I arranged with a young owner-driver of a one-box transport firm that he should take Energise back to his own small transit yard overnight and ferry him on in a day or two to whichever trainer I decided to send him.

'A dark brown horse. Almost black,' I said. 'The gatekeeper will tell you which box he's in. But I don't suppose he'll have a lad with him.'

The owner-driver, it transpired, could provide a lad to look after Energise. 'He'll be right as rain,' he said. 'No need for you to worry.' He had brought two other horses to the course, one of which was in the last race, and he would be away within an hour afterwards, he said. We exchanged telephone numbers and addresses and shook hands on the deal.

After that, more out of politeness than through any

great appetite for racing, I went back to the private
box of the man who had earlier given me lunch and
with whom I'd watched my own horse win.

'Steven, where have you been? We've been waiting
to help you celebrate.'

Charlie Canterfield, my host, held his arms wide in
welcome, with a glass of champagne in one hand and
a cigar in the other. He and his eight or ten other guests
sat on dining chairs round a large central table, its
white cloth covered now not with the paraphernalia of
lunch, but with a jumble of half full glasses, race cards,
binoculars, gloves, handbags and betting tickets. A faint
haze of Havana smoke and the warm smell of alcohol
filled the air, and beyond, on the other side of snugly
closed glass, lay the balcony overlooking the fresh and
windy racecourse.

Four races down and two to go. Mid afternoon.
Everyone happy in the interval between coffee-and-
brandy and cake-and-tea. A cosy little roomful of
chat and friendliness and mild social smugness. Well-
intentioned people doing no one any harm.

I sighed inwardly and raised a semblance of enjoyment for Charlie's sake, and sipped champagne and
listened to everyone telling me it was *great* that Energise had won. They'd all backed it, they said. Lots of
lovely lolly, Steven dear. Such a clever horse ... and
such a clever little trainer, Jody Leeds.

'Mm,' I said, with a dryness no one heard.

Charlie waved me to the empty chair between himself and a lady in a green hat.

'What do you fancy for the next race?' he asked.

I looked at him with a mind totally blank.

'Can't remember what's running,' I said.

Charlie's leisured manner skipped a beat. I'd seen it in him before, this split-second assessment of a new factor, and I knew that therein lay the key to his colossal business acumen. His body might laze, his bonhomie might expand like softly whipped cream, but his brain never took a moment off.

I gave him a twisted smile.

Charlie said, 'Come to dinner.'

'Tonight, do you mean?'

He nodded.

I bit my thumb and thought about it. 'All right.'

'Good. Let's say Parkes, Beauchamp Place, eight o'clock.'

'All right.'

The relationship between Charlie and me had stood for years in that vague area between acquaintanceship and active friendship where chance meetings are enjoyed and deliberate ones seldom arranged. That day was the first time he had invited me to his private box. Asking me for dinner as well meant a basic shift to new ground.

I guessed he had misread my vagueness, but all the same I liked him, and no one in his right mind would pass up a dinner at Parkes. I hoped he wouldn't think it a wasted evening.

Charlie's guests began disappearing to put on bets for the next race. I picked up a spare race card which was lying on the table and knew at once why Charlie had paid me such acute attention: two of the very top hurdlers were engaged in battle and the papers had been talking about it for days.

I looked up and met Charlie's gaze. His eyes were amused.

'Which one, then?' he asked.

'Crepitas.'

'Are you betting?'

I nodded. 'I did it earlier. On the Tote.'

He grunted. 'I prefer the bookmakers. I like to know what odds I'm getting before I lay out my cash.' And considering his business was investment banking that was consistent thinking. 'I can't be bothered to walk down, though.'

'You can have half of mine, if you like,' I said.

'Half of how much?' he said cautiously.

'Ten pounds.'

He laughed. 'Rumour says you can't think in anything less than three noughts.'

'That was an engineering joke,' I said, 'which escaped.'

'How do you mean?'

'I sometimes use a precision lathe. You can just about set it to an accuracy of three noughts . . . point nought nought nought one. One ten-thousandth of an inch. That's my limit. Can't think in less than three noughts.'

He chuckled. 'And you never have a thousand on a horse?'

'Oh, I did that too, once or twice.'

He definitely did, that time, hear the arid undertone. I stood up casually and moved towards the glass door to the balcony.

'They're going down to the post,' I said.

He came without comment, and we stood outside watching the two stars, Crepitas and Waterboy, bouncing past the stands with their jockeys fighting for control.

Charlie was a shade shorter than I, a good deal stouter, and approximately twenty years older. He wore top quality clothes as a matter of course and no one hearing his mellow voice would have guessed his father had been a lorry driver. Charlie had never hidden his origins. Indeed he was justly proud of them. It was simply that under the old educational system he'd been sent to Eton as a local boy on Council money, and had acquired the speech and social habits along with the book learning. His brains had taken him along all his life like a surf rider on the crest of a roller, and it was probably only a modest piece of extra luck that he'd happened to be born within sight of the big school.

His other guests drifted out on to the balcony and claimed his attention. I knew none of them well, most of them by sight, one or two by reputation. Enough for the occasion, not enough for involvement.

The lady in the green hat put a green glove on my arm. 'Waterboy looks wonderful, don't you think?'

'Wonderful,' I agreed.

She gave me a bright myopic smile from behind think lensed glasses. 'Could you just tell me what price they're offering now in the ring?'

'Of course.'

I raised my binoculars and scanned the boards of the bookmakers ranged in front of a sector of stands lying some way to our right. 'It looks like evens Waterboy and five to four Crepitas, as far as I can see.'

'So kind,' said the green lady warmly.

I swung the binoculars round a little to search out Ganser Mays: and there he stood, half way down the row of bookmakers lining the rails separating the Club Enclosure from Tattersall's, a thin man of middle height with a large sharp nose, steel-rimmed spectacles and the manner of a high church clergyman. I had never liked him enough to do more than talk about the weather, but I had trusted him completely, and that had been foolish.

He was leaning over the rails, head bent, talking earnestly to someone in the Club Enclosure, someone hidden from me by a bunch of other people. Then the bunch shifted and moved away and the person behind them was Jody.

The anger in Jody's body came over sharp and clear

and his lower jaw moved vigorously in speech. Ganser Mays' responses appeared more soothing than fierce and when Jody finally strode furiously away, Ganser Mays raised his head and looked after him with an expression more thoughtful than actively worried.

Ganser Mays had reached that point in a book-maker's career where outstanding personal success began to merge into the status of a large and respect-able firm. In gamblers' minds he was moving from an individual to an institution. A multiplying host of betting shops bore his name from Glasgow southwards, and recently he had announced that next Flat season he would sponsor a three-year-old sprint.

He still stood on the rails himself at big meetings to talk to his more affluent customers and keep them faithful. To open his big shark jaws and suck in all the new unwary little fish.

With a wince I swung my glasses away. I would never know exactly how much Jody and Ganser Mays had stolen from me in terms of cash, but in terms of dented self-respect they had stripped me of all but crumbs.

The race started, the super-hurdlers battled their hearts out, and Crepitas beat Waterboy by a length. The Tote would pay me a little because of him, and a great deal because of Energise, but two winning bets in one afternoon weren't enough to dispel my depression. I dodged the tea-and-cakes, thanked Charlie for the lunch and said I'd see him later, and went down towards the weighing room again to see if inspiration would strike in the matter of a choice of trainers.

I heard hurrying footsteps behind me and a hand grabbed my arm.

'Thank goodness I've found you.'

He was out of breath and looking worried. The young owner-driver I'd hired for Energise.

'What is it? Box broken down?'

'No . . . look, you did say your horse was black, didn't you? I mean, I did get that right, didn't I?'

Anxiety sharpened my voice. 'Is there anything wrong with him?'

'No . . . at least . . . not with him, no. But the horse which Mr Leeds has left for me to take is . . . well . . . a chestnut mare.'

I went with him to the stables. The gatekeeper still smiled with pleasure at things going wrong.

'S'right,' he said with satisfaction. 'Leeds went off a quarter of an hour ago in one of them hire boxes, one horse. Said his own box had had an accident and he was leaving Energise here, instructions of the owner.'

'The horse he's left is not Energise,' I said.

'Can't help that, can I?' he said virtuously.

I turned to the young man. 'Chestnut mare with a big white blaze?'

He nodded.

'That's Asphodel. She ran in the first race today. Jody Leeds trains her. She isn't mine.'

'What will I do about her then?'

29

'Leave her here,' I said. 'Sorry about this. Send me a bill for cancellation fees.'

He smiled and said he wouldn't, which almost restored my faith in human nature. I thanked him for bothering to find me instead of keeping quiet, taking the wrong horse and then sending me a bill for work done. He looked shocked that anyone could be so cynical, and I reflected that until I learnt from Jody, I wouldn't have been.

Jody had taken Energise after all.

I burnt with slow anger, partly because of my own lack of foresight. If he had been prepared to urge Andy-Fred to risk running me down I should have known that he wouldn't give up at the first setback. He had been determined to get the better of me and whisk Energise back to his own stable and I'd underestimated both his bloody-mindedness and his nerve.

I could hardly wait to be free of Jody. I went back to my car and drove away from the racecourse with no thoughts but of which trainer I would ask to take my horses and how soon I could get them transferred from one to the other.

Charlie smiled across the golden polished wood of the table in Parkes and pushed away his empty coffee cup. His cigar was half smoked, his port half drunk, and his stomach, if mine were anything to go by, contentedly full of some of the best food in London.

I wondered what he had looked like as a young man, before the comfortable paunch and the beginning of jowls. Big businessmen were all the better for a little weight, I thought. Lean-and-hungry was for the starters, the hotheads in a hurry. Charlie exuded maturity and wisdom with every excess pound.

He had smooth greying hair, thin on top and brushed back at the sides. Eyes deep set, nose large, mouth firmly straight. Not conventionally a good-looking face, but easy to remember. People who had once met Charlie tended to know him next time.

He had come alone, and the restaurant he had chosen consisted of several smallish rooms with three or four tables in each; a quiet place where privacy was easy. He had talked about racing, food, the Prime Minister and the state of the Stock Market, and still had not come to the point.

'I get the impression,' he said genially, 'that you are waiting for something.'

'You've never asked me to dine before.'

'I like your company.'

'And that's all?'

He tapped ash off the cigar. 'Of course not,' he said.

'I thought not,' I smiled. 'But I've probably eaten your dinner under false pretences.'

'Knowingly?'

'Maybe. I don't know exactly what's in your mind.'

'Your vagueness,' he said. 'When someone like you goes into a sort of trance . . .'

'I thought so,' I sighed. 'Well, that was no useful productive otherwhereness of mind, that was the aftermath of a practically mortal row I'd just had with Jody Leeds.'

He sat back in his chair. 'What a pity.'

'Pity about the row, or a pity about the absence of inspiration?'

'Both, I dare say. What was the row about?'

'I gave him the sack.'

He stared. 'What on earth for?'

'He said if I told anyone that, he'd sue me for slander.'

'Oh, did he indeed!' Charlie looked interested all over again, like a horse taking fresh hold of its bit. 'And could he?'

'I expect so.'

Charlie sucked a mouthful of smoke and trickled it out from one corner of his mouth.

'Care to risk it?' he said.

'Your discretion's better than most . . .'

'Absolute,' he said. 'I promise.'

I believed him. I said, 'He found a way of stealing huge sums from me so that I didn't know I was being robbed.'

'But you must have known that *someone* . . .'

I shook my head. 'I dare say I'm not the first the trick's been played on. It's so deadly simple.'

'Proceed,' Charlie said. 'You fascinate me.'

'Right. Now suppose you are basically a good racehorse trainer but you've got a large and crooked thirst for unearned income.'

'I'm supposing,' Charlie said.

'First of all, then,' I said, 'you need a silly mug with a lot of money and enthusiasm and not much knowledge of racing.'

'You?' Charlie said.

'Me.' I nodded ruefully. 'Someone recommends you to me as a good trainer and I'm impressed by your general air of competence and dedication, so I toddle up and ask you if you could find me a good horse, as I'd like to become an owner.'

'And do I buy a good horse cheaply and charge you a fortune for it?'

'No. You buy the very best horse you can. I am delighted, and you set about the training and very soon the horse is ready to run. At this point you tell me you know a very reliable bookmaker and you introduce me to him.'

'Oh hum.'

'As you say. The bookmaker however is eminently respectable and respected and as I am not used to betting in large amounts I am glad to be in the hands of so worthy a fellow. You, my trainer, tell me the horse shows great promise and I might think of a small each way bet on his first race. A hundred pounds each way, perhaps.'

'A small bet!' Charlie exclaimed.

'You point out that is scarcely more than three weeks' training fees,' I said.

'I do?'

'You do. So I gulp a little as I've always bet in tenners before and I stake a hundred each way. But sure enough the horse does run well and finishes third, and the bookmaker pays out a little instead of me paying him.'

I drank the rest of my glass of port. Charlie finished his and ordered more coffee.

'Next time the horse runs,' I went on, 'you say it is really well and sure to win and if I ever want to have a big bet, now's the time, before everyone else jumps on the bandwagon. The bookmaker offers me a good price and I feel euphoric and take the plunge.'

'A thousand?'

I nodded. 'A thousand.'

'And?'

'The word goes round and the horse starts favourite. It is not his day, though. He runs worse than the first time and finishes fifth. You are very upset. You can't understand it. I find myself comforting you and telling you he is bound to run better next time.'

'But he doesn't run better next time?'

'But he does. Next time he wins beautifully.'

'But you haven't backed it?'

'Yes, I have. The price this time isn't five to two as it was before, but six to one. I stake five hundred pounds and win three thousand. I am absolutely delighted. I have regained all the money I had lost and more besides, and I have also gained the prize money for the race. I pay the training bills out of the winnings and I have recouped part of the purchase price of the horse, and I am very happy with the whole business of being an owner. I ask you to buy me another horse. Buy two or three, if you can find them.'

'And this time you get expensive duds?'

'By no means. My second horse is a marvellous two-year-old. He wins his very first race. I have only a hundred on him, mind you, but as it is at ten to one, I am still very pleased. So next time out, as my horse is a hot favourite and tipped in all the papers, you encourage me to have a really big bet. Opportunities like this seldom arise, you tell me, as the opposition is hopeless. I am convinced, so I lay out three thousand pounds.'

'My God,' Charlie said.

'Quite so. My horse sprints out of the stalls and takes the lead like the champion he is and everything is going splendidly. But then half way along the five furlongs a buckle breaks on the saddle and the girths come loose and the jockey has to pull up as best he can because by now he is falling off.'

'Three thousand!' Charlie said.

'All gone,' I nodded. 'You are inconsolable. The strap was new, the buckle faulty. Never mind, I say kindly, gulping hard. Always another day.'

'And there is?'

'You're learning. Next time out the horse is favourite again and I have five hundred on. He wins all right, and although I have not this time won back all I lost, well, it's the second time the horse has brought home a decent prize, and taking all in all I am not out of pocket and I have had a great deal of pleasure and excitement. And I am well content.'

'And so it goes on?'

'And so, indeed, it goes on. I find I get more and more delight from watching horses. I get particular delight if the horses are my own, and although in time of course my hobby costs me a good deal of money, because owners on the whole don't make a profit, I am totally happy and consider it well spent.'

'And then what happens?'

'Nothing really,' I said. 'I just begin to get these niggling suspicions and I thrust them out of my head and think how horribly disloyal I am being to you, after all the winners you have trained for me. But the suspicions won't lie down. I've noticed, you see, that when I have my biggest bets, my horses don't win.'

'A lot of owners could say the same,' Charlie said.

'Oh sure. But I tot up all the big bets which didn't come up, and they come to nearly forty thousand pounds.'

'Good God.'

'I am really ashamed of myself, but I begin to *wonder*. I say to myself, suppose . . . just suppose . . . that every time I stake anything over a thousand, my trainer and my bookmaker conspire together and simply keep the money and make sure my horse doesn't win. Just suppose . . . that if I stake three thousand, they split it fifty fifty, and the horse runs badly, or is left, or the buckle on the girth breaks. Just suppose that next time out my horse is trained to the utmost and the race is carefully chosen and he duly wins, and I am delighted . . . just suppose that this time my bookmaker and my trainer are betting on the horse themselves . . . with the money they stole from me last time.'

Charlie looked riveted.

'If my horse wins, they win. If my horse loses, they haven't lost their own money, but only mine.'

'Neat.'

'Yes. So the weeks pass and now the Flat season is finished, and we are back with the jumpers. And you, my trainer, have found and bought for me a beautiful young hurdler, a really top class horse. I back him a little in his first race and he wins it easily. I am thrilled. I am also worried, because you tell me there is a race absolutely made for him at Sandown Park which he is certain to win, and you encourage me to have a very big bet on him. I am by now filled with horrid doubts and fears, and as I particularly admire this horse I do not want his heart broken by trying to win when he isn't allowed to . . . which I am sure happened to one or two of the others . . . so I say I will not back him.'

'Unpopular?'

'Very. You press me harder than ever before to lay out a large stake. I refuse. You are obviously annoyed and warn me that the horse will win and I will be sorry. I say I'll wait till next time. You say I am making a big mistake.'

'When do I say all this?'

'Yesterday.'

'And today?' Charlie asked.

'Today I am suffering from suspicion worse than ever. Today I think that maybe you will let the horse win if he can, just to prove I was wrong not to back him, so that next time you will have no difficulty at all in persuading me to have a bigger bet than ever.'

'Tut tut.'

'Yes. So today I don't tell you that a little while ago ... because of my awful doubts ... I opened a credit account with the Tote, and today I also don't tell you that I have backed my horse for a thousand pounds on my credit account.'

'Deceitful of you.'

'Certainly.'

'And your horse wins,' Charlie said, nodding.

'He looked superb ...' I smiled wryly. 'You tell me after the race that it is my own fault I didn't back him. You say you did try to get me to. You say I'd do better to take your advice next time.'

'And then?'

'Then,' I sighed, 'all the weeks of suspicion just jelled into certainty. I knew he'd been cheating me in other

ways too. Little ways. Little betrayals of friendship.
Nothing enormous. I told him there wasn't going to be
a next time. I said I would be taking the horses away.'

'What did he say to that?'

'He didn't ask why.'

'Oh dear,' Charlie said.

CHAPTER THREE

I told Charlie everything that had happened that day. All amusement died from his expression and by the end he was looking grim.

'He'll get away with it,' he said finally.

'Oh yes.'

'You remember, I suppose, that his father's a member of the Jockey Club?'

'Yes.'

'Above suspicion, is Jody Leeds.'

Jody's father, Quintus Leeds, had achieved pillar-of-the-Turf status by virtue of being born the fifth son of a sporting peer, owning a few racehorses and knowing the right friends. He had a physically commanding presence, tall, large and handsome, and his voice and handshake radiated firm confidence. He was apt to give people straight piercing looks from fine grey eyes and to purse his mouth thoughtfully and shake his head as if pledged to secrecy when asked for an opinion. I privately thought his appearance and mannerisms were a lot of glossy window-dressing concealing a marked absence of goods, but there was no doubting that he was basically well-meaning and honest.

He was noticeably proud of Jody, puffing up his chest and beaming visibly in unsaddling enclosures from Epsom to York.

In his father's eyes, Jody, energetic, capable and clever, could do no wrong. Quintus would believe him implicitly, and for all his suspect shortness of intelligence he carried enough weight to sway official opinion.

As Jody had said, I couldn't prove a thing. If I so much as hinted at theft he'd slap a lawsuit on me, and the bulk of the Jockey Club would be ranged on his side.

'What will you do?' Charlie said.

'Don't know.' I half smiled. 'Nothing, I suppose.'

'It's bloody unfair.'

'All crime is bloody unfair on the victim.'

Charlie made a face at the general wickedness of the world and called for the bill.

Outside we turned left and walked down Beauchamp Place together, having both, as it happened, parked our cars round the corner in Walton Street. The night was cold, cloudy, dry and still windy. Charlie pulled his coat collar up round his ears and put on thick black leather gloves.

'I hate the winter,' he said.

'I don't mind it.'

'You're young,' he said. 'You don't feel the cold.'

'Not that young. Thirty-five.'

'Practically a baby.'

We turned the corner and the wind bit sharply with Arctic teeth. 'I hate it,' Charlie said.

His car, a big blue Rover 3500, was parked nearer than my Lamborghini. We stopped beside his and he unlocked the door. Down the street a girl in a long dress walked in our direction, the wind blowing her skirt sideways and her hair like flags.

'Very informative evening,' he said, holding out his hand.

'Not what you expected, though,' I said, shaking it.

'Better perhaps.'

He opened his door and began to lower himself into the driver's seat. The girl in the long dress walked past us, her heels brisk on the pavement. Charlie fastened his seat belt and I shut his door.

The girl in the long dress stopped, hesitated and turned back.

'Excuse me,' she said. 'But I wonder...' She stopped, appearing to think better of it.

'Can we help you?' I said.

She was American, early twenties, and visibly cold. Round her shoulders she wore only a thin silk shawl, and under that a thin silk shirt. No gloves. Gold sandals. A small gold mesh purse. In the street lights her skin looked blue and she was shivering violently.

'Get in my car,' Charlie suggested, winding down his window, 'out of the wind.'

She shook her head. 'I guess . . .' She began to turn away.

'Don't be silly,' I said. 'You need help. Accept it.'

'But . . .'

'Tell us what you need.'

She hesitated again and then said with a rush, 'I need some money.'

'Is that all?' I said and fished out my wallet. 'How much?'

'Enough for a taxi . . . to Hampstead.'

I held out a fiver. 'That do?'

'Yes. I . . . where shall I send it back to?'

'Don't bother.'

'But I must.'

Charlie said, 'He's got wads of the stuff. He won't miss it.'

'That's not the point,' the girl said. 'If you won't tell me how to repay it, I can't take it.'

'It is ridiculous to argue about morals when you're freezing,' I said. 'My name is Steven Scott. Address, Regent's Park Malthouse. That'll find me.'

'Thanks.'

'I'll drive you, if you like. I have my car.' I pointed along the street.

'No thanks,' she said. 'How d'you think I got *into* this mess?'

'How then?'

She pulled the thin shawl close. 'I accepted a simple invitation to dinner and found there were strings attached. So I left him at the soup stage and blasted out, and it was only when I was walking away that I realised that I'd no money with me. He'd collected me, you see.' She smiled suddenly, showing straight white teeth. 'Some girls are dumber than others.'

'Let Steven go and find you a taxi, then,' Charlie said.

'Okay.'

It took me several minutes, but she was still huddled against the outside of Charlie's car, sheltering as best she could from the worst of the wind, when I got back. I climbed out of the taxi and she climbed in and without more ado drove away.

'A fool and his money,' Charlie said.

'That was no con trick.'

'It would be a good one,' he said. 'How do you know she's not hopping out of the cab two blocks away and shaking a fiver out of the next Sir Galahad?'

He laughed, wound up the window, waved and pointed his Rover towards home.

Monday morning brought the good news and the bad.

The good was a letter with a five pound note enclosed. Sucks to Charlie, I thought.

Dear Mr Scott,
I was so grateful for your help on Saturday night. I
guess I'll never go out on a date again without the
cab fare home.
Yours sincerely,
Alexandra Ward.

The bad news was in public print: comments in both
newspapers delivered to my door (one sporting, one
ordinary) about the disloyalty of owners who shed their
hardworking trainers. One said:

> Particularly hard on Jody Leeds that after all he
> had done for Mr Scott the owner should see fit to
> announce he would be sending his horses elsewhere.
> As we headlined in this column a year ago, Jody
> Leeds took on the extensive Berksdown Court
> Stables especially to house the expanding Scott
> string. Now without as much as half an hour's
> warning, the twenty-eight-year-old trainer is left flat,
> with all his new liabilities still outstanding. Treachery
> may sound a harsh word. Ingratitude is not.

And the other in more tabloid vein:

> Leeds (28) smarting from the sack delivered by
> ungrateful owner Steven Scott (35) said at Sandown
> on Saturday, 'I am right in the cart now. Scott
> dumped me while still collecting back-slaps for the

win on his hurdler Energise, which I trained. I am sick at heart. You sweat your guts out for an owner, and he kicks you in the teeth.'

High time trainers were protected from this sort of thing. Rumour has it Leeds may sue.

All those Press note books, all those extended Press ears had not been there for nothing. Very probably they did all genuinely believe that Jody had had a raw deal, but not one single one had bothered to ask what the view looked like from where I stood. Not one single one seemed to think that there might have been an overpowering reason for my action.

I disgustedly put down both papers, finished my breakfast and settled down to the day's work, which as usual consisted mostly of sitting still in an armchair and staring vacantly into space.

Around mid-afternoon, stiff and chilly, I wrote to Miss Ward.

Dear Miss Ward,
Thank you very much for the fiver. Will you have dinner with me? No strings attached. I enclose five pounds for the cab fare home.
Yours sincerely,
Steven Scott.

In the evening I telephoned three different race-horse trainers and offered them three horses each. They all accepted, but with the reservations blowing cool in their voices. None actually asked why I had split with Jody though all had obviously read the papers.

One, a blunt north countryman, said, 'I'll want a guarantee you'll leave them with me for at least six months, so long as they don't go lame or something.'

'All right.'

'In writing.'

'If you like.'

'Ay, I do like. You send 'em up with a guarantee and I'll take 'em.'

For Energise I picked a large yard in Sussex where hurdlers did especially well, and under the guarded tones of the trainer Rupert Ramsey I could hear that he thought almost as much of the horse as I did.

For the last three I chose Newmarket, a middle-sized stable of average achievement. No single basket would ever again contain all the Scott eggs.

Finally with a grimace I picked up the receiver and dialled Jody's familiar number. It was not he who answered, however, but Felicity, his wife.

Her voice was sharp and bitter. 'What do you want?'

I pictured her in their luxuriously furnished drawing-room, a thin positive blonde girl, every bit as competent and hardworking as Jody. She would be wearing tight blue jeans and an expensive shirt, there would be six gold bracelets jingling on her wrist and she would smell of a musk-based scent. She held intolerant views on most things and stated them forthrightly, but she had never, before that evening, unleashed on me personally the scratchy side of her mind.

'To talk about transport,' I said.

'So you really are kicking our props away.'

'You'll survive.'

'That's bloody complacent claptrap,' she said angrily. 'I could kill you. After all Jody's done for you.'

I paused. 'Did he tell you why I'm breaking with him?'

'Some stupid little quarrel about ten quid on a bill.'

'It's a great deal more than that,' I said.

'Rubbish.'

'Ask him,' I said. 'In any case, three horseboxes will collect my horses on Thursday morning. The drivers will know the ones each of them has to take and where to take them. You tell Jody that if he mixes them up he can pay the bills for sorting them out.'

The names she called me would have shaken Jody's father to the roots.

'Thursday,' I said. 'Three horseboxes, different destinations. And goodbye.'

No pleasure in it. None at all.

I sat gloomily watching a play on television and hearing hardly a word. At nine forty-five the telephone interrupted and I switched off.

' . . . Just want to know, sir, where I stand.'

Raymond Child. Jump jockey. Middle-ranker, thirty years old, short on personality. He rode competently enough, but the longer I went racing and the more I learnt, the more I could see his short-comings. I was certain also that Jody could not have manipulated my horses quite so thoroughly without help at the wheel.

'I'll send you an extra present for Energise,' I said. Jockeys were paid an official percentage of the winning prize money through a central system, but especially grateful owners occasionally came across with more.

'Thank you, sir.' He sounded surprised.

'I had a good bet on him.'

'Did you, sir?' The surprise was extreme. 'But Jody said . . .' He stopped dead.

'I backed him on the Tote.'

'Oh.'

The silence lengthened. He cleared his throat. I waited.

'Well, sir. Er . . . about the future . . .'

'I'm sorry,' I said, half meaning it. 'I'm grateful for the winners you've ridden. I'll send you the present for Energise. But in the future he'll be ridden by the jockey attached to his new stable.'

This time there was no tirade of bad language. This time, just a slow defeated sigh and the next best thing to an admission.

'Can't really blame you, I suppose.'

He disconnected before I could reply.

Tuesday I should have had a runner at Chepstow, but since I'd cancelled Jody's authority he couldn't send it.

I kicked around my rooms unproductively all morning and in the afternoon walked from Kensington Gardens to the Tower of London. Cold grey damp air with seagulls making a racket over the low-tide mud. Coffee-coloured river racing down on the last of the ebb. I stood looking towards the City from the top of little Tower Hill and thought of all the lives that had ended there under the axe. December mood, through and through. I bought a bag of roast chestnuts and went home by bus.

Wednesday brought a letter.

> Dear Mr Scott,
> When and where?
> Alexandra Ward.

She had kept the five pound note.

On Thursday evening the three new trainers confirmed that they had received the expected horses; on Friday I did a little work and on Saturday I drove down to Cheltenham races. I had not, it was true, exactly expected a rousing cheer, but the depth and extent of the animosity shown to me was acutely disturbing.

Several backs were turned, not ostentatiously but decisively. Several acquaintances lowered their eyes in embarrassment when talking to me and hurried away as soon as possible. The Press looked speculative, the trainers wary and the Jockey Club coldly hostile.

Charlie Canterfield alone came up with a broad smile and shook me vigorously by the hand.

'Have I come out in spots?' I said.

He laughed. 'You've kicked the underdog. The British never forgive it.'

'Even when the underdog bites first?'

'Underdogs are never in the wrong.'

He led me away to the bar. 'I've been taking a small poll for you. Ten per cent think it would be fair to hear your side. Ten per cent think you ought to be shot. What will you drink?'

'Scotch. No ice or water. What about the other eighty per cent?'

'Enough righteous indignation to keep the Mothers' Union going for months.' He paid for the drinks. 'Cheers.'

'And to you too.'

'It'll blow over,' Charlie said.

'I guess so.'

'What do you fancy in the third?'

We discussed the afternoon's prospects and didn't refer again to Jody, but later, alone, I found it hard to ignore the general climate. I backed a couple of horses on the Tote for a tenner each, and lost. That sort of day.

All afternoon I was fiercely tempted to protest that it was I who was the injured party, not Jody. Then I thought of the further thousands he would undoubtedly screw out of me in damages if I opened my mouth, and I kept it shut.

The gem of the day was Quintus himself, who planted his great frame solidly in my path and told me loudly that I was a bloody disgrace to the good name of racing. Quintus, I reflected, so often spoke in clichés.

'I'll tell you something,' he said. 'You would have been elected to the Jockey Club if you hadn't served Jody such a dirty trick. Your name was up for consideration. You won't be invited now, I'll see to that.'

He gave me a short curt nod and stepped aside. I didn't move.

'Your son is the one for dirty tricks.'

'How dare you!'

'You'd best believe it.'

'Absolute nonsense. The discrepancy on your bill was a simple secretarial mistake. If you try to say it was anything else . . .'

'I know,' I said. 'He'll sue.'

'Quite right. He has a right to every penny he can get.'

I walked away. Quintus might be biased, but I knew I'd get a straight answer from the Press.

I asked the senior columnist of a leading daily, a fiftyish man who wrote staccato prose and sucked peppermints to stop himself smoking.

'What reason is Jody Leeds giving for losing my horses?'

The columnist sucked and breathed out a gust of sweetness.

'Says he charged you by mistake for some schooling Raymond Child didn't do.'

'That all?'

'Says you accused him of stealing and were changing your trainer.'

'And what's your reaction to that?'

'I haven't got one.' He shrugged and sucked contemplatively. 'Others ... The consensus seems to be it was a genuine mistake and you've been unreasonable ... to put it mildly.'

'I see,' I said. 'Thanks.'

'Is that all? No story?'

'No,' I said. 'Sorry.'

He put another peppermint in his mouth, nodded non-committally, and turned away to more fertile prospects. As far as he was concerned, I was last week's news. Others, this Saturday, were up for the chop.

I walked thoughtfully down on the Club lawn to watch the next race. It really was not much fun being cast as everyone's villain, and the clincher was delivered by a girl I'd once taken to Ascot.

'Steven dear,' she said with coquettish reproof, 'you're a big rich bully. That poor boy's struggling to make ends meet. Even if he did pinch a few quid off you, why get into such a tizz? So uncool, don't you think?'

53

'You believe the rich should lie down for Robin Hood?'

'What?'

'Never mind.'

I gave it up and went home.

The evening was a great deal better. At eight o'clock I collected Miss Alexandra Ward from an address in Hampstead and took her to dinner in the red and gold grill room of the Café Royal.

Seen again in kinder light, properly warm and not blown to rags by the wind, she was everything last week's glimpse had suggested. She wore the same long black skirt, the same cream shirt, the same cream silk shawl. Also the gold sandals, gold mesh purse and no gloves. But her brown hair was smooth and shining, her skin glowing, her eyes bright, and over all lay the indefinable extra, a typically American brand of grooming.

She opened the door herself when I rang the bell and for an appreciable pause we simply looked at each other. What she saw was, I supposed, about six feet of solidly built chap, dark hair, dark eyes, no warts to speak of. Tidy, clean, house-trained and dressed in a conventional dinner jacket.

'Good evening,' I said.

She smiled, nodded as if endorsing a decision,

stepped out through the door, and pulled it shut behind her.

'My sister lives here,' she said, indicating the house. 'I'm on a visit. She's married to an Englishman.'

I opened the car door for her. She sat smoothly inside, and I started the engine and drove off.

'A visit from the States?' I asked.

'Yes. From Westchester . . . outside New York.'

'Executive ladder-climbing country?' I said, smiling.

She gave me a quick sideways glance. 'You know Westchester?'

'No. Been to New York a few times, that's all.'

We stopped at some traffic lights. She remarked that it was a fine night. I agreed.

'Are you married?' she said abruptly.

'Did you bring the fiver?'

'Yes, I did.'

'Well . . . No, I'm not.'

The light changed to green. We drove on.

'Are you truthful?' she said.

'In that respect, yes. Not married now. Never have been.'

'I like to know,' she said with mild apology.

'I don't blame you.'

'For the sakes of the wives.'

'Yes.'

I pulled up in due course in front of the Café Royal at Piccadilly Circus, and helped her out of the car. As we went in she looked back and saw a small thin man taking my place in the driving seat.

'He works for me,' I said. 'He'll park the car.'

She looked amused. 'He waits around to do that?'

'On overtime, Saturday nights.'

'So he likes it?'

'Begs me to take out young ladies. Other times I do my own parking.'

In the full light inside the hall she stopped for another straight look at what she'd agreed to dine with.

'What do you expect of me?' she said.

'Before I collected you, I expected honesty, directness and prickles. Now that I've known you for half an hour I expect prickles, directness and honesty.'

She smiled widely, the white teeth shining and little pouches of fun swelling her lower eyelids.

'That isn't what I meant.'

'No . . . So what do you expect of me?'

'Thoroughly gentlemanly conduct and a decent dinner.'

'How dull.'

'Take it or leave it.'

'The bar,' I said, pointing, 'is over there. I take it.'

She gave me another flashing smile, younger sister to the first, and moved where I'd said. She drank vodka martini, I drank scotch, and we both ate a few black olives and spat out the stones genteelly into fists.

'Do you usually pick up girls in the street?' she said.

'Only when they fall.'

'Fallen girls?'

I laughed. 'Not those, no.'

'What do you do for a living?'

I took a mouthful of scotch. 'I'm a sort of engineer.'
It sounded boring.

'Bridges and things?'

'Nothing so permanent or important.'

'What then?'

I smiled wryly. 'I make toys.'

'You make . . . *what*?'

'Toys. Things to play with.'

'I know what toys are, damn it.'

'What do you do?' I asked, 'In Westchester.'

She gave me an amused glance over her glass. 'You
take it for granted that I work?'

'You have the air.'

'I cook, then.'

'Hamburgers and French fries?'

Her eyes gleamed. 'Weddings and stuff. Parties.'

'A lady caterer.'

She nodded. 'With a girl friend. Millie.'

'When do you go back?'

'Thursday.'

Thursday suddenly seemed rather close. After a
noticeable pause she added almost defensively, 'It's
Christmas, you see. We've a lot of work then and
around New Year. Millie couldn't do it all alone.'

'Of course not.'

We went into dinner and ate smoked trout and steak

wrapped in pastry. She read the menu from start to finish with professional interest and checked with the head waiter the ingredients of two or three dishes.

'So many things are different over here,' she explained.

She knew little about wine. 'I guess I drink it when I'm given it, but I've a better palate for spirits.' The wine waiter looked sceptical, but she wiped that look off his face later by correctly identifying the brandy he brought with the coffee as Armagnac.

'Where is your toy factory?' she asked.

'I don't have a factory.'

'But you said you made toys.'

'Yes, I do.'

She looked disbelieving. 'You don't mean you actually *make* them. I mean, with your own hands?'

I smiled. 'Yes.'

'But . . .' She looked round the velvety room with the thought showing as clear as spring water: if I worked with my hands how often could I afford such a place.

'I don't often make them,' I said. 'Most of the time I go to the races.'

'Okay,' she said. 'I give in. You've got me hooked. Explain the mystery.'

'Have some more coffee.'

'Mr Scott . . .' She stopped. 'That sounds silly, doesn't it?'

'Yes, Miss Ward, it does.'

'Steven . . .'

'Much better.'

'My mother calls me Alexandra, Millie calls me Al. Take your pick.'

'Allie?'

'For God's sakes.'

'I invent toys,' I said. 'I patent them. Other people manufacture them. I collect royalties.'

'Oh.'

'Does "oh" mean enlightenment, fascination, or boredom to death?'

'It means oh how extraordinary, oh how interesting, and oh I never knew people did things like that.'

'Quite a lot do.'

'Did you invent Monopoly?'

I laughed. 'Unfortunately not.'

'But that sort of thing?'

'Mechanical toys, mostly.'

'How odd . . .' She stopped, thinking better of saying what was in her mind. I knew the reaction well, so I finished the sentence for her.

'How odd for a grown man to spend his life in toyland?'

'You said it.'

'Children's minds have to be fed.'

She considered it. 'And the next bunch of leaders are children today?'

'You rate it too high. The next lot of parents, teachers, louts and layabouts are children today.'

'And you are fired with missionary zeal?'

'All the way to the bank.'

'Cynical.'

'Better than pompous.'

'More honest,' she agreed. Her eyes smiled in the soft light, half mocking, half friendly, greeny-grey and shining, the whites ultra white. There was nothing wrong with the design of her eyebrows. Her nose was short and straight, her mouth curved up at the corners, and her cheeks had faint hollows in the right places. Assembled, the components added up not to a standard type of beauty, but to a face of character and vitality. Part of the story written, I thought. Lines of good fortune, none of discontent. No anxiety, no inner confusion. A good deal of self assurance, knowing she looked attractive and had succeeded in the job she'd chosen. Definitely not a virgin: a girl's eyes were always different, after.

'Are all your days busy,' I asked, 'between now and Thursday?'

'There are some minutes here and there.'

'Tomorrow?'

She smiled and shook her head. 'Not a chink tomorrow. Monday if you like.'

'I'll collect you,' I said. 'Monday morning, at ten.'

CHAPTER FOUR

Rupert Ramsey's voice on the telephone sounded resigned rather than welcoming.

'Yes, of course, do come down to see your horses, if you'd like to. Do you know the way?'

He gave me directions which proved easy to follow, and at eleven thirty, Sunday morning, I drove through his white painted stone gateposts and drew up in the large gravelled area before his house.

He lived in a genuine Georgian house, simple in design, with large airy rooms and elegant plaster-worked ceilings. Nothing self-consciously antique about the furnishings: all periods mingled together in a working atmosphere that was wholly modern.

Rupert himself was about forty-five, intensely ener-getic under a misleadingly languid exterior. His voice drawled slightly. I knew him only by sight and it was to all intents the first time we had met.

'How do you do?' He shook hands. 'Care to come into my office?'

I followed him through the white painted front door,

across the large square hall and into the room he called his office, but which was furnished entirely as a sitting-room except for a dining table which served as a desk, and a grey filing cabinet in one corner.

'Do sit down.' He indicated an armchair. 'Cigarette?'

'Don't smoke.'

'Wise man.' He smiled as if he didn't really think so and lit one for himself.

'Energise,' he said, 'is showing signs of having had a hard race.'

'But he won easily,' I said.

'It looked that way, certainly.' He inhaled, breathing out through his nose. 'All the same, I'm not too happy about him.'

'In what way?'

'He needs building up. We'll do it, don't you fear. But he looks a bit thin at present.'

'How about the other two?'

'Dial's jumping out of his skin. Ferryboat needs a lot of work yet.'

'I don't think Ferryboat likes racing any more.'

The cigarette paused on its way to his mouth.

'Why do you say that?' he asked.

'He's had three races this autumn. I expect you'll have looked up his form. He's run badly every time. Last year he was full of enthusiasm and won three times out of seven starts, but the last of them took a lot of winning ... and Raymond Child cut him raw with his whip ... and during the summer out at grass

Ferryboat seems to have decided that if he gets too
near the front he's in for a beating, so it's only good
sense *not* to get near the front . . . and he consequently
isn't trying.'

He drew deeply on the cigarette, giving himself time.

'Do you expect me to get better results than Jody?'

'With Ferryboat, or in general?'

'Let's say . . . both.'

I smiled. 'I don't expect much from Ferryboat. Dial's
a novice, an unknown quantity. Energise might win the
Champion Hurdle.'

'You didn't answer my question,' he said pleasantly.

'No . . . I expect you to get different results from
Jody. Will that do?'

'I'd very much like to know why you left him.'

'Disagreements over money,' I said. 'Not over the
way he trained the horses.'

He tapped ash off with the precision that meant his
mind was elsewhere. When he spoke, it was slowly.

'Were you always satisfied with the way your horses
ran?'

The question hovered delicately in the air, full of
inviting little traps. He looked up suddenly and met my
eyes and his own widened with comprehension. 'I see
you understand what I'm asking.'

'Yes. But I can't answer. Jody says he will sue me
for slander if I tell people why I left him, and I've no
reason to doubt him.'

'That remark in itself is a slander.'

'Indubitably.'

He got cheerfully to his feet and stubbed out the cigarette. A good deal more friendliness seeped into his manner.

'Right then. Let's go out and look at your horses.'

We went out into his yard, which showed prosperity at every turn. The thin cold December sun shone on fresh paint, wall-to-wall tarmac, tidy flower tubs and well-kept stable lads. There was none of the clutter I was accustomed to at Jody's; no brooms leaning against walls, no rugs, rollers, brushes and bandages lying in ready heaps, no straggles of hay across the swept ground. Jody liked to give owners the impression that work was being done, that care for the horses was non-stop. Rupert, it seemed, preferred to tuck the sweat and toil out of sight. At Jody's, the muck heap was always with you. At Rupert's it was invisible.

'Dial is here.'

We stopped at a box along a row outside the main quadrangle, and with an unobtrusive flick of his fingers Rupert summoned a lad hovering twenty feet away.

'This is Donny,' he said. 'Looks after Dial.'

I shook hands with Donny, a young tough-looking boy of about twenty with unsmiling eyes and a you-can't-con-me expression. From the look he directed first at Rupert and then later at the horse I gathered that this was his overall attitude to life, not an announcement of no confidence in me personally. When we'd looked at and admired the robust little chestnut I tried Donny with a fiver. It raised a nod of thanks, but no smile.

Further along the same row stood Ferryboat, looking out on the world with a lack-lustre eye and scarcely shifting from one leg to the other when we went into his box. His lad, in contrast to Donny, gave him an indulgent smile, and accepted his gift from me with a beam.

'Energise is in the main yard,' Rupert said, leading the way. 'Across in the corner.'

When we were half way there two other cars rolled up the drive and disgorged a collection of men in sheep-skin coats and ladies in furs and jangly bracelets. They saw Rupert and waved and began to stream into the yard.

Rupert said, 'I'll show you Energise in just a moment.'

'It's all right,' I said. 'You tell me which box he's in. I'll look at him myself. You see to your other owners.'

'Number fourteen, then. I'll be with you again shortly.'

I nodded and walked on to number fourteen. Unbolted the door. Went in. The near-black horse was tied up inside. Ready, I supposed, for my visit.

Horse and I looked at each other. My old friend, I thought. The only one of them all with whom I'd ever had any real contact. I talked to him, as in the horsebox, looking guiltily over my shoulder at the open door, for fear someone should hear me and think me nuts.

I could see at once why Rupert had been unhappy about him. He looked thinner. All that crashing about in the horsebox could have done him no good.

Across the yard I could see Rupert talking to the newcomers and shepherding them to their horses. Owners came en masse on Sunday mornings.

I was content to stay where I was. I spent probably twenty minutes with my black horse, and he instilled in me some very strange ideas.

Rupert came back hurrying and apologising. 'You're still here . . . I'm so sorry.'

'Don't be,' I assured him.

'Come into the house for a drink.'

'I'd like to.'

We joined the other owners and returned to his office for lavish issues of gin and scotch. Drinks for visiting owners weren't allowable as a business expense for tax purposes unless the visiting owners were foreign. Jody had constantly complained of it to all and sundry while accepting cases of the stuff from me with casual nods. Rupert poured generously and dropped no hints, and I found it a refreshing change.

The other owners were excitedly making plans for the Christmas meeting at Kempton Park. Rupert made introductions, explaining that Energise, too, was due to run there in the Christmas Hurdle.

'After the way he won at Sandown,' remarked one of the sheepskin coats, 'he must be a cast-iron certainty.'

I glanced at Rupert for an opinion but he was busy with bottles and glasses.

'I hope so,' I said.

The sheepskin coat nodded sagely.

His wife, a cosy-looking lady who had shed her ocelot and now stood five-feet-nothing in bright green wool, looked from him to me in puzzlement.

'But George honey, Energise is trained by that nice young man with the pretty little wife. You know, the one who introduced us to Ganser Mays.'

She smiled happily and appeared not to notice the pole-axed state of her audience. I must have stood immobile for almost a minute while the implications fizzed around my brain, and during that time the conversation between George-honey and the bright green wool had flowed on into the chances of their own chaser in a later race. I dragged them back.

'Excuse me,' I said, 'but I didn't catch your names.'

'George Vine,' said the sheepskin coat, holding out a chunky hand, 'and my wife, Poppet.'

'Steven Scott,' I said.

'Glad to know you.' He gave his empty glass to Rupert, who amiably refilled it with gin and tonic. 'Poppet doesn't read the racing news much, so she wouldn't know you've left Jody Leeds.'

'Did you say,' I asked carefully, 'that Jody Leeds introduced you to Ganser Mays?'

'Oh no,' Poppet said, smiling. 'His wife did.'

'That's right,' George nodded. 'Bit of luck.'

'You see,' Poppet explained conversationally, 'the prices on the Tote are sometimes so awfully small and it's all such a lottery isn't it? I mean, you never know really what you're going to get for your money, like you do with the bookies.'

'Is that what she said?' I asked.

'Who? Oh . . . Jody Leeds' wife. Yes, that's right, she did. I'd just been picking up my winnings on one of our horses from the Tote, you see, and she was doing the same at the next window, the Late-Pay window that was, and she said what a shame it was that the Tote was only paying three to one when the bookies' starting price was five to one, and I absolutely agreed with her, and we just sort of stood there chatting. I told her that only last week we had bought the steeplechaser which had just won and it was our first ever racehorse, and she was so interested and explained that she was a trainer's wife and that sometimes when she got tired of the Tote paying out so little she bet with a bookie. I said I didn't like pushing along the rows with all those men shoving and shouting and she laughed and said she meant one on the rails, so you could just walk up to them and not go through to the bookies' enclosure at all. But of course you have to know them, I mean, they have to know *you*, if you see what I mean. And neither George nor I knew any of them, as I explained to Mrs Leeds.'

She stopped to take a sip of gin. I listened in fascination.

'Well,' she went on, 'Mrs Leeds sort of hesitated and then I got this great idea of asking her if she could possibly introduce us to *her* bookie on the rails.'

'And she did?'

'She thought it was a great idea.'

She would.

'So we collected George and she introduced us to dear Ganser Mays. And,' she finished triumphantly, 'he gives us much better odds than the Tote.'

George Vine nodded several times in agreement.

'Trouble is,' he said, 'you know what wives are, she bets more than ever.'

'George honey.' A token protest only.

'You know you do, love.'

'It isn't worth doing in sixpences,' she said smiling. 'You never win enough that way.'

He patted her fondly on the shoulder and said man-to-man to me, 'When Ganser Mays' account comes, if she's won, she takes the winnings, and if she's lost, I pay.'

Poppet smiled happily. 'George honey, you're sweet.'

'Which do you do most?' I asked her. 'Win or lose?'

She made a face. 'Now that's a naughty question, Mr Scott.'

Next morning, ten o'clock to the second, I collected Allie from Hampstead.

Seen in daylight for the first time she was sparkling

as the day was rotten. I arrived at her door with a big black umbrella holding off slanting sleet, and she opened it in a neat white mackintosh and knee-high black boots. Her hair bounced with new washing, and the bloom on her skin had nothing to do with Max Factor.

I tried a gentlemanly kiss on the cheek. She smelled of fresh flowers and bath soap.

'Good morning,' I said.

She chuckled. 'You English are so formal.'

'Not always.'

She sheltered under the umbrella down the path to the car and sat inside with every glossy hair dry and in place.

'Where are we going?'

'Fasten your lap straps,' I said. 'To Newmarket.'

'Newmarket?'

'To look at horses.' I let in the clutch and pointed the Lamborghini roughly north-east.

'I might have guessed.'

I grinned. 'Is there anything you'd really rather do?'

'I've visited three museums, four picture galleries, six churches, one Tower of London, two Houses of Parliament and seven theatres.'

'In how long?'

'Sixteen days.'

'High time you saw some real life.'

The white teeth flashed. 'If you'd lived with my two

small nephews for sixteen days you couldn't wait to get away from it.'

'Your sister's children?'

She nodded. 'Ralph and William. Little devils.'

'What do they play with?'

She was amused. 'The toy maker's market research?'

'The customer is always right.'

We crossed the North Circular road and took the AI towards Baldock.

'Ralph dresses up a doll in soldier's uniforms and William makes forts on the stairs and shoots dried beans at anyone going up.'

'Healthy aggressive stuff.'

'When I was little I hated being given all those educational things that were supposed to be good for you.'

I smiled. 'It's well known there are two sorts of toys. The ones that children like and the ones their mothers buy. Guess which there are more of?'

'You're cynical.'

'So I'm often told,' I said. 'It isn't true.'

The wipers worked overtime against the sleet on the windscreen and I turned up the heater. She sighed with what appeared to be contentment. The car purred easily across Cambridgeshire and into Suffolk, and the ninety minute journey seemed short.

It wasn't the best of weather but even in July the stable I'd chosen for my three young flat racers would have looked depressing. There were two smallish quadrangles side by side, built tall and solid in Edwardian brick. All the doors were painted a dead dull dark brown. No decorations, no flowers, no grass, no gaiety of spirit in the whole place.

Like many Newmarket yards it led straight off the street and was surrounded by houses. Allie looked around without enthusiasm and put into words exactly what I was thinking.

'It looks more like a prison.'

Bars on the windows of the boxes. Solid ten foot tall gates at the road entrance. Jagged glass set in concrete along the top of the boundary wall. Padlocks swinging on every bolt on every door in sight. All that was missing was a uniformed figure with a gun, and maybe they had those too, on occasion.

The master of all this security proved pretty dour himself. Trevor Kennet shook hands with a smile that looked an unaccustomed effort for the muscles involved and invited us into the stable office out of the rain.

A bare room; linoleum, scratched metal furniture, strip lighting and piles of paper work. The contrast between this and the grace of Rupert Ramsey was remarkable. A pity I had taken Allie to the wrong one.

'They've settled well, your horses.' His voice dared me to disagree.

'Splendid,' I said mildly.

'You'll want to see them, I expect.'

As I'd come from London to do so, I felt his remark silly.

'They're doing no work yet, of course.'

'No,' I agreed. The last Flat season had finished six weeks ago. The next lay some three months ahead. No owner in his senses would have expected his Flat horses to be in full work in December. Trevor Kennet had a genius for the obvious.

'It's raining,' he said. 'Bad day to come.'

Allie and I were both wearing macs, and I carried the umbrella. He looked lengthily at these preparations and finally shrugged.

'Better come on, then.'

He himself wore a raincoat and a droopy hat that had suffered downpours for years. He led the way out of the office and across the first quadrangle with Allie and me close under my umbrella behind him.

He flicked the bolts on one of the dead chocolate doors and pulled both halves open.

'Wrecker,' he said.

We went into the box. Wrecker moved hastily away across the peat which covered the floor, a leggy bay yearling colt with a nervous disposition. Trevor Kennet made no effort to reassure him but stood four square looking at him with an assessing eye. Jody for all his faults had been good with young stock, fondling them and talking to them with affection. I thought I might have chosen badly, sending Wrecker here.

'He needs a gentle lad,' I said.

Kennet's expression was open to scorn. 'Doesn't do to molly coddle them. Soft horses win nothing.'

End of conversation.

We went out into the rain and he slammed the bolts home. Four boxes further along he stopped again.

'Hermes.'

Again the silent appraisal. Hermes, from the experience of two full racing seasons, could look at humans without anxiety and merely stared back. Ordinary to look at, he had won several races in masterly fashion ... and lost every time I'd seriously backed him. Towards the end of the Flat season he had twice trailed in badly towards the rear of the field. Too much racing, Jody had said. Needed a holiday.

'What do you think of him?' I asked.

'He's eating well,' Kennet said.

I waited for more, but nothing came. After a short pause we trooped out again into the rain and more or less repeated the whole depressing procedure in the box of my third colt, Bubbleglass.

I had great hopes of Bubbleglass. A late-developing two-year-old, he had run only once so far, and without much distinction. At three, though, he might be fun. He had grown and filled out since I'd seen him last. When I said so, Kennet remarked that it was only to be expected.

We all went back to the office, Kennet offered us coffee and looked relieved when I said we'd better be going.

'What an utterly dreary place,' Allie said, as we drove away.

'Designed to discourage owners from calling too often, I dare say.'

She was surprised. 'Do you mean it?'

'Some trainers think owners should pay their bills and shut up.'

'That's crazy.'

I glanced sideways at her.

She said positively, 'If I was spending all that dough, I'd sure expect to be welcomed.'

'Biting the hand that feeds is a national sport.'

'You're all nuts.'

'How about some lunch?'

We stopped at a pub which did a fair job for a Monday, and in the afternoon drove comfortably back to London. Allie made no objections when I pulled up outside my own front door and followed me in through it with none of the prickly reservations I'd feared.

I lived in the two lower floors of a tall narrow house in Prince Albert Road overlooking Regent's Park. At street level, garage, cloakroom, workshop. Upstairs, bed, bath, kitchen and sitting-room, the last with a balcony half as big as itself. I switched on lights and led the way.

'A bachelor's pad if ever I saw one,' Allie said, looking around her. 'Not a frill in sight.' She walked across and looked out through the sliding glass wall to the balcony. 'Don't you just hate all that traffic?'

Cars drove incessantly along the road below, yellow sidelights shining through the glistening rain.

'I quite like it,' I said. 'In the summer I practically live out there on the balcony ... breathing in great lungfuls of exhaust fumes and waiting for the clouds to roll away.'

She laughed, unbuttoned her mac and took it off. The red dress underneath looked as unruffled as it had at lunch. She was the one splash of bright colour in that room of creams and browns, and she was feminine enough to know it.

'Drink?' I suggested.

'It's a bit early ...' She looked around her as if she had expected to see more than sofas and chairs. 'Don't you keep any of your toys here?'

'In the workshop,' I said. 'Downstairs.'

'I'd love to see them.'

'All right.'

We went down to the hall again and turned towards the back of the house. I opened the civilised wood-panelled door which led straight from carpet to concrete, from white collar to blue, from champagne to tea breaks. The familiar smell of oil and machinery waited there in the dark. I switched on the stark bright lights and stood aside for her to go through.

'But it *is* ... a factory.' She sounded astonished.

'What did you expect?'

'Oh, I don't know. Something much smaller, I guess.'

The workshop was fifty feet long and was the reason

I had bought the house on my twenty-third birthday with money I had earned myself. Selling off the three top floors had given me enough back to construct my own first floor flat, but the heart of the matter lay here, legacy of an old-fashioned light engineering firm that had gone bust.

The pulley system that drove nearly the whole works from one engine was the original, even if now powered by electricity instead of steam, and although I had replaced one or two and added another, the old machines still worked well.

'Explain it to me,' Allie said.

'Well ... this electric engine here ...' I showed her its compact floor-mounted shape. ' ... drives that endless belt, which goes up there round that big wheel.'

'Yes.' She looked up where I pointed.

'The wheel is fixed to that long shaft which stretches right down the workshop, near the ceiling. When it rotates, it drives all those other endless belts going down to the machines. Look, I'll show you.'

I switched on the electric motor and immediately the big belt from it turned the wheel, which rotated the shaft, which set the other belts circling from the shaft down to the machines. The only noises were the hum of the engines, the gentle whine of the spinning shaft and the soft slapping of the belts.

'It looks alive,' Allie said. 'How do you make the machines work?'

'Engage a sort of gear inside the belt, then the belt revolves the spindle of the machine.'

'Like a sewing machine,' Allie said.

'More or less.'

We walked down the row. She wanted to know what job each did, and I told her.

'That's a milling machine, for flat surfaces. That's a speed lathe; I use that for wood as well as metal. That tiny lathe came from a watchmaker for ultra-fine work. That's a press. That's a polisher. That's a hacksaw. And that's a drilling machine; it bores holes downwards.'

I turned round and pointed to the other side of the workshop.

'That big one on its own is an engine lathe, for heavier jobs. It has its own electric power.'

'It's incredible. All this.'

'Just for toys?'

'Well . . .'

'These machines are all basically simple. They just save a lot of time.'

'Do toys have to be so . . . well . . . *accurate*?'

'I mostly make the prototypes in metal and wood. Quite often they reach the shops in plastic, but unless the engineering's right in the first place the toys don't work very well, and break easily.'

'Where do you keep them?' She looked around at the bare well-swept area with no work in sight.

'Over there. In the right-hand cupboard.'

I went over with her and opened the big double doors. She pulled them wider with outstretched arms.

'Oh!' She looked utterly astounded.

She stood in front of the shelves with her mouth open and her eyes staring, just like a child.

'Oh,' she said again, as if she could get no breath to say anything else. 'Oh . . . They're the Rola toys!'

'Yes, that's right.'

'Why didn't you say so?'

'Habit, really. I never do.'

She gave me a smile without turning her eyes away from the bright coloured rows in the cupboard. 'Do so many people ask for free samples?'

'It's just that I get tired of talking about them.'

'But I played with them myself.' She switched her gaze abruptly in my direction, looking puzzled. 'I had a lot of them in the States ten or twelve years ago.' Her voice plainly implied that I was too young to have made those.

'I was only fifteen when I did the first one,' I explained. 'I had an uncle who had a workshop in his garage . . . he was a welder, himself. He'd shown me how to use tools from the time I was six. He was pretty shrewd. He made me take out patents before I showed my idea to anyone, and he raised and lent me the money to pay for them.'

'Pay?'

'Patents are expensive and you have to take out one

for each different country, if you don't want your idea pinched. Japan, I may say, costs the most.'

'Good heavens.' She turned back to the cupboard, put out her hand and lifted out the foundation of all my fortunes, the merry-go-round.

'I had the carousel,' she said. 'Just like this, but different colours.' She twirled the centre spindle between finger and thumb so that the platform revolved and the little horses rose and fell on their poles. 'I simply can't believe it.'

She put the merry-go-round back in its slot and one by one lifted out several of the others, exclaiming over old friends and investigating the strangers. 'Do you have a Rola-base down here?'

'Sure,' I said, lifting it from the bottom of the cupboard.

'Oh do let me . . . please?' She was as excited as if she'd still been little. I carried the base over to the workbench and laid it there, and she came over with four of the toys.

The Rola-base consisted of a large flat box, in this case two feet square by six inches deep, though several other sizes had been made. From one side protruded a handle for winding, and one had to have that side of the Rola-base aligned with the edge of the table, so that winding was possible. Inside the box were the rollers which gave the toy its phonetic Rola name; wide rollers carrying a long flat continuous belt inset with many rows of sideways facing cogwheel teeth. In

the top of the box were corresponding rows of holes:
dozen of holes altogether. Each of the separate mechanical toys, like the merry-go-round and a hundred
others, had a central spindle which protruded down
from beneath the toy and was grooved like a cog-wheel.
When one slipped any spindle through any hole it
engaged on the belt of cog teeth below, and when one
turned the single handle in the Rola-base, the wide belt
of cog teeth moved endlessly round and all the spindles
rotated and all the toys performed their separate tasks.
A simple locking device on the base of each toy
engaged with stops by each hole to prevent the toy
rotating as a whole.

Allie had brought the carousel and the roller-coaster
from the fairground set, and a cow from the farm set,
and the firing tank from the army set. She slotted the
spindles through random holes and turned the handle.
The merry-go-round went round and round, the trucks
went up and down the roller-coaster, the cow nodded
its head and swished its tail, and the tank rotated with
sparks coming out of its gun barrel.

She laughed with pleasure.

'I don't believe it. I simply don't believe it. I never
dreamt you could have made the Rola toys.'

'I've made others, though.'

'What sort?'

'Um . . . the latest in the shops is a coding machine.
It's doing quite well this Christmas.'

'You don't mean the Secret Coder?'

'Yes.' I was surprised she knew of it.

'Do show me. My sister's giving one each to the boys, but they were already gift-wrapped.'

So I showed her the coder, which looked like providing me with racehorses for some time to come, as a lot of people besides children had found it compulsive. The new adult version was much more complicated but also much more expensive, which somewhat increased the royalties.

From the outside the children's version looked like a box, smaller than a shoe box, with a sloping top surface. Set in this were letter keys exactly like a conventional typewriter, except that there were no numbers, no punctuation and no space bar.

'How does it work?' Allie asked.

'You type your message and it comes out in code.'

'Just like that?'

'Try it.'

She gave me an amused look, turned so that I couldn't see her fingers, and with one hand expertly typed about twenty-five letters. From the end of the box a narrow paper strip emerged, with letters typed on it in groups of five.

'What now?'

'Tear the strip off,' I said.

She did that. 'It's like ticker-tape,' she said.

'It is. Same size, anyway.'

She held it out to me. I looked at it and came as close to blushing as I'm ever likely to.

'Can you read it just like that?' she exclaimed. 'Some coder, if you can read it at a glance.'

'I invented the damn thing,' I said. 'I know it by heart.'

'How does it work?'

'There's a cylinder inside with twelve complete alphabets on it, each arranged in a totally random manner and all different. You set this dial here . . . see,' I showed her, 'to any number from one to twelve. Then you type your message. Inside, the keys don't print the letter you press on the outside, but the letter that's aligned with it inside. There's an automatic spring which jumps after every five presses, so the message comes out in groups of five.'

'It's fantastic. My sister says the boys have been asking for them for weeks. Lots of children they know have them, all sending weird messages all over the place and driving their mothers wild.'

'You can make more involved codes by feeding the coded message through again, or backwards,' I said. 'Or by switching the code number every few letters. All the child receiving the message needs to know is the numbers he has to set on his own dial.'

'How do I decode this?'

'Put that tiny lever . . . there . . . down instead of up, and just type the coded message. It will come out as it went in, except still in groups of five letters, of course. Try it.'

She herself looked confused. She screwed up the tape and laughed, 'I guess I don't need to.'

'Would you like one?' I asked diffidently.

'I sure would.'

'Blue or red?'

'Red.'

In another cupboard I had a pile of manufactured coders packed like those in the shops. I opened one of the cartons, checked that the contents had a bright red plastic casing and handed it over.

'If you write me a Christmas message,' she said, 'I'll expect it in code number four.'

I took her out to dinner again as I was on a bacon-and-egg level myself as a cook, and she was after all on holiday to get away from the kitchen.

There was nothing new in taking a girl to dinner. Nothing exceptional, I supposed, in Allie herself. I liked her directness, her naturalness. She was supremely easy to be with, not interpreting occasional silences as personal insults, not coy or demanding, nor sexually a tease. Not a girl of hungry intellect, but certainly of good sense.

That wasn't all, of course. The spark which attracts one person to another was there too, and on her side also, I thought.

I drove her back to Hampstead and stopped outside her sister's house.

'Tomorrow?' I said.

She didn't answer directly. 'I go home on Thursday.'

'I know. What time is your flight?'

'Not till the evening. Six-thirty.'

'Can I drive you to the airport?'

'I could get my sister . . .'

'I'd like to.'

'Okay.'

We sat in a short silence.

'Tomorrow,' she said finally. 'I guess . . . If you like.'

'Yes.'

She nodded briefly, opened the car door, and spoke over her shoulder. 'Thank you for a fascinating day.'

She was out on the pavement before I could get round to help her. She smiled. Purring and contented, as far as I could judge.

'Good night.' She held out her hand.

I took it, and at the same time leant down and kissed her cheek. We looked at each other, her hand still in mine. One simply cannot waste such opportunities. I repeated the kiss, but on her lips.

She kissed as I'd expected, with friendliness and reservations. I kissed her twice more on the same terms.

'Good night,' she said again, smiling.

I watched her wave before she shut her sister's front door, and drove home wishing she were still with me. When I got back I went into the workshop and retrieved the screwed up piece of code she'd thrown in the litter bin. Smoothing it, I read the jumbled up letters again.

No mistake. Sorted out, the words were still a pat on the ego.

The toy man is as great as his toys.

I put the scrap of paper in my wallet and went upstairs to bed feeling the world's biggest fool.

CHAPTER FIVE

On Wednesday morning Charlie Canterfield telephoned at seven-thirty. I stretched a hand sleepily out
of bed and groped for the receiver.

'Hullo?'

'Where the hell have you been?' Charlie said. 'I've
been trying your number since Sunday morning.'

'Out.'

'I know that.' He sounded more amused than irri-
tated. 'Look . . . can you spare me some time today?'

'All of it, if you like.'

My generosity was solely due to the unfortunate fact
that Allie had felt bound to spend her last full day with
her sister, who had bought tickets and made plans. I
had gathered that she'd only given me Monday and
Tuesday at the expense of her other commitments, so
I couldn't grumble. Tuesday had been even better than
Monday, except for ending in exactly the same way.

'This morning will do,' Charlie said. 'Nine-thirty?'

'Okay. Amble along.'

'I want to bring a friend.'

'Fine. Do you know how to get here?'

'A taxi will find it,' Charlie said and disconnected.

Charlie's friend turned out to be a large man of Charlie's age with shoulders like a docker and language to match.

'Bert Huggerneck,' Charlie said, making introductions.

Bert Huggerneck crunched my bones in his muscular hand. 'Any friend of Charlie's is a friend of mine,' he said, but with no warmth or conviction.

'Come upstairs,' I said. 'Coffee? Or breakfast?'

'Coffee,' Charlie said. Bert Huggerneck said he didn't mind, which proved in the end to be bacon and tomato ketchup on toast twice, with curried baked beans on the side. He chose the meal himself from my meagre store cupboard and ate with speed and relish.

'Not a bad bit of bleeding nosh,' he observed, 'considering.'

'Considering what?' I asked.

He gave me a sharp look over a well-filled fork and made a gesture embracing both the flat and its neighbourhood. 'Considering you must be a rich bleeding capitalist, living here.' He pronounced it '*capit*alist', and clearly considered it one of the worst of insults.

'Come off it,' Charlie said amiably. 'His breeding's as impeccable as yours and mine.'

'Huh.' Total disbelief didn't stop Bert Huggerneck accepting more toast. 'Got any jam?' he said.

'Sorry.'

He made do with half a jar of marmalade.

'What's that about breeding?' he said suspiciously to Charlie. 'Capitalists are all snobs.'

'His grandfather was a mechanic,' Charlie said. 'Same as mine was a milkman and yours a navvie.'

I was amused that Charlie had glossed over my father and mother, who had been school teacher and nurse. Far more respectable to be able to refer to the grandfather-mechanic, the welder-uncle and the host of card-carrying cousins. If politicians of all sorts searched diligently amongst their antecedents for proletarianism and denied aristocratic contacts three times before cockcrow every week-day morning, who was I to spoil the fun? In truth the two seemingly divergent lines of manual work and schoolmastering had given me the best of both worlds, the ability to use my hands and the education to design things for them to make. Money and experience had done the rest.

'I gather Mr Huggerneck is here against his will,' I observed.

'Don't you believe it,' Charlie said. 'He wants your help.'

'How does he act if he wants to kick you in the kidneys?'

'He wouldn't eat your food.'

Fair enough, I thought. Accept a man's salt, and you didn't boot him. Times hadn't collapsed altogether where that still held good.

We were sitting round the kitchen table with Charlie smoking a cigarette and using his saucer as an ashtray and me wondering what he considered so urgent. Bert wiped his plate with a spare piece of toast and washed that down with coffee.

'What's for lunch?' he said.

I took it as it was meant, as thanks for breakfast.

'Bert,' said Charlie, coming to the point, 'is a bookie's clerk.'

'Hold on,' Bert said. 'Not is. Was.'

'Was,' Charlie conceded, 'and will be again. But at the moment the firm he worked for is bankrupt.'

'The boss went spare,' Bert said, nodding. 'The bums come and took away all the bleeding office desks and that.'

'And all the bleeding typists?'

'Here,' said Bert, his brows suddenly lifting as a smile forced itself at last into his eyes. 'You're not all bad, then.'

'Rotten to the core,' I said. 'Go on.'

'Well, see, the boss got all his bleeding sums wrong, or like he said, his mathematical computations were based on a misconception.'

'Like the wrong horse won?'

Bert's smile got nearer. 'Cotton on quick, don't you? A whole bleeding row of wrong horses. Here, see, I've been writing for him for bleeding years. All the big courses, he was . . . well, he had . . . a pitch in Tatt's and down in the Silver Ring too, and I've been writing for him myself most of the time, for him personally, see?'

'Yes.' Bookmakers always took a clerk to record all bets as they were made. A bookmaking firm of any size sent out a team of two men or more to every allowed enclosure at most race meetings in their area: the bigger the firm, the more meetings they covered.

'Well, see, I warned him once or twice there was a leary look to his book. See, after bleeding years you get a nose for trouble, don't you? This last year or so he's made a right bleeding balls-up more than once and I told him he'd have the bums in if he went on like that, and I was right, wasn't I?'

'What did he say?'

'Told me to mind my own bleeding business,' Bert said. 'But it was my bleeding business, wasn't it? I mean, it was my job at stake. My livelihood, same as his. Who's going to pay my H.P. and rent and a few pints with the lads, I asked him, and he turned round and said not to worry, he had it all in hand, he knew what he was doing.' His voice held total disgust.

'And he didn't,' I remarked.

'Of course he bleeding didn't. He didn't take a blind bit of notice of what I said. Bleeding stupid, he was. Then ten days ago he really blew it. Lost a bleeding packet. The whole works. All of us got the push. No redundancy either. He's got a bleeding big overdraft in the bank and he's up to the eyeballs in debt.'

I glanced at Charlie who seemed exclusively interested in the ash on his cigarette.

'Why,' I asked Bert, 'did your boss ignore your warnings and rush headlong over the cliff?'

'He didn't jump over no cliff, he's getting drunk every night down the boozer.'

'I meant . . .'

'Hang on, I get you. Why did he lose the whole bleeding works? Because someone fed him the duff gen, that's my opinion. Cocky as all get out, he was, on the way to the races. Then coming home he tells me the firm is all washed up and down the bleeding drain. White as chalk, he was. Trembling, sort of. So I told him I'd warned him over and over. And that day I'd warned him too that he was laying too much on that Energise and not covering himself, and he'd told me all jolly like to mind my own effing business. So I reckon someone had told him Energise was fixed not to win, but it bleeding did win, and that's what's done for the firm.'

Bert shut his mouth and the silence was as loud as bells. Charlie tapped the ash off and smiled.

I swallowed.

'Er . . .' I said eventually.

'That's only half of it,' Charlie said, interrupting smoothly. 'Go on, Bert, tell him the rest.'

Bert seemed happy to oblige. 'Well, see, there I was in the boozer Saturday evening. Last Saturday, not the day Energise won. Four days ago, see? After the bums had been, and all that. Well, in walks Charlie like he sometimes does and we had a couple of jars together, him and me being old mates really on account of we lived next door to each other when we were kids and he was going to that la-di-da bleeding Eton and someone had to take him down a peg or two in the holidays. So, anyway, there we were in the boozer and I pour out all my troubles and Charlie says he has another friend who'd like to hear them, so ... well ... here we are.'

'What are the other troubles, then?' I asked.

'Oh ... Yeah. Well, see, the boss had a couple of betting shops. Nothing fancy, just a couple of betting shops in Windsor and Staines, see. The office, now, where the bailiffs came and took everything, that was behind the shop in Staines. So there's the boss holding his head and wailing like a siren because all his bleeding furniture's on its way out, when the phone rings. Course by this time the phone's down on the floor because the desk it was on is out on the pavement. So the boss squats down beside it and there's some geezer on the other end offering to buy the lease.'

He paused more for dramatic effect than breath.

'Go on,' I said encouragingly.

'Manna from Heaven for the boss, that was,' said Bert, accepting the invitation. 'See, he'd have had to go on paying the rent for both places even if they were shut. He practically fell on the neck of this geezer in a manner of speaking, and the geezer came round and paid him in cash on the nail, three hundred smackers, that very morning and the boss has been getting drunk on it ever since.'

A pause. 'What line of business,' I asked, 'is this geezer in?'

'Eh?' said Bert, surprised. 'Bookmaking, of course.'

Charlie smiled.

'I expect you've heard of him,' Bert said. 'Name of Ganser Mays.'

It was inevitable, I supposed.

'In what way,' I asked, 'do you want me to help?'

'Huh?'

'Charlie said you wanted my help.'

'Oh that. I dunno, really. Charlie just said it might help to tell you what I'd told him, so I done it.'

'Did Charlie tell you,' I asked, 'who owns Energise?'

'No, Charlie didn't,' Charlie said.

'What the bleeding hell does it matter who owns it?' Bert demanded.

'I do,' I said.

Bert looked from one of us to the other several times. Various thoughts took their turn behind his eyes, and Charlie and I waited.

'Here,' he said at last. 'Did you bleeding fix that race?'

'The horse ran fair and square, and I backed it on the Tote,' I said.

'Well, how come my boss thought . . .'

'I've no idea,' I said untruthfully.

Charlie lit another cigarette from the stub of the last. They were his lungs, after all.

'The point is,' I said, 'who gave your boss the wrong information?'

'Dunno.' He thought it over, but shook his head. 'Dunno.'

'Could it have been Ganser Mays?'

'Blimey!'

'Talk about slander,' Charlie said. 'He'd have you for that.'

'I merely ask,' I said. 'I also ask whether Bert knows of any other small firms which have gone out of business in the same way.'

'Blimey,' Bert said again, with even more force.

Charlie sighed with resignation, as if he hadn't engineered the whole morning's chat.

'Ganser Mays,' I said conversationally, 'has opened a vast string of betting shops during the past year or so. What has happened to the opposition?'

'Down the boozer getting drunk,' Charlie said.

Charlie stayed for a while after Bert had gone, sitting more comfortably in one of my leather armchairs and reverting thankfully to his more natural self.

'Bert's a great fellow,' he said. 'But I find him tiring.' His Eton accent, I noticed, had come back in force and I realised with mild surprise how much he tailored voice and manner to suit his company. The Charlie

Canterfield I knew, the powerful banker smoking a cigar who thought of a million as everyday currency, was not the face he had shown to Bert Huggerneck. It occurred to me that of all the people I had met who had moved from one world to another, Charlie had done it with most success. He swam through big business like a fish in water but he could still feel completely at home with Bert in a way that I, who had made a less radical journey, could not.

'Which is the villain,' Charlie asked, 'Ganser Mays or Jody Leeds?'

'Both.'

'Equal partners?'

We considered it. 'No way of knowing at the moment,' I said.

'At the moment?' His eyebrows went up.

I smiled slightly. 'I thought I might have a small crack at . . . would you call it justice?'

'The law's a bad thing to take into your own hands.'

'I don't exactly aim to lynch anyone.'

'What, then?'

I hesitated. 'There's something I ought to check. I think I'll do it today. After that, if I'm right, I'll make a loud fuss.'

'Slander actions notwithstanding?'

'I don't know.' I shook my head. 'It's infuriating.'

'What are you going to check?' he asked.

'Telephone tomorrow morning and I'll tell you.'

Charlie, like Allie, asked before he left if I would

show him where I made the toys. We went down to the workshop and found Owen Idris, my general helper, busy sweeping the tidy floor.

'Morning, Owen.'

'Morning, sir.'

'This is Mr Canterfield, Owen.'

'Morning, sir.'

Owen appeared to have swept without pause but I knew the swift glance he had given Charlie was as good as a photograph. My neat dry little Welsh factotum had a phenomenal memory for faces.

'Will you want the car today, sir?' he said.

'This evening.'

'I'll just change the oil, then.'

'Fine.'

'Will you be wanting me for the parking?'

I shook my head. 'Not tonight.'

'Very good, sir.' He looked resigned. 'Any time,' he said.

I showed Charlie the machines but he knew less about engineering than I did about banking.

'Where do you start, in the hands or in the head?'

'Head,' I said. 'Then hands, then head.'

'So clear.'

'I think of something, I make it, I draw it.'

'Draw it?'

'Machine drawings, not an artistic impression.'

'Blue prints,' said Charlie, nodding wisely.

'Blue prints are copies . . . The originals are black on white.'

'Disillusioning.'

I slid open one of the long drawers which held them and showed him some of the designs. The fine spidery lines with a key giving details of materials and sizes of screw threads looked very different from the bright shiny toys which reached the shops, and Charlie looked from design to finished article with a slowly shaking head.

'Don't know how you do it.'

'Training,' I said. 'Same way that you switch money round ten currencies in half an hour and end up thousands richer.'

'Can't do that so much these days,' he said gloomily. He watched me put designs and toys away. 'Don't forget though that my firm can always find finances for good ideas.'

'I won't forget.'

'There must be a dozen merchant banks,' Charlie said, 'all hoping to be nearest when you look around for cash.'

'The manufacturers fix the cash. I just collect the royalties.'

He shook his head. 'You'll never make a million that way.'

'I won't get ulcers either.'

'No ambition?'

'To win the Derby and get even with Jody Leeds.'

*

I arrived at Jody's expensive stable uninvited, quietly, at half past midnight, and on foot. The car lay parked half a mile behind me, along with prudence.

Pale fitful moonlight lit glimpses of the large manor house with its pedimented front door and rows of uniform windows. No lights shone upstairs in the room Jody shared with Felicity, and none downstairs in the large drawing-room beneath. The lawn, rough now and scattered with a few last dead leaves, stretched peacefully from the house to where I stood hidden in the bushes by the gate.

I watched for a while. There was no sign of anyone awake or moving, and I hadn't expected it. Jody like most six-thirty risers was usually asleep by eleven at the latest, and telephone calls after ten were answered brusquely if at all. On the other hand he had no reservations about telephoning others in the morning before seven. He had no patience with life-patterns unlike his own.

To the right and slightly to the rear of the house lay the dimly gleaming roofs of the stables. White railed paddocks lay around and beyond them, with big planned trees growing at landscaped corners. When Berksdown Court had been built, cost had come second to excellence.

Carrying a large black rubber-clad torch, unlit, I walked softly up the drive and round towards the horses. No dogs barked. No all-night guards sprang out to ask my business. Silence and peace bathed the whole place undisturbed.

My breath, all the same, came faster. My heart thumped. It would be bad if anyone caught me. I had tried reassuring myself that Jody would do me no actual physical harm, but I hadn't found myself convinced. Anger, as when I'd stood in the path of the horsebox, was again thrusting me into risk.

Close to the boxes one could hear little more than from a distance. Jody's horses stood on sawdust now that straw prices had trebled, and made no rustle when they moved. A sudden equine sneeze made me jump.

Jody's yard was not a regular quadrangle but a series of three-sided courts of unequal size and powerful charm. There were forty boxes altogether, few enough in any case to support such a lavish establishment, but since my horses had left I guessed there were only about twenty inmates remaining. Jody was in urgent need of another mug.

He had always economised on labour, reckoning that he and Felicity between them could do the work of four. His inexhaustible energy in fact ensured that no lads stayed in the yard very long as they couldn't stand the pace. Since the last so-called head lad had left in dudgeon because Jody constantly usurped his authority, there had been no one but Jody himself in charge. It was unlikely, I thought, that in present circumstances he would have taken on another man, which meant that the cottage at the end of the yard would be empty.

There were at any rate no lights in it, and no anxious figure came scurrying out to see about the stranger in the night. I went with care to the first box in the first court and quietly slid back the bolts.

Inside stood a large chestnut mare languidly eating hay. She turned her face unexcitedly in the torchlight. A big white blaze down her forehead and nose. Asphodel.

I shut her door, inching home the bolts. Any sharp noise would carry clearly through the cold calm air and Jody's subconscious ears would never sleep. The second box contained a heavy bay gelding with black points, the third a dark chestnut with one white sock. I went slowly round the first section of stables, shining the torch at each horse.

Instead of settling, my nerves got progressively worse. I had not yet found what I'd come for, and every passing minute made discovery more possible. I was careful with the torch. Careful with the bolts. My breath was shallow. I decided I'd make a rotten burglar.

Box number nine, in the next section, contained a dark brown gelding with no markings. The next box housed an undistinguished bay, the next another and the next another. After that came an almost black horse, with a slightly Arab looking nose, another very dark horse, and two more bays. The next three boxes all contained chestnuts, all unremarkable to my eyes. The last inhabited box held the only grey.

I gently shut the door of the grey and returned to the box of the chestnut next door. Went inside. Shone my torch over him carefully inch by inch.

I came to no special conclusion except that I didn't know enough about horses.

I'd done all I could. Time to go home. Time for my heart to stop thudding at twice the speed of sound. I turned for the door.

Lights came on in a blaze. Startled I took one step towards the door. Only one.

Three men crowded into the opening.

Jody Leeds.

Ganser Mays.

Another man whom I didn't know, whose appearance scarcely inspired joy and confidence. He was large, hard and muscular, and he wore thick leather gloves, a cloth cap pulled forward and, at two in the morning, sunglasses.

Whomever they had expected, it wasn't me. Jody's face held a mixture of consternation and anger, with the former winning by a mile.

'What the bloody hell are you doing here?' he said.

There was no possible answer.

'He isn't leaving,' Ganser Mays said. The eyes behind the metal rims were narrowed with ill intent and the long nose protruded sharply like a dagger. The urbane manner which lulled the clients while he relieved them of their cash had turned into the naked viciousness of the threatened criminal. Too late to worry that I'd cast myself in the role of threat.

'What?' Jody turned his face to him, not understanding.

'He isn't leaving.'

Jody said, 'How are you going to stop him?'

Nobody told him. Nobody told me, either. I took two steps towards the exit and found out.

The large man said nothing at all, but it was he who moved. A large gloved fist crashed into my ribs at the business end of a highly efficient short jab. Breath left my lungs faster than nature intended and I had difficulty getting it back.

Beyond schoolboy scuffles I had never seriously had to defend myself. No time to learn. I slammed an elbow at Jody's face, kicked Ganser Mays in the stomach and tried for the door.

Muscles in cap and sunglasses knew all that I didn't. An inch or two taller, a stone or two heavier, and warmed to his task. I landed one respectable punch on the junction of his nose and mouth in return for a couple of bangs over the heart, and made no progress towards freedom.

Jody and Ganser Mays recovered from my first onslaught and clung to me like limpets, one on each arm. I staggered under their combined weight. Muscles measured his distance and flung his bunched hand at my jaw. I managed to move my head just in time and felt the leather glove burn my cheek. Then the other fist came round, faster and crossing, and hit me square. I fell reeling across the box, released suddenly by Ganser Mays and Jody, and my head smashed solidly into the iron bars of the manger.

Total instant unconsciousness was the result.

Death must be like that, I suppose.

CHAPTER SIX

Life came back in an incomprehensible blur.

I couldn't see properly. Couldn't focus. Heard strange noises. Couldn't control my body, couldn't move my legs, couldn't lift my head. Tongue paralysed. Brain whirling. Everything disconnected and hazy.

'Drunk,' someone said distinctly.

The word made no sense. It wasn't I who was drunk.

'Paralytic.'

The ground was wet. Shining. Dazzled my eyes. I was sitting on it. Slumped on it, leaning against something hard. I shut my eyes against the drizzle and that made the whirling worse. I could feel myself falling. Banged my head. Cheek in the wet. Nose in the wet. Lying on the hard wet ground. There was a noise like rain.

'Bloody amazing,' said a voice.

'Come on, then, let's be having you.'

Strong hands slid under my armpits and grasped my ankles. I couldn't struggle. Couldn't understand where I was or what was happening.

It seemed vaguely that I was in the back of a car. I could smell the upholstery. My nose was on it. Someone was breathing very loudly. Almost snoring. Someone spoke. A jumbled mixture of sounds that made no words. It couldn't have been me. Couldn't have been.

The car jerked to a sudden stop. The driver swore. I rolled off the seat and passed out.

Next thing, bright lights and people carrying me as before.

I tried to say something. It came out in a jumble. This time I knew the jumble came from my own mouth.

'Waking up again,' someone said.

'Get him out of here before he's sick.'

March, march. More carrying. Loud boots on echoing floors.

'He's bloody heavy.'

'Bloody nuisance.'

The whirling went on. The whole building was spinning like a merry-go-round.

Merry-go-round.

The first feeling of identity came back. I wasn't just a lump of weird disorientated sensations. Somewhere, deep inside, I was . . . somebody.

Merry-go-rounds swam in and out of consciousness. I found I was lying on a bed. Bright lights blinded me every time I tried to open my eyes. The voices went away.

Time passed.

I began to feel exceedingly ill. Heard someone moaning. Didn't think it was me. After a while, I knew it was, which made it possible to stop.

Feet coming back. March march. Two pairs at least.

'What's your name?'

What was my name? Couldn't remember.

'He's soaking wet.'

'What do you expect? He was sitting on the pavement in the rain.'

'Take his jacket off.'

They took my jacket off, sitting me up to do it. I lay down again. My trousers were pulled off and someone put a blanket over me.

'He's dead drunk.'

'Yes. Have to make sure though. They're always an infernal nuisance like this. You simply can't risk that they haven't bumped their skulls and got a hairline fracture. You don't want them dying on you in the night.'

I tried to tell him I wasn't drunk. Hairline fracture . . . Christ . . . I didn't want to wake up dead in the morning.

'What did you say?'

I tried again. 'Not drunk,' I said.

Someone laughed without mirth.

'Just smell his breath.'

How did I know I wasn't drunk? The answer eluded me. I just knew I wasn't drunk . . . because I knew I hadn't drunk enough ... or any ... alcohol. How did I know? I just knew. How did I know?

While these hopeless thoughts spiralled around in the chaos inside my head a lot of strange fingers were feeling around in my hair.

'He *has* banged his head, damn it. There's quite a large swelling.'

'He's no worse than when they brought him in, doc. Better if anything.'

'Scott,' I said suddenly.

'What's that?'

'Scott.'

'Is that your name?'

I tried to sit up. The lights whirled giddily.

'Where ... am I?'

'That's what they all say.'

'In a cell, my lad, that's where.'

In a cell.

'What?' I said.

'In a cell at Savile Row police station. Drunk and incapable.'

I couldn't be.

'Look, constable, I'll just take a blood test. Then I'll do those other jobs, then come back and look at him, to make sure. I don't think we've a fracture here, but we can't take the chance.'

'Right, doc.'

The prick of a needle reached me dimly. Waste of time, I thought. Wasn't drunk. What was I ... besides ill, giddy, lost and stuck in limbo? Didn't know. Couldn't be bothered to think. Slid without struggling into a whirling black sleep.

The next awakening was in all ways worse. For a start, I wasn't ready to be dragged back from the dark. My head ached abominably, bits of my body hurt a good deal and overall I felt like an advanced case of seasickness.

'Wakey, wakey, rise and shine. Cup of tea for you and you don't deserve it.'

I opened my eyes. The bright light was still there but now identifiable not as some gross moon but as a simple electric bulb near the ceiling.

I shifted my gaze to where the voice had come from. A middle-aged policeman stood there with a paper cup in one hand. Behind him, an open door to a corridor. All round me, the close walls of a cell. I lay on a reasonably comfortable bed with two blankets keeping me warm.

'Sobering up, are you?'

'I wasn't . . . drunk.' My voice came out hoarse and my mouth felt as furry as a mink coat.

The policeman held out the cup. I struggled on to one elbow and took it from him.

'Thanks.' The tea was strong, hot and sweet. I wasn't sure it didn't make me feel even sicker.

'The doc's been back twice to check on you. You were drunk all right. Banged your head, too.'

'But I wasn't . . .'

'You sure were. The doc did a blood test to make certain.'

'Where are my clothes?'

'Oh yeah. We took 'em off. They were wet. I'll get them.'

He went out without shutting the door and I spent the few minutes he was away trying to sort out what was happening. I could remember bits of the night, but hazily. I knew who I was. No problem there. I looked at my watch: seven-thirty. I felt absolutely lousy.

The policeman returned with my suit which was wrinkled beyond belief and looked nothing like the one I'd set out in.

Set out . . . Where to?

'Is this . . . Savile Row? West end of London?'

'You remember being brought in then?'

'Some of it. Not much.'

'The patrol car picked you up somewhere in Soho at around four o'clock this morning.'

'What was I doing there?'

'I don't know, do I? Nothing, as far as I know. Just sitting dead drunk on the pavement in the pouring rain.'

'Why did they bring me here if I wasn't doing anything?'

'To save you from yourself,' he said without rancour. 'Drunks make more trouble if we leave them than if we bring them in, so we bring them in. Can't have drunks wandering out into the middle of the road and causing accidents or breaking their silly skulls falling over or waking up violent and smashing shop windows as some of them do.'

'I feel ill.'

'What d'you expect? If you're going to be sick there's a bucket at the end of the bed.'

He gave me a nod in which sympathy wasn't entirely lacking, and took himself away.

About an hour later I was driven with three other gentlemen in the same plight to attend the Marlborough Street Magistrates' Court. Drunks, it seemed, were first on the agenda. Every day's agenda.

In the interim I had become reluctantly convinced of three things.

First was that even though I could not remember drinking, I had at four a.m. that morning been hopelessly intoxicated. The blood test, analysed at speed because of the bang on my head, had revealed a level of two hundred and ninety milligrammes of alcohol per centilitre of blood which, I had been assured, meant that I had drunk the equivalent of more than half a bottle of spirits during the preceding few hours.

The second was that it would make no difference at all if I could convince anyone that at one-thirty I had been stone cold sober seventy miles away in Berkshire. They would merely say I had plenty of time to get drunk on the journey.

And the third and perhaps least welcome of all was that I seemed to have collected far more sore spots than I could account for.

I had remembered, bit by bit, my visit to Jody. I remembered trying to fight all three men at once, which was an idiotic sort of thing to attempt in the first place, even without the casual expertise of the man in sun glasses. I remembered the squashy feel when my fist connected with his nose and I knew all about the punches he'd given me in return. Even so . . .

I shrugged. Perhaps I didn't remember it all, like I didn't remember getting drunk. Or perhaps . . . Well, Ganser Mays and Jody both had reason to dislike me, and Jody had been wearing jodhpur boots.

The court proceedings took ten minutes. The charge was 'drunk in charge'. In charge of what, I asked. In charge of the police, they said.

'Guilty or not guilty?'

'Guilty,' I said resignedly.

'Fined five pounds. Do you need time to pay?'

'No, sir.'

'Good. Next, please.'

Outside, in the little office where I was due to pay the fine, I telephoned Owen Idris. Paying after all had been a problem, as there had proved to be no wallet in my rough-dried suit. No cheque book either, nor, when I came to think of it, any keys. Were they all by any chance at Savile Row, I asked. Someone telephoned. No, they weren't. I had nothing at all in my pockets when picked up. No means of identification, no money, no keys, no pen, no handkerchief.

'Owen? Bring ten pounds and a taxi to Marlborough Street Court.'

'Very good, sir.'

'Right away.'

'Of course.'

I felt hopelessly groggy. I sat in an upright chair to wait and wondered how long it took for half a bottle of spirits to dry out.

Owen came in thirty minutes and handed me the money without comment. Even his face showed no surprise at finding me in such a predicament and unshaven into the bargain. I wasn't sure that I appreciated his lack of surprise. I also couldn't think of any believable explanation. Nothing to do but shrug it off, pay the five pounds and get home as best I could. Owen sat beside me in the taxi and gave me small sidelong glances every hundred yards.

I made it upstairs to the sitting-room and lay down flat on the sofa. Owen had stayed downstairs to pay the taxi and I could hear him talking to someone down in the hall. I could do without visitors, I thought. I could do without everything except twenty-four hours of oblivion.

The visitor was Charlie.

'Your man says you're in trouble.'

'Mm.'

'Good God.' He was standing beside me, looking down. 'What on earth have you been doing?'

'Long story.'

'Hm. Will your man get us some coffee?'

'Ask him . . . he'll be in the workshop. Intercom over there.' I nodded towards the far door and wished I hadn't. My whole brain felt like a bruise.

Charlie talked to Owen on the intercom and Owen came up with his ultra-polite face and messed around with filters in the kitchen.

'What's the matter with you?' Charlie asked.

'Knocked out, drunk and . . .' I stopped.

'And what?'

'Nothing.'

'You need a doctor.'

'I saw a police surgeon. Or rather . . . he saw me.'

'You can't see the state of your eyes,' Charlie said seriously. 'And whether you like it or not, I'm getting you a doctor.' He went away to the kitchen to consult Owen and I heard the extension bell there tinkling as he kept his promise. He came back.

'What's wrong with my eyes?'

'Pinpoint pupils and glassy daze.'

'Charming.'

Owen brought the coffee, which smelled fine, but I found I could scarcely drink it. Both men looked at me with what I could only call concern.

'How did you get like this?' Charlie asked.

'Shall I go, sir?' Owen said politely.

'No. Sit down, Owen. You may as well know too ...'
He sat comfortably in a small armchair, neither per-
ching on the front nor lolling at ease in the depths. The
compromise of Owen's attitude to me was what made
him above price, his calm understanding that although
I paid for work done, we each retained equal dignity
in the transaction. I had employed him for less than a
year: I hoped he would stay till he dropped.

'I went down to Jody Leeds' stable, last night, after
dark,' I said. 'I had no right at all to be there. Jody and
two other men found me in one of the boxes looking
at a horse. There was a bit of a struggle and I banged
my head ... on the manger, I think ... and got knocked
out.'

I stopped for breath. My audience said nothing at
all.

'When I woke up, I was sitting on a pavement in
Soho, dead drunk.'

'Impossible,' Charlie said.

'No. It happened. The police scooped me up, as they
apparently do to all drunks littering the footpaths. I
spent the remains of the night in a cell and got fined
five pounds, and here I am.'

There was a long pause.

Charlie cleared his throat. 'Er ... various questions
arise.'

'They do indeed.'

Owen said calmly, 'The car, sir. Where did you leave

the car?' The car was his especial love, polished and cared for like silver.

I told him exactly where I'd parked it. Also that I no longer had its keys. Nor the keys to the flat or the workshop, for that matter.

Both Charlie and Owen showed alarm and agreed between themselves that the first thing Owen would do, even before fetching the car, would be to change all my locks.

'I made those locks,' I protested.

'Do you want Jody walking in here while you're asleep?'

'No.'

'Then Owen changes the locks.'

I didn't demur any more. I'd been thinking of a new form of lock for some time, but hadn't actually made it. I would soon, though. I would patent it and make it as a toy for kids to lock up their secrets, and maybe in twenty years' time half the doors in the country would be keeping out burglars that way. My lock didn't need keys or electronics, and couldn't be picked. It stood there, clear and sharp in my mind, with all its working parts meshing neatly.

'Are you all right?' Charlie said abruptly.

'What?'

'For a moment you looked . . .' He stopped and didn't finish the sentence.

'I'm not dying, if that's what you think. It's just that I've an idea for a new sort of lock.'

Charlie's attention sharpened as quickly as it had at Sandown.

'Revolutionary?' he asked hopefully.

I smiled inside. The word was apt in more ways than one, as some of the lock's works would revolve.

'You might say so,' I agreed.

'Don't forget ... my bank.'

'I won't.'

'No one but you would be inventing things when he's half dead.'

'I may look half dead,' I said, 'but I'm not.' I might feel half dead, too, I thought, but it would all pass.

The door bell rang sharply.

'If it's anyone but the doctor,' Charlie told Owen, 'tell them our friend is out.'

Owen nodded briefly and went downstairs, but when he came back he brought not the doctor but a visitor less expected and more welcome.

'Miss Ward, sir.'

She was through the door before he had the words out, blowing in like a gust of fresh air, her face as smooth and clean and her clothes as well-groomed as mine were dirty and squalid. She looked like life itself on two legs, her vitality lighting the room.

'Steven!'

She stopped dead a few feet from the sofa, staring down. She glanced at Charlie and at Owen. 'What's the matter with him?'

'Rough night on the tiles,' I said. 'D'you mind if I don't get up?'

'How do you do?' Charlie said politely. 'I am Charlie Canterfield. Friend of Steven's.' He shook hands with her.

'Alexandra Ward,' she replied, looking bemused.

'You've met,' I said.

'What?'

'In Walton Street.'

They looked at each other and realised what I meant. Charlie began to tell Allie how I had arrived in this sorry state and Owen went out shopping for locks. I lay on the sofa and drifted. The whole morning seemed disjointed and jerky to me, as if my thought processes were tripping over cracks.

Allie pulled up a squashy leather stool and sat beside me, which brought recovery nearer. She put her hand on mine. Better still.

'You're crazy,' she said.

I sighed. Couldn't have everything.

'Have you forgotten I'm going home this evening?'

'I have not,' I said. 'Though it looks now as though I'll have to withdraw my offer of driving you to the airport. I don't think I'm fit. No car, for another thing.'

'That's actually what I came for.' She hesitated. 'I have to keep peace with my sister . . .' She stopped, leaving a world of family tensions hovering unspoken. 'I came to say goodbye.'

'What sort of goodbye?'

'What do you mean?'

'Goodbye for now,' I said, 'or goodbye for ever?'

'Which would you like?'

Charlie chuckled. 'Now there's a double-edged question if I ever heard one.'

'You're not supposed to be listening,' she said with mock severity.

'Goodbye for now,' I said.

'All right.' She smiled the flashing smile. 'Suits me.'

Charlie wandered round the room looking at things but showed no signs of going. Allie disregarded him. She stroked my hair back from my forehead and kissed me gently. I can't say I minded.

After a while the doctor came. Charlie went down to let him in and apparently briefed him on the way up. He and Allie retired to the kitchen where I heard them making more coffee.

The doctor helped me remove all clothes except underpants. I'd have been much happier left alone. He tapped my joints for reflexes, peered through lights into my eyes and ears and prodded my many sore spots. Then he sat on the stool Allie had brought, and pinched his nose.

'Concussion,' he said. 'Go to bed for a week.'

'Don't be silly,' I protested.

'Best,' he said succinctly.

'But the jump jockeys get concussion one minute and ride winners the next.'

'The jump jockeys are bloody fools.' He surveyed

me morosely. 'If you'd been a jump jockey I'd say you'd been trampled by a field of horses.'

'But as I'm not?'

'Has someone been beating you?'

It wasn't the sort of question somehow that one expected one's doctor to ask. Certainly not as matter-of-factly as this.

'I don't know,' I said.

'You must do.'

'I agree it feels a bit like it, but if they did, I was unconscious.'

'With something big and blunt,' he added. 'They're large bruises.' He pointed to several extensive reddening patches on my thighs, arms and trunk.

'A boot?' I said.

He looked at me soberly. 'You've considered the possibility?'

'Forced on me.'

He smiled. 'Your friend, the one who let me in, told me you say you got drunk also while unconscious.'

'Yes. Tube down the throat?' I suggested.

'Tell me the time factors.'

I did as nearly as I could. He shook his head dubiously. 'I wouldn't have thought pouring neat alcohol straight into the stomach would produce that amount of intoxication so quickly. It takes quite a while for a large quantity of alcohol to be absorbed into the bloodstream through the stomach wall.' He pondered, thinking aloud. 'Two hundred and ninety milligrammes ... and you were maybe unconscious from the bang on the head for two hours or a little more. Hm.'

He leaned forward, picked up my left forearm and peered at it closely, front and back. Then he did the same thing with the right, and found what he was looking for.

'There,' he exclaimed. 'See that? The mark of a needle. Straight into the vein. They've tried to disguise it by a blow on top to bruise all the surrounding tissue. In a few more hours the needle mark will be invisible.'

'Anaesthetic?' I said dubiously.

'My dear fellow. No. Probably gin.'

'*Gin!*'

'Why not? Straight into the bloodstream. Much more efficient than a tube to the stomach. Much quicker results. Deadly, really. And less effort, on the whole.'

'But ... how? You can't harness a gin bottle to a hypodermic.'

He grinned. 'No, no. You'd set up a drip. Sterile glucose saline drip. Standard stuff. You can buy it in plastic bags from any chemist. Pour three quarters of a pint of gin into one bag of solution, and drip it straight into the vein.'

'But, how long would that take?'

'Oh, about an hour. Frightful shock to the system.'

I thought about it. If it had been done that way I had been transported to London with gin dripping into

121

my blood for most of the journey. There hadn't been time to do it first and set off after.

'Suppose I'd started to come round?' I asked.

'Lucky you didn't, I dare say. Nothing to stop someone bashing you back to sleep, as far as I can see.'

'You take it very calmly,' I said.

'So do you. And it's interesting, don't you think?'

'Oh very,' I said dryly.

CHAPTER SEVEN

Charlie and Allie stayed for lunch, which meant that they cooked omelettes for themselves and found some reasonable cheese to follow. Out in the kitchen Charlie seemed to have been filling in gaps because when they carried their trays into the sitting-room it was clear that Allie knew all that Charlie did.

'Do you feel like eating?' Charlie asked.

'I do not.'

'Drink?'

'Shut up.'

'Sorry.'

The body rids itself of alcohol very slowly, the doctor had said. Only at a rate of ten milligrammes per hour. There was no way of hastening the process and nothing much to be done about hangovers except endure them. People who normally drank little suffered worst, he said, because their bodies had no tolerance. Too bad, he'd said, smiling about it.

Two hundred and ninety milligrammes came into the paralytic bracket. Twenty-nine hours to be rid of it. I'd lived through about ten so far. No wonder I felt so awful.

Round a mouthful of omelette Charlie said, 'What are you going to do about all this?' He waved his fork from my heels to my head, still prostrate on the sofa.

'Would you suggest going to the police?' I asked neutrally.

'Er . . .'

'Exactly. The very same police who gave me hospitality last night and know for a certainty that I was so drunk that anything I might complain of could be explained away as an alcoholic delusion.'

'Do you think that's why Jody and Ganser Mays did it?'

'Why else? And I suppose I should be grateful that all they did was discredit me, not bump me right off altogether.'

Allie looked horrified, which was nice. Charlie was more prosaic.

'Bodies are notoriously difficult to get rid of,' he said. 'I would say that Jody and Ganser Mays made a rapid assessment and reckoned that dumping you drunk in London was a lot less dangerous than murder.'

'There was another man as well,' I said, and described my friend with sunglasses and muscles.

'Ever seen him before?' Charlie asked.

'No, never.'

'The brawn of the organisation?'

'Maybe he has brain, too. Can't tell.'

'One thing is sure,' Charlie said. 'If the plan was to discredit you, your little escapade will be known all round the racecourse by tomorrow afternoon.'

How gloomy, I thought. I was sure he was right. It would make going to the races more uninviting than ever.

Allie said, 'I guess you won't like it, but if I were trying to drag your name through the mud I'd have made sure there was a gossip columnist in court this morning.'

'Oh hell.' Worse and worse.

'Are you just going to lie there,' Charlie said, 'and let them crow?'

'He's got a problem,' Allie said with a smile. 'How come he was wandering around Jody's stable at that time anyway?'

'Ah,' I said. 'Now that's the nub of the matter, I agree. And if I tell you, you must both promise me on your souls that you will not repeat it.'

'Are you serious?' Allie said in surprise.

'You don't sound it,' Charlie commented.

'I am, though. Deadly serious. Will you promise?'

'You play with too many toys. It's childish.'

'Many civil servants swear an oath of secrecy.'

'Oh all right,' Charlie said in exasperation. 'On my soul.'

'And on mine,' Allie said lightheartedly. 'Now do get on with it.'

'I own a horse called Energise,' I said. They both

nodded. They knew. 'I spent half an hour alone with him in a crashed horsebox at Sandown.' They both nodded again. 'Then I sent him to Rupert Ramsey and last Sunday morning I spent half an hour alone with him again.'

'So what?' Charlie said.

'So the horse at Rupert Ramsey's is not Energise.'

Charlie sat bolt upright so quickly that his omelette plate fell on the carpet. He bent down, feeling around for bits of egg with his astounded face turned up to mine.

'Are you sure?'

'Definitely. He's very like him, and if I hadn't spent all that time in the crashed horsebox I would never have known the difference. Owners often don't know which their horse is. It's a standing joke. But I *learnt* Energise that day at Sandown. So when I visited Rupert Ramsey's I knew he had a different horse.'

'So,' said Charlie slowly, 'you went to Jody's stable last night to see if Energise was still there.'

'Yes.'

'And is he?'

'Yes.'

'Absolutely certain?'

'Positive. He has a slightly Arab nose, a nick near the tip of his left ear, a bald spot about the size of a twopenny piece on his shoulder. He was in box number thirteen.'

'Is that where they found you?'

'No. You remember, Allie, that we went to Newmarket?'

'How could I forget?'

'Do you remember Hermes?'

She wrinkled her nose. 'Was that the chestnut?'

'That's right. Well, I went to Trevor Kennet's stable that day with you because I wanted to see if I could tell whether the Hermes he had was the Hermes Jody had had . . . if you see what I mean.'

'And was he?' she said, fascinated.

'I couldn't tell. I found I didn't know Hermes well enough and anyway if Jody did switch Hermes he probably did it before his last two races last summer, because the horse did no good at all in those and trailed in at the back of the field.'

'Good God,' Charlie said. 'And did you find Hermes at Jody's place too?'

'I don't know. There were three chestnuts there. No markings, same as Hermes. All much alike. I couldn't tell if any of them was Hermes. But it was in one of the chestnuts' boxes that Jody and the others found me, and they were certainly alarmed as well as angry.'

'But what would he get out of it?' Allie asked.

'He owns some horses himself,' I said. 'Trainers often do. They run them in their own names, then if they're any good, they sell them at a profit, probably to owners who already have horses in the stable.'

'You mean . . .' she said, 'that he sent a horse he owned himself to Rupert Ramsey and kept Energise.

Then when Energise wins another big race he'll sell him to one of the people he trains for, for a nice fat sum, and keep on training him himself?'

'That's about it.'

'Wow.'

'I'm not so absolutely sure,' I said with a sardonic smile, 'that he hasn't in the past sold me my own horse back after swopping it with one of his own.'

'Je-*sus*,' Charlie said.

'I had two bay fillies I couldn't tell apart. The first one won for a while, then turned sour. I sold her on Jody's advice and bought the second, which was one of his own. She started winning straight away.'

'How are you going to prove it?' Allie said.

'I don't see how you can,' said Charlie. 'Especially not after this drinking charge.'

We all three contemplated the situation in silence.

'Gee, dammit,' said Allie finally and explosively. 'I just don't see why that guy should be allowed to rob you and make people despise you and get away with it.'

'Give me time,' I said mildly, 'and he won't.'

'Time?'

'For thinking,' I explained. 'If a frontal assault would land me straight into a lawsuit for slander, which it would, I'll have to come up with a sneaky scheme which will creep up on him from the rear.'

Allie and Charlie looked at each other.

Charlie said to her, 'A lot of the things he's invented as children's toys get scaled up very usefully.'

'As if Cockerell had made the first Hovercraft for the bath tub?'

'Absolutely.' Charlie nodded at her with approval. 'And I dare say it was a gentle-seeming man who thought up gunpowder.'

She flashed a smiling look from him to me and then looked suddenly at her watch and got to her feet in a hurry.

'Oh golly! I'm late. I should have gone an hour ago. My sister will be so mad. Steven . . .'

Charlie looked at her resignedly and took the plates out to the kitchen. I shifted my lazy self off the sofa and stood up.

'I wish you weren't going,' I said.

'I really have to.'

'Do you mind kissing an unshaven drunk?'

It seemed she didn't. It was the best we'd achieved.

'The Atlantic has shrunk,' I said, 'since Columbus.'

'Will you cross it?'

'Swim, if necessary.'

She briefly kissed my bristly cheek, laughed and went quickly. The room seemed darker and emptier. I wanted her back with a most unaccustomed fierceness. Girls had come and gone in my life and each time afterwards I had relapsed thankfully into singleness. Maybe at thirty-five, I thought fleetingly, what I wanted was a wife.

Charlie returned from the kitchen carrying a cup and saucer.

'Sit down before you fall down,' he said. 'You're swaying about like the Empire State.'

I sat on the sofa.

'And drink this.'

He had made a cup of tea, not strong, not weak, and with scarcely any milk. I took a couple of sips and thanked him.

'Will you be all right if I go?' he said. 'I've an appointment.'

'Of course, Charlie.'

'Take care of your damned silly self.'

He buttoned his overcoat, gave me a sympathetic wave and departed. Owen had long since finished changing the locks and had set off with a spare set of keys to fetch the car. I was alone in the flat. It seemed much quieter than usual.

I drank the rest of the tea, leaned back against the cushions, and shut my eyes, sick and uncomfortable from head to foot. Damn Jody Leeds, I thought. Damn and blast him to hell.

No wonder, I thought, that he had been so frantically determined to take Energise back with him from Sandown. He must already have had the substitute in his yard, waiting for a good moment to exchange them. When I'd said I wanted Energise to go elsewhere immediately he had been ready to go to any lengths to prevent it. I was pretty sure now that had Jody been driving the horsebox instead of Andy-Fred I would have ended up in hospital if not the morgue.

I thought about the passports which were the identity cards of British thoroughbreds. A blank passport form bore three stylised outlines of a horse, one from each side and one from head on. At the time when a foal was named, usually as a yearling or two-year-old, the veterinary surgeon attending the stable where he was being trained filled in his markings on the form and completed a written description alongside. The passport was then sent to the central racing authorities who stamped it, filed it and sent a photocopy back to the trainer.

I had noticed from time to time that my horses had hardly a blaze, star or white sock between them. It had never struck me as significant. Thousands of horses had no markings. I had even preferred them without.

The passports, once issued, were rarely used. As far as I knew, apart from travelling abroad, they were checked only once, which was on the day of the horse's very first race; and that not out of suspicion, but simply to make sure the horse actually did match the vet's description.

I didn't doubt that the horse now standing instead of Energise at Rupert Ramsey's stable matched Energise's passport in every way. Details like the shape of the nose, the slant of the stomach, the angle of the hock, wouldn't be on it.

I sighed and shifted a bit to relieve various aches. Didn't succeed. Jody had been generous with his boots.

I remembered with satisfaction the kick I'd landed in Ganser Mays' stomach. But perhaps he too had taken revenge.

It struck me suddenly that Jody wouldn't have had to rely on Raymond Child to ride crooked races. Not every time, anyway. If he had a substitute horse of poor ability, all he had to do was send him instead of the good one whenever the race had to be lost.

Racing history was packed with rumours of ringers, the good horses running in the names of the bad. Jody, I was sure, had simply reversed things and run bad horses in the names of good.

Every horse I'd owned, when I looked back, had followed much the same pattern. There would be at first a patch of sporadic success, but with regular disasters every time I staked a bundle, and then a long tail-off with no success at all. It was highly likely that the no success was due to my now having the substitute, which was running way out of its class.

It would explain why Ferryboat had run badly all autumn. Not because he resented Raymond Child's whip, but because he wasn't Ferryboat. Wrecker, too. And at least one of the three older horses I'd sent up north.

Five at least, that made. Also the filly. Also the first two, now sold as flops. Eight. I reckoned I might still have the real Dial and I might still have the real Bubbleglass, because they were novices who had yet to prove their worth. But they too would have been matched, when they had.

A systematic fraud. All it needed was a mug.

I had been ignorantly happy. No owner expected to win all the time and there must have been many days when Jody's disappointment too had been genuine. Even the best-laid bets went astray if the horses met faster opposition.

The money I'd staked with Ganser Mays had been small change compared with the value of the horses.

Impossible ever to work out just how many thousands had vanished from there. It was not only that the re-sale value of the substitutes after a string of bad races was low, but there was also the prize money the true horses might have won for me and even, in the case of Hermes, the possibility of stud fees. The real Hermes might have been good enough. The substitute would fail continually as a four-year-old and no one would want to breed from him. In every way, Jody had bled every penny he could.

Energise . . .

Anger deepened in me abruptly. For Energise I felt more admiration and affection than for any of the others. He wasn't a matter of cash value. He was a person I'd got to know in a horsebox. One way or another I was going to get him back.

I moved restlessly, standing up. Not wise. The headache I'd had all day began imitating a pile-driver. Whether it was still alcohol, or all concussion, it made little difference to the wretched end result. I went impatiently into the bedroom, put on a dressing-gown over shirt and trousers and lay down on the bed. The short December afternoon began to close in with creeping grey shadows and I reckoned it was twelve hours since Jody had dumped me in the street.

I wondered whether the doctor was right about the gin dripping into my vein. The mark he had said was a needle prick had, as predicted, vanished into a larger area of bruising. I doubted whether it had ever been there. When one thought it over it seemed an unlikely method because of one simple snag: the improbability of Jody just happening to have a bag of saline lying around handy. Maybe it was true one could buy it from any chemist, but not in the middle of the night.

The only all-night chemists were in London. Would there have been time to belt up the M4, buy the saline, and drip it in while parked in central London? Almost certainly not. And why bother? Any piece of rubber tubing down the throat would have done instead.

I massaged my neck thoughtfully. No soreness around the tonsils. Didn't prove anything either way.

It was still less likely that Ganser Mays, on a visit to Jody, would be around with hypodermic and drip. My absolutely stinking luck, I reflected gloomily, that I had chosen to snoop around on one of the rare evenings Jody had not been to bed by ten thirty. I supposed that for all my care the flash of my torch had been visible from outside. I supposed that Jody had come out of his house to see off his guests and they'd spotted the wavering light.

Ganser Mays. I detested him in quite a different way from Jody because I had never at any time liked him personally. I felt deeply betrayed by Jody, but the trust I'd given Ganser Mays had been a surface thing, a matter of simple expectation that he would behave with professional honour.

From Bert Huggerneck's description of the killing-off of one small bookmaking business it was probable Ganser Mays had as much professional honour as an octopus. His tentacles stretched out and clutched and sucked the victim dry. I had a vision of a whole crowd of desperate little men sitting on their office floors because the bailiffs had taken the furniture, sobbing with relief down their telephones while Ganser Mays offered to buy the albatross of their lease for peanuts: and another vision of the same crowd of little men getting drunk in dingy pubs, trying to obliterate the pain of seeing the bright new shop fronts glowing over the ashes of their closed books.

Very likely the little men had been stupid. Very likely they should have had more sense than to believe even the most reliable-seeming information, even though the reliable-seeming information had in the past proved to be correct. Every good card-sharper knew that the victim who had been allowed to win to begin with would part with the most in the end.

If on a minor level Ganser Mays had continually

worked that trick on me, and others like me, then how much more had he stood to gain by entangling every vulnerable little firm he could find. He'd sucked the juices, discarded the husks, and grown fat.

Proof, I thought, was impossible. The murmurs of wrong information could never be traced and the crowd of bankrupt little men probably thought of Ganser Mays as their saviour, not the architect of the skids.

I imagined the sequence of events as seen by Jody and Ganser Mays when Energise ran at Sandown. To begin with, they must have decided that I should have a big bet and the horse would lose. Or even ... that the substitute would run instead. Right up until the day before the race, that would have been the plan. Then I refused to bet. Persuasion failed. Quick council of war. I should be taught a lesson, to bet when my trainer said so. The horse ... Energise himself ... was to run to win.

Fine. But Bert Huggerneck's boss went off to Sandown expecting, positively *knowing*, that Energise would lose. The only people who could have told him so were Ganser Mays and Jody. Or perhaps Raymond Child. I thought it might be informative to find out just when Bert Huggerneck's boss had been given the news. I might get Bert to ask him.

My memory wandered to Rupert Ramsey's office and the bright green wool of Poppet Vine. She and her husband had started to bet with Ganser Mays and Felicity Leeds had engineered it. Did Felicity, I wondered sourly, know all about Jody's plundering ways? I supposed that she must, because she knew all their horses. Lads might come and go, discouraged by having to work too hard, but Felicity rode out twice every morning and groomed and fed in the evenings. Felicity assuredly would know if a horse had been switched.

She might be steering people to Ganser Mays out of loyalty, or for commission, or for some reason unguessed at; but everything I heard or learned seemed to make it certain that although Jody Leeds and Ganser Mays might benefit in separate ways, everything they did was a joint enterprise.

There was also, I supposed, the third man, old muscle and sunglasses. The beef of the organisation. I didn't think I would ever forget him: raincoat over heavy shoulders, cloth cap over forehead, sunglasses over eyes ... almost a disguise. Yet I hadn't known him. I was positive I'd never seen him anywhere before. So why had he needed a disguise at one-thirty in the morning when he hadn't expected to be seen by me in the first place?

All I knew of him was that at some point he had learned to box. That he was of sufficient standing in the trio to make his own decisions, because neither of the others had told him to hit me: he'd done it of his own accord. That Ganser Mays and Jody felt they needed his extra muscle, because neither of them was large, though Jody in his way was strong, in case any of the swindled victims cut up rough.

The afternoon faded and became night. All I was doing, I thought, was sorting through the implications and explanations of what had happened. Nothing at all towards getting myself out of trouble and Jody in. When I tried to plan that, all I achieved was a blank.

In the silence I clearly heard the sound of the street door opening. My heart jumped. Pulse raced again, as in the stable. Brain came sternly afterwards like a schoolmaster, telling me not to be so bloody silly.

No one but Owen had the new keys. No one but Owen would be coming in. All the same I was relieved when the lights were switched on in the hall and I could hear his familiar tread on the stairs.

He came into the dark sitting-room.

'Sir?'

'In the bedroom,' I called.

He came into the doorway, silhouetted against the light in the passage.

'Shall I turn the light on?'

'No, don't bother.'

'Sir . . .' His voice suddenly struck me as being odd. Uncertain. Or distressed.

'What's the matter?'

'I couldn't find the car.' The words came out in a rush. The distress was evident.

'Go and get yourself a stiff drink and come back and tell me about it.'

He hesitated a fraction but went away to the sitting-room and clinked glasses. I fumbled around with an outstretched hand and switched on the bedside light. Squinted at my watch. Six-thirty. Allie would be at Heathrow, boarding her aeroplane, waving to her sister, flying away.

Owen returned with two glasses, both containing scotch and water. He put one glass on my bedside table and interrupted politely when I opened my mouth to protest.

'The hair of the dog. You know it works, sir.'

'It just makes you drunker.'

'But less queasy.'

I waved towards my bedroom armchair and he sat in it easily as before, watching me with a worried expression. He held his glass carefully, but didn't drink. With a sigh I propped myself on one elbow and led the way. The first sip tasted vile, the second passable, the third familiar.

'Okay,' I said. 'What about the car?'

Owen took a quick gulp from his glass. The worried expression intensified.

'I went down to Newbury on the train and hired a taxi, like you said. We drove to where you showed me on the map, but the car didn't seem to be there. So I got the taxi driver to go along every possible road leading away from Mr Leeds' stable and I still couldn't find it. The taxi driver got pretty ratty in the end. He said there wasn't anywhere else to look. I got him to drive around in a larger area, but you said you'd walked from the car to the stables so it couldn't have been more than a mile away, I thought.'

'Half a mile, no further,' I said.

'Well, sir, the car just wasn't there.' He took another swig. 'I didn't really know what to do. I got the taxi to take me to the police in Newbury, but they knew nothing about it. They rang around two or three local nicks because I made a bit of a fuss, sir, but no one down there had seen hair or hide of it.'

I thought a bit. 'They had the keys, of course.'

'Yes, I thought of that.'

'So the car could be more or less anywhere by now.'

He nodded unhappily.

'Never mind,' I said. 'I'll report it stolen. It's bound to turn up somewhere. They aren't ordinary car thieves. When you come to think of it we should have expected it to be gone, because if they were going to deny I had ever been in the stables last night they wouldn't want my car found half a mile away.'

'Do you mean they went out looking for it?'

'They would know I hadn't dropped in by parachute.'

He smiled faintly and lowered the level in his glass to a spoonful.

'Shall I get you something to eat, sir?'

'I don't feel . . .'

'Better to eat. Really it is. I'll pop out to the take-away.' He put his glass down and departed before I could argue and came back in ten minutes with a wing of freshly roasted chicken.

'Didn't think you'd fancy the chips,' he said. He put the plate beside me, fetched knife, fork and napkin, and drained his own glass.

'Be going now, sir,' he said, 'if you're all right.'

CHAPTER EIGHT

Whether it was Owen's care or the natural course of events, I felt a great deal better in the morning. The face peering back at me from the bathroom mirror, though adorned now with two days' stubble, had lost the grey look and the dizzy eyes. Even the bags underneath were retreating to normal.

I shaved first and bathed after, and observed that at least twenty per cent of my skin was now showing bruise marks. I supposed I should have been glad I hadn't been awake when I collected them. The bothersome aches they had set up the day before had more or less abated, and coffee and breakfast helped things along fine.

The police were damping on the matter of stolen Lamborghinis. They took particulars with pessimism and said I might hear something in a week or so; then within half an hour they were back on the line bristling with irritation. My car had been towed away by colleagues the night before last because I'd parked it on a space reserved for taxis in Leicester Square. I could find it in the pound at Marble Arch and there would be a charge for towing.

Owen arrived at nine with a long face and was hugely cheered when I told him about the car.

'Have you seen the papers, sir?'

'Not yet.'

He held out one of his own. 'You'd better know,' he said. I unfolded it. Allie had been right about the gossip columnist. The paragraph was short and sharp and left no one in any doubt.

Red-face day for Steven Scott (35), wealthy race-horse owner, who was scooped by police from a Soho gutter early yesterday. At Marlborough Street Court, Scott, looking rough and crumpled, pleaded guilty to a charge of drunk and incapable. Save your sympathy. Race-followers will remember Scott recently dumped Jody Leeds (28), trainer of all his winners, without a second's notice.

I looked through my own two dailies and the *Sporting Life*. They all carried the story and in much the same vein, even if without the tabloid heat. Smug satisfaction that the kicker-of-underdogs had himself bitten the dust.

It was fair to assume that the story had been sent to every newspaper and that most of them had used it. Even though I'd expected it, I didn't like it. Not a bit.

'It's bloody unfair,' Owen said, reading the piece in the *Life*.

I looked at him with surprise. His usually non-committal face was screwed into frustrated anger and I wondered if his expression was a mirror-image of my own.

'Kind of you to care.'

'Can't help it, sir.' The features returned more or less to normal, but with an effort. 'Anything I can do, sir?'

'Fetch the car?'

He brightened a little. 'Right away.'

His brightness was short-lived because after half an hour he came back white-faced and angrier than I would have thought possible.

'Sir!'

'What is it?'

'The car, sir. The car.'

His manner said it all. He stammered with fury over the details. The nearside front wing was crumpled beyond repair. Headlights smashed. Hub cap missing. Bonnet dented. All the paintwork on the nearside scratched and scored down to the metal. Nearside door a complete write-off. Windows smashed, handle torn away.

'It looks as if it was driven against a brick wall, sir. Something like that.'

I thought coldly of the nearside of Jody's horsebox,

identically damaged. My car had been smashed for vengeance.

'Were the keys in it?' I asked.

He shook his head. 'It wasn't locked. Couldn't be, with one lock broken. I looked for your wallet, like you said, but it wasn't there. None of your things, sir.'

'Is the car drivable?'

He calmed down a little. 'Yes, the engine's all right. It must have been going all right when it was driven into Leicester Square. It looks a proper wreck, but it must be going all right, otherwise how could they have got it there?'

'That's something, anyway.'

'I left it in the pound, sir. It'll have to go back to the coach builders, and they might as well fetch it from there.'

'Sure,' I agreed. I imagined he couldn't have borne to have driven a crumbed car through London; he was justly proud of his driving.

Owen took his tangled emotions down to the workshop and I dealt with mine upstairs. The fresh blight Jody had laid on my life was all due to my own action in creeping into his stable by night. Had it been worth it, I wondered. I'd paid a fairly appalling price for a half-minute's view of Energise: but at least I now *knew* Jody had swapped him. It was a fact, not a guess.

I spent the whole morning on the telephone straightening out the chaos. Organising car repairs and arranging a hired substitute. Telling my bank manager and about ten assorted others that I had lost my cheque book and credit cards. Assuring various enquiring relatives, who had all of course read the papers, that I was neither in jail nor dipsomaniac. Listening to a shrill lady, whose call inched in somehow, telling me it was disgusting for the rich to get drunk in gutters. I asked her if it was okay for the poor, and if it was, why should they have more rights than I. Fair's fair, I said. Long live equality. She called me a rude word and rang off. It was the only bright spot of the day.

Last of all I called Rupert Ramsey.

'What do you mean, you don't want Energise to run?' His voice sounded almost as surprised as Jody's at Sandown.

'I thought,' I said diffidently, 'that he might need more time. You said yourself he needed building up. Well, it's only a week or so to that Christmas race and I don't want him to run below his best.'

Relief distinctly took the place of surprise at the other end of the wire.

'If you feel like that, fine,' he said. 'To be honest, the horse has been a little disappointing on the gallops. I gave him a bit of fast work yesterday upsides a hurdler he should have made mincemeat of, and he couldn't even lie up with him. I'm a bit worried about him. I'm sorry not to be able to give you better news.'

'It's all right,' I said. 'If you'll just keep him and do your best, that'll be fine with me. But don't run him anywhere. I don't mind waiting. I just don't want him raced.'

'You made your point.' The smile came down the wire with the words. 'What about the other two?'

'I'll leave them to your judgement. Nothing Ferryboat does will disappoint me, but I'd like to bet on Dial whenever you say he's ready.'

'He's ready now. He's entered at Newbury in a fortnight. He should run very well there, I think.'

'Great,' I said.

'Will you be coming?' There was a load of meaning in the question. He too had read the papers.

'Depends on the state of my courage,' I said flippantly. 'Tell you nearer the day.'

In the event, I went.

Most people's memories were short and I received no larger slice than I expected of the cold shoulder. Christmas had come and gone, leaving perhaps a trace of goodwill to all men even if they had been beastly to poor Jody Leeds and got themselves fined for drunkenness. I collected more amused sniggers than active disapproval, except of course from Quintus Leeds, who went out of his way to vent himself of his dislike. He told me again that I would certainly never be elected to the Jockey Club. Over his dead body, he said. He and Jody were both addicted to the phrase.

I was in truth sorry about the Jockey Club. Whatever

one thought of it, it was still a sort of recognition to be asked to become a member. Racing's freedom of the city: along those lines. If I had meekly allowed Jody to carry on robbing, I would have been in. As I hadn't, I was out. Sour joke.

Dial made up for a lot by winning the four-year-old hurdle by a length, and not even Quintus telling everyone it was solely due to Jody's groundwork could dim my pleasure in seeing him sprint to the post.

Rupert Ramsey, patting Dial's steaming sides, sounded all the same apologetic.

'Energise isn't his old self yet, I'm afraid.'

Truer than you know, I thought. I said only, 'Never mind. Don't run him.'

He said doubtfully, 'He's entered for the Champion Hurdle. I don't know if it's worth leaving him in at the next forfeit stage.'

'Don't take him out,' I said with haste. 'I mean . . . I don't mind paying the extra entrance fee. There's always hope that he'll come right.'

'Ye-es.' He was unconvinced, as well he might be. 'As you like, of course.'

I nodded. 'Drink?' I suggested.

'A quick one, then. I've some other runners.'

He gulped his scotch in friendly fashion, refused a refill, and cantered away to the saddling boxes. I wandered alone to a higher point in the stands and looked idly over the cold windy racecourse.

During the past fortnight I'd been unable to work

out just which horse was doubling for Energise. Nothing on Jody's list of horses-in-training seemed to match. Near-black horses were rarer than most, and none on his list were both the right colour and the right age. The changeling at Rupert's couldn't be faulted on colour, age, height, or general conformation. Jody, I imagined, hadn't just happened to have him lying around: he would have had to have searched for him diligently. How, I wondered vaguely, would one set about buying a ringer? One could hardly drift about asking if anyone knew of a spitting image at bargain prices.

My wandering gaze jolted to a full stop. Down among the crowds among the rows of bookmakers' stands I was sure I had seen a familiar pair of sunglasses.

The afternoon was grey. The sky threatened snow and the wind searched every crevice between body and soul. Not a day, one would have thought, for needing to fend off dazzle to the eyes.

There they were again. Sitting securely on the nose of a man with heavy shoulders. No cloth cap, though. A trilby. No raincoat; sheepskin.

I lifted my race glasses for a closer look. He had his back towards me with his head slightly turned to the left. I could see a quarter profile of one cheek and the tinted glasses which showed plainly as he looked down to a race card.

Mousey brown hair, medium length. Hands in

pigskin gloves. Brownish tweed trousers. Binoculars slung over one shoulder. A typical racegoer among a thousand others. Except for those sun specs.

I willed him to turn round. Instead he moved away, his back still towards me, until he was lost in the throng. Impossible to know without getting closer.

I spent the whole of the rest of the afternoon looking for a man, any man, wearing sunglasses, but the only thing I saw in shades was an actress dodging her public.

Inevitably, at one stage, I came face to face with Jody.

Newbury was his local meeting and he was running three horses, so I had been certain he would be there. A week earlier I had shrunk so much from seeing him that I had wanted to duck going, but in the end I had seen that it was essential. Somehow or other I had to convince him that I had forgotten most of my nocturnal visit, that the crack on the head and concussion had between them wiped the memory slate clean.

I couldn't afford for him to be certain I had seen and recognised Energise and knew about the swap. I couldn't afford it for exactly the same reason that I had failed to go to the police. For the same reason that I had quite seriously sworn Charlie and Allie to secrecy.

Given a choice of prosecution for fraud and getting rid of the evidence, Jody would have jettisoned the evidence faster than sight. Energise would have been dead and dogmeat long before an arrest.

The thought that Jody had already killed him was

one I tried continually to put out of my head. I reasoned that he couldn't be sure I'd seen the horse, or recognised him even if I had. They had found me down one end of the line of boxes: they couldn't be sure that I hadn't started at that far end and was working back. They couldn't really be sure I had been actually searching for a ringer, or even that I suspected one. They didn't know for certain why I'd been in the yard.

Energise was valuable, too valuable to destroy in needless panic. I guessed, and I hoped, that they wouldn't kill him unless they had to. Why else would they have gone to such trouble to make sure my word would be doubted. Transporting me to London and making me drunk had given them ample time to whisk Energise to a safer place, and I was sure that if I'd gone belting back there at once with the police I would have been met by incredulous wide-eyed innocence.

'Come in, come in, search where you like,' Jody would have said.

No Energise anywhere to be seen.

'Of course, if you were drunk, you dreamt it all, no doubt.'

End of investigation, and end of Energise, because after that it would have been too risky to keep him.

Whereas if I could convince Jody I knew nothing, he might keep Energise alive and somehow or other I might get him back.

I accidentally bumped into him outside the weighing

room. We both half-turned to each other to apologise, and recognition froze the words in our mouths.

Jody's eyes turned stormy and I suppose mine also.

'Get out of my bloody way,' he said.

'Look, Jody,' I said, 'I want your help.'

'I'm as likely to help you as kiss your arse.'

I ignored that and put on a bit of puzzle. 'Did I, or didn't I, come to your stables a fortnight ago?'

He was suddenly a great deal less violent, a great deal more attentive.

'What d'you mean?'

'I know it's stupid ... but somehow or other I got drunk and collected concussion from an almighty bang on the head, and I thought ... it seemed to me, that the evening before, I'd set out to visit you, though with things as they are between us I can't for the life of me think why. So what I want to know is, did I arrive at your place, or didn't I?'

He gave me a straight narrow-eyed stare.

'If you came, I never saw you,' he said.

I looked down at the ground as if disconsolate and shook my head. 'I can't understand it. In the ordinary way I never drink much. I've been trying to puzzle it out ever since, but I can't remember anything between about six one evening and waking up in a police station next morning with a frightful headache and a lot of bruises. I wondered if you could tell me what I'd done in between, because as far as I'm concerned it's a blank.'

I could almost feel the procession of emotions flowing out of him. Surprise, elation, relief and a feeling that this was a totally unexpected piece of luck.

He felt confident enough to return to abuse.

'Why the bloody hell should you have wanted to visit me? You couldn't get shot of me fast enough.'

'I don't know,' I said glumly. 'I suppose you didn't ring me up and ask me . . .'

'You're so right I didn't. And don't you come hanging round. I've had a bellyful of you and I wouldn't have you back if you crawled.'

He scowled, turned away and strode off, and only because I knew what he must be thinking could I discern the twist of satisfied smile that he couldn't entirely hide. He left me in much the same state. If he was warning me so emphatically to stay away from his stables there was the best of chances that Energise was back there, alive and well.

I watched his sturdy backview threading through the crowd, with people smiling at him as he passed. Everyone's idea of a bright young trainer going places. My idea of a ruthless little crook.

At Christmas I had written to Allie in code four.

'Which is the first night you could have dinner with me and where? I enclose twenty dollars for cab fare home.'

On the morning after Newbury races I received her reply, also in groups of five letters, but not in code four. She had jumbled her answer ingeniously enough for it to take me two minutes to unravel it. Very short messages were always the worst, and this was brief indeed.

'January fifth in Miami.'

I laughed aloud. And she had kept the twenty bucks.

The *Racing Calendar* came in the same post. I took it and a cup of coffee over to the big window on the balcony and sat in an armchair there to read. The sky over the Zoo in Regent's Park looked as heavy and grey as the day before, thick with the threat of snow. Down by the canal the bare branches of trees traced tangled black lines across the brown water and grassy banks, and the ribbon traffic as usual shattered the illusion of rural peace. I enjoyed this view of life which, like my work, was a compromise between old primitive roots and new glossy technology. Contentment, I thought, lay in being succoured by the first and cosseted by the second. If I'd had a pagan god, it would have been electricity, which sprang from the skies and galvanised machines. Mysterious lethal force of nature, harnessed and insulated and delivered on tap. My welder-uncle had made electricity seem a living person to me as a child. 'Electricity will catch you if you don't look out.' He said it as a warning; and I thought of Electricity as a fiery monster hiding in the wires and waiting to pounce.

The stiff yellowish pages of the *Racing Calendar* crackled familiarly as I opened their double spread and folded them back. The *Calendar*, racing's official weekly publication, contained lists of horses entered for forthcoming races, pages and pages of them, four columns to a page. The name of each horse was accompanied by the name of its owner and trainer, and also by its age and the weight it would have to carry if it ran.

With pencil in hand to act as insurance against skipping a line with the eye, I began painstakingly, as I had the previous week and the week before that, to check the name, owner and trainer of every horse entered in hurdle races.

Grapevine (Mrs R. Wantage) B. Fritwell 6 11 11
Pirate Boy (Lord Dresden) A. G. Barnes 10 11 4
Hopfield (Mr Paul Hatheleigh) K. Poundsgate 5 11 2

There were reams of them. I finished the Worcester entries with a sigh. Three hundred and sixty-eight down for one novice hurdle and three hundred and forty-nine for another, and not one of them what I was looking for.

My coffee was nearly cold. I drank it anyway and got on with the races scheduled for Taunton.

Hundreds more names, but nothing.

Ascot, nothing. Newcastle, nothing. Warwick, Teesside, Plumpton, Doncaster, nothing.

I put the *Calendar* down for a bit and went out onto the balcony for some air. Fiercely cold air, slicing down to the lungs. Primeval arctic air carrying city gunge: the mixture as before. Over in the Park the zoo creatures were quiet, sheltering in warmed houses. They always made more noise in the summer.

Return to the task.

Huntingdon, Market Rasen, Stratford on Avon . . . I sighed before starting Stratford and checked how many more still lay ahead. Nottingham, Carlisle and Wetherby. I was in for another wasted morning, no doubt.

Turned back to Stratford, and there it was.

I blinked and looked again carefully, as if the name would vanish if I took my eyes off it.

Half way down among sixty-four entries for the Shakespeare Novice Hurdle.

Padellic (Mr J. Leeds) J. Leeds 5 10 7

Padellic.

It was the first time the name had appeared in association with Jody. I knew the names of all his usual horses well, and what I had been searching for was a new one, an unknown. Owned, if my theories were right, by Jody himself. And here it was.

Nothing in the *Calendar* to show Padellic's colour or markings. I fairly sprinted over to the shelf where I kept a few form books and looked him up in every index.

Little doubt, I thought. He was listed as a black or brown gelding, five years old, a half-bred by a thoroughbred sire out of a hunter mare. He had been trained by a man I'd never heard of and he had run three times in four-year-old hurdles without being placed.

I telephoned to the trainer at once, introducing myself as a Mr Robinson trying to buy a cheap novice.

'Padellic?' he said in a forthright Birmingham accent. 'I got shot of that bugger round October time. No bloody good. Couldn't run fast enough to keep warm. Is he up for sale again? Can't say as I'm surprised. He's a right case of the slows, that one.'

'Er . . . where did you sell him?' I asked tentatively.

'Sent him to Doncaster mixed sales. Right bloody lot they had there. He fetched four hundred quid and I reckon he was dear at that. Only the one bid, you see. I reckon the bloke could've got him for three hundred if he'd tried. I was right pleased to get four for him, I'll tell you.'

'Would you know who bought him?'

'Eh?' He sounded surprised at the question. 'Can't say. He paid cash to the auctioneers and didn't give his name. I saw him make his bid, that's all. Big fellow. I'd never clapped eyes on him before. Wearing sunglasses. I didn't see him after. He paid up and took the horse away and I was right glad to be shot of him.'

'What is the horse like?' I asked.

'I told you, bloody slow.'

'No, I mean to look at.'

'Eh? I thought you were thinking of buying him.'

'Only on paper, so to speak. I thought,' I lied, 'that he still belonged to you.'

'Oh, I see. He's black, then. More or less black, with a bit of brown round the muzzle.'

'Any white about him?'

'Not a hair. Black all over. Black 'uns are often no good. I bred him, see? Meant to be bay, he was, but he turned out black. Not a bad looker, mind. He fills the eye. But nothing where it matters. No speed.'

'Can he jump?'

'Oh ay. In his own good time. Not bad.'

'Well, thanks very much.'

'You'd be buying a monkey,' he said warningly. 'Don't say as I didn't tell you.'

'I won't buy him,' I assured him. 'Thanks again for your advice.'

I put down the receiver reflectively. There might of course be dozens of large untraceable men in sunglasses going round the sales paying cash for slow black horses with no markings; and then again there might not.

The telephone bell rang under my hand. I picked up the receiver at the first ring.

'Steven?'

No mistaking that cigar-and-port voice. 'Charlie.'

'Have you lunched yet?' he said. 'I've just got off a train round the corner at Euston and I thought . . .'

'Here or where?' I said.

'I'll come round to you.'

'Great.'

He came, beaming and expansive, having invested three million somewhere near Rugby. Charlie, unlike some merchant bankers, liked to see things for himself. Reports on paper were all very well, he said, but they didn't give you the smell of a thing. If a project smelt wrong, he didn't disgorge the cash. Charlie followed his nose and Charlie's nose was his fortune.

The feature in question buried itself gratefully in a large scotch and water.

'How about some of that nosh you gave Bert?' he suggested, coming to the surface. 'To tell you the truth I get tired of eating in restaurants.'

We repaired amicably to the kitchen and ate bread and bacon and curried beans and sausages, all of which did no good at all to anyone's waistline, least of all Charlie's. He patted the bulge affectionately. 'Have to get some weight off, one of these days. But not today,' he said.

We took coffee back to the sitting-room and settled comfortably in armchairs.

'I wish I lived the way you do,' he said. 'So easy and relaxed.'

I smiled. Three weeks of my quiet existence would have driven him screaming to the madhouse. He thrived on bustle, big business, fast decisions, financial juggling and the use of power. And three weeks of all *that*, I thought in fairness, would have driven me mad even quicker.

'Have you made that lock yet?' he asked. He was lighting a cigar round the words and they sounded casual, but I wondered all of a sudden if that was why he had come.

'Half,' I said.

He shook his match to blow it out. 'Let me know,' he said.

'I promise.'

He drew in a lungful of Havana and nodded, his eyes showing unmistakably now that his mind was on duty for his bank.

'Which would you do most for,' I asked. 'Friendship or the lock?'

He was a shade startled. 'Depends what you want done.'

'Practical help in a counter-offensive.'

'Against Jody?'

I nodded.

'Friendship,' he said. 'That comes under the heading of friendship. You can count me in.'

His positiveness surprised me. He saw it and smiled.

'What he did to you was diabolical. Don't forget, I was here. I saw the state you were in. Saw the humiliation of that drink charge, and the pain from God knows what else. You looked a little below par and that's a fact.'

'Sorry.'

'Don't be. If it was just your pocket he'd bashed, I would probably be ready with cool advice but not active help.'

I hadn't expected anything like this. I would have thought it would have been the other way round, that the loss of property would have angered him more than the loss of face.

'If you're sure . . .' I said uncertainly.

'Of course.' He was decisive. 'What do you want done?'

I picked up the *Racing Calendar*, which was lying on the floor beside my chair, and explained how I'd looked for and found Padellic.

'He was bought at Doncaster sales for cash by a large man in sunglasses and he's turned up in Jody's name.'

'Suggestive.'

'I'd lay this house to a sneeze,' I said, 'that Rupert Ramsey is worrying his guts out trying to train him for the Champion Hurdle.'

Charlie smoked without haste. 'Rupert Ramsey has Padellic, but thinks he has Energise. Is that right?'

I nodded.

161

'And Jody is planning to run Energise at Stratford on Avon in the name of Padellic?'

'I would think so,' I said.

'So would I.'

'Only it's not entirely so simple.'

'Why not?'

'Because,' I said, 'I've found two other races for which Padellic is entered, at Nottingham and Lingfield. All the races are ten to fourteen days ahead and there's no telling which Jody will choose.'

He frowned. 'What difference does it make, which he chooses?'

I told him.

He listened with his eyes wide open and the eyebrows disappearing upwards into his hair. At the end, he was smiling.

'So how do you propose to find out which race he's going for?' he asked.

'I thought,' I said, 'that we might mobilise your friend Bert. He'd do a lot for you.'

'What, exactly?'

'Do you think you could persuade him to apply for a job in one of Ganser Mays' betting shops?'

Charlie began to laugh. 'How much can I tell him?'

'Only what to look for. Not why.'

'You slay me, Steven.'

'And another thing,' I said, 'how much do you know about the limitations of working hours for truck drivers?'

CHAPTER NINE

Snow was falling when I flew out of Heathrow, thin scurrying flakes in a driving wind. Behind me I left a half-finished lock, a half-mended car and a half-formed plan.

Charlie had telephoned to say Bert Huggerneck had been taken on at one of the shops formerly owned by his ex-boss and I had made cautious enquiries from the auctioneers at Doncaster. I'd had no success. They had no record of the name of the person who'd bought Padellic. Cash transactions were common. They couldn't possibly remember who had bought one particular cheap horse three months earlier. End of enquiry.

Owen had proclaimed himself as willing as Charlie to help in any way he could. Personal considerations apart, he said, whoever had bent the Lamborghini deserved hanging. When I came back, he would help me build the scaffold.

The journey from snow to sunshine took eight hours. Seventy-five degrees at Miami airport and only a shade cooler outside the hotel on Miami Beach; and it felt great. Inside the hotel the air-conditioning brought things nearly back to an English winter, but my sixth-floor room faced straight towards the afternoon sun. I drew back the closed curtains and opened the window, and let heat and light flood in.

Below, round a glittering pool, tall palm trees swayed in the sea wind. Beyond, the concrete edge to the hotel grounds led immediately down to a narrow strip of sand and the frothy white waves edging the Atlantic, with mile upon mile of deep blue water stretching away to the lighter blue horizon.

I had expected Miami Beach to be garish and was unprepared for its beauty. Even the ranks of huge white slabs of hotels with rectangular windows piercing their façades in a uniform geometrical pattern held a certain grandeur, punctuated and softened as they were by scattered palms.

Round the pool people lay in rows on day beds beside white fringed sun umbrellas, soaking up ultra-violet like a religion. I changed out of my travel-sticky clothes and went for a swim in the sea, paddling lazily in the warm January water and sloughing off cares like dead skin. Jody Leeds was five thousand miles away, in another world. Easy, and healing, to forget him.

Upstairs again, showered and dressed in slacks and cotton shirt I checked my watch for the time to tele-phone Allie. After the letters, we had exchanged cables, though not in code because the cable company didn't like it.

I sent, 'What address Miami?'

She replied: 'Telephone four two six eight two after six any evening.'

When I called her it was five past six on January fifth, local time. The voice which answered was not hers and for a soggy moment I wondered if the Western Union had jumbled the message as they often did, and that I should never find her.

'Miss Ward? Do you mean Miss Alexandra?'

'Yes,' I said with relief.

'Hold the line, please.'

After a pause came the familiar voice, remembered but suddenly fresh. 'Hallo?'

'Allie . . . It's Steven.'

'Hi.' Her voice was laughing. 'I've won close on fifty dollars if you're in Miami.'

'Collect it,' I said.

'I don't believe it.'

'We have a date,' I said reasonably.

'Oh sure.'

'Where do I find you?'

'Twelve twenty-four Garden Island,' she said. 'Any cab will bring you. Come right out, it's time for cocktails.'

Garden Island proved to be a shady offshoot of land with wide enough channels surrounding it to justify its name. The cab rolled slowly across twenty yards of decorative iron bridge and came to a stop outside twelve twenty-four. I paid off the driver and rang the bell.

From the outside the house showed little. The white-washed walls were deeply obscured by tropical plants and the windows by insect netting. The door itself looked solid enough for a bank.

Allie opened it. Smiled widely. Gave me a non-committal kiss.

'This is my cousin's house,' she said. 'Come in.'

Behind its secretive front the house was light and large and glowing with clear, uncomplicated colours. Blue, sea-green, bright pink, white and orange; clear and sparkling.

'My cousin Minty,' Allie said, 'and her husband, Warren Barbo.'

I shook hands with the cousins. Minty was neat, dark and utterly self-possessed in lemon-coloured beach pyjamas. Warren was large, sandy and full of noisy good humour. They gave me a tall, iced, unspecified drink and led me into a spacious glass-walled room for a view of the setting sun.

Outside in the garden the yellowing rays fell on a lush lawn, a calm pool and white painted lounging chairs. All peaceful and prosperous and a million miles from blood, sweat and tears.

'Alexandra tells us you're interested in horses,' Warren said, making host-like conversation. 'I don't know how long you reckon on staying, but there's a racemeet at Hialeah right now, every day this week. And the bloodstock sales, of course, in the evenings. I'll be going myself some nights and I'd be glad to have you along.'

The idea pleased me, but I turned to Allie.

'What are your plans?'

'Millie and I split up,' she said without visible regret. 'She said when we were through with Christmas and New Year she would be off to Japan for a spell, so I grabbed a week down here with Minty and Warren.'

'Would you come to the races, and the sales?'

'Sure.'

'I have four days,' I said.

She smiled brilliantly but without promise. Several other guests arrived for drinks at that point and Allie said she would fetch the canapés. I followed her to the kitchen.

'You can carry the stone crabs,' she said, putting a large dish into my hands. 'And okay, after a while we can sneak out and eat some place else.'

For an hour I helped hand round those understudies for a banquet, American-style canapés. Allie's delicious work. I ate two or three and like a true male chauvinist meditated on the joys of marrying a good cook.

I found Minty at my side, her hand on my arm, her gaze following mine.

'She's a great girl,' she said. 'She swore you would come.'

'Good,' I said with satisfaction.

167

Her eyes switched sharply to mine with a grin breaking out. 'She told us to be careful what we said to you, because you always understood the implications, not just the words. And I guess she was right.'

'You've only told me that she wanted me to come and thought I liked her enough to do it.'

'Yeah, but . . .' She laughed. 'She didn't actually say all that.'

'I see what you mean.'

She took out of my hands a dish of thin pastry boats filled with pink chunks of lobster in pale green mayonnaise. 'You've done more than your duty here,' she smiled. 'Get on out.'

She lent us her car. Allie drove it northwards along the main boulevard of Collins Avenue and pulled up at a restaurant called Stirrup and Saddle.

'I thought you might feel at home here,' she said teasingly.

The place was crammed. Every table in sight was taken, and as in many American restaurants, the tables were so close together that only emaciated waiters could inch around them. Blow-ups of racing scenes decorated the walls and saddles and horseshoes abounded.

Dark decor, loud chatter and, to my mind, too much light.

A slightly harassed head waiter intercepted us inside the door.

'Do you have reservations, sir?'

I began to say I was sorry, as there were dozens of people already waiting round the bar, when Allie interrupted.

'Table for two, name of Barbo.'

He consulted his lists, smiled, nodded. 'This way, sir.'

There was miraculously after all one empty table, tucked in a corner but with a good view of the busy room. We sat comfortably in dark wooden-armed chairs and watched the head waiter turn away the next customers decisively.

'When did you book this table?' I asked.

'Yesterday. As soon as I got down here.' The white teeth gleamed. 'I got Warren to do it; he likes this place. That's when I made the bets. He and Minty said it was crazy, you wouldn't come all the way from England just to take me out to eat.'

'And you said I sure was crazy enough for anything.'

'I sure did.'

We ate bluepoint oysters and barbecued baby ribs with salad alongside. Noise and clatter from other tables washed around us and waiters towered above with huge loaded trays. Business was brisk.

'Do you like it here?' Allie asked, tackling the ribs.

'Very much.'

She seemed relieved. I didn't add that some quiet candlelight would have done even better. 'Warren says all horse people like it, the same way he does.'

'How horsey is Warren?'

'He owns a couple of two-year-olds. Has them in

training with a guy in Aiken, North Carolina. He was hoping they'd be running here at Hialeah but they've both got chipped knees and he doesn't know if they'll be any good any more.'

'What are chipped knees?' I asked.

'Don't you have chipped knees in England?'

'Heaven knows.'

'So will Warren.' She dug into the salad, smiling down at the food. 'Warren's business is real estate but his heart beats out there where the hooves thunder along the homestretch.'

'Is that how he puts it?'

Her smile widened. 'It sure is.'

'He said he'd take us to Hialeah tomorrow, if you'd like.'

'I might as well get used to horses, I suppose.' She spoke with utter spontaneity and then in a way stood back and looked at what she'd said. 'I mean . . .' she stuttered.

'I know what you mean,' I said smiling.

'You always do, dammit.'

We finished the ribs and progressed to coffee. She asked how fast I'd recovered from the way she had seen me last and what had happened since. I told her about the gossip columns and the car, and she was fiercely indignant; mostly, I gathered, because of the car.

'But it was so beautiful!'

'It will be again.'

'I'd like to murder that Jody Leeds.'

She scarcely noticed, that time, that she was telling me what she felt for me. The sense of a smoothly deepening relationship filled me with contentment: and it was also great fun.

After three cups of dawdled coffee I paid the bill and we went out to the car.

'I can drop you off at your hotel,' Allie said. 'It's quite near here.'

'Certainly not. I'll see you safely home.'

She grinned. 'There isn't much danger. All the alligators in Florida are a hundred miles away in the Everglades.'

'Some alligators have two feet.'

'Okay, then.' She drove slowly southwards, the beginnings of a smile curling her mouth all the way. Outside her cousin's house she put on the handbrake but left the engine running.

'You'd better borrow this car to go back. Minty won't mind.'

'No, I'll walk.'

'You can't. It's all of four miles.'

'I like seeing things close. Seeing how they're made.'

'You sure are nuts.'

I switched off the engine, put my arm round her shoulders and kissed her the same way as at home, several times. She sighed deeply but not, it seemed, with boredom.

*

171

I hired an Impala in the morning and drove down to Garden Island. A cleaner answered the door and showed me through to where Warren and Minty were in swimsuits, standing by the pool in January sunshine as warm as July back home.

'Hi,' said Minty in welcome. 'Alexandra said to tell you she'll be right back. She's having her hair fixed.'

The fixed hair, when it appeared, looked as smooth and shining as the girl underneath. A black-and-tan sleeveless cotton dress did marvellous things for her waist and stopped in plenty of time for the legs. I imagine appreciation was written large on my face because the wide smile broke out as soon as she saw me.

We sat by the pool drinking cold fresh orange juice while Warren and Minty changed into street clothes. The day seemed an interlude, a holiday, to me, but not to the Barbos. Warren's life, I came to realise, was along the lines of perpetual summer vacation interrupted by short spells in the office. Droves of sharp young men did the leg-work of selling dream retirement homes to elderly sun-seekers and Warren, the organiser, went to the races.

Hialeah Turf Club was a sugar-icing racecourse, as pretty as lace. Miami might show areas of cracks and rust and sun-peeled poverty on its streets, but in the big green park in its suburb the lush life survived and seemingly flourished.

Bright birds in cages beguiled visitors the length

of the paddock, and a decorative pint-sized railway trundled around. Tons of ice cream added to weight problems and torn up Tote tickets fluttered to the ground like snow.

The racing itself that day was moderate, which didn't prevent me losing my bets. Allie said it served me right, gambling was a nasty habit on a par with jumping off cliffs.

'And look where it's got you,' she pointed out.

'Where?'

'In Ganser Mays' clutches.'

'Not any more.'

'Which came first,' she said, 'the gamble or the race?'

'All life's a gamble. The fastest sperm fertilizes the egg.'

She laughed. 'Tell that to the chickens.'

It was the sort of day when nonsense made sense. Minty and Warren met relays of drinking pals and left us much alone, which suited me fine, and at the end of the racing programme we sat high up on the stands looking over the course while the sunlight died to yellow and pink and scarlet. Drifts of flamingoes on the small lakes in the centre of the track deepened from pale pink to intense rose and the sky on the water reflected silver and gold.

'I bet it's snowing in London,' I said.

After dark and after dinner Warren drove us round to the sales paddock on the far side of the racecourse, where spotlights lit a scene that was decidedly more rustic than the stands. Sugar icing stopped with the tourists: horse-trading had its feet on the grass.

There were three main areas linked by short undefined paths and well-patronised open-fronted bars; there was the sale ring, the parade ring and long barns lined with stalls, where the merchandise ate hay and suffered prods and insults and people looking at its teeth.

Warren opted for the barns first and we wandered down the length of the nearest while he busily consulted his catalogue. Minty told him they were definitely not buying any more horses until the chipped knees were all cleared up. 'No dear,' Warren said soothingly, but with a gleam in his eye which spelt death to the bank balance.

I looked at the offerings with interest. A mixed bunch of horses which had been raced, from three years upwards. Warren said the best sales were those for two-year-olds at the end of the month and Minty said why didn't he wait awhile and see what they were like.

The lights down the far end of the barn were dim and the horse in the last stall of all was so dark that at first I thought the space was empty. Then an eye shimmered and a movement showed a faint gleam on a rounded rump.

A black horse. Black like Energise.

I looked at him first because he was black, and then more closely, with surprise. He was indeed very like Energise. Extremely like him.

The likeness abruptly crystallised an idea I'd already been turning over in my mind. A laugh fluttered in my throat. The horse was a gift from the gods and who was I to look it in the mouth.

'What have you found?' Warren asked, advancing with good humour.

'I've a hurdler like this at home.'

Warren looked at the round label stuck onto one hindquarter which bore the number sixty-two.

'Hip number sixty-two,' he said, flicking the pages of the catalogue. 'Here it is. Black Fire, five-year-old gelding. Humph.' He read quickly down the page through the achievements and breeding. 'Not much good and never was much good, I guess.'

'Pity.'

'Yeah.' He turned away. 'Now there's a damned nice looking chestnut colt along there . . .'

'No, Warren,' said Minty despairingly.

We all walked back to look at the chestnut colt. Warren knew no more about buying horses than I did, and besides, the first thing I'd read on the first page of the catalogue was the clear warning that the auctioneers didn't guarantee the goods were of merchantable quality. In other words, if you bought a lame duck it was your own silly fault.

'Don't pay no attention to that,' said Warren expansively. 'As long as you don't take the horse out of the sales paddock, you can get a veterinarian to check a horse you've bought, and if he finds anything wrong

175

you can call the deal off. But you have to do it within twenty-four hours.'

'Sounds fair.'

'Sure. You can have x-rays even. Chipped knees would show on an x-ray. Horses can walk and look okay with chipped knees but they sure can't race.'

Allie said with mock resignation, 'So what exactly are chipped knees?'

Warren said, 'Cracks and compressions at the ends of the bones at the knee joint.'

'From falling down?' Allie asked.

Warren laughed kindly. 'No. From too much hard galloping on dirt. The thumping does it.'

I borrowed the sales catalogue from Warren again for a deeper look at the regulations and found the twenty-four hour inspection period applied only to brood mares, which wasn't much help. I mentioned it diffidently to Warren. 'It says here,' I said neutrally, 'that it's wise to have a vet look at a horse for soundness before you bid. After is too late.'

'Is that so?' Warren retrieved his book and peered at the small print. 'Well, I guess you're right.' He received the news good-naturedly. 'Just shows how easy it is to go wrong at horse sales.'

'And I hope you remember it,' Minty said with meaning.

Warren did in fact seem a little discouraged from his chestnut colt but I wandered back for a second look at Black Fire and found a youth in jeans and grubby sweat shirt bringing him a bucket of water.

'Is this horse yours?' I asked.

'Nope. I'm just the help.'

'Which does he do most, bite or kick?'

The boy grinned. 'Reckon he's too lazy for either.'

'Would you take him out of that dark stall so I could have a look at him in the light?'

'Sure.' He untied the halter from the tethering ring and brought Black Fire out into the central alley, where the string of electric lights burned without much enthusiasm down the length of the barn.

'There you go, then,' he said, persuading the horse to arrange its legs as if for a photograph. 'Fine looking fella, isn't he?'

'What you can see of him,' I agreed.

I looked at him critically, searching for differences. But there was no doubt he was the same. Same height, same elegant shape, even the same slightly dished Arab-looking nose. And black as coal, all over. When I walked up and patted him he bore it with fortitude. Maybe his sweet nature, I thought. Or maybe tranquillisers.

On the neck or head of many horses the hair grew in one or more whorls, making a pattern which was entered as an identifying mark on the passports. Energise had no whorls at all. Nor had Padellic. I looked carefully at the forehead, cheeks, neck and shoulders of Black Fire and ran my fingers over his coat. As far

177

as I could feel or see in that dim light, there were no whorls on him either.

'Thanks a lot,' I said to the boy, stepping back.

He looked at me with surprise. 'You don't aim to look at his teeth or feel his legs?'

'Is there something wrong with them?'

'I guess not.'

'Then I won't bother,' I said and left unsaid the truth understood by us both, that even if I'd inspected those extremities I wouldn't have been any the wiser.

'Does he have a tattoo number inside his lip?' I asked.

'Yeah, of course.' The surprise raised his eyebrows to peaks like a clown. 'Done when he first raced.'

'What is it?'

'Well, gee, I don't know.' His tone said he couldn't be expected to and no one in his senses would have bothered to ask.

'Take a look.'

'Well, okay.' He shrugged and with the skill of practice opened the horse's mouth and turned down the lower lip. He peered closely for a while during which time the horse stood suspiciously still, and then let him go.

'Far as I can see there's an F and a six and some others, but it's not too light in here and anyway the numbers get to go fuzzy after a while, and this fella's five now so the tattoo would be all of three years old.'

'Thanks anyway.'

'You're welcome.' He pocketed my offered five bucks and took the very unfiery Black Fire back to his stall.

I turned to find Allie, Warren and Minty standing in a row, watching. Allie and Minty both wore indulgent feminine smiles and Warren was shaking his head.

'That horse has won a total of nine thousand three hundred dollars in three years' racing,' he said. 'He won't have paid the feed bills.' He held out the catalogue opened at Black Fire's page, and I took it and read the vaguely pathetic race record for myself.

'At two, unplaced. At three, three wins, four times third. At four, twice third. Total: three wins, six times third, earned $9,326.'

A modest success as a three-year-old, but all in fairly low-class races. I handed the catalogue back to Warren with a smile of thanks, and we moved unhurriedly out of that barn and along to the next. When even Warren had had a surfeit of peering into stalls we went outside and watched the first entries being led into the small wooden-railed collecting ring.

A circle of lights round the rails lit the scene, aided by spotlights set among the surrounding trees. Inside, as on a stage, small bunches of people anxiously added the finishing touches of gloss which might wring a better price from the unperceptive. Some of the horses' manes were decorated with a row of bright wool pompoms, arching along the top of the neck from ears to withers as if ready for the circus. Hip No. 1, resplendent in scarlet pompoms, raised his long bay head and whinnied theatrically.

I told Allie and the Barbos I would be back in a minute and left them leaning on the rails. A couple of enquiries and one misdirection found me standing in the cramped office of the auctioneers in the sale ring building.

'A report from the veterinarian? Sure thing. Pay in advance, please. If you don't want to wait, return for the report in half an hour.'

I paid and went back to the others. Warren was deciding it was time for a drink and we stood for a while in the fine warm night near one of the bars drinking Bacardi and Coke out of throwaway cartons.

Brilliant light poured out of the circular sales building in a dozen places through open doors and slatted windows. Inside, the banks of canvas chairs were beginning to fill up, and down on the rostrum in the centre the auctioneers were shaping up to starting the evening's business. We finished the drinks, duly threw away the cartons and followed the crowd into the show.

Hip No. 1 waltzed in along a ramp and circled the rostrum with all his pompoms nodding. The auctioneer began his sing-song selling, amplified and insistent, and to me, until my ears adjusted, totally unintelligible. Hip No. 1 made five thousand dollars and Warren said the prices would all be low because of the economic situation.

Horses came and went. When Hip No. 15 in orange pompoms had fetched a figure which had the crowd murmuring in excitement I slipped away to the office and found that the veterinary surgeon himself was there, dishing out his findings to other enquiries.

'Hip number sixty-two?' he echoed. 'Sure, let me find my notes.' He turned over a page or two in a notebook. 'Here we are. Dark bay or brown gelding, right?'

'Black,' I said.

'Uh, uh. Never say black.' He smiled briefly, a busy middle-aged man with an air of a clerk. 'Five years. Clean bill of health.' He shut the notebook and turned to the customer.

'Is that all?' I said blankly.

'Sure,' he said briskly. 'No heart murmur, legs cool, teeth consistent with given age, eyes normal, range of movement normal, trots sound. No bowed tendons, no damaged knees.'

'Thanks,' I said.

'You're welcome.'

'Is he tranquillised?'

He looked at me sharply, then smiled. 'I guess so. Acepromazine probably.'

'Is that usual, or would he be a rogue?'

'I wouldn't think he'd had much. He should be okay.'

'Thanks again.'

I went back to the sale ring in time to see Warren fidgeting badly over the sale of the chestnut colt. When the price rose to fifteen thousand Minty literally clung on to his hands and told him not to be a darned fool.

'He must be sound,' Warren protested, 'to make that money.'

The colt made twenty-five thousand in thirty seconds' brisk bidding and Warren's regrets rumbled on all evening. Minty relaxed as if the ship of state had safely negotiated a killing reef and said she would like a breath of air. We went outside and leaned again on the collecting ring rails.

There were several people from England at the sales. Faces I knew, faces which knew me. No close friends, scarcely acquaintances, but people who would certainly notice and remark if I did anything unexpected.

I turned casually to Warren.

'I've money in New York,' I said. 'I can get it tomorrow. Would you lend me some tonight?'

'Sure,' he said good-naturedly, fishing for his wallet. 'How much do you need?'

'Enough to buy that black gelding.'

'What?' His hand froze and his eyes widened.

'Would you buy it for me?'

'You're kidding.'

'No.'

He looked at Allie for help. 'Does he mean it?'

'He's sure crazy enough for anything,' she said.

'That's just what it is,' Warren said. 'Crazy. Crazy to

buy some goddamned useless creature, just because he looks like a hurdler you've got back home.'

To Allie this statement suddenly made sense. She smiled vividly and said, 'What are you going to do with him?'

I kissed her forehead. 'I tend to think in circles,' I said.

CHAPTER TEN

Warren, enjoying himself hugely, bought Black Fire for four thousand six hundred dollars. Bid for it, signed for it, and paid for it.

With undiminished good nature he also contracted for its immediate removal from Hialeah and subsequent shipment by air to England.

'Having himself a ball,' Minty said.

His good spirits lasted all the way back to Garden Island and through several celebratory nightcaps.

'You sure bought a stinker,' he said cheerfully, 'but boy, I haven't had so much fun in years. Did you see that guy's face, the one I bid against? He thought he was getting it for a thousand.' He chuckled. 'At four thousand five he sure looked mad and he could see I was going on for ever.'

Minty began telling him to make the most of it, it was the last horse he'd be buying for a long time, and Allie came to the door to see me off. We stood outside for a while in the dark, close together.

'One day down. Three to go,' she said.

'No more horses,' I promised.

'Okay.'

'And fewer people.'

A pause. Then again, 'Okay.'

I smiled and kissed her good night and pushed her indoors before my best intentions should erupt into good old-fashioned lust. The quickest way to lose her would be to snatch.

She said how about Florida Keys and how about a swim and how about a picnic. We went in the Impala with a cold box of goodies in the boot and the Tropic of Cancer flaming away over the horizon ahead.

The highway to Key West stretched for mile after mile across a linked chain of causeways and small islands. Palm trees, sand dunes, sparkling water and scrubby grass. Few buildings. Sun-bleached wooden huts, wooden landing stages, fishing boats. Huge skies, hot sun, vast seas. Also Greyhound buses on excursions and noisy families in station wagons with Mom in pink plastic curlers.

Allie had brought directions from Warren about one of the tiny islands where he fished, and when we reached it we turned off the highway on to a dusty side road that was little more than a track. It ended abruptly under two leaning palms, narrowing to an Indian file path through sand dunes and tufty grass towards the sea. We took the picnic box and walked, and found ourselves surprisingly in a small sandy hollow from which neither the car nor the road could be seen.

'That,' said Allie, pointing at the sea, 'is Hawk Channel.'

'Can't see any hawks.'

'You'd want cooks in Cook Strait.'

She took off the loose white dress she'd worn on the way down and dropped it on the sand. Underneath she wore a pale blue and white bikini, and underneath that, warm honey coloured skin.

She took the skin without more ado into the sea and I stripped off shirt and trousers and followed her. We swam in the free warm-cool water and it felt the utmost in luxury.

'Why are these islands so uninhabited?' I asked.

'Too small, most of them. No fresh water. Hurricanes, as well. It isn't always so gentle here. Sizzling hot in the summer and terrible storms.'

The wind in the palm tree tops looked as if butter wouldn't melt in its mouth. We splashed in the shallows and walked up the short beach to regain the warm little hollow, Allie delivering on the way a fairly non-stop lecture about turtles, bonefish, marlin and tarpon. It struck me in the end that she was talking fast to hide that she was feeling self-conscious.

I fished in my jacket pocket and brought out a twenty dollar bill.

'Bus fare home,' I said, holding it out to her.

She laughed a little jerkily. 'I still have the one you sent from England.'

'Did you bring it?'

She smiled, shook her head, took the note from me, folded it carefully and pushed it into the wet top half of her bikini.

'It'll be safe there,' she said matter-of-factly. 'How about a vodka martini?'

She had brought drinks, ice and delicious food. The sun in due course shifted thirty degrees round the sky, and I lay lazily basking in it while she put the empties back in the picnic box and fiddled with spoons.

'Allie?'

'Mm?'

'How about now?'

She stopped the busy rattling. Sat back on her ankles. Pushed the hair out of her eyes and finally looked at my face.

'Try sitting here,' I said, patting the sand beside me with an unemphatic palm.

She tried it. Nothing cataclysmic seemed to happen to her in the way of fright.

'You've done it before,' I said persuasively, stating a fact.

'Yeah . . . but . . .'

'But what?'

'I didn't really like it.'

'Why not?'

'I don't know. I didn't like the boy enough, I expect.'

187

'Then why the hell sleep with him?'

'You make it sound so simple. But at college, well, one sort of had to. Three years ago, most of one summer. I haven't done it since. I've been not exactly afraid to, but afraid I would . . . be unfair . . .' She stopped.

'You can catch a bus whenever you like,' I said.

She smiled and bit by bit lay down beside me. I knew she wouldn't have brought me to this hidden place if she hadn't been willing at least to try. But acquiescence, in view of what she'd said, was no longer enough. If she didn't enjoy it, I couldn't.

I went slowly, giving her time. A touch. A kiss. An undemanding smoothing of hand over skin. She breathed evenly through her nose, trusting but unaroused.

'Clothes off?' I suggested. 'No one can see us.'

' . . . Okay.'

She unhitched the bikini top, folded it over the twenty dollars, and put it on the sand beside her. The pants in a moment followed. Then she sat with her arms wrapped round her knees, staring out to sea.

'Come on,' I said, smiling, my shorts joining hers. 'The fate worse than death isn't all that bad.'

She laughed with naturalness and lay down beside me, and it seemed as if she'd made up her mind to do her best, even if she found it unsatisfactory. But in a while she gave the first uncontrollable shiver of authentic pleasure, and after that it became not just all right but very good indeed.

'Oh God,' she said in the end, half laughing, half gasping for air. 'I didn't know . . .'

'Didn't know what?' I said, sliding lazily down beside her.

'At college . . . he was clumsy. And too quick.'

She stretched out her hand, fumbled in the bikini and picked up the twenty dollar note.

She waved it in the air, holding it between finger and thumb. Then she laughed and opened her hand and the wind blew her fare home away along the beach.

CHAPTER ELEVEN

London was cold enough to encourage emigration. I arrived back early Tuesday morning with sand in my shoes and sympathy for Eskimos, and Owen collected me with a face pinched and blue.

'We've had snow and sleet and the railways are on strike,' he said, putting my suitcase in the hired Cortina. 'Also the mild steel you ordered hasn't come and there's a cobra loose somewhere in Regent's Park.'

'Thanks very much.'

'Not at all, sir.'

'Anything else?'

'A Mr Kennet rang from Newmarket to say Hermes has broken down. And ... sir ...'

'What?' I prompted, trying to dredge up resignation.

'Did you order a load of manure, sir?'

'Of course not.'

The total garden in front of my house consisted of three tubs of fuchsia, an old walnut tree and several square yards of paving slabs. At the rear, nothing but workshop.

'Some has been delivered, sir.'

'How much?'

'I can't see the dustmen moving it.'

He drove steadily from Heathrow to home, and I dozed from the jet-lag feeling that it was midnight. When we stopped it was not in the driveway but out on the road, because the driveway was completely blocked by a dung-hill five feet high.

It was even impossible to walk round it without it sticking to one's shoes. I crabbed sideways with my suitcase to the door, and Owen drove off to find somewhere else to park.

Inside, on the mat, I found the delivery note. A postcard handwritten in ball point capitals, short and unsweet.

'*Shit to the shit.*'

Charming little gesture. Hardly original, but disturbing all the same, because it spoke so eloquently of the hatred prompting it.

Felicity, I wondered?

There was something remarkably familiar about the consistency of the load. A closer look revealed half rotted horse droppings mixed with a little straw and a lot of sawdust. Straight from a stable muck heap, not from a garden supplier: and if looked exactly like Jody's own familiar muck heap, that wasn't in itself conclusive. I dared say one vintage was much like another.

Owen came trudging back and stared at the smelly obstruction in disgust.

'If I hadn't been using the car to go home, like you said, I wouldn't have been able to get out of the garage this morning to fetch you.'

'When was it dumped?'

'I was here yesterday morning, sir. Keeping an eye on things. Then this morning I called round to switch on the central heating, and there it was.'

I showed him the card. He looked, read, wrinkled his nose in distaste, but didn't touch.

'There'll be fingerprints on that, I shouldn't wonder.'

'Do you think it's worth telling the police?' I asked dubiously.

'Might as well, sir. You never know, this nutter might do something else. I mean, whoever went to all this trouble is pretty sick.'

'You're very sensible, Owen.'

'Thank you, sir.'

We went indoors and I summoned the constabulary, who came in the afternoon, saw the funny side of it, and took away the card in polythene.

'What are we going to do with the bloody stuff?' said Owen morosely. 'No one will want it on their flower beds, it's bung full of undigested hay seeds and that means weeds.'

'We'll shift it tomorrow.'

'There must be a ton of it.' He frowned gloomily.

'I didn't mean spadeful by spadeful,' I said. 'Not you and I. We'll hire a grab.'

Hiring things took the rest of the day. Extraordinary

what one could hire if one tried. The grab proved to be one of the easiest on a long list.

At about the time merchant bankers could reasonably be expected to be reaching for their hats, I telephoned to Charlie.

'Are you going straight home?' I asked.

'Not necessarily.'

'Care for a drink?'

'On my way,' he said.

When he arrived, Owen took his Rover to park it and Charlie stood staring at the muck heap, which looked no more beautiful under the street lights and was moreover beginning to ooze round the edges.

'Someone doesn't love me,' I said with a grin. 'Come on in and wipe your feet rather thoroughly on the mat.'

'What a stink.'

'Lavatory humour,' I agreed.

He left his shoes alongside mine on the tray of newspaper Owen had prudently positioned near the front door and followed me upstairs in his socks.

'Who?' he said, shaping up to a large scotch.

'A shit is what Jody's wife Felicity called me after Sandown.'

'Do you think she did it?'

'Heaven knows. She's a capable girl.'

'Didn't anyone see the . . . er . . . delivery?'

'Owen asked the neighbours. No one saw a thing. No one ever does, in London. All he discovered was that the muck wasn't there at seven yesterday evening when the man from two doors along let his labrador make use of my fuchsia tubs.'

He drank his whisky and asked what I'd done in Miami. I couldn't stop the smile coming. 'Besides that,' he said.

'I bought a horse.'

'You're a glutton for punishment.'

'An understudy,' I said, 'for Energise.'

'Tell all to your Uncle Charlie.'

I told, if not all, most.

'The trouble is though, that although we must be ready for Saturday at Stratford, he might choose Nottingham on Monday or Lingfield on Wednesday,' I said.

'Or none of them.'

'And it might freeze.'

'How soon would we know?' Charlie asked.

'He'll have to declare the horse to run four days before the race, but he then has three days to change his mind and take him out again. We wouldn't know for sure until the runners are published in the evening papers the day before. And even then we need the nod from Bert Huggerneck.'

He chuckled. 'Bert doesn't like the indoor life. He's itching to get back on the racecourse.'

'I hope he'll stick to the shop.'

'My dear fellow!' Charlie lit a cigar and waved the match. 'Bert's a great scrapper by nature and if you could cut him in on the real action he'd be a lot happier. He's taken a strong dislike to Ganser Mays, and he says that for a capitalist you didn't seem half bad. He knows there's something afoot and he said if there's a chance of anyone punching Ganser Mays on the long bleeding nose he would like it to be him.'

I smiled at the verbatim reporting. 'All right. If he really feels like that, I do indeed have a job for him.'

'Doing what?'

'Directing the traffic.'

He puffed at the cigar. 'Do you know what your plan reminds me of?' he said. 'Your own Rola toys. There you are, turning the single handle, and all the little pieces will rotate on their spindles and go through their allotted acts.'

'You're no toy,' I said.

'Of course I am. But at least I know it. The real trick will be programming the ones who don't.'

'Do you think it will all work?'

He regarded me seriously. 'Given ordinary luck, I don't see why not.'

'And you don't have moral misgivings?'

His sudden huge smile warmed like a fire. 'Didn't you know that merchant bankers are pirates under the skin?'

Charlie took Wednesday off and we spent the whole day prospecting the terrain. We drove from London to Newbury, from Newbury to Stratford on Avon, from Stratford to Nottingham, and from Nottingham back to Newbury. By that time the bars were open, and we repaired to the Chequers for revivers.

'There's only the one perfect place,' Charlie said, 'and it will do for both Stratford and Nottingham.'

I nodded. 'By the fruit stall.'

'Settle on that, then?'

'Yes.'

'And if he isn't down to run at either of those courses we spend Sunday surveying the road to Lingfield?'

'Right.'

He smiled vividly. 'I haven't felt so alive since my stint in the army. However this turns out, I wouldn't have missed it for the world.'

His enthusiasm was infectious and we drove back to London in good spirits.

Things had noticeably improved in the garden. The muck heap had gone and Owen had sloshed to some effect with buckets of water, though without obliterating the smell. He had also stayed late, waiting for my return. All three of us left our shoes in the hall and went upstairs.

'Too Japanese for words,' Charlie said.

'I stayed, sir,' Owen said, 'because a call came from America.'

'Miss Ward?' I said hopefully.

'No, sir. About a horse. It was a shipping firm. They said a horse consigned to you would be on a flight to Gatwick Airport tonight as arranged. Probable time of arrival, ten a.m. tomorrow morning. I wrote it down.'

He pointed to the pad beside the telephone. 'But I thought I would stay in case you didn't see it. They said you would need to engage transport to have the horse met.'

'You,' I said, 'will be meeting it.'

'Very good, sir,' he said calmly.

'Owen,' Charlie said, 'if he ever kicks you out, come to me.'

We all sat for a while discussing the various arrangements and Owen's part in them. He was as eager as Charlie to make the plan work, and he too seemed to be plugged into some inner source of excitement.

'I'll enjoy it, sir,' he said, and Charlie nodded in agreement. I had never thought of either of them as being basically adventurous and I had been wrong.

I was wrong also about Bert Huggerneck, and even in a way about Allie, for they too proved to have more fire than reservations.

Charlie brought Bert with him after work on Thursday and we sat round the kitchen table poring over a large scale map.

'That's the A34,' I said, pointing with a pencil to a red line running south to north. 'It goes all the way from Newbury to Stratford. For Nottingham, you branch off just north of Oxford. The place we've chosen is some way south of that. Just here . . .' I marked it with the pencil. 'About a mile before you reach the Abingdon by-pass.'

197

'I know that bleeding road,' Bert said. 'Goes past the Harwell atomic.'

'That's right.'

'Yeah. I'll find that. Easy as dolly-birds.'

'There's a roadside fruit stall there,' I said. 'Shut, at this time of year. A sort of wooden hut.'

'Seen dozens of 'em,' Bert nodded.

'It has a good big space beside it for cars.'

'Which side of the road?'

'On the near side, going north.'

'Yeah. I get you.'

'It's on a straight stretch after a fairly steep hill. Nothing will be going very fast there. Do you think you could manage?'

'Here,' he complained to Charlie. 'That's a bleeding insult.'

'Sorry,' I said.

'Is that all I do, then? Stop the bleeding traffic?' He sounded disappointed; and I'd thought he might have needed to be persuaded.

'No,' I said. 'After that you do a lot of hard work extremely quickly.'

'What, for instance?'

When I told him, he sat back on his chair and positively beamed.

'That's more bleeding like it,' he said. 'Now that's a daisy, that is. Now you might think I'm slow on my feet, like, with being big, but you'd be bleeding wrong.'

'I couldn't do it at all without you.'

'Hear that?' he said to Charlie.

'It might even be true,' Charlie said.

Bert at that point described himself as peckish and moved in a straight line to the store cupboard. 'What've you got here, then? Don't you ever bleeding eat? Do you want this tin of ham?'

'Help yourself,' I said.

Bert made a sandwich inch-deep in mustard and ate it without blinking. A couple of cans of beer filled the cracks.

'Can I chuck the betting shop, then?' he asked between gulps.

'What have you learned about Ganser Mays?'

'He's got a bleeding nickname, that's one thing I've learned. A couple of smart young managers run his shops now, you'd never know they was the same place. All keen and sharp and not a shred of soft heart like my old boss.'

'A soft-hearted bookmaker?' Charlie said. 'There's no such thing.'

'Trouble was,' Bert said, ignoring him, 'he had a bleeding soft head and all.'

'What is Ganser Mays' nickname?' I asked.

'Eh? Oh yeah. Well, these two smart alecs, who're sharp enough to cut themselves, they call him Squeezer. Squeezer Mays. When they're talking to each other, of course, that is.'

'Squeezer because he squeezes people like your boss out of business?'

199

'You don't hang about, do you? Yeah, that's right. There's two sorts of squeezer. The one they did on my boss, telling him horses were fixed to lose when they wasn't. And the other way round, when the smart alecs know a horse that's done no good before is fixed to win. Then they go round all the little men putting thousands on, a bit here and a bit there, and all the little men think it's easy pickings because they think the bad horse can't win in a month of bleeding Sundays. And then of course it does, and they're all down the bleeding drain.'

'They owe Ganser Mays something like the National Debt.'

'That's right. And they can't raise enough bread. So then Mr pious bleeding Mays comes along and says he'll be kind and take the shop to make up the difference. Which he does.'

'I thought small bookies were more clued up nowadays,' I said.

'You'd bleeding well think so, wouldn't you? They'll tell you they are, but they bleeding well aren't. Oh sure, if they find afterwards there's been a right fiddle, like, they squeal blue murder and refuse to pay up, but take the money in the first place, of course they do. Like bleeding innocent little lambs.'

'I don't think there would be any question of anyone thinking it a fiddle, this time,' I said.

'There you are, then. Quite a few would all of a

bleeding sudden be finding they were swallowed up by that smarmy bastard. Just like my poor old boss.'

I reflected for a minute or two. 'I think it would be better if you stayed in the betting shop until we're certain which day the horse is going to run. I don't imagine they would risk letting him loose without backing him, so we must suppose that his first race is IT. But if possible I'd like to be sure. And you might hear something, if you're still in the shop.'

'Keep my ears flapping, you mean?'

'Absolutely. And eyes open.'

'Philby won't have nothing on me,' Bert said.

Charlie stretched out to the makings of the sandwich and assembled a smaller edition for himself.

'Now, transport,' I said. 'I've hired all the vehicles we need from a firm in Chiswick. I was there this morning, looking them over. Owen took a Land-Rover and trailer from there to Gatwick to meet Black Fire and ferry him to his stable, and he's coming back by train. Then there's the caravan for you, Charlie, and the car to pull it. Tomorrow Owen is driving those to Reading and leaving them in the station car park, again coming back by train. I got two sets of keys for the car and caravan, so I'll give you yours now.' I went through to the sitting-room and came back with the small jingling bunch. 'Whichever day we're off, you can go down to Reading by train and drive from there.'

'Fine,' Charlie said, smiling broadly.

'The caravan is one they hire out for horse shows

and exhibitions and things like that. It's fitted out as a sort of office. No beds or cookers, just a counter, a couple of desks, and three or four folding chairs. Owen and I will load it with all the things you'll need before he takes it to Reading.'

'Great.'

'Finally there's the big van for Owen. I'll bring that here tomorrow and put the shopping in it. Then we should be ready.'

'Here,' said Bert. 'How's the cash, like?'

'Do you want some, Bert?'

'It's only, well, seeing as how you're hiring things left right and centre, well, I wondered if it wouldn't be better to hire a car for me too, like. Because my old banger isn't all that bleeding reliable, see? I wouldn't like to miss the fun because of a boiling bleeding radiator or some such.'

'Sure,' I said. 'Much safer.' I went back to the sitting-room, fetched some cash, and gave it to Bert.

'Here,' he said. 'I don't need that much. What do you think I'm going to hire, a bleeding golden coach?'

'Keep it anyway.'

He looked at me dubiously. 'I'm not doing this for bread, mate.'

I felt humbled. 'Bert . . . Give me back what you don't use. Or send it to the Injured Jockeys' Fund.'

His face lightened. 'I'll take my old boss down the boozer a few times. Best bleeding charity there is!'

Charlie finished his sandwich and wiped his fingers

on his handkerchief. 'You won't forget the sign-writing, will you?' he said.

'I did it today,' I assured him. 'Want to see?'

We trooped down to the workshop, where various painted pieces of the enterprise were standing around drying.

'Blimey,' Bert said. 'They look bleeding real.'

'They'd have to be,' Charlie nodded.

'Here,' Bert said, 'seeing these makes it seem, well, as if it's all going to happen.'

Charlie went home to a bridge-playing wife in an opulent detached in Surrey and Bert to the two-up two-down terraced he shared with his fat old mum in Staines. Some time after their departure I got the car out and drove slowly down the M4 to Heathrow.

I was early. About an hour early. I had often noticed that I tended to arrive prematurely for things I was looking forward to, as if by being there early one could make them happen sooner. It worked in reverse that time. Allie's aeroplane was half an hour late.

'Hi,' she said, looking as uncrushed as if she'd travelled four miles, not four thousand. 'How's cold little old England?'

'Warmer since you're here.'

The wide smile had lost none of its brilliance, but now there was also a glow in the eyes, where the Miami sun shone from within.

'Thanks for coming,' I said.

'I wouldn't miss this caper for the world.' She gave me a kiss of excitement and warmth. 'And I haven't told my sister I'm coming.'

'Great,' I said with satisfaction; and took her home to the flat.

The change of climate was external. We spent the night, our first together, warmly entwined under a goosefeather quilt: more comfortable, more relaxed and altogether more cosy than the beach or the fishing boat or my hotel bedroom on an air-conditioned afternoon in Miami.

We set off early next morning while it was still dark, shivering in the chill January air and impatient for the car heater to make an effort. Allie drove, concentrating fiercely on the left-hand business, telling me to watch out that she didn't instinctively turn the wrong way at crossings. We reached the fruit stall on the A34 safely in two hours and drew up there in the wide sweep of car-parking space. Huge lorries ground past on the main route from the docks at Southampton to the heavy industry area at Birmingham; a road still in places too narrow for its traffic.

Each time a heavy truck breasted the adjoining hill and drew level with us, it changed its gears, mostly with a good deal of noise. Allie raised her voice. 'Not the quietest of country spots.'

I smiled. 'Every decibel counts.'

We drank hot coffee from a thermos flask and

watched the slow grey morning struggle from gloomy to plain dull.

'Nine o'clock,' said Allie, looking at her watch. 'The day sure starts late in these parts.'

'We'll need you here by nine,' I said.

'You just tell me when to start.'

'Okay.'

She finished her coffee. 'Are you certain sure he'll come this way?'

'It's the best road and the most direct, and he always does.'

'One thing about having an ex-friend for an enemy,' she said. 'You know his habits.'

I packed away the coffee and we started again, turning south.

'This is the way you'll be coming,' I said. 'Straight up the A34.'

'Right.'

She was driving now with noticeably more confidence, keeping left without the former steady frown of anxiety. We reached a big crossroads and stopped at the traffic lights. She looked around and nodded. 'When I get here, there'll only be a couple of miles to go.'

We pressed on for a few miles, the road climbing and descending over wide stretches of bare downlands, bleak and windy and uninviting.

'Slow down a minute,' I said. 'See that turning there, to the left? That's where Jody's stables are. About a mile along there.'

'I really hate that man,' she said.

'You've never met him.'

'You don't have to know snakes to hate them.'

We went round the Newbury by-pass, Allie screwing her head round alarmingly to learn the route from the reverse angle.

'Okay,' she said. 'Now what?'

'Still the A34. Signposts to Winchester. But we don't go that far.'

'Right.'

Through Whitchurch, and six miles beyond we took a narrow side road on the right, and in a little while turned into the drive of a dilapidated looking country house with a faded paint job on a board at the gate.

HANTSFORD MANOR RIDING SCHOOL.
FIRST CLASS INSTRUCTION. RESIDENTIAL ACCOMMODATION.
PONIES AND HORSES FOR HIRE OR AT LIVERY.

I had chosen it from an advertisement in the *Horse and Hound* because of its location, to make the drive from there to the fruit stall as simple as possible for Allie, but now that I saw it, I had sinking doubts.

There was an overall air of life having ended, of dust settling, weeds growing, wood rotting and hope dead. Exaggerated, of course. Though the house indoors smelt faintly of fungus and decay, the proprietors were still alive. They were two much-alike sisters, both about seventy, with thin wiry bodies dressed in jodhpurs, hacking jackets and boots. They both had kind faded blue eyes, long strong lower jaws, and copious iron grey hair in businesslike hairnets.

They introduced themselves as Miss Johnston and Mrs Fairchild-Smith. They were glad to welcome Miss Ward. They said they hoped her stay would be comfortable. They never had many guests at this time of year. Miss Ward's horse had arrived safely the day before and they were looking after him.

'Yourselves?' I asked doubtfully.

'Certainly, ourselves.' Miss Johnston's tone dared me to imply they were incapable. 'We always cut back on staff at this time of year.'

They took us out to the stables, which like everything else were suffering from advancing years and moreover appeared to be empty. Among a ramshackle collection of wooden structures whose doors any self-respecting toddler could have kicked down, stood three or four brick-built boxes in a sturdy row; in one of these we found Black Fire.

He stood on fresh straw. There was clean water in his bucket and good-looking hay in his net, and he had his head down to the manger, munching busily at oats and bran. All too clear to see where any profits of the business disappeared: into the loving care of the customers.

'He looks fine,' I said, and to myself, with relief, confirmed that he really was indeed the double of

Energise, and that in the warm distant Miami night I hadn't been mistaken.

Allie cleared her throat. 'Er . . . Miss Johnston, Mrs Fairchild-Smith . . . Tomorrow morning I may be taking Black Fire over to some friends, to ride with them. Would that be okay?'

'Of course,' they said together.

'Leaving at eight o'clock?'

'We'll see he's ready for you, my dear,' said Miss Johnston.

'I'll let you know for sure when I've called my friends. If I don't go tomorrow, it may be Monday, or Wednesday.'

'Whenever you say, my dear.' Miss Johnston paused delicately. 'Could you give us any idea how long you'll be staying?'

Allie said without hesitation, 'I guess a week's board would be fair, both for Black Fire and me, don't you think? We may not be here for all of seven days, but obviously at this time of year you won't want to be bothered with shorter reservations.'

The sisters looked discreetly pleased and when Allie produced cash for the bulk of the bill in advance, a faint flush appeared on their thin cheeks and narrow noses.

'Aren't they the weirdest?' Allie said as we drove out of the gates. 'And how do you shift these damned gears?'

She sat this time at the wheel of the Land-Rover I'd

hired from Chiswick, learning her way round its unusual levers.

'That one with the red knob engages four-wheeled drive, and the yellow one is for four ultra-low gears, which you shouldn't need as we're not aiming to cross ploughed fields or drag tree stumps out of the ground.'

'I wouldn't rule them out when you're around.'

She drove with growing ease, and before long we returned to hitch on the two-horse trailer. She had never driven with a trailer before and reversing, as always, brought the worst problems. After a fair amount of swearing on all sides and the best part of an hour's trundling around Hampshire she said she guessed she would reach the fruit stall if it killed her. When we returned to Hantsford Manor after refuelling she parked with the Land-Rover's nose already facing the road, so that at least she wouldn't louse up the linkage, as she put it, before she'd even started.

'You'll find the trailer a good deal heavier with a horse in it,' I said.

'You don't say.'

Without encountering the sisters we returned to Black Fire and I produced from an inner pocket a hair-cutting gadget in the form of a razor blade incorporated into a comb.

'What are you going to do with that?' Allie said.

'If the two old girls materialise, keep them chatting,' I said. 'I'm just helping the understudy to look like the star.'

I went into the box and as calmly as possible approached Black Fire. He wore a head collar, but was not tied up, and the first thing I did was attach him to the tethering chain. I ran my hand down his neck and patted him a few times and said a few soothing non-senses. He didn't seem to object to my presence, so rather gingerly I laid the edge of the hair-cutting comb against his black coat.

I had been told often that nervous people made horses nervous also. I wondered if Black Fire could feel my fumbling inexperience. I thought that after all this I would really have to spend more time with horses, that owning them should entail the obligation of intimacy.

His muscles twitched. He threw his head up and down. He whinnied. He also stood fairly still, so that when I'd finished my delicate scraping he had a small bald patch on his right shoulder, the same size and in the same place as the one on Energise.

Allie leant her elbows on the closed bottom half of the stable door and watched through the open top half.

'Genius,' she said smiling, 'is nine tenths an infinite capacity for taking pains.'

I straightened, grinned, patted Black Fire almost familiarly, and shook my head. 'Genius is infinite pain,' I said. 'I'm happy. Too bad.'

'How do you know, then? About genius being pain?'

'Like seeing glimpses of a mountain from the valley.'

'And you'd prefer to suffer on the peaks?'

I let myself out of the loose box and carefully fastened all the bolts.

'You're either issued with climbing boots, or you aren't,' I said. 'You can't choose. Just as well.'

The sisters reappeared and invited us to take sherry: a double thimbleful in unmatched cut glasses. I looked at my watch and briefly nodded, and Allie asked if she might use the telephone to call the friends.

In the library, they said warmly. This way. Mind the hole in the carpet. Over there, on the desk. They smiled, nodded and retreated.

Beside the telephone stood a small metal box with a stuck-on notice. *Please pay for calls.* I dialled the London number of the Press Association and asked for the racing section.

'Horses knocked out of the novice hurdle at Stratford?' said a voice. 'Well, I suppose so, but we prefer people to wait for the evening papers. These enquiries waste our time.'

'Arrangements to make as soon as possible . . .' I murmured.

'Oh, all right. Wait a sec. Here we are . . .' He read out about seven names rather fast. 'Got that?'

'Yes, thank you very much,' I said.

I put down the telephone slowly, my mouth suddenly dry. Jody had declared Padellic as a Saturday Stratford runner three days ago. If he intended not to go there, he would have had to remove his name by a Friday morning deadline of eleven o'clock . . .

Eleven o'clock had come and gone. None of the horses taken out of the novice hurdle had been Padellic. 'Tomorrow,' I said. 'He runs tomorrow.'

'Oh.' Allie's eyes were wide. 'Oh golly!'

CHAPTER TWELVE

Eight o'clock, Saturday morning.

I sat in my hired Cortina in a lay-by on the road over the top of the Downs, watching the drizzly dawn take the eye-strain out of the passing headlights.

I was there much too early because I hadn't been able to sleep. The flurry of preparations all Friday afternoon and evening had sent me to bed still in top gear and from then on my brain had whirred relentlessly, thinking of all the things which could go wrong.

Snatches of conversation drifted back.

Rupert Ramsey expressing doubts and amazement on the other end of the telephone.

'You want to do *what*?'

'Take Energise for a ride in a horsebox. He had a very upsetting experience in a horsebox at Sandown, in a crash . . . I thought it might give him confidence to go for an uneventful drive.'

'I don't think it would do much good,' he said.

'All the same I'm keen to try. I've asked a young chap called Pete Duveen, who drives his own box, just to pick him up and take him for a ride. I thought tomorrow would be a good day. Pete Duveen says he can collect him at seven thirty in the morning. Would you have the horse ready?'

'You're wasting your money,' he said regretfully. 'I'm afraid there's more wrong with him than nerves.'

'Never mind. And ... will you be at home tomorrow evening?'

'After I get back from Chepstow races, yes.'

The biggest race meeting of the day was scheduled for Chepstow, over on the west side of the Bristol Channel. The biggest prizes were on offer there and most of the top trainers, like Rupert, would be going.

'I hope you won't object,' I said, 'but after Energise returns from his ride, I'd like to hire a security firm to keep an eye on him.'

Silence from the other end. Then his voice, carefully polite. 'What on earth for?'

'To keep him safe,' I said reasonably. 'Just a guard to patrol the stable and make regular checks. The guard wouldn't be a nuisance to anybody.'

I could almost feel the shrug coming down the wire along with the resigned sigh. Eccentric owners should be humoured. 'If you want to, I suppose ... But why?'

'If I called at your house tomorrow evening,' I suggested diffidently, 'I could explain.'

'Well ...' He thought for a bit. 'Look, I'm having a few friends to dinner. Would you care to join us?'

'Yes, I would,' I said positively. 'I'd like that very much.'

I yawned in the car and stretched. Despite anorak, gloves and thick socks the cold encroached on fingers and toes, and through the drizzle-wet windows the bare rolling Downs looked thoroughly inhospitable. Straight ahead through the windscreen wipers I could see a good two miles of the A34. It came over the brow of a distant hill opposite, swept down into a large valley and rose again higher still to cross the Downs at the point where I sat.

A couple of miles to my rear lay the crossroads with the traffic lights, and a couple of miles beyond that, the fruit stall.

Bert Huggerneck, wildly excited, had telephoned at six in the evening.

'Here, know what? There's a squeezer on tomorrow!'

'On Padellic?' I said hopefully.

'What else? On bleeding little old Padellic.'

'How do you know?'

'Listened at the bleeding door,' he said cheerfully. 'The two smart alecs was talking. Stupid bleeding gits. All over the whole bleeding country Ganser Mays is going to flood the little bookies' shops with last minute bets on Padellic. The smart alecs are all getting their girl friends, what the little guys don't know by sight, to

215

go round putting on the dough. Hundreds of them, by the sound of it.'

'You're a wonder, Bert.'

'Yeah,' he said modestly. 'Missed my bleeding vocation.'

Owen and I had spent most of the afternoon loading the big hired van from Chiswick and checking that we'd left nothing out. He worked like a demon, all energy and escaping smiles.

'Life will seem flat after this,' he said.

I had telephoned Charlie from Hantsford Manor and caught him before he went to lunch.

'We're off,' I said. 'Stratford, tomorrow.'

'Tally bloody ho!'

He rang me from his office again at five. 'Have you seen the evening papers?'

'Not yet,' I said.

'Jody has two definite runners at Chepstow as well.'

'Which ones?'

'Cricklewood in the big race and Asphodel in the handicap chase.'

Cricklewood and Asphodel both belonged to the same man, who since I'd left had become Jody's number one owner. Cricklewood was now also ostensibly the best horse in the yard.

'That means,' I said, 'that Jody himself will almost certainly go to Chepstow.'

'I should think so,' Charlie agreed. 'He wouldn't want to draw attention to Padellic by going to Stratford, would you think?'

'No, I wouldn't.'

'Just what we wanted,' Charlie said with satisfaction. 'Jody going to Chepstow.'

'We thought he might.'

Charlie chuckled. '*You* thought he might.' He cleared his throat. 'See you tomorrow, in the trenches. And Steven . . .'

'Yes?'

'Good luck with turning the handle.'

Turning the handle . . .

I looked at my watch. Still only eight-thirty and too early for any action. I switched on the car's engine and let the heater warm me up.

All the little toys, revolving on their spindles, going through their programmed acts. Allie, Bert, Charlie and Owen. Felicity and Jody Leeds, Ganser Mays. Padellic and Energise and Black Fire. Rupert Ramsey and Pete Duveen.

And one little toy I knew nothing about.

I stirred, thinking of him uneasily.

A big man who wore sunglasses. Who had muscles, and knew how to fight.

What else?

Who had bought Padellic at Doncaster Sales?

I didn't know if he had bought the horse after Jody had found it, or if he knew Energise well enough to look for a double himself; and there was no way of finding out.

I'd left no slot for him in today's plan. If he turned up like a joker, he might entirely disrupt the game.

I picked up my raceglasses which were lying on the seat beside me and started watching the traffic crossing the top of the opposite distant hill. From two miles away, even with strong magnification, it was difficult to identify particular vehicles, and in the valley and climbing the hill straight towards me they were head-on and foreshortened.

What looked like car and trailer came over the horizon. I glanced at my watch. If it was Allie, she was dead on time.

I focused on the little group. Watched it down into the valley. Definitely a Land-Rover and animal trailer. I got out of the car and watched it crawling up the hill, until finally I could make out the number plate. Definitely Allie.

Stepping a pace on to the road, I flagged her down. She pulled into the lay-by, opened her window, and looked worried.

'Is something wrong?'

'Not a thing.' I kissed her. 'I got here too early, so I thought I'd say good morning.'

'You louse. When I saw you standing there waving I thought the whole darned works were all fouled up.'

'You found the way, then.'

'No problem.'

'Sleep well?'

She wrinkled her nose. 'I guess so. But oh boy, that's some crazy house. Nothing works. If you want to flush the john you have to get Miss Johnston. No one else has the touch. I guess they're really sweet, though, the poor old ducks.'

'Shades of days gone by,' I said.

'Yeah, that's exactly right. They showed me their scrap books. They were big in the horse world thirty-forty years ago. Won things at shows all over. Now they're struggling on a fixed income and I guess they'll soon be starving.'

'Did they say so?'

'Of course not. You can see it, though.'

'Is Black Fire all right?'

'Oh sure. They helped me load him up, which was lucky because I sure would have been hopeless on my own.'

'Was he any trouble?'

'Quiet as a little lamb.'

I walked round to the back of the trailer and looked in over the three-quarter door. Black Fire occupied the left-hand stall. A full hay net lay in the right. The ladies might starve, but their horses wouldn't.

I went back to Allie. 'Well . . .' I said. 'Good luck.'

'To you too.'

She gave me the brilliant smile, shut the window and with care pulled out of the lay-by into the stream of northbound traffic.

Time and timing, the two essentials.

I sat in the car metaphorically chewing my nails and literally looking at my watch every half minute.

Padellic's race was the last of the day, the sixth race, the slot often allotted to that least crowd-pulling of events, the novice hurdle. Because of the short January afternoon, the last race was scheduled for three-thirty.

Jody's horses, like those of most other trainers, customarily arrived at a racecourse about two hours before they were due to run. Not often later, but quite often sooner.

The journey by horsebox from Jody's stable to Stratford on Avon racecourse took two hours. The very latest, therefore, that Jody's horsebox would set out would be eleven-thirty.

I thought it probable it would start much sooner than that. The latest time allowed little margin for delays on the journey or snags on arrival and I knew that if I were Jody and Ganser Mays and had so much at stake, I would add a good hour for contingencies.

Ten-thirty . . . But suppose it was earlier . . .

I swallowed. I had had to guess.

If for any reason Jody had sent the horse very early and it had already gone, all our plans were for nothing.

If he had sent it the day before . . . If he had sent it with another trainer's horses, sharing the cost . . . If for some unimaginable reason the driver took a different route . . .

The ifs multiplied like stinging ants.

Nine-fifteen.

I got out of the car and extended the aerial of a large efficient walkie-talkie. No matter that British civilians were supposed to have permission in triple triplicate before operating them: in this case we would be cluttering the air for seconds only, and lighting flaming beacons on hill-tops would have caused a lot more fuss.

'Charlie?' I said, transmitting.

'All fine here.'

'Great.' I paused for five seconds, and transmitted again. 'Owen?'

'Here, sir.'

'Great.'

Owen and Charlie could both hear me but they couldn't hear each other, owing to the height of the Downs where I sat. I left the aerial extended and the switches to 'receive', and put the gadget back in the car.

The faint drizzle persisted, but my mouth was dry.

I thought about the five of us, sitting and waiting. I wondered if the others like me were having trouble with their nerves.

The walkie-talkie crackled suddenly. I picked it up.

'Sir?'

'Owen?'

'Pete Duveen just passed me.'

'Fine.'

I could hear the escaping tension in my own voice and the excitement in his. The on-time arrival of Pete Duveen signalled the real beginning. I put the walkie-talkie down and was disgusted to see my hand shaking.

Pete Duveen in his horsebox drove into the lay-by nine and a half minutes after he had passed Owen, who was stationed in sight of the road to Jody's stable. Pete owned a pale blue horse-box with his name, address and telephone number painted in large black and red letters on the front and back. I had seen the box and its owner at race meetings and it was he, in fact, whom I had engaged at Sandown on my abortive attempt to prevent Jody taking Energise home.

Pete Duveen shut down his engine and jumped from the cab.

'Morning, Mr Scott.'

'Morning,' I said, shaking hands. 'Glad to see you.'

'Anything to oblige.' He grinned cheerfully, letting me know both that he thought I was barmy and also that I had every right to be, as long as I was harmless and, moreover, paying him.

He was well-built and fair, with weatherbeaten skin and a threadbare moustache. Open-natured, sensible and honest. A one-man transport firm, and making a go of it.

'You brought my horse?' I said.

'Sure thing.'

'And how has he travelled?'

'Not a peep out of him the whole way.'

'Mind if I take a look at him?' I said.

'Sure thing,' he said again. 'But honest, he didn't act up when we loaded him and I wouldn't say he cared a jimmy riddle one way or another.'

I unclipped and opened the part of the side of the horse-box which formed the entrance ramp for the horses. It was a bigger box than Jody's but otherwise much the same. The horse stood in the front row of stalls in the one furthest across from the ramp, and he looked totally uninterested in the day's proceedings.

'You never know,' I said, closing the box again. 'He might be all the better for the change of routine.'

'Maybe,' Pete said, meaning he didn't think so.

I smiled. 'Like some coffee?'

'Sure would.'

I opened the boot of my car, took out a thermos, and poured us each a cup.

'Sandwich?' I offered.

Sandwich accepted. He ate beef-and-chutney with relish. 'Early start,' he said, explaining his hunger. 'You said to get here soon after nine-thirty.'

'That's right,' I agreed.

'Er . . . why so early?'

'Because,' I said reasonably, 'I've other things to do all the rest of the day.'

He thought me even nuttier, but the sandwich plugged the opinion in his throat.

The sky began to brighten and the tiny-dropped drizzle dried away. I talked about racing in general and Stratford on Avon in particular, and wondered how on earth I was to keep him entertained if Jody's box should after all not leave home until the last possible minute.

By ten-fifteen we had drunk two cups of coffee each and he had run out of energy for sandwiches. He began to move restively and make ready-for-departure signs of which I blandly took no notice. I chatted on about the pleasures of owning racehorses and my stomach bunched itself into anxious knots.

Ten-twenty. Ten-twenty-five. Ten-thirty. Nothing.

It had all gone wrong, I thought. One of the things which could have sent everything awry had done so.

Ten-thirty-five.

'Look,' Pete said persuasively. 'You said you had a great deal to do today, and honestly, I don't think . . .'

The walkie-talkie crackled.

I practically leapt towards the front of the car and reached in for it.

'Sir?'

'Yes, Owen.'

'A blue horsebox just came out of his road and turned south.'

'Right.'

I stifled my disappointment. Jody's two runners setting off to Chepstow, no doubt.

'What's that?' Pete Duveen said, his face appearing at my shoulder full of innocent enquiry.

'Just a radio.'

'Sounded like a police car.'

I smiled and moved away back to the rear of the car, but I had hardly got Pete engaged again in useless conversation when the crackle was repeated.

'Sir?'

'Go ahead.'

'A fawn coloured box with a red slash, sir. Just turned north.'

His voice trembled with excitement.

'That's it, Owen.'

'I'm on my way.'

I felt suddenly sick. Took three deep breaths. Pressed the transmit button.

'Charlie?'

'Yes.'

'The box is on its way.'

'Halle-bloody-lujah.'

Pete was again looking mystified and inquisitive. I ignored his face and took a travelling bag out of the boot of my car.

'Time to go,' I said pleasantly. 'I think, if you don't

mind, I'd like to see how my horse behaves while going along, so could you start the box now and take me up the road a little way?'

He looked very surprised, but then he had found the whole expedition incomprehensible.

'If you like,' he said helplessly. 'You're the boss.'

I made encouraging signs to him to get into his cab and start the engine and while he was doing it I stowed my bag on the passenger side. The diesel engine whirred and coughed and came to thunderous life, and I went back to the Cortina.

Locked the boot, shut the windows, took the keys, locked the doors, and stood leaning against the wing holding binoculars in one hand and walkie-talkie in the other.

Pete Duveen had taken nine and a half minutes from Jody's road to my lay-by and Jody's box took exactly the same. Watching the far hill through raceglasses I saw the big dark blue van which contained Owen come over the horizon, followed almost immediately by an oblong of fawn.

Watched them down into the valley and on to the beginning of the hill.

I pressed the transmit button.

'Charlie?'

'Go ahead.'

'Seven minutes. Owen's in front.'

'Right.'

I pushed down the aerial of the walkie-talkie and

took it and myself along to the passenger door of Pete's box. He looked across and down at me enquiringly, wondering why on earth I was still delaying.

'Just a moment,' I said, giving no explanation, and he waited patiently, as if humouring a lunatic.

Owen came up the hill, changed gears abreast of the lay-by, and slowly accelerated away. Jody's horsebox followed, doing exactly the same. The scrunched near-side front had been hammered out, I saw, but respraying lay in the future. I had a quick glimpse into the cab: two men, neither of them Jody, both unknown to me; a box driver who had replaced Andy-Fred and the lad with the horse. Couldn't be better.

I hopped briskly up into Pete's box.

'Off we go, then.'

My sudden haste looked just as crazy as the former dawdling, but again he made no comment and merely did what I wanted. When he had found a gap in the traffic and pulled out on to the road there were four or five vehicles between Jody's box and ourselves, and this seemed to me a reasonable number.

I spent the next four miles trying to look as if nothing in particular was happening while listening to my heart beat like a discotheque. Owen's van went over the traffic lights at the big crossroads a half second before they changed to amber and Jody's box came to a halt as they showed red. The back of Owen's van disappeared round a bend in the road.

Between Jody's box and Pete's there were three

private cars and one small van belonging to an electrical firm. When the lights turned green one of the cars peeled off to the left and I began to worry that we were getting too close.

'Slow down just a fraction,' I suggested.

'If you like ... but there's not a squeak from the horse.' He glanced over his shoulder to where the black head looked patiently forward through a small observation hatch, as nervous as a suet pudding.

A couple of private cars passed us. We motored sedately onwards and came to the bottom of the next hill. Pete changed his gears smoothly and we lumbered noisily up. Near the top, his eye took in a notice board on a tripod at the side of the road.

'Damn,' he said.

'What is it?' I asked.

'Did you see that?' he said. 'Census point ahead.'

'Never mind, we're not in a hurry.'

'I suppose not.'

We breasted the hill. The fruit stall lay ahead on our left, with the sweep of car park beside it. Down the centre of the road stood a row of red and white cones used for marking road obstructions and in the northbound lane, directing the traffic, stood a large man in navy blue police uniform with a black and white checked band round his cap.

As we approached he waved the private cars past and then directed Pete into the fruit stall car park, walking in beside the horsebox and talking to him through the window.

'We'll keep you only a few minutes, sir. Now, will you pull right round in a circle and park facing me just here, sir?'

'All right,' Pete said resignedly and followed the instructions. When he pulled the brake on we were facing the road. On our left, about ten feet away, stood Jody's box, but facing in the opposite direction. On the far side of Jody's box was Owen's van. And beyond Owen's van, across about twenty yards of cindery park, lay the caravan, its long flat windowless side towards us.

The Land-Rover and trailer which Allie had brought stood near the front of Jody's box. There was also the car hitched to the caravan and the car Bert had hired, and all in all the whole area looked populated, official, and busy.

A second large notice on a tripod faced the car park from just outside the caravan.

DEPARTMENT OF THE ENVIRONMENT
CENSUS POINT

and near a door at one end of the caravan a further notice on a stand said '*Way In*'.

Jody's horsebox driver and Jody's lad were following its directions, climbing the two steps up to the caravan and disappearing within.

'Over there, please sir.' A finger pointed

authoritatively. 'And take your driving licence and log book, please.'

Pete shrugged, picked up his papers, and went. I jumped out and watched him go.

The second he was inside Bert slapped me on the back in a most unpolicemanlike way and said, 'Easy as Blackpool tarts.'

We zipped into action. Four minutes maximum, and a dozen things to do.

I unclipped the ramp of Jody's horsebox and let it down quietly. The one thing which would bring any horsebox driver running, census or no census, was the sound of someone tampering with his cargo; and noise, all along, had been one of the biggest problems.

Opened Pete Duveen's ramp. Also the one on Allie's trailer.

While I did that, Bert brought several huge rolls of three-inch thick latex from Owen's van and unrolled them down all the ramps, and across the bare patches of car park in between the boxes. I fetched the head collar bought for the purpose from my bag and stepped into Jody's box. The black horse looked at me incuriously, standing there quietly in his travelling rug and four leg-guards. I checked his ear for the tiny nick and his shoulder for the bald pennyworth, and wasted a moment in patting him.

I knew all too well that success depended on my being able to persuade this strange four-footed creature to go with me gently and without fuss, and wished passionately for more expertise. All I had were nimble hands and sympathy, and they would have to be enough.

I unbuckled his rug at high speed and thanked the gods that the leg-guards Jody habitually used for travelling his horses were not laboriously wound-on bandages but lengths of plastic-backed foam rubber fastened by strips of velcro.

I had all four off before Bert had finished the sound-proofing. Put the new head collar over his neck; unbuckled and removed his own and left it swinging, still tied to the stall. Fitted and fastened the new one, and gave the rope a tentative tug. Energise took one step, then another, then with more assurance followed me sweetly down the ramp. It felt miraculous, but nothing like fast enough.

Hurry. Get the other horses, and hurry.

They didn't seem to mind walking on the soft spongy surface, but they wouldn't go fast. I tried to take them calmly, to keep my urgency to myself, to stop them taking fright and skittering away and crashing those metal-capped feet on to the car park.

Hurry. Hurry.

I had to get Energise's substitute into his place, wearing the right rug, the right bandages, and the right collar, before the box driver and the lad came out of the caravan.

Also his hooves . . . Racing plates were sometimes put on by the blacksmith at home, who then rubbed on oil to obliterate the rasp marks of the file and give the feet a well-groomed appearance. I had brought hoof oil in my bag in case Energise had already had his shoes changed and he had.

'Hurry for gawd's sake,' said Bert, seeing me fetch the oil. He was running back to the van with relays of re-rolled latex and grinning like a Pools winner.

I painted the hooves a glossy dark. Buckled on the swinging head collar without disturbing the tethering knot, as the lad would notice if it were tied differently. Buckled the rug round the chest and under the belly. Fastened the velcro strips on all four leg-guards. Shut the folding gates to his stall exactly as they had been before, and briefly looked back before closing the ramp. The black head was turned incuriously towards me, the liquid eye patient and unmoved. I smiled at him involuntarily, jumped out of the box, and with Bert's help eased shut the clips on the ramp.

Owen came out of the caravan, ran across, and fastened the ramp on the trailer. I jumped in with the horse in Pete's box. Bert lifted the ramp and did another silent job on the clips.

Through the windscreen of Pete's box the car park looked quiet and tidy.

Owen returned to the driving seat of his van and Bert walked back towards the road.

At the same instant Jody's driver and lad hurried out of the caravan and trampled across to their horsebox. I ducked out of sight, but I could hear one of them say, as he re-embarked, 'Right lot of time-wasting cobblers, that was.'

Then the engine throbbed to life, the box moved off, and Bert considerately held up a car or two so that it should have a clear passage back to its interrupted journey. If I hadn't had so much still to do I would have laughed.

I fastened the rug. Tied the head collar rope. Clipped on the leg guards. I'd never worked so fast in my life.

What else? I glanced over my beautiful black horse, seeking things undone. He looked steadfastly back. I smiled at him, too, and told him he was a great fellow. Then Pete came out of the caravan and I scrambled through to the cab, and tried to sit in the passenger seat as if bored with waiting instead of sweating with effort and with a heart racing like tappets.

Pete climbed into his side of the cab and threw his log book and licence disgustedly on to the glove shelf.

'They're always stopping us nowadays. Spot check on log books. Spot check on vehicles. Half an hour a time, those. And now a census.'

'Irritating,' I agreed, making my voice a lot slower than my pulse.

His usual good nature returned in a smile. 'Actually the checks are a good thing. Some lorries, in the old days, were death on wheels. And some drivers, I dare say.' He stretched his hand towards the ignition. 'Where to?' he said.

'Might as well go back. As you say, the horse is quiet. If you could take me back to my car?'

'Sure thing,' he said. 'You're the boss.'

Bert shepherded us solicitously on to the south-bound lane, holding up the traffic with a straight face and obvious enjoyment. Pete drove steadfastly back to the lay-by and pulled in behind the Cortina.

'I expect you think it a wasted day,' I said. 'But I assure you from my point of view it's been worth it.'

'That's all that matters,' he said cheerfully.

'Take good care of this fellow going home,' I said, looking back at the horse. 'And would you remind the lads in Mr Ramsey's yard that I've arranged for a security guard to patrol the stable at night for a while? He should be arriving there later this afternoon.'

'Sure,' he said, nodding.

'That's all then, I guess.' I took my bag and jumped down from the cab. He gave me a final wave through the window and set off southwards along the A34.

I leaned against the Cortina, watching him go down the hill, across the valley, and up over the horizon on the far side.

I wondered how Energise would like his new home.

CHAPTER THIRTEEN

Charlie, Allie, Bert and Owen were all in the caravan when I drove back there, drinking coffee and laughing like kids.

'Here,' Bert said, wheezing with joy. 'A bleeding police car came along a second after I'd picked up the census notices and all those cones. Just a bleeding second.'

'It didn't stop, I hope.'

'Not a bleeding chance. Mind you, I'd taken off the fancy clobber. First thing. The fuzz don't love you for impersonating them, even if your hatband is only a bit of bleeding ribbon painted in checks.'

Charlie said more soberly, 'It was the only police car we've seen.'

'The cones were only in the road for about ten minutes,' Allie said. 'It sure would have been unlucky if the police had driven by in that time.'

She was sitting by one of the desks looking neat but unremarkable in a plain skirt and jersey. On the desk stood my typewriter, uncovered, with piles of stationery alongside. Charlie, at the other desk, wore an elderly suit, faintly shabby and a size too small. He had parted his hair in the centre and brushed it flat with water, and had somehow contrived a look of middling bureaucracy instead of world finance. Before him, too, lay an impressive array of official forms and other literature and the walls of the caravan were drawing-pinned with exhortative Ministry posters.

'How did you get all this bleeding junk?' said Bert, waving his hand at it.

'Applied for it,' I said. 'It's not difficult to get government forms or information posters. All you do is ask.'

'Blimey.'

'They're not census forms, of course. Most of them are application forms for driving licences and passports and things like that. Owen and I just made up the census questions and typed them out for Charlie, and he pretended to put the answers on the forms.'

Owen drank his coffee with a happy smile and Charlie said, chuckling, 'You should have seen your man here putting on his obstructive act. Standing there in front of me like an idiot and either answering the questions wrong or arguing about answering them at all. The two men from the horsebox thought him quite funny and made practically no fuss about being kept waiting. It was the other man, Pete Duveen, who was getting tired of it, but as he was at the back of the queue he couldn't do much.'

'Four minutes,' Owen said. 'You said you needed a minimum of four. So we did our best.'

'You must have given me nearer five,' I said gratefully. 'Did you hear anything?'

Allie laughed. 'There was so much darned racket going on in here. Owen arguing, me banging away on the typewriter, the traffic outside, pop radio inside, and that heater . . . How did you fix that heater?'

We all looked at the calor gas heater which warmed the caravan. It clattered continually like a broken fan.

'Screwed a small swinging flap up at the top here, inside. The rising hot air makes it bang against the casing.'

'Switch it off,' Charlie said. 'It's driving me mad.'

I produced instead a screwdriver and undid the necessary screws. Peace returned to the gas and Charlie said he could see the value of a college education.

'Pete Duveen knew the other box driver,' Allie said conversationally. 'Seems they're all one big club.'

'See each other every bleeding day at the races,' Bert confirmed. 'Here, that box driver made a bit of a fuss when I said the lad had to go into the caravan too. Like you said, they aren't supposed to leave a racehorse unguarded. So I said I'd bleeding guard it for him. How's that for a laugh? He said he supposed it was okay, as I was the police. I said I'd got instructions that everyone had to go into the census, no exceptions.'

'People will do anything if it looks official enough,' Charlie said, happily nodding.

'Well...' I put down my much needed cup of coffee and stretched my spine. 'Time to be off, don't you think?'

'Right,' Charlie said. 'All this paper and stuff goes in Owen's van.'

They began moving slowly, the reminiscent smiles still in place, packing the phoney census into carrier bags. Allie came out with me when I left.

'We've had more fun...' she said. 'You can't imagine.'

I supposed that I felt the same way, now that the flurry was over. I gave her a hug and a kiss and told her to take care of herself, and she said you, too.

'I'll call you this evening,' I promised.

'I wish I was coming with you.'

'We can't leave that here all day,' I said, pointing to the Land-Rover and the trailer.

She smiled. 'I guess not. Charlie says we'd all best be gone before anyone starts asking what we're doing.'

'Charlie is a hundred per cent right.'

I went to Stratford upon Avon races.

Drove fast, thinking of the righting of wrongs without benefit of lawyers. Thinking of the ephemeral quality of racehorses and the snail pace of litigation. Thinking that the best years of a hurdler's life could be wasted in stagnation while the courts deliberated to whom he belonged. Wondering what Jody would do when he found out about the morning's work and hoping that I knew him well enough to have guessed right.

When I drew up in the racecourse car park just before the first race, I saw Jody's box standing among a row of others over by the entrance to the stables. The ramp was down and from the general stage of activity I gathered that the horse was still on board.

I sat in my car a hundred yards away, watching through race glasses. I wondered when the lad would realise he had the wrong horse. I wondered if he would realise at all, because he certainly wouldn't expect to set off with one and arrive with another, and he would quite likely shrug off the first stirring of doubt. He was new in the yard since I had left and with average luck, knowing Jody's rate of turnover, he would be neither experienced nor very bright.

Nothing appeared to be troubling him at that moment. He walked down the ramp carrying a bucket and a bundle of other equipment and went through the gate to the stables. He looked about twenty. Long curly hair. Slight in build. Wearing flashy red trousers. I hoped he was thinking more of his own appearance than his horse's. I put the glasses down and waited.

My eye was caught by a woman in a white coat striding across the car park towards the horseboxes, and it took about five seconds before I realised with a jolt who she was.

Felicity Leeds.

Jody might have taken his knowing eyes to Chepstow, but Felicity had brought hers right here.

I hopped out of the car as if stung and made speed in her direction.

The lad came out of the stable, went up the ramp and shortly reappeared, holding the horse's head. Felicity walked towards him as he began to persuade the horse to disembark.

'Felicity,' I called.

She turned, saw me, looked appalled, threw a quick glance over her shoulder at the descending horse and walked decisively towards me.

When she stopped I looked over her shoulder and said with the sort of puzzlement which takes little to tip into suspicion, 'What horse is that?'

She took another hurried look at the black hindquarters now disappearing towards the stable and visibly gathered her wits.

'Padellic. Novice hurdler. Not much good.'

'He reminds me . . .' I said slowly.

'First time out, today,' Felicity said hastily. 'Nothing much expected.'

'Oh,' I said, not sounding entirely reassured. 'Are you going into the stables to see him, because I . . .'

'No,' she said positively. 'No need. He's perfectly all right.' She gave me a sharp nod and walked briskly away to the main entrance to the course.

Without an accompanying trainer no one could go into the racecourse stables. She knew I would have to contain my curiosity until the horse came out for its race and until then, from her point of view, she was safe.

I, however, didn't want her visiting the stables herself. There was no particular reason why she should, as trainers mostly didn't when the journey from home to course was so short. All the same I thought I might as well fill up so much of her afternoon that she scarcely had time.

I came up with her again outside the weighing room, where she vibrated with tension from her patterned silk headscarf to her high-heeled boots. There were sharp patches of colour on her usually pale cheeks and the eyes which regarded me with angry apprehension were as hot as fever.

'Felicity,' I said. 'Do you know anything about a load of muck that was dumped in my front garden?'

'A what?' The blank look she gave me was not quite blank enough.

I described at some length the component parts and all-over consistency of the obstruction and remarked on their similarity to the discard pile at her own home.

'All muck heaps are alike,' she said. 'You couldn't tell where one particular load came from.'

'All you'd need is a sample for forensic analysis.'

'Did you take one?' she said sharply.

'No,' I admitted.

'Well, then.'

'You and Jody seem the most likely to have done it.'

She looked at me with active dislike. 'Everyone on the racecourse knows what a shit you've been to us. It doesn't surprise me at all that someone has expressed the same opinion in a concrete way.'

'It surprises me very much that anyone except you should bother.'

'I don't intend to talk about it,' she said flatly.

'Well I do,' I said, and did, at some length, repetitively.

The muck heap accounted for a good deal of the afternoon, and Quintus, in a way, for the rest.

Quintus brought his noble brow and empty mind on to the stands and gave Felicity a peck on the cheek, lifting his hat punctiliously. To me he donated what could only be called a scowl.

Felicity fell upon him as if he were a saviour.

'I didn't know you were coming!' She sounded gladder than glad that he had.

'Just thought I would, you know, my dear.'

She drew him away from me out of earshot and began talking to him earnestly. He nodded, smiling, agreeing with her. She talked some more. He nodded benignly and patted her shoulder.

I homed in again like an attacking wasp.

'Oh for God's sake, leave the bloody subject alone,' Felicity exploded.

'What's the fella talking about?' Quintus said.

'A muck heap on his doorstep.'

'Oh,' Quintus said. 'Ah . . .'

I described it all over again. I was getting quite attached to it, in retrospect.

Quintus was distinctly pleased. Chuckles quivered in his throat and his eyes twinkled with malice.

'Serves you right, what?' he said.

'Do you think so?'

'Shit to a shit,' he said, nodding with satisfaction.

'*What* did you say?'

'Er . . . nothing.'

Realisation dawned on me with a sense of fitness. 'You did it yourself,' I said with conviction.

'Don't be ridiculous.' He was still vastly amused.

'Lavatory humour would be just your mark.'

'You are insulting.' Less amusement, more arrogance.

'And the police took away the card you left to test it for fingerprints.'

His mouth opened and shut. He looked blank. 'The police?'

'Fellows in blue,' I said.

Felicity said furiously, 'Trust someone like you not to take a joke.'

'I'll take an apology,' I said mildly. 'In writing.'

Their objections, their grudging admissions and the eventual drafting of the apology took care of a lot of time. Quintus had hired a tip-up truck for his delivery and had required his gardener to do the actual work. Jody and Felicity had generously contributed the load.

Quintus had supervised its disposal and written his
message.

He also, in his own hand and with bravado-ish flour-
ishes, wrote the apology. I thanked him courteously
and told him I would frame it, which didn't please him
in the least.

By that time the fifth race was over and it was time
to saddle the horses for the sixth.

Felicity, as the trainer's wife, was the natural person
to supervise the saddling of their runner, and I knew
that if she did she would know she had the wrong
horse.

On the other hand if she did the saddling she
couldn't stop me, as a member of the public, taking a
very close look, and from her point of view that was
a risk she didn't want to take.

She solved her dilemma by getting Quintus to see
to the saddling.

She herself, with a superhuman effort, laid her hand
on my arm in a conciliatory gesture and said, 'All right.
Let bygones be bygones. Let's go and have a drink.'

'Sure,' I said, expressing just the right amount of
surprise and agreement. 'Of course, if you'd like.'

So went off to the bar where I bought her a large
gin and tonic and myself a scotch and water, and we
stood talking about nothing much while both busy
with private thoughts. She was trembling slightly from
the force of hers, and I too had trouble preventing
mine from showing. There we were, both trying our

darnedest to keep the other away from the horse, she because she thought it was Energise and I because I knew it wasn't. I could feel the irony breaking out in wrinkles round my eyes.

Felicity dawdled so long over her second drink that the horses were already leaving the parade ring and going out to the course when we finally made our way back to the heart of things. Quintus had understudied splendidly and was to be seen giving a parting slap to the horse's rump. Felicity let her breath out in a sigh and dropped most of the pretence of being nice to me. When she left me abruptly to rejoin Quintus for the race, I made no move to stop her.

The horse put up a good show, considering.

There were twenty-two runners, none of them more than moderate, and they delivered the sort of performance Energise would have left in the next parish. His substitute was running in his own class and finished undisgraced in sixth place, better than I would have expected. The crowd briefly cheered the winning favourite, and I thought it time to melt prudently and inconspicuously away.

I had gone to Stratford with more hope than certainty that the horse would actually run without the exchange being noticed. I had been prepared to do anything I reasonably could to achieve it, in order to give Ganser Mays the nasty shock of losing every penny he'd laid out on his squeezer.

What I hadn't actually bargained for was the effect the lost race would have on Felicity.

I saw her afterwards, though I hadn't meant to, when she went to meet her returning horse. The jockey, a well-known rider who had doubtless been told to win, was looking strained enough, but Felicity seemed on the point of collapse.

Her face was a frightening white, her whole body shook and her eyes looked as blank as marbles.

If I had ever wanted any personal revenge, I had it then, but I drove soberly away from the racecourse feeling sorry for her.

CHAPTER FOURTEEN

Rupert Ramsey met me with a stony face, not at all the expression one would normally expect from a successful trainer who had invited one of his owners to dinner.

'I'm glad you're early,' he said forbiddingly. 'Please come into the office.'

I followed him across the hall into the familiar room which was warm with a living log fire. He made no move to offer me a drink and I thought I might as well save him some trouble.

'You're going to tell me,' I said, 'that the horse which left here this morning is not the one which returned.'

He raised his eyebrows. 'So you don't deny it?'

'Of course not.' I smiled. 'I wouldn't have thought all that much of you if you hadn't noticed.'

'The lad noticed. Donny. He told the head lad, and the head lad told me, and I went to see for myself. And what I want is an explanation.'

'And it had better be good,' I added, imitating his schoolmasterly tone. He showed no amusement.

'This is no joke.'

'Maybe not. But it's no crime, either. If you'll calm down a fraction, I'll explain.'

'You have brought me a ringer. No trainer of any sense is going to stand for that.' His anger was cold and deep.

I said, 'The horse you thought was Energise was the ringer. And I didn't send him here, Jody did. The horse you have been trying to train for the Champion Hurdle and which left here this morning, is a fairly useless novice called Padellic.'

'I don't believe it.'

'As Energise,' I pointed out, 'you have found him unbelievably disappointing.'

'Well...' The first shade of doubt crept into his voice.

'When I discovered the wrong horse had been sent here, I asked you expressly not to run him in any races, because I certainly did not want you to be involved in running a ringer, nor myself for that matter.'

'But if you knew... why on earth didn't you immediately tell Jody he had made a mistake?'

'He didn't,' I said simply. 'He sent the wrong one on purpose.'

He walked twice round the room in silence and then still without a word poured us each a drink.

'Right,' he said, handing me a glass. 'Pray continue.'

I continued for quite a long while. He gestured to me

to sit down and sat opposite me himself, and listened attentively with a serious face.

'And this security firm . . .' he said at the end. 'Are you expecting Jody to try to get Energise back?'

I nodded. 'He's an extremely determined man. I made the mistake once of underestimating his vigour and his speed, and that's what lost me Energise in the first place. I think when he got home from Chepstow and heard what Felicity and the box driver and the lad had to say, he would have been violently angry and would decide to act at once. He's not the sort to spend a day or so thinking about it. He'll come tonight. I think and hope he will come tonight.'

'He will be sure Energise is here?'

'He certainly should be,' I said. 'He'll ask his box driver about the journey and his box driver will tell him about the census. Jody will question closely and find that Pete Duveen was there too. Jody will, I think, telephone to ask Pete Duveen if he saw anything unusual and Pete, who has nothing to hide, will tell him he brought a black horse from here. He'll tell him he took a black horse home again. And he'll tell him I was there at the census point. I didn't ask him not to tell and I am sure he will, because of his frank and open nature.'

Rupert's lips twitched into the first hint of a smile. He straightened it out immediately. 'I don't really approve of what you've done.'

'Broken no laws,' I said neutrally, neglecting to

249

mention the shadowy area of Bert's police-impression uniform.

'Perhaps not.' He thought it over. 'And the security firm is both to prevent the theft of Energise and to catch Jody redhanded?'

'Exactly so.'

'I saw them in the yard this evening. Two men. They said they were expecting instructions from you when you arrived, though frankly at that point I was so angry with you that I was paying little attention.'

'I talked to them on my way in,' I agreed. 'One will patrol the yard at regular intervals and the other is going to sit outside the horse's box. I told them both to allow themselves to be enticed from their posts by any diversion.'

'To *allow*?'

'Of course. You have to give the mouse a clear view of the cheese.'

'Good God.'

'And I wondered . . . whether you would consider staying handy, to act as a witness if Jody should come a-robbing.'

It seemed to strike him for the first time that he too was Jody's victim. He began to look almost as Charlie had done, and certainly as Bert had done, as if he found counter-measures attractive. The tugging smile reappeared.

'It depends of course on what time Jody comes . . . if he comes at all . . . but two of my guests tonight would be the best independent witnesses you could get. A lady magistrate and the local vicar.'

'Will they stay late?' I asked.

'We can try.' He thought for a bit. 'What about the police?'

'How quickly can they get here if called?'

'Um . . . Ten minutes. Quarter of an hour.'

'That should be all right.'

He nodded. A bell rang distantly in the house, signalling the arrival of more guests. He stood up, paused a moment, frowned and said, 'If the guard is to allow himself to be decoyed away why plant him outside the horse's door in the first place?'

I smiled. 'How else is Jody to know which box to rob?'

The dinner party seemed endless, though I couldn't afterwards remember a word or a mouthful. There were eight at table, all better value than myself, and the vicar particularly shone because of his brilliance as a mimic. I half-heard the string of imitated voices and saw everyone else falling about with hysterics and could think only of my men outside in the winter night and of the marauder I hoped to entice.

To groans from his audience the vicar played Cinderella at midnight and took himself off to shape up to Sunday, and three others shortly followed. Rupert pressed the last two to stay for nightcaps: the lady magistrate and her husband, a quiet young colonel with an active career and a bottomless capacity for port. He settled happily enough at the sight of a fresh decanter, and she with mock resignation continued a mild flirtation with Rupert.

The wheels inside my head whirred with the same doubts as in the morning. Suppose I had been wrong. Suppose Jody didn't come. Suppose he did come, but came unseen, and managed to steal the horse successfully.

Well . . . I'd planned for that, too. I checked for the hundredth time through the ifs. I tried to imagine what I hadn't already imagined, see what I hadn't seen, prepare for the unprepared. Rupert cast an amused glance or two at my abstracted expression and made no attempt to break it down.

The door bell rang sharply, three long insistent pushes.

I stood up faster than good manners.

'Go on,' Rupert said indulgently. 'We'll be right behind you, if you need us.'

I nodded and departed, and crossed the hall to open the front door. My man in a grey flannel suit stood outside, looking worried and holding a torch.

'What is it?'

'I'm not sure. The other two are patrolling the yard and I haven't seen them for some time. And I think we have visitors, but they haven't come in a horsebox.'

'Did you see them? The visitors?'

'No. Only their car. Hidden off the road in a patch of wild rhododendrons. At least . . . there is a car there which wasn't there half an hour ago. What do you think?'

'Better take a look,' I said.

He nodded. I left the door of Rupert's house ajar and we walked together towards the main gate. Just inside it stood the van which had brought the security guards, and outside, less than fifty yards along the road, we came to the car in the bushes, dimly seen even by torchlight.

'It isn't a car I recognise,' I said. 'Suppose it's just a couple of lovers?'

'They'd be inside it on a night like this, not out snogging in the freezing undergrowth.'

'You're right.'

'Let's take the rotor arm, to make sure.'

We lifted the bonnet and carefully removed the essential piece of electrics. Then, shining the torch as little as possible and going on grass whenever there was a choice, we hurried back towards the stable. The night was windy enough to swallow small sounds, dark enough to lose contact at five paces and cold enough to do structural damage to brass monkeys.

At the entrance to the yard we stopped to look and listen.

No lights. The dark heavy bulk of buildings was more sensed than seen against the heavily overcast sky.

No sounds except our own breath and the greater lungs of the wind. No sign of our other two guards.

'What now?'

'We'll go and check the horse,' I said.

We went into the main yard and skirted round its edges, which were paved with quieter concrete. The centre was an expanse of crunchy gravel, a giveaway even for cats.

Box fourteen had a chair outside it. A wooden kitchen chair planted prosaically with its back to the stable wall. No guard sat on it.

Quietly I slid back the bolts on the top half of the door and looked inside. There was a soft movement and the sound of a hoof rustling the straw. A second's flash of torch showed the superb shape patiently standing half-asleep in the dark, drowsing away the equine night.

I shut the door and made faint grating noises with the bolt.

'He's fine,' I said. 'Let's see if we can find the others.'

He nodded. We finished the circuit of the main yard and started along the various branches, moving with caution and trying not to use the torch. I couldn't stop the weird feeling growing that we were not the only couple groping about in the dark. I saw substance in shadows and reached out fearfully to touch objects which were not there, but only darker patches in the pervading black. We spent five or ten minutes feeling our way, listening, taking a few steps, listening, going on. We completed the tour of the outlying rows of boxes, and saw and heard nothing.

'This is no good,' I said quietly. 'There isn't a sign of them, and has it occurred to you that they are hiding from us, thinking we are the intruders?'

'Just beginning to wonder.'

'Let's go back to the main yard.'

We turned and retraced our steps, taking this time a short cut through a narrow alleyway between two sections of boxes. I was in front, so it was I who practically tripped over the huddled bundle on the ground.

I switched on the torch. Saw the neat navy uniform and the blood glistening red on the forehead. Saw the shut eyes and the lax limbs of the man who should have been sitting on the empty kitchen chair.

'Oh God,' I said desperately, and thought I would never ever forgive myself. I knelt beside him and fumbled for his pulse.

'He's alive,' said my friend in the grey flannel suit. He sounded reassuring and confident. 'Look at him breathing. He'll be all right, you'll see.'

All I could see was a man who was injured because I'd stationed him in the path of danger. 'I'll get a doctor,' I said, standing up.

'What about the horse?'

'Damn the horse. This is more important.'

'I'll stay here with him till you get back.'

255

I nodded and set off anxiously towards the house, shining the torch now without reservations. If permanent harm came to that man because of me ...

I ran.

Burst in through Rupert's front door and found him standing there in the hall talking to the lady magistrate and the colonel, who were apparently just about to leave. She was pulling a cape around her shoulders and Rupert was holding the colonel's coat. They turned and stared at me like a frozen tableau.

'My guard's been attacked. Knocked out,' I said. 'Could you get him a doctor?'

'Sure,' Rupert said calmly. 'Who attacked him?'

'I didn't see.'

'Job for the police?'

'Yes, please.'

He turned to the telephone, dialling briskly. 'What about the horse?'

'They didn't come in a horsebox.'

We both digested implications while he got the rescue services on the move. The colonel and the magistrate stood immobile in the hall with their mouths half open and Rupert, putting down the telephone, gave them an authoritative glance.

'Come out into the yard with us, will you?' he said. 'Just in case we need witnesses?'

They weren't trained to disappear rapidly at the thought. When Rupert hurried out of the door with me at his heels they followed more slowly after.

Everything still looked entirely quiet outside.

'He's in a sort of alley between two blocks of boxes,' I said.

'I know where you mean,' Rupert nodded. 'But first we'll check on Energise.'

'Later.'

'No. Now. Why bash the guard if they weren't after the horse?'

He made straight for the main yard, switched on all six external lights, and set off across the brightly illuminated gravel.

The effect was like a flourish of trumpets. Noise, light and movement filled the space where silence and dark had been total.

Both halves of the door of box fourteen swung open about a foot, and two dark figures catapulted through the gap.

'Catch them!' Rupert shouted.

There was only one way out of the yard, the broad entrance through which we had come. The two figures ran in curving paths towards the exit, one to one side of Rupert and me, one to the other.

Rupert rushed to intercept the smaller who was suddenly, as he turned his head to the light, recognisable as Jody.

I ran for the larger. Stretched out. Touched him.

He swung a heavy arm and threw out a hip and I literally bounced off him, stumbling and falling.

The muscles were rock hard. The sunglasses glittered.

The joker was ripping through the pack.

Jody and Rupert rolled on the gravel, one clutching, one punching, both swearing. I tried again at Muscles with the same useless results. He seemed to hesitate over going to Jody's help, which was how I'd come to be able to reach him a second time, but finally decided on flight. By the time I was again staggering to my feet he was on his way to the exit with the throttle wide open.

A large figure in navy blue hurtled straight at him from the opposite direction and brought him down with a diving hug round the knees. The sunglasses flew off in a shiny arc and the two blue figures lay in a writhing entwined mass, the blue uniform uppermost and holding his own. I went to his help and sat on Muscles' ankles, crushing his feet sideways with no compunction at all. He screeched with pain and stopped struggling, but I fear I didn't immediately stand up.

Jody wrenched himself free from Rupert and ran past me. The colonel, who with his lady had been watching the proceedings with astonishment, decided it was time for some soldierly action and elegantly stuck out his foot.

Jody tripped over and fell sprawling. The colonel put more energy into it, leant down and took hold of

the collar of Jody's coat. Rupert, rallying, came to his
aid, and between them they too more or less sat on
Jody, pinning him to the ground.

'What now?' Rupert panted.

'Wait for the police,' I said succinctly.

Muscles and Jody both heaved about a good deal
at this plan but didn't succeed in freeing themselves.
Muscles complained that I'd broken his ankle. Jody,
under the colonel's professional ministrations, seemed
to have difficulty saying anything at all. The colonel
was in fact so single-handedly efficient that Rupert
stood up and dusted himself down and looked at me
speculatively.

I jerked my head in the direction of box fourteen,
where the door still stood half open, showing only
darkness within. He nodded slowly and went that way.
Switched on the light. Stepped inside. He came back
with a face of stone and three bitter words.

'Energise is dead.'

CHAPTER FIFTEEN

Rupert fetched some rope with which he ignominiously tied Jody's hands behind his back before he and the colonel let him get up, and the colonel held the free end of rope so that Jody was to all intents on a lead. Once up, Jody aimed a kick at the colonel and Rupert told him to stop unless he wanted his ankles tied as well.

Rupert and my man in blue uniform did a repeat job on Muscles, whose ankles were not in kicking shape and whose language raised eyebrows even on the lady magistrate, who had heard more than most.

The reason for Muscles' ubiquitous sunglasses was at once apparent, now that one could see his face. He stood glowering like a bull, seething with impotent rage, hopping on one foot and pulling against the tethering rope which led back from his wrists to my man in blue. His eyelids, especially the lower, were grossly distorted, and even in the outside lighting looked bright pink with inflammation. One could pity his plight, which was clearly horrid.

'I know you,' Rupert said suddenly, looking at him closely. 'What's the matter with your eyes?'

'Mind your own effing business.'

'Macrahinish. That's what your name is. Macrahinish.'

Muscles didn't comment. Rupert turned to me. 'Don't you know him? Perhaps he was before your time. He's a vet. A struck-off vet. Struck off the vets' register and warned off the racecourse. And absolutely not allowed to set foot in a racing stable.'

Muscles-Macrahinish delivered himself of an unflattering opinion of racing in general and Rupert in particular.

Rupert said, 'He was convicted of doping and fraud and served a term in jail. He ran a big doping ring and supplied all the drugs. He looks older and there's something wrong with his eyes, but that's who this is, all right. Macrahinish.'

I turned away from the group and walked over to the brightly lit loosebox. Swung the door wide. Looked inside.

My beautiful black horse lay flat on his side, legs straight, head flaccid on the straw. The liquid eye was dull and opaque, mocking the sheen which still lay on his coat, and he still had pieces of unchewed hay half in and half out of his mouth. There was no blood, and no visible wound. I went in and squatted beside him, and patted him sadly with anger and regret.

Jody and Macrahinish had been unwillingly

propelled in my wake. I looked up to find them inside the box, with Rupert, the colonel, his wife and the man in blue effectively blocking the doorway behind them.

'How did you kill him?' I asked, the bitterness apparent in my voice.

Macrahinish's reply did not contain the relevant information.

I straightened up and in doing so caught sight of a flat brown attaché case half hidden in the straw by the horse's tail. I bent down again and picked it up. The sight of it brought a sound and a squirm from Macrahinish, and he began to swear in earnest when I balanced it on the manger and unfastened the clips.

The case contained regular veterinarian equipment, neatly stowed in compartments. I touched only one thing, lifting it carefully out.

A plastic bag containing a clear liquid. A bag plainly proclaiming the contents to be sterile saline solution.

I held it out towards Jody and said, 'You dripped alcohol straight into my veins.'

'You were unconscious,' he said disbelievingly.

'Shut up, you stupid fool,' Macrahinish screamed at him.

I smiled. 'Not all the time. I remember nearly everything about that night.'

'He said he didn't,' Jody said defensively to Macrahinish and was rewarded by a look from the swollen eyes which would have made a non-starter of Medusa.

'I went to see if you still had Energise,' I said. 'And I found you had.'

'You don't know one horse from another,' he sneered. 'You're just a mug. A blind greedy mug.'

'So are you,' I said. 'The horse you've killed is not Energise.'

'It is!'

'Shut up,' screamed Macrahinish in fury. 'Keep your stupid sodding mouth shut.'

'No,' I said to Jody. 'The horse you've killed is an American horse called Black Fire.'

Jody looked wildly down at the quiet body.

'It damn well is Energise,' he insisted. 'I'd know him anywhere.'

'Jesus,' Macrahinish shouted. 'I'll cut your tongue out.'

Rupert said doubtfully to me, 'Are you sure it's not Energise?'

'Positive.'

'He's just saying it to spite me,' said Jody furiously. 'I know it's Energise. See that tiny bald patch on his shoulder? That's Energise.'

Macrahinish, beyond speech, tried to attack him, tied hands and dicky ankle notwithstanding. Jody gave him a vague look, concentrating only on the horse.

'You are saying,' Rupert suggested, 'that you came to kill Energise and that you've done it.'

'Yes,' said Jody triumphantly.

The word hung in the air, vibrating. No one said

anything. Jody looked round at each watching face, at first with defiant angry pride, then with the first creeping of doubt, and finally with the realisation of what Macrahinish had been trying to tell him, that he should never have been drawn into admitting anything. The fire visibly died into glum and chilly embers.

'I didn't kill him,' he said suddenly. 'Macrahinish did. I didn't want to kill him at all, but Macrahinish insisted.'

A police car arrived with two young and persistent constables who seemed to find nothing particularly odd in being called to the murder of a horse.

They wrote in their notebooks that five witnesses, including a magistrate, had heard Jody Leeds admit that he and a disbarred veterinary surgeon had broken into a racing stable after midnight with the intention of putting to death one of the horses. They noted that a horse was dead. Cause of death, unknown until an autopsy could be arranged.

Hard on their heels came Rupert's doctor, an elderly man with a paternal manner. Yawning but uncomplaining, he accompanied me to find my security guard, who to my great relief was sitting on the ground with his head in his hands, awake and groaning healthily. We took him into Rupert's office, where the doctor stuck a plaster on the dried wound on his forehead, gave him some tablets and told him to lay off work for a couple of days. He smiled weakly and said it depended if his boss would let him.

One of the young policemen asked if he'd seen who had hit him.

'Big man with sunglasses. He was creeping along behind me, holding a ruddy great chunk of wood. I heard something . . . I turned and shone my torch, and there he was. He swung at my head. Gave me a right crack, he did. Next thing I knew, I was lying on the ground.'

Reassured by his revival I went outside again to see what was happening.

The magistrate and the colonel seemed to have gone home, and Rupert was down in the yard talking to some of his own stable staff who had been woken by the noise.

Macrahinish was hopping about on one leg, accusing me of having broken the other and swearing he'd have me prosecuted for using undue force to protect my property. The elderly doctor phlegmatically examined the limb in question and said that in his opinion it was a sprain.

The police had rashly untied the Macrahinish wrists and were obviously relying on the leg injury to prevent escape. At the milder word sprain they produced handcuffs and invited Macrahinish to stick his arms out. He refused and resisted and because they, as I had done, underestimated both his strength and his violence, it took a hectic few minutes for them to make him secure.

'Resisting arrest,' they panted, writing it in the notebooks. 'Attacking police officers in the course of their duty.'

Macrahinish's sunglasses lay on the gravel in the main yard, where he had lost them in the first tackle. I walked down to where they shone in the light and picked them up. Then I took them slowly back to him and put them in his handcuffed hands.

He stared at me through the raw-looking eyelids. He said nothing. He put the sunglasses on, and his fingers were trembling.

'Ectropion,' said the doctor, as I walked away.

'What?' I said.

'The condition of his eyes. Ectropion. Poor fellow.'

The police made no mistakes with Jody. He sat beside Macrahinish in the back of the police car with handcuffs on his wrists and the Arctic in his face. When the police went to close the doors ready to leave, he leant forward and spoke to me through rigid lips.

'You *shit*,' he said.

Rupert invited the rest of my security firm indoors for warmth and coffee and in his office I introduced them to him.

'My friend in grey flannel,' I said, 'is Charlie Canterfield. My big man in blue is Bert Huggerneck. My injured friend with the dried blood on his face is Owen Idris.'

Rupert shook hands with each and they grinned at him. He sensed immediately that there was more in their smiles than he would have expected, and he turned his enquiring gaze on me.

'Which firm do they come from?' he asked.

'Charlie's a merchant banker, Bert's a bookies' clerk, and Owen helps in my workshop.'

Charlie chuckled and said in his fruitiest Eton, 'We also run a nice line in a census, if you should ever need one.'

Rupert shook his head helplessly and fetched brandy and glasses from a cupboard.

'If I ask questions,' he said, pouring lavishly, 'will you answer them?'

'If we can,' I said.

'That dead horse in the stable. Is it Energise?'

'No. Like I said, it's a horse I bought in the States called Black Fire.'

'But the bald patch . . . Jody was so certain.'

'I did that bald patch with a razor blade. The horses were extraordinarily alike, apart from that. Especially at night, because of being black. But there's one certain way of identifying Black Fire. He has his American racing number tattooed inside his lip.'

'Why did you bring him here?'

'I didn't want to risk the real Energise. Before I saw Black Fire in America I couldn't see how to entice Jody safely. Afterwards, it was easier.'

'But I didn't get the impression earlier this evening,'

Rupert said pensively, 'that you expected them to kill the horse.'

'No . . . I didn't know about Macrahinish. I mean, I didn't know he was a vet, or that he could over-rule Jody. I expected Jody just to try to steal the horse and I wanted to catch him in the act. Catch him physically committing a positive criminal act which he couldn't possibly explain away. I wanted to force the racing authorities, more than the police, to see that Jody was not the innocent little underdog they believed.'

Rupert thought it over. 'Why didn't you think he would kill him?'

'Well . . . it did cross my mind, but on balance I thought it unlikely, because Energise is such a good horse. I thought Jody would want to hide him away somewhere so that he could make a profit on him later, even if he sold him as a point-to-pointer. Energise represents money, and Jody has never missed a trick in that direction.'

'But Macrahinish wanted him dead,' Rupert said.

I sighed. 'I suppose he thought it safer.'

Rupert smiled. 'You had put them in a terrible fix. They couldn't risk you being satisfied with getting your horse back. They couldn't be sure you couldn't somehow prove they had stolen it originally. But if you no longer had it, you would have found it almost impossible to make allegations stick.'

'That's right,' Charlie agreed. 'That's exactly what Steven thought.'

'Also,' I said, 'Jody wouldn't have been able to bear the thought of me getting the better of him. Apart from safety and profit, he would have taken Energise back simply for revenge.'

'You know what?' Charlie said. 'It's my guess that he probably put his entire bank balance on Padellic at Stratford, thinking it was Energise, and when Padellic turned up sixth he lost the lot. And that in itself is a tidy little motive for revenge.'

'Here,' Bert said appreciatively. 'I wonder how much Ganser bleeding Mays is down the drain for! Makes you bleeding laugh, don't it? There they all were, thinking they were backing a ringer, and we'd gone and put the real Padellic back where he belonged.'

'Trained by Rupert,' I murmured, 'to do his best.'

Rupert looked at us one by one and shook his head. 'You're a lot of rogues.'

We drank our brandy and didn't dispute it.

'Where did the American horse come from?' Rupert asked.

'Miami.'

'No . . . This morning.'

'A quiet little stable in the country,' I said. 'We had him brought to the census point . . .'

'And you should have bleeding seen him,' Bert interrupted gleefully. 'Our ca*pit*alist here, I mean. Whizzing those three horses in and out of horseboxes faster than the three card trick.'

'I must say,' Rupert said thoughtfully, 'that I've wondered just how he managed it.'

'He took bleeding Energise out of Jody's box and put it in the empty stall of the trailer which brought Black Fire. Then he put Padellic where Energise had been, in Jody's box. Then he put bleeding Black Fire where Padellic had been, in your box, that is. All three of them buzzing in a circle like a bleeding merry-go-round.'

Charlie said, smiling, 'All change at the census. Padellic started from here and went to Stratford. Black Fire started from the country and came here. And Energise started from Jody's . . .' He stopped.

'And went to where?' Rupert asked.

I shook my head. 'He's safe, I promise you.' Safe with Allie at Hantsford Manor, with Miss Johnston and Mrs Fairchild-Smith. 'We'll leave him where he is for a week or two.'

'Yeah,' Bert said, explaining. 'Because, see, we've had Jody Leeds and that red-eyed hunk of muscle of his exploding all over us with temper-temper, but what about that other one? What about that other one we've kicked right where it hurts, eh? We don't want to risk Energise getting the chop after all from Mr Squeezer bleeding Ganser down the bleeding drain Mays.'

CHAPTER SIXTEEN

Owen and I went back to London. I drove, with him sitting beside me fitfully dozing and pretending in between times that he didn't have a headache.

'Don't be silly,' I said. 'I know what it feels like. You've got a proper thumper and notwithstanding that snide crack to the doctor about your boss not letting you take a couple of days off that's what you're going to get.'

He smiled.

'I'm sorry about your head,' I said.

'I know.'

'How?'

'Charlie said.'

I glanced across at him. His face in the glow from the dashboard looked peaceful and contented. 'It's been,' he said drowsily, 'a humdinger of a day.'

It was four in the morning when we reached the house and pulled into the driveway. He woke up slowly and shivered, his eyes fuzzy with fatigue.

'You're sleeping in my bed,' I said, 'and I'm taking the sofa.' He opened his mouth. 'Don't argue,' I added.

'All right.'

I locked the car and we walked to the front door, and that's where things went wrong.

The front door was not properly shut. Owen was too sleepy to realise at once, but my heart dropped to pavement level the instant I saw it.

Burglars, I thought dumbly. Today of all days.

I pushed the door open. Everything was quiet. There was little furniture in the hall and nothing looked disturbed. Upstairs, though, it would be like a blizzard . . .

'What is it?' said Owen, realising that something was wrong.

'The workshop door,' I said, pointing.

'Oh no!'

That too was ajar, and there was no question of the intruder having used a key. The whole area was split, the raw wood showing in jagged layers up and down the jamb.

We walked along the carpeted passage, pushed the door wider, and took one step through on to concrete.

One step, and stopped dead.

The workshop was an area of complete devastation.

All the lights were on. All the cupboard doors and drawers were open, and everything which should have been in them was out and scattered and smashed. The work benches were overturned and the racks of tools were torn from their moorings and great chunks of plaster had been gouged out of the walls.

All my designs and drawings had been ripped to pieces. All the prototype toys seemed to have been stamped on.

Tins of oil and grease had been opened, and the contents emptied on to the mess, and the paint I'd used on the census notices was splashed on everything the oil had missed.

The machines themselves . . .

I swallowed. I was never going to make anything else on those machines. Not ever again.

Not burglars, I thought aridly.

Spite.

I felt too stunned to speak and I imagine it was the same with Owen because for an appreciable time we both just stood there, immobile and silent. The mess before us screamed out its message of viciousness and evil, and the intensity of the hate which had committed such havoc made me feel literally sick.

On feet which seemed disconnected from my legs I took a couple of steps forward.

There was a flicker of movement on the edge of my vision away behind the half-open door. I spun on my toe with every primeval instinct raising hairs in instant alarm, and what I saw allowed no reassurance whatsoever.

Ganser Mays stood there, waiting like a hawk. The long nose seemed a sharp beak, and his eyes behind the metal-rimmed spectacles glittered with mania. He was positioning his arms for a scything downward swing, which was the movement I'd seen, and in his hands he held a heavy long-handled axe.

I leapt sideways a thousandth of a second before the killing edge swept through the place where I'd been standing.

'Get help,' I shouted breathlessly to Owen. 'Get out and get help.'

I had a blurred impression of his strained face, mouth open, eyes huge, dried blood still dark on his cheek. For an instant he didn't move and I thought he wouldn't go, but when I next caught a glimpse of the doorway, it was empty.

Whether or not he'd been actively lying in wait for me, there was no doubt that now that I was there Ganser Mays was trying to do to me what he'd already done to my possessions. I learned a good deal from him in the next few minutes. I learned about mental terror. Learned about extreme physical fear. Learned that it was no fun at all facing unarmed and untrained a man with the will and the weapon for murder.

What was more, it was my own axe.

We played an obscene sort of hide and seek round the wrecked machines. It only needed one of the ferocious chops to connect, and I would be without arm or leg if not without life. He slashed whenever he could get near enough, and I hadn't enough faith in my speed or strength to try to tackle him within slicing range. I dodged always and precariously just out of total disaster, circling the ruined lathe . . . the milling machine . . . the hacksaw . . . back to the lathe . . . putting the precious bulks of metal between me and death.

Up and down the room, again and again.

There was never a rigid line between sense and insanity and maybe by some definitions Ganser Mays was sane. Certainly in all that obsessed destructive fury he was aware enough that I might escape through the door. From the moment I'd first stepped past him into the workshop, he gave me no chance to reach safety that way.

There were tools scattered on the floor from the torn-down racks, but they were mostly small and in any case not round the machines but on the opposite side of the workshop. I could leave the shelter of the row of machines and cross open space to arm myself . . . but nothing compared in weight or usefulness with that axe, and chisels and saws and drill bits weren't worth the danger of exposure.

If Owen came back with help, maybe I could last out . . .

Shortage of breath . . . I was averagely fit, but no athlete . . . couldn't pull in enough oxygen for failing muscles . . . felt fatal weaknesses slowing my movements . . . knew I couldn't afford to slip on the oil or stumble over the bolts mooring the base plates to the floor or leave my hands holding on to anything for more than a second for fear of severed fingers.

He seemed tireless, both in body and intent. I kept my attention more on the axe than his face, but the fractional views I caught of his fixed, fanatical and curiously rigid expression gave no room for hope that he would stop before he had achieved his object. Trying to reason with him would have been like arguing with an avalanche. I didn't even try.

Breath sawed through my throat. Owen ... why didn't he bloody well hurry ... if he didn't hurry he might as well come back tomorrow for all the good it would do me ...

The axe crashed down so close to my shoulder that I shuddered from imagination and began to despair. He was going to kill me. I was going to feel the bite of that heavy steel ... to know the agony and see the blood spurt ... to be chopped and smashed like everything else.

I was up at one end, where the electric motor which worked all the machines was located. He was four feet away, swinging, looking merciless and savage. I was shaking, panting and still trying frantically to escape, and it was more to distract him for a precious second than from any devious plan that I took the time to kick the main switch from off to on.

The engine hummed and activated the main belt, which turned the big wheel near the ceiling and rotated the long shaft down the workshop. All the belts to the machines began slapping as usual, except that this time half of them had been cut right through and the free ends flapped in the air like streamers.

It took his eye off me for only a blink. I circled the electric motor which was much smaller than the machines and not good cover, and he brought his head back towards me with a snap.

He saw that I was exposed. A flash of triumph crossed his pale sweating face. He whipped the axe back and high and struck at me with all his strength.

I jumped sideways in desperation and slipped and fell, and thought as I went down that this was it ... this was the end ... he would be on me before I could get up.

I half saw the axe go up again. I lunged out with one foot in a desperate kick at his ankles. Connected. Threw him a fraction off balance. Only a matter of a few inches: and it didn't affect the weight of his downward swing, but only its direction. Instead of burying itself in me, the blade sank into the main belt driving the machines, and for one fatal moment Ganser Mays hung on to the shaft. Whether he thought I had somehow grasped the axe and was trying to tug it away from him, heaven knows. In any case he gripped tight, and the whirling belt swept him off his feet.

The belt moved at about ten feet a second. It took one second for Ganster Mays to reach the big wheel above. I dare say he let go of the shaft at about that point, but the wheel caught him and crushed him in the small space between itself and the ceiling.

He screamed . . . a short loud cry of extremity, chokingly cut off.

The wheel inexorably whirled him through and out the other side. It would have taken more than a soft human body to stop a motor which drove machine tools.

He fell from the high point and thumped sickeningly on to the concrete not far from where I was still scrambling to get up. It had happened at such immense speed that he had been up to the ceiling and down again before I could find my feet.

The axe had been dislodged and had fallen separately beside him. Near his hand, as if all he had to do was stretch out six inches and he would be back in business.

But Ganser Mays was never going to be back in business. I stood looking down at him while the engine hummed and the big killing wheel rotated impersonally as usual, and the remaining belts to the machines slapped quietly as they always did.

There was little blood. His face was white. The spectacles had gone and the eyes were half open. The sharp nose was angled grotesquely sideways. The neck was bent at an impossible angle; and whatever else had broken, that was enough.

I stood there for a while panting for breath and sweating and trembling from fatigue and the screwed tension of past fear. Then whatever strength I had left drained abruptly away and I sat on the floor beside the electric motor and drooped an arm over it for support like a wilted lily. Beyond thought. Beyond feeling. Just dumbly and excruciatingly exhausted.

It was at that moment that Owen returned. The help he'd brought wore authentic navy blue uniform and a real black and white checkered band on his cap. He took a long slow look and summoned reinforcements.

Hours later, when they had all gone, I went back downstairs to the workshop.

Upstairs nothing, miraculously, had been touched. Either our return had interrupted the programme before it had got that far, or the workshop had been the only intended target. In any case my first sight of the peaceful sitting-room had been a flooding relief.

Owen and I had flopped weakly around in armchairs while the routine police work ebbed and flowed, and after lengthy question-and-answer sessions and the departure of the late Mr Mays we had found ourselves finally alone.

It was already Sunday morning. The sun, with no sense of fitness, was brightly shining. Regent's Park sparkled with frost and the puddles were glazed with ice.

'Go to bed,' I said to Owen.

He shook his head. 'Think I'll go home.'

'Come back when you're ready.'

He smiled. 'Tomorrow,' he said. 'For a spot of sweeping up.'

When he'd gone I wandered aimlessly about, collecting coffee cups and emptying ashtrays and thinking disconnected thoughts. I felt both too tired and too unsettled for sleep, and it was then that I found myself going back to the devastation in the workshop.

The spirit of the dead man had gone. The place no longer vibrated with violent hate. In the morning light it looked a cold and sordid shambles, squalid debris of a spent orgy.

I walked slowly down the room, stirring things with my toe. The work of twenty years lay there in little pieces. Designs torn like confetti. Toys crushed flat. Nothing could be mended or saved.

I supposed I could get duplicates at least of the design drawings if I tried, because copies were lodged in the patents' office. But the originals, and all the hand-made prototype toys, were gone for good.

I came across the remains of the merry-go-round which I had made when I was fifteen. The first Rola; the beginning of everything. I squatted down and stirred the pieces, remembering that distant decisive summer when I'd spent day after day in my uncle's workshop with ideas gushing like newly-drilled oil out of a brain that was half child, half man.

I picked up one of the little horses. The blue one,

with a white mane and tail. The one I'd made last of the six.

The golden barley-sugar rod which had connected it to the revolving roof was snapped off jaggedly an inch above the horse's back. One of the front legs was missing, and one of the ears.

I turned it over regretfully in my hands and looked disconsolately around at the mess. Poor little toys. Poor beautiful little toys, broken and gone.

It had cost me a good deal, one way and another, to get Energise back.

Turn the handle, Charlie had said, and all the little toys would revolve on their spindles and do what they should. But people weren't toys, and Jody and Macrahinish and Ganser Mays had jumped violently off their spindles and stripped the game out of control.

If I hadn't decided to take justice into my own hands I wouldn't have been kicked or convicted of drunkenness. I would have saved myself the price of Black Fire and a host of other expenses. I wouldn't have put Owen at risk as a guard, and I wouldn't have felt responsible for the ruin of Jody and Felicity, the probable return to jail of Macrahinish, and the death of Ganser Mays.

Pointless to say that I hadn't meant them so much harm, or that their own violence had brought about their own doom. It was I who had given them the first push.

Should I have done it?

Did I wish I hadn't?

I straightened to my feet and smiled ruefully at the shambles, and knew that the answer to both questions was no.

EPILOGUE

I gave Energise away.

Six weeks after his safe return to Rupert's stable he ran in the Champion Hurdle and I took a party to Cheltenham to cheer him on. A sick tycoon having generously lent his private box, we went in comfort, with lunch before and champagne after and a lot of smiling in between.

The four newly-registered joint-owners were having a ball and slapping each other on the back with glee: Bert, Allie, Owen and Charlie, as high in good spirits as they'd been at the census.

Charlie had brought the bridge-playing wife and Bert his fat old mum, and Owen had shyly and unexpectedly produced an unspoiled daughter of sixteen. The oddly mixed party proved a smash-hit success, my four conspirators carrying it along easily on the strength of liking each other a lot.

While they all went off to place bets and look at the horses in the parade ring, I stayed up in the box. I stayed there most of the afternoon. I had found it

impossible, as the weeks passed, to regain my old innocent enthusiasm for racing. There was still a massive
movement of support and sympathy for Jody, which I
supposed would never change. Letters to sporting
papers spoke of sympathy for his misfortunes and
disgust for the one who had brought them about.
Racing columnists, though reluctantly convinced of his
villainy, referred to him still as the 'unfortunate' Jody.
Quintus, implacably resentful, was ferreting away
against me in the Jockey Club and telling everyone it
was my fault his son had made 'misjudgements'. I had
asked him how it could possibly be my fault that Jody
had made the misjudgement of taking Macrahinish and
Ganser Mays for buddy-buddies, and had received no
answer.

I had heard unofficially the results of the autopsy
on Black Fire. He had been killed by a massive dose
of chloroform injected between the ribs straight into
the heart. Quick, painless, and positively the work of a
practised hand.

The veterinary bag found beside the dead horse had
contained a large hypodermic syringe with a sufficient
length of needle; traces of chloroform inside the syringe
and Macrahinish's fingerprints outside.

These interesting facts could not be generally broad-
cast on account of the forthcoming trial, and my high-
up police informant had made me promise not to repeat
them.

Jody and Macrahinish were out on bail, and the

racing authorities had postponed their own enquiry until the law's verdict should be known. Jody still technically held his trainer's licence.

The people who to my mind had shown most sense had been Jody's other owners. One by one they had melted apologetically away, reluctant to be had for mugs. They had judged without waiting around for a jury, and Jody had no horses left to train. And that in itself, in many eyes, was a further crying shame to be laid at my door.

I went out on the balcony of the kind tycoon's box and stared vacantly over Cheltenham racecourse. Moral victory over Jody was impossible, because too many people still saw him, despite everything, as the poor hardworking little man who had fallen foul of the rich robber baron.

Charlie came out on the balcony in my wake.

'Steven? What's the matter? You're too damned quiet.'

'What we did,' I said sighing, 'has changed nothing.'

'Of course it has,' he said robustly. 'You'll see. Public opinion works awful slowly. People don't like doing about-turns and admitting they were fooled. But you trust your Uncle Charlie, this time next year, when they've got over their red faces, a lot of people will quietly be finding you're one of their best friends.'

'Yeah,' I said.

'Quintus,' he said positively, 'is doing himself a lot of personal no good just now with the hierarchy. The *on dit* round the bazaars is that if Quintus can't see his son is a full-blown criminal he is even thicker than anyone thought. I tell you, the opinion where it matters is one hundred per cent for you, and our little private enterprise is the toast of the cigar circuit.'

I smiled. 'You make me feel better even if you do lie in your teeth.'

'As God's my judge,' he said, virtuously, and spoiled it by glancing a shade apprehensively skywards.

'I saw Jody,' I said. 'Did you know?'

'No!'

'In the City,' I nodded. 'Him and Felicity, coming out of some law offices.'

'What happened?'

'He spat,' I said.

'How like him.'

They had both looked pale and worried and had stared at me in disbelief. Jody's ball of mucus landed at my feet, punctuation mark of how he felt. If I'd known they were likely to be there I would have avoided the district by ten miles, but since we were accidentally face to face I asked him straight out the question I most wanted answered.

'Did you send Ganser Mays to smash my place up?'

'He told him how to make you suffer,' Felicity said spitefully. 'Serves you right.'

She cured in that one sentence the pangs of conscience I'd had about the final results of the Energise shuttle.

'You're a bloody fool, Jody,' I said. 'If you'd dealt straight with me I'd've bought you horses to train for the Classics. With your ability, if you'd been honest, you could have gone to the top. Instead, you'll be warned off for life. It is you, believe me, who is the mug.'

They had both stared at me sullenly, eyes full of frustrated rage. If either of them should have a chance in the future to do me further bad turns I had no doubt that they would. There was no one as vindictive as the man who'd done you wrong and been found out.

Charlie said beside me, 'Which do you think was the boss? Jody or Macrahinish or Ganser Mays?'

'I don't know,' I said. 'How does a triumvirate grab you?'

'Equal power?' He considered. 'Might well be, I suppose. Just three birds of a feather drawn to each other by natural evil, stirring it in unholy alliance.'

'Are all criminals so full of hate?'

'I dare say. I don't know all that many. Do you?'

'No.'

'I should think,' Charlie said, 'that the hate comes first. Some people are just natural haters. Some bully the weak, some become anarchists, some rape women, some steal with maximum mess... and all of them enjoy the idea of the victim's pain.'

'Then you can't cure a hater,' I said.

'With hardliners, not a chance.'

Charlie and I contemplated this sombre view and

the others came back waving Tote tickets and bubbling over with good humour.

'Here,' Bert said, slapping me on the back. 'Know what I just heard? Down in the ring, see. All those bleeding little bookies that we saved from going bust over Padellic, they're passing round the bleeding hat.'

'Just what, Bert,' said Allie, 'do you bleeding mean?'

'Here!' A huge grin spread across Bert's rugged features. 'You're a right smashing bit of goods, you are, Allie, and that's a fact. What I mean is, those little guys are making a bleeding collection all round the country, and every shop the smart alecs tried it on with, they're all putting a fiver in, and they're going to send it to the Injured Jockeys' bleeding Fund in honour of the firm of Scott, Canterfield, Ward, Idris and Huggerneck, what saved them all from disappearing down the bleeding plug-hole.'

We opened a bottle of champagne on the strength of it and Charlie said it was the eighth wonder of the world.

When the time came for the Champion Hurdle we all went down to see Energise saddled. Rupert, busy fastening buckles, looked at the ranks of shining eyes and smiled with the indulgence of the long-time professional. The horse himself could scarcely stand still, so full was he of oats and health and general excitement. I patted his elegant black neck and he tossed his head and sprayed me with a blow through his nostrils.

I said to Rupert, 'Do you think I'm too old to learn to ride?'

'Racehorses?' He pulled tight the second girth and fastened the buckle.

'Yes.'

He slapped the black rump. 'Come down Monday morning and make a start.'

'In front of all the lads?'

'Well?' He was amused, but it was an exceptional offer. Few trainers would bother.

'I'll be there,' I said.

Donny led Energise from the saddling boxes to the parade ring, closely followed by Rupert and the four new owners.

'But you're coming as well,' Allie said, protesting.

I shook my head. 'Four owners to one horse is enough.'

Bert and Charlie tugged her with them and they all stood in a little smiling group with happiness coming out of their ears. Bert's mum, Owen's daughter and Charlie's wife went off to plunder the Tote, and I, with the most reputable bookmaking firm in the business, bet five hundred pounds to three thousand that Energise would win.

We watched him from the balcony of the private box with hearts thumping like jungle drums. It was for this that we had gone to so much trouble, this few minutes ahead. For the incredible pleasure of seeing a superb creature do what he was bred, trained, endowed and eager for. For speed, for fun, for exhilaration, for love.

The tapes went up and they were away, the fourteen best hurdlers in Britain out to decide which was king.

Two miles of difficult undulating track. Nine flights of whippy hurdles. They crossed the first and the second and swept up the hill past the stands, with Energise lying sixth and moving easily, his jockey still wearing my distinctive bright blue colours because none of his new owners had any.

'Go on boyo,' Owen said, his face rapt. 'Slaughter the bloody lot of them.' Generations of fervent Welshmen echoed in his voice.

Round the top of the course. Downhill to the dip. More jumps, then the long climb on the far side. One horse fell, bringing a gasp like a gale from the stands and a moan from Allie that she couldn't bear to watch. Energise flowed over the hurdles with the economy of all great jumpers and at the top of the far hill he lay fourth.

'Get your bleeding skates on,' muttered Bert, whose knuckles showed white with clutching his raceglasses. 'Don't bleeding hang about.'

Energise obeyed the instructions. Down the leg-twisting slope he swooped like a black bird, racing level with the third horse, level with the second, pressing on the leader.

Over the next, three of them in a line like a wave. Round the last bend swept all three in a row, with nothing to choose and all to be fought for over the last of the hurdles and the taxing, tiring, pull-up to the winning post.

'I can't bear it,' Allie said. 'Oh come on, you great . . . gorgeous . . .'

'Slaughter them, boyo . . .'

'Shift, you bleeding . . .'

The voices shouted, the crowd yelled, and Charlie had tears in his eyes.

They came to the last flight all in a row, with Energise nearest the rails, furthest from the stands. He met it right, and jumped it cleanly and I had stopped breathing.

The horse in the middle hit the top of the hurdle, twisted in the air, stumbled on landing, and fell in a skidding, sliding, sprawling heap. He fell towards Energise, who had to dodge sideways to avoid him.

Such a little thing. A half-second's hesitation before he picked up his stride. But the third of the three, with a clear run, started away from the hurdle with a gain of two lengths.

Energise put his soul into winning that race. Stretched out and fought for every inch. Showed what gut and muscle could do on the green turf. Shortened the gap and closed it, and gained just a fraction at every stride.

Allie and Owen and Bert and Charlie were

screaming like maniacs, and the winning post was too near, too near.

Energise finished second, by a short head.

It's no good expecting fairytale endings, in racing.